PRECIPICE:
THE BEGINNING

KEVIN J. HOWARD

outskirtspress
DENVER, COLORADO

Precipice: The Beginning
All Rights Reserved.
Copyright © 2013 Kevin J. Howard
v2.0

Cover Photo © 2013 JupiterImages Corporation. All rights reserved - used with permission.

Outskirts Press, Inc.
http://www.outskirtspress.com

ISBN: 978-1-4787-1693-8

Outskirts Press and the "OP" logo are trademarks belonging to Outskirts Press, Inc.

PRINTED IN THE UNITED STATES OF AMERICA

This book is dedicated to my son
Logan Anthony Howard.
For him I'd walk to Mars and back.

1

"I swear to God, turn that damn thing off." Beth mumbled beneath her arm, covering her eyes from the camcorder's light. She withdrew her arm and opened her eyes, rubbing away the lingering shards of sleep. Above her stood her husband of only four days, Sebastian, holding the camcorder they'd owned for only three days. Purchased the day before they'd boarded the largest ship to ever set sail, Festival of the Seas from the Presidential Cruise Lines. "Are you going to give it a rest or do I have to smack you in the balls?" Beth sat up with a smile.

"Sounds kinky," Sebastian said, turning with his camcorder held before him, moving slowly to capture every inch of their balcony suite. He stepped before the mirror and waved, hamming it up for the home audience that would see it upon their return in seven more days. Sebastian began focusing in on the vanity, the small fridge and then toward the door.

"I don't think we need to remember the bathroom." Beth swung her legs over the side of the bed, resting her elbows on her knees. A light headache wouldn't cease in the back of her head, steadily rising to a muffled roar. Too many drink specials last night during the show. She'd spent two hours of last night double fisting tropical drinks that can only be found aboard a cruise, drinking them with an ever-growing buzz while watching a musical journey through America's night clubs. It had been a pretty decent show.

"One of these days, like twenty years from now, we're going to be watching this and wishing I'd gotten the bathroom. Not to mention the closet here." Sebastian opened the narrow door and filmed the interior, two white robes and two folded life jackets. Sebastian closed the door and turned back toward his wife, zooming in on her open mouth as she yawned. "Show me those pearly whites." He turned the button from record to standby and set the camcorder on the vanity. He walked over to his wife and took her by the hands, pulling her to her feet to plant a firm kiss on her dry lips. "Drinks didn't agree with you I take it," he said as he pulled away, tasting her morning breath within his own mouth.

Beth gave him a firm poke to his ribs and a wink before moving to the balcony door. She paused a moment to wrap the red floral pattern sarong her mother had given her about her waist. The sun was making its way into the morning sky, maybe just an hour or two past seven. She opened the door and closed her eyes against the warm gust of wind. The air was fresh, nothing like she was used to in Southern California. The sky over the water was blue and clear; no trace of the brown smog that hung over her hometown of Fullerton every day of her life. This truly was a wonderful choice for a honeymoon.

"Here, have some or you'll get a headache." Sebastian handed Beth a small cup of coffee. He took a seat beside her in a lounge chair and let out a content breath. "Now this is the life."

"Worth the extra money to be on the back of the ship like this."

Sebastian nodded, feeling there was no need for words. Moments of contentment such as this were few and far between. Not that he'd ever admit this to another living soul but he had trouble finding moments of peace, even the smallest ones. His genetics took hold of him at times, anger brewing through his bloodstream as it had through his father and grandfather, even his two sisters. Was there such a thing as genetic rage? Sebastian had never really put too much thought into it. He just used it to fall back on when people watched him snap, keeping their distance on the highway as he flew by with his middle finger held up high and his mouth streaming vulgarities. That had become his everyday routine, anger on the road, trouble with the bills, and then there was the slowly growing issue of his increasing waistline. Beth had helped him immensely. Her beautiful smile melted the rage like ice on the surface of the sun. Because of her he was able to come home to their apartment, take a deep breath, and show his teeth in something other than a snarl. Because of his darling wife, he was able to lie back in the lounge chair and let himself go. Even if for only a week or so, knowing full well the vacation would end and he'd be back on that same highway trudging through thick traffic an hour each way. But for now, this very moment, he let his lips stretch across his face as he slipped on the shades he purchased in Honolulu.

"Are we going to the art auction today?"

Beth thought a moment, shaking her head. "Kind of boring."

"True, but if we go to all three of them they enter us into a raffle to win a free piece of art." Sebastian let the words hang a moment, wondering if he himself even wanted to go. They didn't have a ton of money to spend, but art was his favorite souvenir. He'd purchased an oil painting of a small Mexican village on their trip to Mazatlan. "I mean, they will have free champagne," Sebastian said, sweetening the deal.

"No more booze…until dinner." Beth smiled.

Beth sat forward and slapped Sebastian in the shoulder. She was a physical person by nature, hitting him playfully, but with a surprising amount of strength whenever she remembered something or thought something was really funny. "I'm going to get the sunscreen." Beth stood, stepping over the chair while reaching for the door. "Need anything?"

"No."

Beth went into the room and lifted the suitcase onto the bed, shuffling through layers of shorts and tank tops for the sunscreen they'd purchased from the gift shop on the fourth deck. A twenty-seven dollar bottle of sunscreen was well worth a thorough search. Sebastian turned in his chair and lifted up his shades, watching her through the tinted window. The outline of her blue bathing suit bottoms could be made out beneath the thin fabric of the sarong. His mood shifted quickly as it often did, giving him the incentive he needed to rise from his chair and sneak back into his cabin. Beth heard the door and looked slightly back over her shoulder as he snuck up behind her, knowing full well where his normal dirty mind had taken him. After all, this was a vacation for them both.

"What do you think you're doing?" Beth said

coyly, turning to wrap her arms about his neck.

Sebastian leaned forward and kissed his wife, taking it slow as they had more than enough time to lead into the inevitable.

Their passion was doused by an overhead alarm beeping continuous at an unbearable volume. They covered their ears and ran toward the door, opening it to peek out into the hallway. An extremely over-weight man of perhaps fifty years of age ran by them, huffing as he went.

"What's going on?" Sebastian screamed, his voice either buried beneath the alarm or ignored by the portly fellow.

"This is your captain speaking." The captain's voice echoed throughout the ship, his thick Italian accent making it sometimes difficult to distinguish most of his announcements. "All passengers and crew quickly return to your rooms or the nearest enclosed space. Put your life vests on and brace yourselves for impact. Repeat. All passengers and crew put your life vests on. This is not a drill." The intercom clicked off but the alarm continued to sound.

"Impact from what?" Beth was screaming, her voice shaken from the captain's words.

Sebastian felt his stomach shrink and became nauseous, lightheaded from the noise and the confu-sion. He turned toward the bathroom and then back to the balcony. The captain's voice had been crisper than normal, perhaps knowing the importance of the delivery. He went to the closet and pulled open the door, grabbing the life vest. He slipped the vest over his neck and handed one to Beth, both of them struggling over the three sets of ties in the front.

"What do we do?" Beth asked.

Sebastian held out his hands and motioned for Beth to stay put as he hurried over to the balcony. The word "impact" circled his mind as if an airplane were towing a message for him to read over and over again. If they were going to hit something he might be able to see it, to put this into perspective. He threw open the door and stepped out onto the balcony, turning his neck as he saw the distance between the ocean and the horizon rapidly merging.

"Oh my God," Beth said softly as she stepped beside him, looking up into the wave as it rose above them, dwarfing the ship to look more like a tub toy than an all impressive ocean liner.

Beth took her husband's hand and squeezed it tightly as the wave took them.

2

Lieutenant Travis Daniels sat up straight, his chest rising fast and his body dripped with sweat. The small cell was still dark, but he could make out all the familiar markings. The hand-carved drawing of his sweet Annie's face on the wall opposite the bed, the single chair pushed into the thin table. Travis let out a deep breath and swung his feet out of bed, letting his bare soles hover over the floor, knowing it would burn from the cold as soon as he stepped down. Slowly, preparing himself for the oncoming sting, he lowered his feet and pressed them lightly to the ground. As with every morning, the bottoms of his feet stung and danced from a combination of lingering sleep and frosty temperatures. He would have slept with his socks on, but it was always warmest at night, then the heat kicked off around four in the morning, staying off until two in the afternoon. He wasn't quite clear on how the heating systems were run, but he was certain the integrity of the Martian facility could be maintained with an extra three hours of heat.

Travis stood, holding out his arms as he stretched, turning his torso to and fro. He turned his head from side to side and took a seat on the floor, folding his legs beneath him as he took a moment to collect himself. Bad thoughts still settled in the front of his mind, wrapping around his normal routine. With his eyes closed, he pushed them away, pulling them from his mind like a gardener ripping pesky weeds from the soil, tossing them back into the shadow of his brain until they would surface again tomorrow. It never failed. Day after day he would awake to the same awful images. The days of his past back on Earth had traveled with him the millions of miles to Mars, whether he'd wanted them to or not. Not all baggage could be checked and neatly stored overheard, or in this case hopefully lost. The decisions he'd made would follow him to the day he died.

Logan

Travis's eyes opened at the thought of his son, the name carrying with it so much emotion. The guilt he felt toward abandoning his only child, his toddler, overwhelmed him with tears as it always did. Travis didn't need to guard his emotions while in his cell, so he let the tears roll. They ran down his cheeks in a thin line, collected a moment and then fell to his bare shoulders. Travis lost himself in the few memories he had of his son. Only twice in the year he'd been stationed aboard the Martian facility had he seen his son, two brief moments; each visit through a viewing monitor with a distance of over fifty-five million miles between them. Annie would hold him up to the camera to show his daddy how big he'd gotten, what new words he could say. Simple everyday milestones to a normal parent, but to Travis they were amazing feats, each one worthy of a holiday in Logan's honor.

Travis took a deep breath and gave his head a hard single shake, shedding his mind of the negative emotions that would keep him from making it through yet another day. He lay back and cringed as his bare skin connected to the floor. It took a moment for his flesh to adapt to the tingle that surged through him, but the sensation faded. Travis crossed his arms about his chest and sat forward, laying back to repeat the motion a hundred times, maybe even two hundred if the automated lights allowed him the time.

Exercise was the key to keeping himself sane. It gave him focus, drive, strength, but more importantly it gave him something to do. Travis counted, throwing out the next consecutive number as the breaths grew shorter, his lungs thirstily grabbing for the next helping of stale, recycled air. With every upward movement he would mentally pull one bad memory from his mind, set it on his stomach and crunch it like a car compactor in a junkyard. Then he'd let his body fall back to rise up again, setting out the next troubling thought. This one was his wife's crying face as she told him she was pregnant, knowing full well he would not be there to see the birth.

"Ninety-eight!" Travis said as he crunched the image, laying back to set up the next one.

Travis pulled out an image of Sean Jeffries, the pilot that had been assigned to take them in on their last mission. He saw him sitting in his cell back on Earth, slumped forward with a letter clutched tightly in his right hand, tears streaming from his eyes in an uncontrollable flow of raw emotion. He muttered his father's name over and over as he shook his head, his body slightly rocking as if in synch with an unheard melody. Then Sean had looked up and met Travis' eyes from across the hall. So much hate in those eyes.

"Ninety-nine!"

Travis lay back as the automated lights buzzed into life, shining down on him without mercy. He sat up to make it an even one hundred and rolled upward to a standing position. He turned to his metal locker and opened it to find his few possessions. Four white shirts, a blue jumpsuit with his name "Daniels" stitched in black thread across the left breast, two pairs of black boots, three pairs of socks and underwear. This was all he had to work with. He dressed himself quickly, knowing full well the automated door wouldn't wait. Travis zipped up the jumpsuit and took a seat on his bed, crossing his leg atop the other to pull on his thick socks.

"Stand clear. Door will open in thirty seconds."

Travis stepped into his boots, wondering what he had to stand clear of. The door slid sideways and disappeared into the wall, nothing too exciting or dangerous. Still, it's nice to hear a woman's voice first thing every morning, even if it was robotic and annoyingly repetitive. He stood and approached the door, already seeing men passing by.

"Another day."

3

Travis followed the line of men through a sterile grey corridor passing more than a dozen cells duplicate to his own. They didn't like to refer to them as cells. The men and the security personnel universally referred to them as "private quarters," but a prison cell is a prison cell. Travis didn't know the names of the men he closely followed to the cafeteria. These were workers, men trained for the sole purpose of mining the Martian soil or building and maintaining the facility. Travis didn't concern himself with finding out their names or where they came from. He wasn't like them. Travis had come with a group of four men and one woman and they were the only ones he'd allow a moment of his time. They were the only ones that could possibly understand why he'd come to be millions of miles from his home.

Travis got in line and grabbed a plastic tray off the stack, sliding it along the thin metal bars. He thought back to when he'd been in high school, so many days spent in line behind an empty tray looking through a glass enclosure at what might have one day been eatable food. The scenery and the date sure had changed, but the gelatinous goop of food obviously hadn't.

"Looks like someone threw up in a bowl," Travis said, looking down into the bowl full of grey slop.

"It's got all your vitamins," Jerome McKinney said from behind him. "Kind of like porridge or gruel." Jerome laughed as he took his bowl from the man behind the counter. "Tastes like total shit of course, but at least it's good for you."

"Something this terrible could only be good for you," Travis said as he filled a plastic cup full of water and set it on the tray, turning from the counter to walk through rows of packed tables. A soft medley of classical music drifted down from the speakers above as it did every day.

Travis looked down at the men as he passed by, the tables full with burley men eating from plastic bowls with the same depressing food. The table directly ahead sat three people that didn't quite fit in. The closest man to him was TJ Ames, thirty-one years old and their equipment specialist. He was six-foot-six and had the darkest skin Travis had ever seen. What set him above the rest was his vast training in hand-to-hand combat. There was Morgan Ellis, originally from Las Vegas, forty-nine years old and a mechanical genius. He had an uncanny way of looking at machinery and just knowing how it all fit together, like some kind of extra sense. On the opposite side of the table was Christina Perez, the only woman on the facility but not someone you could take advantage of. She was thirty-six, five-foot-six and very beautiful. Her blonde hair and hazel eyes could draw your attention from across the room, but her combat training and hand-to-hand combat went unmatched, except maybe by TJ. The final member of their special ops team was not found at their table. Across the room, sitting alone with his head down was Sean Jeffries, their pilot. He looked up from his bowl as Travis took a seat, giving him a scowl before returning to his loneliness.

"Don't worry about him," TJ said, speaking over a mouth full of food.

"Even with all these men, TJ, your sexiness just stands out," Christina said with a smile.

"You know you want this goodness," TJ said after taking another bite, making it a point to speak through as much food as possible for added effect.

The table shared a single laugh, glad to have the tension eased if only for a moment. Day in and day out they shared the same expression, longing to be back home where the grass was green and they could smell dew in the air. In the facility, the air always smelled stale. The huge drawback of recycled air was just that; it was recycled. Nothing was fresh here. The food was frozen or made from a powder, the water heavily filtered and reused from their own urine. Morgan had done repairs numerous times on the filtration devices within the toilets. It made him shudder with every sip from his plastic cup, looking over the rim at the men around him to wonder just who had deposited the liquid he was now consuming.

"Next week marks our eleventh month," Christina said, holding up her cup for a toast. "Let us all give thanks for a job well done."

"I guess we can drink to that," Travis said, gently tapping cups so as not to spill a single drop. They were only rationed so much water a day, no exceptions. "Okay, where did we last leave off?" Travis set his cup on the table and leaned back, thinking back to yesterday to recall the last person to name off an item. It was a game they played, something to help pass the time while keeping Earth fresh in their minds. Sadly, after almost a year of mindless routine, Travis found it difficult to remember even the previous day. They all seemed to mesh together, like rain falling into the ocean until there was nothing but an endless blur. "I think it was TJ?"

"No, it was Jerome," TJ said quickly, folding his arms about his chest as he passed the duties to Jerome with a sly smile. "I'm on deck."

"Deck my ass," Jerome laughed. "You just can't stand the pressure." Jerome took a spoonful and smiled over the awful taste, like mayo and sand served at room temperature. "Okay, let me run this through the massive computer that is my mind." Jerome put his hands to his forehead and closed his eyes, shaking a bit for dramatic effect. He smiled as he often did, unable to keep a serious expression if his life depended on it. "I think the one thing I would like to see again would be a baseball game. Doesn't matter the team. Just to sit down in the stands, a hotdog in one hand and a beer in the other." Jerome closed his eyes and took a deep breath. "Would be very nice."

"Okay Morgan, how about it," Daniels said, passing the duty to Morgan.

"That's a pretty tough one to pass up." Morgan took a moment to think. "Probably drive-thru burgers." He rubbed his stomach while licking his lips. "King Charlie's drive-thru in Michigan. That would be so awesome right about now. I took my first girlfriend there on our first date."

"Wow, what a big spender," Jerome said with a laugh.

"Come on, fast food can be very romantic if done

right," Christina defended.

"All right little Casanova, what's yours?" Jerome asked.

Christina smiled, closing her eyes as she ran through memories like a photo album, snagging the one that made her the happiest. "I would have to say that the thing I miss the most, right now, would be a nice warm bubble bath. Candles burning with the light off while watching a movie."

They all nodded in unison as the image appealed to them, maybe not the bath itself, but the feeling of being encased in warmth and comfort. The air was always drafty and the water from the showers was icy and timed to conserve water.

"What about you, sir?" Christina asked Travis.

"Same as it is every day, my wife and son." Travis looked down to the ring on his finger, tracing it absently as he thought back to the last time he'd felt the warmth of his wife's touch.

The classical music overhead screeched to a halt and there was a brief pause. "Travis Daniels." The voice was automated, echoing loudly through the large cafeteria. "Please report to sector seven for your monthly evaluation."

"Nothing like a beautiful train ride through the country side," Travis said sarcastically as he stood, leaving more than half his breakfast in the bowl for one of his men to finish if they so desired.

Travis gave them a brief nod before heading out the door, glancing over briefly to Sean as he passed. Sean looked up and gave him a stone cold glare before returning back to his food. Travis took a deep breath and let it out slowly, knowing there were some things he had to simply let go.

4

Travis exited the cafeteria and took a long walk down a corridor he traveled daily, only this time he'd be taking a slight alteration. Everyday his routine was exactly the same. He'd be summoned from his "living quarters" with the rest of the men to go have a hearty breakfast of tasteless snot. They were given forty minutes to shoot the shit while consuming their liquids and vitamins, then the door on the opposite wall of the door he'd taken today would slide open, the light above turning from red to green. Each of them would slide their food trays into the slot beside the door and follow a very short corridor into the staging area. There the men would get their suits from the lockers and suit up for the elevator ride deep within the planet. Those were the daily routines for the miners such as himself. If you were working on the systems maintenance, the atmospheric processors, or general construction, you'd grab your suits from the same lockers but continue down a corridor that ran behind the elevator and let out into Grand Central Station, as they called it, the main terminal for the network of trains that ran over the surface of the planet. These weren't your average trains. They were airtight shuttles that ran along narrow tracks to the scientific facility set near the northern ice cap, the atmospheric processor at the southern pole, an adjoining dome shaped structure that housed the corporate honchos and the shrink, or one of three thousand thermal vents set up to vent greenhouse gasses into the atmosphere.

Travis entered the locker room and opened the one with his last name across the front. He stepped inside the tight fitting brown suit and zipped up the inner lining. Once the suit was sealed he fastened the outer straps and then the clamps over the front of the suit, making it airtight. He stuck his hands into the matching gloves and grabbed his helmet, kicking the locker shut with the back of his foot, the metallic bang echoing through the cavernous locker room. It was strange to see it empty. Travis turned toward the corridor at the opposite end of the wall, looking to the sealed airlock with the elevator behind, wondering if this little trip would last long enough to keep him from mining for the rest of the day. Travis turned his attention back to the hall and continued forth, figuring it really didn't matter. Mining was at least a way to pass the time.

"Please step forward and scan your identification." The train operator said as Travis came to the end of the hall and entered the loading dock of the train station.

Travis approached the podium with the train operator and extended his right hand, pulling the glove back. He rested it on the podium while the man ran a red laser over the barcode. Travis looked up to the screen behind the operator, a man named Danny Alino by the nametag, and saw his own face turning from side to side with the serial number they assigned him blinking beneath his head.

"Please enter the train and keep clear of the track," the operator said without emotion. "Have your helmet securely fastened and take a seat. Do not stand."

Travis placed his helmet over his head and turned it clockwise until he heard that all too familiar click, instantly followed by a cool rush of oxygen. The train went through the air blowers and crawled into the station at three miles an hour, coming to a jerky stop. The doors parted with a loud hiss, giving Travis only thirty seconds to enter before they sealed shut, that same hydraulic hiss as the metal door eased its way into the airtight rubber seal. Travis took a seat as the train took off, giving the man behind the controls a brief wave that was not returned.

The train rolled into a dark tunnel and stopped, waiting a brief moment for the station door to seal behind it before going forward toward the outer door. The train, if you could call it that with only four compartments, shook as it went up a slight incline. It moved toward two thick metal doors that slowly parted, allowing the light to fill in the darkness of the train's interior. There was always a moment of fear, just a slight twinge somewhere in the back of him, that as soon as the train leveled out on the Martian surface the thick glass windows would shatter or there'd be a malfunction in the rubber sealant. Any number of things could happen to allow the deadly conditions outside to come rushing in. He knew it to be a completely foolish thing to worry about, especially while wearing a suit capable of withstanding the Martian environment, but fears often were foolish. He figured it'd be something to tell the shrink about.

The trip was brief, but very enjoyable. Anything to break up the day and add a dash of variety. The train emerged from the dark tunnel and leveled out upon the Martian surface, turning in an arch toward the small dome structure set just beside the main facility. Travis pressed his helmet to the glass and looked out on the alien landscape, taken back as he always was. This wasn't like a casual drive through the Sahara or some kind of NASA look-alike to train their astronauts and rovers; this was the real deal. An eerie red soil as far as the eye could see, stretching off into the infinite. Mountains towered in the distance that made Earth's Mt. Everest look like a molehill. But what got him the most was the vast darkness of the trench to his right, so deep you couldn't see the bottom. Both the main facility and the corporate structure were built into the side of the canyon; only the tip of the dome from the corporate structure was visible from the surface. Travis had heard a few different reasons for this. One being that the meteorite activity was a concern and this would add much needed protection, which of course he was for. Another has something to do with the supply ship having an easier time docking from inside the walls of the canyons, like it cut down the wind resistance from the numerous sand storms or something. Such details were seldom shared with people in Travis's situation.

The train made a complete one hundred and eighty degree turn and moved toward the dome at twenty miles an hour. Four minutes later and the train angled downward into a short cement tunnel, slowing to a complete stop. Powerful hoses ran the length of the train, spraying off any access soil. The doors to the only train station in this smaller structure opened to an exact duplicate of the scene he'd just left. An empty terminal with a single operator standing behind a podium-style control board with a vacant expression, barely bringing himself to look up as the train stopped and the doors parted.

"Please scan your identification," the man said with a stone cold expression. The excitement of being stationed on the fourth planet from the sun had long since worn off.

Travis stuck his arm, wrist side up, under the red laser and let the light scan the barcode. His face popped up on the screen and spun slowly with his facility ID underneath. It was a little uncomfortable to see his severed head spinning like that.

"You have a scheduled session with Dr. Hoffman. Please take the corridor to your left and follow it 'til you reach the last door on the right." The man spoke in monotone, tilting his head to the right slightly from sheer boredom.

"Quite the life isn't it?" Travis said with a joking smile.

"Just move along." The man shooed him away with his hands.

Travis turned from the wonderfully exciting conversation with the train's operator and headed down the corridor as instructed. He passed by numerous doors, all of them made of thin metal that slid inward. He passed the Communication Uplink Specialist, Mineral Analysis, Human Resources, Vice President of Off-World Mining. He couldn't help but laugh. He and his men had all but been forced to come here, faced with both a court marshal and life in prison or work detail on Mars until the atmosphere was deemed breathable and the permanent facilities were all up and running. But the men and women behind those doors had fought hard to take the hundred-day trek across space to fulfill these pointless positions. The one that tickled him the most was the Human Resources Director, imagining him sitting behind his desk with a "Hang in There" kitty poster on the wall, listening to big strapping miners talk about how so and so sexually harassed them. It made him laugh. But that's how the world worked. Even out here across the vastness of space you couldn't escape the politics of big business and all the bullshit that went with it. Still, lame positions meant more jobs. Only in an environment such as this, more positions meant more of their air being sucked up by these wastes of space.

Travis controlled his wide smile and good humor, shaking the giggle from his face before knocking on the last door at the end of the hall, this one with Dr. Hoffman written across the front in black bold letters.

"Aw, thank you for accepting my invitation, Mr. Daniels," Dr. Hoffman said as the door opened. He stood from his leather recliner and hurried across the small office, shaking his hand. "Please, why don't you come in and have a seat."

Travis crossed the flat carpet to the couch, taking a seat. His humor fought hard to surface as he took in the surroundings, looking from the evenly stacked books in the waist-high bookshelf and ending with the trinkets on his desk that seemed to be handed out as soon as you got your doctorate. A bronzed statue of Freud's head, a globe with a brass axis. The desk organizer with the pens lined perfectly beside the pad of paper set dead in its center. What brought the smile to his face were not the items themselves, but just the need for them. Travis could picture Dr. Hoffman in his office back on Earth, deciding which couch would make the men more comfortable or which pieces of art might create the most calming atmosphere. But that was the real trick to every perfectly placed piece or art to the small half-moon shaped rug beneath Travis's feet—to create the most calming atmosphere. To make everyone that stepped into his office feel as if they were right back home.

"What's so funny?" Dr. Hoffman asked while taking his seat, patiently resting his right leg over his left knee. This position said: *You can talk to me. I'll take the time to listen because I want to.*

"I just find it interesting how things were brought over from Earth to create an 'at home' like feeling. Like the pictures you have on the wall. A man playing catch with his dog, a boy and his sailboat…I don't know. It's just humorous to me." Travis sat back and folded his arms, not really knowing where he was going with this. He was letting his nerves get the best of him. Truth be told, Dr. Hoffman was the best friend they had on this distant red rock. He's the man that could get you rest vouchers, calls from home, medication if you're so inclined.

"You're right. Everything I've brought with me has been hand selected to create a sense of comfort and peace. After all my main function here is to monitor the stress and overall mental state of the men stationed here. You and your unit especially." Dr. Hoffman read the look on Travis' face. "Part of your condition for being here is that you and your men undergo routine mental tests and monitoring. With your extensive military training you are the best suited for this type of isolation, but it is quite common for men to snap, experience heightened levels of aggression as your training seeks for a means." The doc smiled, holding out his hands to ease the tension he saw rising in Travis's shoulder. "Fortunately I don't see a single instance that would arouse any concern. But…there are two issues I would like to review with you."

"Sure," Travis said, leaning forward to rest his elbows on his knees.

"I see you're having trouble sleeping?" Dr. Hoffman asked with a concerned look.

"Just bad dreams. Plus the bed isn't very comfortable."

"I should imagine not," the doc said as they shared an uncomfortable chuckle that quickly died. "Is there anything in particular you remember or care to discuss?"

Travis thought for a moment, shaking his head.

"Do they center around an individual?"

"No, just restless sleep."

The doc nodded as he scribbled something on the legal pad on his lap. "My last concern is over Mr. Jeffries. I've noticed some more tension there and I want to hear if there's anything on your mind."

"No, just some bitterness toward me is all." Travis rubbed his hands together. "Really nothing I can do about it."

"Have you ever tried to open a line of communication with him?"

"Not in a few weeks, and it wasn't very pleasant."

Dr. Hoffman nodded as he made some more squiggles.

"I'm not all that concerned with him," Travis lied,

hiding his guilt as best he could. "I don't foresee any problems there."

"I have here your monthly report to General Campbell. Have there been any changes in your superiors or other coworkers? Any concerns over how the facility is being run? The General wants you to be as specific as possible."

"Nothing that stands out." Travis thought for a moment. "Maybe some better food or leisure activities for the men, games and cards. But other than that I can't think of too much right now."

"Excellent. Now, what about your family? I'm sure you miss them terribly." Dr. Hoffman tapped his knee, hoping to get some kind of emotional response from his patient. These sessions were getting rather boring and he was starting to miss his practice back on earth. These men were so tightlipped, too well trained in shedding emotions.

"Every single day," Travis said, his throat becoming choked with emotion. "I think about them, what they might be doing, where they are as I'm starting my day. But I feel better about our situations. At least up here I'm able to contact them every so often and let my son know that his father loves him."

"Well then, I have excellent news for you. I've gone through your quarterly review and have arranged for a communications link with our facility back on Earth. I've already had them contact your wife and she's in the comms room waiting to talk to you."

"Oh that is fantastic." Travis could hardly contain his excitement. "What about my son? Will I get to see Logan as well?"

"We informed Mrs. Daniel's that it would be an excellent idea to bring your son." Dr. Hoffman smiled. "I was told she reacted quite enthusiastically to the notion."

"Oh thank you." Travis stood and took Dr. Hoffman's hand, pumping it rapidly. "I really do appreciate this."

"Well you better hurry if you want to make the most out of it. You only have twenty minutes of uplink," the doc said with a smile as he hurried to the door, stepping aside as it opened. "Just go down to the door with Communication Uplink Specialist across the front."

5

Annie Daniels stood before the mirror atop her dresser, tying a blue ribbon in her hair. She wore a blue housedress with a white floral print, one she knew her husband enjoyed. Travis had told her once that she had such an amazing figure and that this dress did a great job of featuring all his favorite highlights. Annie smiled as she watched his face light up in her memory. Seeing him sitting on the bed with such a goofy expression across his face. Travis had always managed to make her smile. It was his sense of humor that had drawn her to him in the first place. When they'd met fifteen years ago, he had been in plain clothes. It was only after they'd spent three hours talking that he let it slip he was in the armed forces. For every man up until Travis she would have politely smiled and walked away. She hated the military. Thought they were nothing but a bunch of slimy bastards bent on destroying the world. But there was nothing evil behind his smile, no dark laid plans within his eyes, only honesty. She loved him the instant he had bumped into her at the park, running backwards to catch a Frisbee until he'd stumbled into her and knocked them both down. They shared a laugh and started a four-hour conversation. Annie's mother told her later that same week that they would end up together, that good couples always had an excellent story of how they first met. And they had been a perfect couple, loving and living for each other. Longing for him when he was called away for one of his secret missions. Twelve years of perfect marriage that was finally blessed with a pregnancy. She had been unable to contain her excitement. Late at night she'd run to the corner drugstore and purchased a pregnancy test. Alone in the bathroom at four in the morning, pacing with one hand on her hip and the other against her forehead, waiting anxiously as Travis slept without a clue. Her heartbeat tripled as she saw the blue plus sign slowly appear in the little window. Running out of the bathroom with the test in her hand, she'd hopped into bed and awoken her husband with the great news. They both held each other. So much love in their arms. Eight and a half months later and Logan was born…then this mess had happened.

Annie finished tying the ribbon about her hair, exhaling a long breath while eyeing herself in the mirror. The stress was beginning to take its toll. There were lines about her eyes, creeping over her face like the dry bottom of a lakebed. Laugh lines that couldn't be further from the truth. She didn't laugh much anymore and when she did it was usually followed by a fresh batch of tears. But that wasn't going to be the case today. This was going to be a very happy day for all of them.

"Logie!" Annie yelled over her shoulder, loud enough for her voice to travel out her bedroom door and down the stairs to her son on the couch. "Remember not to play on the floor and get your clothes dirty."

"Okay mom," Logan's little voice called up, barely audible.

Annie leaned in close to the mirror, gently applying a thin layer of eye shadow. She put on some light pink lipstick and a few drops of foundation on her cheeks, rubbing the liquid into her skin. One of the most common compliments her husband paid her was how she didn't need makeup to look great. Travis said she was a natural beauty. She believed her husband, but still, a woman needed a little mascara every now and then. Just that extra smear of confidence to stand out and feel secure. Annie wiped off her hands and stood back, turning her face from side to side for inspection.

Having given herself a passing score, Annie left the bedroom, cursing under her breath as she lifted up her bare foot to examine the sharp pinch she'd felt. Lying on the floor was one of Logan's numerous army men sprawled on its back with its plastic bayonet pointed skyward, blending perfectly with the dark green carpeting. The hideous color had been mutually decided upon when they'd considered how well it would hide the many stains left by a child, or one day quite possibly, children.

"At ease soldier." Annie kicked the plastic man aside with her hurt foot, shaking her head at the numerous times she stepped on something. At least this time it hadn't been something soft and squishy.

Annie came down the stairs and went into the kitchen, shaking her head with a little smile as she saw Logan sitting on the floor, digging through his toy box with determination. One thing she loved about her son was his compulsive behavior. If he wanted to play with a certain dinosaur you'd better believe he was going to find it, even if it took him two hours of searching through the multiple stacks of toys throughout the house. Today he was content with the few action figures he'd pulled out of the toy box, laying them down on the floor as he hovered over them, acting out the different voices. Annie knew she should have been angry at his complete disregard for her words, but a good parent knows when to pick a battle and when to simple laugh it off. Annie figured the poor guy had it hard enough without her harping over every little thing. Besides, Travis won't care if there's a small patch of dirt on his son's slacks.

"Are you still hungry?" Annie asked as she poured some apple juice into a travel cup.

"Can I have fruit snacks?" Logan asked without looking up, his mind deeply locked on the strategic battle between a red robot and some kind of superhero.

"A fruit snack? I don't see an empty bowl of cereal," Annie said in a playful manner, tapping the counter beside his partially eaten breakfast. She knew this was an argument that would get her nowhere. How children could eat so sparsely and still grow was beyond her.

"Please," Logan said with a wide grin, hamming it up.

Annie shook her head and walked over to the pantry, tossing her son a small packet of fruit snack. She watched him rip them open and shove half the pack into his mouth. Before the day was out he'd probably consume two to three more packs. Annie just rationalized his eating habits with the knowledge that at least they're made from real fruit.

"Are you looking forward to seeing daddy?" Annie

asked as she took the travel bag from the pantry and set it on the counter, adding three more packets of fruit snacks for good measure.

"I want to show him the new Power Bot you got me," Logan said brightly, holding up the robot for his mother to admire.

"I think he'd really like that."

Annie took a moment to watch her son play on the floor, seeing the similarities in his face to Travis'. They both had the same nose and cheekbones. The eyes were hers, but the smile was pure Travis. Every smile made her want to cry, seeing her husband in those stretched lips. Annie couldn't control the emotion; it overwhelmed her. She turned her back to her son and wept softly, kicking herself for being so weak. It was her goal to keep sadness from their lives. To go on as if this was just a transitional phase and that daddy would be home someday. She knew better of course, but Logie didn't need to accept that. Not at the tender age of three. He deserved to play with his daddy's smile and his new toys. Annie wiped the tears and took a slow, calming breath. She turned around and gripped the counter, shaking the lingering depression from her head.

"Okay Pook, let's get going," Annie said as she glanced up at the clock above the stove. "Come on. We don't want to be late and miss daddy's call."

Annie took Logan's hands and pulled him to his feet, helping him carry an armload of this and that out to the car. She tossed the toys beside his car seat in their station wagon and buckled him in. He made the process difficult as he leaned over to grab his toys and of course his blue blanket with the satin trim. You could never leave the house without blankey. God have mercy on your soul if you wandered away without it. Travis had purchased the blanket two months before Logan was born. Since his birth it had never left his side. Once Logie was securely fastened with his mound of toys and stuffed animals nearly engulfing him, Annie came around the front of the car and got behind the wheel.

For the next three and a half hours they passed the time singing children's songs, playing road trip games like I Spy or the alphabet game. Logan got bored easily and put his attention to the comfort blankey offered between his cheek and the padded headrest of the booster seat. Within ten seconds he was sleeping with his mouth slightly agape. Annie looked up into the rearview repeatedly to steal a glimpse of his precious face.

This was a long trek, but it wasn't as simple as picking up a phone when it came to calling another planet. The only communication link between the Martian facility and Earth was through TransWorld

Inc., the company that built the place. Thankfully the main building was just north of Salem, VA. Better than having to hop on a plane and fly to California or Florida just for a twenty minute conversation with her husband. The company was building the off-world facilities under government contracts and thus was under fire with the public. They saw TransWorld Inc. as an extension of the military being sent to Mars to eventually test weapons of mass destruction or engineer new viruses, perfecting them before they unleashed them back home. Travis had told her what was really going down. There was nothing remotely exciting happening off-world, no doomsday devices or giant laser cannons being constructed with Earth in the crosshairs. But it was the connection with the military that had offered Travis and his unit an alternative to a death sentence. Annie closed her eyes a brief moment to mentally block out the headache. Thinking of her husband being locked away for something that wasn't his fault made her stomach sour. Sometimes life could be so unfair.

Annie exited off highway 220 just north of Salem and headed down a dirt road that looked too rural for a high tech facility with billion-dollar government funding, but it was there. Anyone within a hundred miles could tell you where they were located after witnessing the last launch of the gargantuan supply ship just over three months ago, looking like a metallic version of Noah's ark. The road narrowed, lined with tall trees to keep the massive structure relatively hidden. Annie slowed to a crawl as she approached the gate, rolling down her window as three soldiers armed with machine guns approached the car.

"Please turn off your engine and exit the car ma'am," the soldier standing beside her driver side door ordered in a firm voice. He was the only soldier of the three not aiming a weapon. The soldier stepped aside and stood stiff as a rail while Annie swung the door open and cautiously exited the car, smoothing out her dress as she stood. "I need to see your identification and letter of admittance."

"Okay, hold onto your panties." Annie tried to lighten the tension. She ducked back into the car and grabbed her purse, digging through the normal clutter until she found her wallet. She undid the snap and pulled out her driver's license and the small piece of paper she'd received in the mail. A piece of mail she'd been waiting for since her last communication with Travis four months prior. "Here you go."

The soldier took the license and the letter and turned back toward the small booth set beside the metal gate. Annie set her arm atop the car and leaned into the open door, waiting patiently as she watched the solider get on the phone and do the standard checks.

"Ma'am, we will need to search your car for con-traband," the soldier standing by the front right tire said as he lowered his weapon, swinging it under his arm so it rested on the strap behind his back.

"Knock yourself out."

The soldier opened the passenger side door and began looking beneath the seat and through the glove box.

"Don't move!" The third soldier yelled, pointing the gun at Logan through the window as he awoke.

"Take your goddamn gun out of my son's face!" Annie yelled, her face red. The veins beneath her skin were visible as her blood boiled through them. "I said now, before I rip off your fucking balls and beat you with them. Does that compute soldier!"

The soldier lowered his weapon and moved to the front of the car, keeping his distance. He may have had the weapon, but the heated look on Annie's face said no amount of bullets were going to bring her down. The soldier slightly averted his gaze to look at the hood of the car, backing down from the hard stare from Annie. She gave him a single nod and turned her attention back to the first soldier as he stepped out of the booth.

"Your clearance has been approved." The soldier handed Annie back the paperwork and her license.

"Please follow the road to the main turnaround at the front of the building. Leave your keys in the car and turn the engine off." Without another word the man turned and entered the booth, triggering the thick metal gate to slowly pull apart.

Annie started the car back up and drove toward the gate, pausing at the booth while rolling down the window. "I'd keep that soldier off the front lines if I were you," Annie said to the man in the booth, motioning with her head toward the soldier that had pulled the gun on Logie. "He seems a bit squeamish to me."

Annie didn't wait for a response; she just turned back toward the thin dirt road and headed through the gate. The road wound through the dense trees for a few hundred yards, the dirt road smoothing out to black pavement looking less than a year old. The paved road took her another thirty yards through the forest and then to a turnaround before a very sterile building, TransWorld Inc. across the front in large silver letters made of sculpted steel. The 'O' in world had been replaced with a globe of Earth. Annie thought it looked a bit too much, like pulling up to the observatory. She parked the car before the entrance and killed the engine, waiting a brief moment. There was a strange vibe to these types of facilities. No one was ever eating their lunch on the lawns, no landscapers working on the bushes. It always looked so deserted from the outside, as if designed this way to give intruders their last chance to say, "Oh look honey, this place must be deserted. Let's just go."

"Are we going to see daddy?" Logan asked, finishing the sentence with a big yawn. His cheeks were red and there were sleep lines across his face. The right side of his head was matted with sweat.

Annie couldn't help but smile, letting her previous tension over the gun incident melt away as if it'd never happened. She left the keys in the ignition and got out of the car, walking around the front to open the back door for her son. She undid the seatbelt and helped him out of his car seat.

"Carry me," Logan said, resting his head on Annie's shoulder.

"Come on, you're a big boy. You can walk." Annie bent down to set him on the ground.

"No, carry me." Logie burrowed his head deep into the flesh of her neck and shoulder, like a cat rubbing against your legs to try and coax some treats out of you.

"Let's go. You're walking Mr. Man," Annie said as she got down on her knees, bending forward until he had no choice but to stand. This was a routine of theirs, no matter where they went. Normally she'd put in one or two firm commands and then eventually give in. It was hard not to when she was all he had. Annie felt responsible to make him feel as loved as possible since she was left to do it alone, even if the consequence might be slightly harmful down the road. But for now, this one time, she wanted her little boy to walk in their on his own, to stand tall and proud for his daddy to see. Annie reached over her son's shoulder and grabbed the travel bag and Logie's blankey off the seat. "Okay, march mister."

"Yeah, we're going to see daddy!" Logan said as he hurried toward the door, hopping up and down with the argument moments ago already gone from his mind.

Annie kicked the back door shut with her foot and hurried over to her son, taking hold of his hand. She held the door and allowed him to enter first, smiling down at how excited he'd become. Logan hopped up and down before the large sculpture of a glass hand holding a planet in the palm of its hand. Carved into the glass was the company's mission state-ment: Building Better Worlds Today For A Brighter Tomorrow. A little corny for sure, but Annie thought the sculpture was perfect. A giant hand holding the planet in its grip is a perfect representation for how they saw things. Annie gave Logie a single tug and got him moving, following the dark blue floor to the metal detector and the guard stationed there. Much like the airport, Annie set their possessions on a conveyor belt, including the contents of their pockets. She walked through the metal detector, turning to see if she'd passed the test or if the green light would go red. It stayed green. Annie grabbed their stuff off the belt and held out her hand to Logie as he walked through. The green light dinged red.

"Please empty your pockets son," the man said, holding out a plastic container to Logan.

Logan had a guilty expression, lowering his head as he pulled a spoon from his pocket and dropped it into the container. There was a faded ring of peanut butter around the tip, now coated in lint. The man took the container and gave Annie a little wink, waving them through.

"Excuse me?" Annie said to Logan as she took his hand, giving him a playful shake.

They followed the blue floor past a few offices and the break room, finally coming to the end of the hall where a man in a black suit was waiting for them.

"Nice to see you again Mrs. Daniels," Francis Sparks said with a slight nod. He was a giant man, standing at six-foot-seven, with giant banana hands she was always a bit uncomfortable to shake. "We have made an excellent connection with the Martian facility and are ready for you. If you and your son will please follow me to room three."

"Thank you," Annie said, her tone fake. This man didn't care if she thanked him or called him a Nazi baby killer. Either way he wouldn't have heard her. And if he did the plastic smile across his tan face would have never faltered. This was a company PR man, someone that ate bullshit for breakfast with a grin every single morning while reading the sports page.

"I bet you've been looking forward to this. Must be very lonely with your husband so far away," Francis said, sneaking a glance from the corner of his eye.

"It is very difficult. But my husband is worth the wait," Annie said sharply, leaving out any hope of advancement on Sharp's part.

Annie followed Mr. Sharp through the door to their left, passing an office with a very large man sitting behind the desk eating donuts. He briefly looked up as they passed, his mouth caked with powdered sugar. Annie smiled and continued on, feeling anxious as they passed a door with Room One written across the front. Mr. Sharp paused before the door on their right, this one being the third room. He opened the door and stepped back, allowing them entrance.

"Now the link has been established and your husband is waiting on his end. Just press the green button there and you're good to go. Please remember that there is a three to five second delay."

"We will, thank you."

Mr. Sharp nodded and shut the door. Annie felt a bit uncomfortable around him. She could feel his eyes watching her the entire time he'd led them down the hall, picturing what her ass might look like in a black thong. Licking his lips like a predator. Annie shook her head, not wanting to give that prick another moment of her time. She took a seat before the monitor and lifted Logan up on her lap, her skin breaking out in bumps from excitement. She bounced Logie on her knee as the screen went from black to blue, an hourglass turning slowly in the screens center. Annie became overwhelmed with emotion as her husband's face appeared. They both began to cry. Unable to contain the flow of tears as she looked at the man she loved.

"You need to shave," Annie laughed.

"I'll have to get around to it," Daniels said after a three second pause. He wiped the tears from his eyes and looked at his son. "You have gotten so big."

"Hi daddy," Logan said cheerfully, waving with excitement. "Look, I have a new robot!" Logan held up the little toy his mother had gotten him, waving it back and forth.

"That is an awesome robot, Logie." Travis took a deep breath and held it, feeling a fresh batch of tears forming. "Are you being a good boy for your mother?"

"Yes, daddy," Logan said sweetly, looking down

as he felt shy.

"Do you miss your daddy?"

"I miss you daddy," Logan said, smiling.

"I miss you too, every day sweetheart." Travis turned away from the screen and talked to someone out of view, nodding with disappointment. "I love you Logie, but I need to talk to mommy for a minute."

"Okay daddy, I love you."

Travis kissed his hand and touched the screen, unable to hold back the tears. Logie touched the screen and pressed his small hand to his father's large hand. Annie helped Logan off the chair and led him out into the hallway and into the room across from them, set up as a little daycare with toys and videos. Knowing her time was incredibly short, she turned on a video and smiled at the young woman in charge of watching her son before hurrying back across the hall.

"He's getting so much older." Travis shook his head. "I'm so sorry you have to raise our son all alone."

"I know." She touched the screen and caressed the image of her husband's face. The feel was of cold glass, not that of the rough texture of her husband's face, his skin always carrying a five o'clock shadow. She'd gotten on his case so many times over the years to keep up his grooming, telling him his face felt like sandpaper. At this moment she'd take his rough cheeks in a heartbeat. To feel the warmth of his breath running over the back of her neck. "How are you carrying on?"

"It's so very different here." Travis looked about his surroundings. He himself was in a telecommunications booth, similar to the one his wife was in, only his room was dark and cold. Unlike her room, his would not lead to a hallway that ended in a sunny day. "It's always so dark here. So very cold."

"The nights have grown so cold here as well. Without you…" Annie shook her head, angry with herself. She'd given a little pep talk in the mirror before she'd come out, telling herself not to waste any precious time discussing things that might upset her husband. No point making him feel worse than he already did.

"That's something I've been wanting to talk to you about." Travis leaned back and scratched his head, a nervous tick he'd had as far back as she'd known him. "I know this has not been easy for you and Logie. I bet it's been hell. So I know how hard it can be to keep things together while being on your own. I just…I want you to know…" Travis cleared his throat, finding it difficult to continue. "If you need help raising our son, I want you to know that I won't hold it against you." Travis took a deep breath, holding back the tears to make his request clear and direct. "My only wish is that you find someone that is kindhearted and good with Logan."

"Are you giving me permission to date?" Annie shook her head.

"I know how lonely you are."

"And you're not?"

"Please, this isn't…"

"Stop," Annie interrupted, holding out her hands. "I know what you're trying to do, but it's not going to happen. It is incredibly difficult to raise a small child on your own, to shield them from the negative criticism they get for having a father sentenced to life of hard labor. But you and I are husband and wife, for better or worse. You're my husband, the father of my only son. And I will not find some temporary replacement just because the nights are a little rough."

"I love you so much." Travis touched the screen.

"I love you too," Annie said, pressing her hand to his. Her attention was called up to a red blinking light in the corner of the screen. "They're giving us the two minute countdown. I can't believe it's over so quickly."

"Can I say goodbye to Logie real quick?"

Annie stood from her chair and opened the door, rushing across the hall to grab her son's hand and take him from the nursery.

"Hi daddy." Logie held up his red robot and

waved it back and forth. "I have blanky with me."

"I know. You're turning into such a big boy." Daniels leaned close and smiled. "I want you to listen to your mother and help her out with whatever she needs. Can you do that for me?"

"Sure daddy."

"I love you both so much."

Her husband's face disappeared and the screen had gone black, broken by the words "Transmission Severed" in the screen's center. Annie shook her head, agitated she hadn't been given the chance to say goodbye. Machines weren't known for their compassion. Annie looked to her son and smiled, gripping his chin while shaking his head slightly.

"You were a good boy for daddy." Annie ran a hand through his hair.

6

Travis sat for a moment with his hand on the screen, touching the cold blackness as if his fingertips might conjure up the image of his wife's face. Never had he felt so far from his family then he did right now.

"Please exit the telecommunications room and return to your assigned duty."

Travis removed his hand and looked up to the small camera mounted in the corner, wiping his eyes. This wasn't a prison, but still never a great idea to show weakness, especially so far from home. Travis took a final look at the black screen, imagining his wife on the other side, holding their son. He hoped he hadn't hurt her feelings, suggesting such a radical means to living. But he knew it was better to give her the permission and have her choose a good and suitable man to help raise their son, then to have her fling herself out there in an act of desperation and bring home a wife beater while feeling guilty for offending their marriage. Deep down Travis knew Annie would wave it off, dismissing the notion as nothing more than a suggestion. She was too strong to disgrace their marriage vows, to look weak in the eyes of their son. That's one of the numerous reasons he loved her so much.

Travis stood and exited the room, heading down the hall with his head down, his mind full of worry. He had been so overwhelmed with the beauty and simple presence of his wife that he hadn't taken the time to really look her over to see the bags under her eyes or the wrinkles spreading across her face. The kind of wrinkles that came from stress, cracking the skin like the delicate surface of a dried leaf.

"Please stand clear of the track," the operator said as Travis stepped onto the platform.

Travis walked up the yellow line and waited patiently for the train to roll into the station. As before, he placed his helmet atop his head and screwed it into position, feeling the cool rush of air. Travis entered the train and took a seat, staying quiet as the train made its slow trip up the incline and out onto the Martian surface, circling around to enter the main terminal of the head facility.

"I hope everything is okay back on the homestead." Alvin Kerch stood on the platform with his hands folded behind his back.

Travis exited the train and unscrewed his helmet, pulling it away from his head with a hiss of air. He took in a deep breath and tucked the helmet beneath his right arm. "It's always greener on the other side."

Alvin gave out a deep laugh. "Hell's greener than this place."

"Am I under arrest?" Travis stopped a foot short of Alvin's impressive six-foot-seven frame.

"I've just been asked to take you to the mines. Like an escort to the prom."

Travis turned and walked side by side with Alvin, the only security personnel he took the time to get along with. Alvin was in his early fifties, well toned with a slight belly to him. His skin was very dark, a shade of black that looked almost too dark. Not that Travis would ever admit to such a thing, but he thought the darkness of his skin to be beautiful. No sexual attraction, just an observation.

"How was your son?" Alvin asked, keeping his tone down as they passed another security officer.

"Logan. He's growing up so damn fast." Travis thought back to his son's face, the smile he shared as he shook his toy back and forth. Such an innocent and simple gesture, but it meant so much to him. "Makes me so sick to see him growing up every few months on some monitor."

"I don't think you're the only one that wouldn't rather be somewhere else."

They shared a laugh and spoke as friends. Just two men on their way to work on any ordinary day. They entered the locker room and passed through the door on the opposite side of the wall. Just a short walk down a dim hallway to the elevator.

"This is where we part." Alvin stood beside the elevator with his hand held out. "After you my good sir."

"Why thank you boss man." Travis was feeling good for perhaps the first time in days.

The elevator doors parted with a strong hiss of air, blowing their hair back. Travis put the helmet over his head and turned it clockwise, taking in a deep breath of stale air. With his helmet and suit secure, he stepped into the elevator, turning to give Alvin a single wave.

"Don't work too hard now." Alvin disappeared from view as the doors sealed shut.

Travis gripped the railing and held on as the elevator dropped rapidly, falling deep within the planet's interior. The quickness of the drop always made his stomach ill, rising into his throat. Travis counted the seconds it took for the elevator to drop to the coring entrance. It took eight seconds to reach the mining station. The elevator came to a jerky halt, nearly knocking him off his feet.

"Please ensure that your helmet is securely locked in place with a steady flow of oxygen." An automated voice called down from the speaker above him. "If there is a malfunction with mining equipment or the security suit, please hit the red button located beside the door to return the elevator to the surface. Airlock opening in ten seconds."

Travis tapped his legs ten times, listening to the echoing of his own breath within the helmet. On the tenth tap, the thick steel doors of the elevator pulled apart, exposing him to the Martian environment. Travis kept his vision low as the lights above were blinding, shining down on the narrow tunnel carved in the rock. It was a long walk to the heart of the mining operation. Spanning beneath the surface of the planet for miles.

"Mr. Daniels, I was wondering when you were going to arrive. I had to radio Alvin to start a search."

"Just had to complete my psych evaluation, Mr. Chen."

"Load up your gear and take tunnel number three to meet your unit by the six mile marker." Mr. Chen scribbled something on his clipboard, looking up for a brief moment to confirm his orders had been heard. "Today, Daniels."

Travis went to the equipment shed and loaded

a laser drill and the strong arm controller set to his genetic coding and got into the front row of the mine cart. He secured the seatbelt across his lap and took a deep breath, signaling to Mr. Chen to send him on his way.

"Keep your hands inside the cart and stay seated," Mr. Chen said as he hit the green button on the panel to his right. The small cart took off down the track, gaining speed.

Travis kept a tight hand on the mining equipment on the seat beside him, remembering the long hours of training videos and instruction they'd been made to watch. The training video about mining cart safety had shown a cartoon man zipping down the track at the top speed of twelve miles an hour. He wore an unnaturally wide smile as he cruised through the belly of the planet. The mine cart shifted and his equipment bounced over the side of his cart, falling onto the track as the wheels ran over it and the cart was flung wildly against the walls. The video stated the proper transport of any such mining equipment was to strap it into the seat beside them with the supplied restraints. The video had been laughable to say the least, but the imagery had been clear enough. The last thing he needed was a cave in or a nasty accident. Despite the constant danger, he couldn't help but let out a smile. The scenery was dark and dreadful, added with the robotic sounded breathing from within his own helmet. But the fear subsided with the Disneyland-like cart he was currently riding in. It sat three miners with their equipment beside them. The cart slowed to a stop. Travis unlocked his mining equipment and stepped out a second before it took off down the track to return to Mr. Chen.

"Well look who it is," Jerome said with a chuckle, holding a laser drill tightly. He released the firing mechanism long enough to sass his friend as he walked toward them. "I thought you were walking back to Earth or something."

"Do you think this thing carries that much air?" Travis took position between Jerome and TJ. "Anything interesting happen?" Travis asked as he gripped the handle of the laser cutter, pressing his fingertips to the rubber grips and waited briefly for the equipment to power up. It shook for a moment before giving out a loud ding, the small display on the handle showing his face and identification number. Something beneath the skin in his arm, maybe imbedded in the ink used in his tattooed ID barcode, sent out a signal that set everything he used to only be used by him. Everything off-world was designed to keep everyone in check and accountable.

"Oh yeah, you missed a whole lot of fantastic shit," TJ said. "We unearthed a Martian carcass with a TV Guide clutched between its three thick fingers."

Christina laughed, annoyed how her breath fogged up the facemask. She lifted her left hand to wipe it clear and shook her head, feeling stupid. Taking off the helmet might make it easier to clean, but it wouldn't do any good once her head exploded.

"How is the family looking?" Morgan asked, cursing under his breath as his grip on the drill handle slipped.

"Logan is looking so much like his mother," Travis yelled as his drill powered up. He twisted the handgrip and aimed the thin red light into the rocks before him, chipping away the thick iron like bits of cornflakes. "I thank God he has his mother's beautiful features."

"Anything's better than having your chimp ass complexion." Jerome gave a laugh.

"Hey, chimps are known as extremely cute creatures," Travis shouted to be heard over the loud whine of his drill.

"At least they used to be," Christina added, her voice hidden beneath the loud machinery. She thought back to the last time she'd seen a chimp, at the zoo in Chicago on a date when she was fifteen. Back then there had been a few left, but much like the polar bear and the elephant, they were nothing more than a distant thought and a photo in a book.

"What about Annie?" Morgan asked, knowing from a previous conversation he'd had with Travis on the topics he was going to discuss with his wife.

"She's doing very well." Travis looked over to Morgan and made eye contact, telling him with his gaze that he'd given his wife the option and she'd said no. He and Morgan had been very close and were well versed in reading the other's body language.

"So what's your little man up to these days? Can he speak Latin or what?" Jerome asked.

"He can say just about anything really. Hard to believe he's come so far in just a few years. Makes me so angry to have to miss out on so much of his life." Travis thought about how well his son was speaking now and how he hadn't been there to hear his first word, to see his first steps, or to rock him to sleep at night.

"Just be thankful he gets to see your face," Morgan offered as a little bit of comfort.

Travis felt comfortable around his unit, having handpicked them all from their files years ago, even Sean Jeffries had been one of his select few. He had been the best pilot in the army, running helicopter missions into enemy territory and maintaining a zero casualty rating with whatever unit he happened to be transporting. Sean had then spent a few years as a test pilot, flying the fastest jets below radar or zipping them out of the atmosphere without break-ing a sweat. Now Sean drove a laser drill. Travis looked over his shoulder and saw Sean looking right back, giving him a heated stare as he shut off his drill, lowering it to rest against his leg.

"Just keep it friendly, boss." Jerome leaned over his drill to stand between them. "You know this is the last place on Earth you'd want to start something."

"That's true, but we're not on Earth anymore," TJ said, slightly egging him on. "Besides, he needs his ass smacked down just a little."

"Leave it alone!" Christina looked from TJ to Sean.

Sean caught sight of Christina and let out a long sigh, releasing his anger toward Travis like a deflat-ing balloon. He picked up his drill and went back to work, standing alone with his head down.

Travis waited a moment, staring at his back.

"Let it go," Morgan said, pulling at his arm.

Travis took up his own drill and went back to work, losing himself in the mundane, wishing he could take the drill to his mind and chip away the thick layers of bad memories and guilt like so much Martian soil.

7

The USS Roosevelt was a scientific vessel sent out on special assignment by the National Oceanic and Atmospheric Administration to investigate some recent seismic activity twelve hundred miles off the coast of California. Captain Vladimir Mallard stood annoyed in his cabin, pouring himself a second cup of coffee. He took it black. No need for any artificial sweeteners or fake cream that can sit out for days and still be consumed. Whatever happened to expiration dates? Captain Mallard walked over to the large window that looked off the port side of the ship. The ocean was rough today, strong winds picking up and clouds seeming to form out of nowhere. Captain Mallard had seen weather like this before, but not so quickly. The sea was mysterious to say the least, but after spending thirty-seven years bobbing on it like a content duck in a pond, he'd grown to know and love it as if it were a part of him. He supposed in many ways that it was more a part of him than anything. Yet despite his deep love of the sea and his experience on its surface and below it, he couldn't take his eyes off the growing cloud coverage. Heavy and black, stretching out like a vortex.

"Captain, you're needed on the bridge."

Captain Mallard nodded to the request from his executive officer. He took a sip of coffee and closed his eyes, enjoying the only vise he carried with him out to sea. The warmth rolled over his tongue and heated his stomach. With an exhale of content, he set the mug down on the table and left his quarters. He walked through crowded corridors of men and women bustling by. He took a flight of stairs and entered the bridge, nodding to the crew as they acknowledged his presence.

"Captain, we're preparing to send out Blue Boy and Blue Boy Two."

"Excellent. Anything coming back from the sonar?" the captain asked as he stood behind the long line of monitors.

"We're sending down an active ping, but there are some unusual responses."

"Meaning?" Captain Mallard looked up, his eyebrows furrowed.

"The imaging keeps shifting." Tamara Brown rubbed the back of her neck, thinking of how to phrase her words. "The depth of the ocean's floor has increased exponentially over the last few hours."

"If the plates are shifting, we might be bearing witness to the birth of an oceanic trench," Captain Mallard said as he straightened, losing himself in the light of discovery. "Send out the blue boys and keep active sonar. I'd like to know if we're facing another earthquake." Captain Mallard took a deep breath and looked down to the screen. "We need to know what's coming before we lose something larger than a cruise ship."

8

Travis and his unit had secured their mining equipment and took the mining carts to the elevator. They entered the elevator and stood slightly slouched, their bodies tired and exhausted. Ten hours worth of drilling away the thick iron within the Martian interior had taken its toll. One person within each cluster of miners took control of the strong arm, a large mechanical arm that picked up the large chunks of iron and ore that broke free from the wall and loaded it into the carts. The carts were then taken up the tracks and dumped onto a conveyer belt that pulled the heavy chunks through the belly of the facility to a large room where it's dumped and sorted. It gets melted down and reused as needed throughout the facility. It's too difficult and not efficient to wait for building supplies from the large cargo ship that made the long trek from Earth every six months with food and requested items, mostly machinery for the scientific division or replacement parts for the air purifiers. Aside from expanding the facility, the mining of iron and other useful ore was the lifeblood to their happy little world.

"Damn this shit makes me smell." Jerome removed his helmet, tucking it under his arm while taking a deep breath.

"I don't think it's the suit that's making that smell," Christina said with a smirk.

"Laugh all you want. Ultimately you're the one that really has to suffer from it." Jerome lifted up his arm and took a whiff, pointing it toward Christina while exhaling.

The doors opened and the four men and Christina exited the elevator and entered the locker room, joining three hundred other miners stripping off their thin outer suits and setting their helmets back within their designated space in the locker. As they did every shift, the four men undressed shoulder to shoulder with Christina tucked away from the other men. The penalty for sexual assault within the facility, regardless of gender, was punishable by death. But still, it was never easy for Christina to be the only woman within the facility; all those men looking from the corners of their eyes, hormones coming off them in waves. But Christina was tough and they all knew it. Not chick tough, but military tough. In the sense that she not only knew how to defend herself, but she could be lethal with pretty much anything she could get her hands on. Her unit knew how dangerous she was yet they still stood shoulder to shoulder to keep her dignity in check.

Travis was the last to step into the blue coveralls they were given from the facility. Each person stationed there was given five pairs. All of them identical blue overalls with a red circle over the right chest, their last names on the opposite side in black thread.

"Slush is on me tonight." Morgan held up his hands like a high roller ready to share the wealth.

They followed Morgan out of the locker room and up a flight of stairs that took them to a smaller version of the cafeteria, called the recreation room by the company, the Pit by the miners. It had several pool tables, some pinball machines, two ping-pong tables and a few card tables. There were five identical machines set up along a table in the back of the room, each of them dispensing a different flavored slushed beverage they called the slush, for obvious reasons. They all took a seat at a table in the back of the room, wanting to be alone to hold private conversations.

"Man I would sell my very soul for a drink," TJ said with a sigh.

"I think giving alcohol to a bunch of burly miners

isolated in this facility might lead to some very bad things. Especially when I'm the only woman in this entire shithole." Christina's eyes went wide, thinking of all the savage men going after her goodies in a drunken brawl. She could kick some major ass, but not three hundred asses. Christina couldn't help but crack a smile at the image. "Besides, the last thing you need is a drink. I don't want to have to fight your pathetic advances all night."

"Look who's all high and mighty," TJ laughed. "You might encourage a man to take a few sips, might make you look good." TJ elbowed Morgan playfully.

Morgan excused himself and stepped to the back of the room, loading up the tray with five plastic glasses full of slush mixtures; the cups' contents swirling with blue, red and white. Morgan carried the tray back to the table and set it down in the center.

"Excuse me, waitress," TJ smiled. "I believe we ordered appetizers."

"I don't cater to small tippers." Morgan took his cup of slush and took a sip, wincing from the cold as it ran over his teeth. Morgan was a very brave man, always willing to take point in dangerous situations or charge in blindly to protect a fellow soldier. But when it came to the dentist, Morgan was a scared little kitten.

"So what did the head shrink think?" Jerome

spoke over the lip of his cup, letting out a refreshing sigh after his first sip. The taste brought him back to his childhood. So many summer days spent in the parking lot of the local gas station convenient store, sitting on the sidewalk with some friends while drinking a similar beverage of a much higher quality. The main difference to the drink in his memory and the one in his hand now was the sugar. He missed the sweet treats so badly.

"Same old garbage. Told me I need to get some more rest or I might go insane."

"Has this quack ever tried sleeping in one of our beds?" Jerome laughed, elbowing Morgan with a wink. "Besides, might not be so bad going insane. At least a hallucination or two might make things a little more interesting." Jerome set his cup down and looked forward with a cold expression, his eyes vacant. "I've gone crazy. I'm looking off into space. Looks like I need a transfer to the Bahamas."

They shared a laugh, secretly wishing they could somehow conjure up a transfer. But they all knew they were most likely never getting off this red ball so far from Earth. So far from their home.

"How was your little phone call home, E.T.?" Sean Jeffries asked from behind Travis, his hands clenching in and out of fists at his side.

Travis turned his head slightly to speak over his

shoulder, keeping his tone nice and level to avoid conflict. "It was fine."

"Must be nice to be able to call home and speak to your loved ones." Sean's voice was heated.

"Please don't," Christina pleaded, tilting her head slightly to give Sean some compassion and understanding.

"Let's not do this now." Travis turned in his seat, holding out his hands to show he meant no harm. "Why don't you join us for a drink?"

"Come on, Sean." Morgan pulled an empty chair from the table behind them up to the table, patting the seat.

Sean reached out and knocked Travis' drink into his lap. Travis stood and swatted at his blue jumper to alleviate the cold wetness spreading across his groin.

"Get your ass out of here!" Jerome pointed toward the door as he stood, his voice elevated.

"What? I can't reach out and touch someone." Sean took a step back, holding out his hands as if he were the victim. Everyone at the table were now on their feet, standing behind Travis with the same disappointed look on their faces. "How fucking typical. Travis and his faithful companions against Mr. Jeffries."

"No one's against you," Travis said, absently wiping the uncomfortable dampness from his lap.

"Let it go, man." TJ shook his head, feeling deflated from the same old scene.

Sean saw them all staring at him and felt his blood boil. None of them had even taken the time to realize what their great and powerful leader had done to them. Or the pain his decisions had caused him. They didn't lose the only family they had. Having had enough, Sean punched Travis hard across the face, jumping forward to fall on him. He brought his fist repeatedly into Travis' side as the rest of his unit gripped his jumpsuit to pull him off. To Sean's surprise, Travis raised his hands to block his face but did not fight back. He winced from the blows to his ribs, but the pacifist routine was only fueling Sean's anger. Sean thrashed furiously against the tight grip of TJ and Jerome, Christina standing beside the table shaking her head as Morgan wrapped his arm about his neck, cutting off his air as he pulled him back. But the disappointed look on Christina's face hurt him worse than the stranglehold or the tight hands over his forearms.

"Break it up!" Homer Andrews, head of security, yelled from the doorway. "Stand clear!"

Sean released his grip on Travis' shirt and allowed his former group of friends to pull him to his feet. He smoothed out his uniform and stood erect as if nothing had happened. Jerome took Travis by the hand and helped him to his feet, giving Sean an angry glare.

"Who started this?" Andrews asked, stepping forward with a shock-wand in his right hand, tapping it against his leg to call attention to its presence. "Well?"

They all stood stiff with their hands clasped behind their back, tight lipped and looking ready for inspection. No one moved an inch when Andrews asked for a culprit.

"Someone had to have started this." Andrews paced before them, looking each of them in the eye. He stood before Travis and smiled. "Word is that your man here doesn't respect you anymore. Is that true?"

"Just a disagreement is all." Travis took a quick look at Sean, seeing the anger still clinging to his face.

"Just a minor scuffle?" Andrews nodded, turning his back to the men as he motioned for the four security officers standing in the doorway to come forward. "I guess we're going to have to punish both of you tight lipped bastards. Take them both to solitary." Andrews stepped aside as his officers followed orders. "A few days of peace and quiet are exactly what you need." Andrews gave a wicked smile. "The rest of you, pick this shit up."

The officers stepped behind Travis and Sean and followed them out of the room.

9

Harold Dasher, or Dasher to his friends of which he had none, sat behind the wheel of an idling black sedan. The engine coughed and struggled but kept running. He would have opted for a quieter getaway car, but if he'd had the money to fulfill such requests he wouldn't be in this situation. As it was, he didn't have a choice. He'd borrowed twenty thousand dollars from Edward Dupree and the time for collection had come and gone. And Edward Dupree was not the kind of man to give extensions. But Dasher didn't have a choice. He needed to borrow the twenty thousand to pay back the ten thousand he'd borrowed from Hector Gomez. With interest, his debt to Hector had increased from ten to eighteen. Dasher looked out the driver side window and watched the bank, wondering how such mindless thugs like Edward and Hector could be so good with math and figures. Dasher himself was quite intelligent, but not very good at following directions. His mother had called him too "jittery" for school. That was just a nice way of telling him he wasn't cut out for a structured learning environment, so he'd left school in the sixth grade. After having it out with his mother for such a "stupid ass decision," her exact words, she'd taken the cigarette from her cracked lips and pressed it to the back of his hand, leaving a scar he carried to this day. So he'd wiped away the tears and left home. Since then he'd had what many would consider a rough life. Hopefully all that was going to change in the next few minutes. One large score and he could not only settle his debts, but maybe have a little something extra to live on, to pull himself out from under the large rock God seemed to have set on him.

"Let's milk this bitch!" Nick bounced anxiously in the passenger seat.

Dasher knew Nick as well as he knew any of the in and out people he'd met over the years, introduced as a friend of a friend, someone to snort some coke with on a Thursday night or shoot pool with at Finnegan's. But he was a twitcher, bouncing and shaking as if his mind were a cell phone set to vibrate. Nick made Dasher nervous. He himself was a bit of a hothead, easily set off and always ready for a fight, but Nick was unpredictable—a very dangerous combination when he gets pissed off or drunk. Dasher remembers an incident three months ago behind Dugan's Theatre in the downtown district. He'd gone with Nick and some really fat guy they called Butch to the alley for a score, supposedly an average pickup of some meth. Dasher found out that most normal things are always twisted to and fro when handled by Nick. So they'd met their contact in the alley and offered up the money in exchange for the goods, but the dealer had tried to pull one over on them. Weighing down the bag instead of the real deal. Without needing to confirm this, Nick grabbed a discarded beer bottle and beat the dealer to death, then proceeded to urinate on the corpse while humming "Twinkle Twinkle Little Star." To say the very least, Nick made Dasher very nervous. Especially at this moment as Nick sat with the shotgun lying across his lap, petting it sensually.

The two men in the back seat were both friends of Nick, people Dasher had never met but were willing to do the job. Dasher shuttered to think what type of characters these two thugs were, but he let it go. He'd come up with a good plan, laid it out to Nick and was thankful for the help. At their level in society, any help was better than none.

"Are we ready?" Dasher spoke to the rearview, looking back at the two men as they nodded in unison, no real expression across their rough exteriors. "Nick?"

"Oh I was born ready baby. Let's rip this whore apart!" Nick let out a little howl, mimicking an old horny fox from a cartoon he remembered as a child. "I want it. I want it."

"Just stick to the plan." Dashed poked Nick on the shoulder to gain his full attention. "Do you got it?"

"Don't worry. Stick to the plan." Nick nodded eagerly.

Dasher took a deep breath and put the car in drive and pulled up to the curb in front of the bank. He left the engine running and threw open the door, pulling down on the knit mask to cover his face. The men hopped out of the back, all four of them on the curb with shotguns in hand. Dasher led them inside, firing a little announcement shot into the ceiling.

"Everyone get down on the floor and stay cool!" Dasher yelled over the screaming customers. "Just get down on the floor and keep quiet. This money is insured by the government so there's no need to risk your own lives."

Nick ran up to the counter and pointed his shotgun at the young teller. "Get the fucking money out!"

"Where's the manager?"

A scrawny man raised his hand from behind the counter, his arm shaking. He looked as if a strong breeze could blow him over.

"You're going to take me to the safe," Dasher ordered as he hopped over the counter, pressing the barrel of his shotgun into the middle of the man's back.

Dasher followed the manager past the tellers into the back room, taking a brief look back over his shoulder to make sure his partners were doing their part. The two meatballs were guarding the entrance while Nick moved from teller to teller with his bag open, begging like a desperate trick-or-treater. Looked like things were actually going according to his plan.

"Just open the safe and lay on the floor, okay?" Dasher instructed the bank manager as they reached the vault door. Dasher saw the man's body trembling beneath his black suit coat and it made him feel bad. "Look, just open the safe and lay down, that's it. All we want is the money." Dasher tried to reassure, but the manager's shoulders continued to shake.

The manager pulled a plastic badge with his picture on it from his pocket. He waved the card before a sensor and entered a ten-digit code in the keypad beside the door. The light changed from red to green as the door's numerous locks began to retract. With a final click, the thick door swung open.

"Get down and keep still," Dasher ordered, pressing down firmly on the manager's shoulders as he moved to the ground, lacing his hands behind his head like a child hiding from a scary shadow at bedtime.

Dasher stepped into the vault, lowering his weapon to his side, temporarily forgetting it was even there as he became overwhelmed with emotion. Before him were tall stacks of hundred dollar bills sitting neatly on three shelves, just sitting there as if waiting for him to come and collect them. It was a thing of pure beauty, like a dream being placed inside a balloon and handed to you, something tangible. Time itself slowed to a crawl so he could process this range of emotion. This was his moment. The thing he dreamt about while sleeping on hard cement sidewalks in the rain or digging through the trashcans behind some random restaurant. Dasher felt as if he were hyperventilating. He took a deep breath and pulled himself back into the present, remembering where he was and the stakes at hand. Dasher pulled a canvas bag from the back of his pants and held it open, throwing in the stacks of money as neatly as he could despite the trembling of his hands.

Nick was growing impatient. Now that all the registers had been emptied, he had nothing to do. He set the bag full of money by the front door, maybe a few thousand dollars worth, definitely a nice haul. Nick began to pace, looking over the scared faces of the customers as they cowered on the floor.

"What are you cocks staring at?!" Nick screamed, his voice booming in the silence of the bank. "Listen." Nick hushed the harsh breathing of the two morons behind him. He cocked his head toward the front entrance, cupping his ear with his right hand to filter out the everyday city noises. "Oh shit! The fucking pigs." Nick paced frantically, shaking his head violently from side to side as the sirens grew in the distance. "Let's go."

"What about Dash?" Thug number one asked with a distant glare. From the vacant expression, one could surmise that it took all his knowledge to formulate such a simple question.

"Screw that bitch. I'm not getting busted for anyone," Nick declared as he grabbed the bag of money on his way out.

With a slight hesitation, the two hired guns ran out of the bank and got into the car a second before Nick peeled away from the curb, turning the corner just as four police cruisers pulled up to the banks entrance.

Dasher crammed as much money into the bag as humanly possible. He had to press down on the cash while pulling on the zipper just to get it closed. He looked up to the two shelves and wished greedily that he could take it all, but he'd burned enough time in the vault. Dasher squatted down and gripped the bag, remembering a commercial he'd seen once of some fatty at work, telling him to lift with his knees so as not to strain his back. Dasher lifted up, shocked by the weight. He put his arm through the strap and swung the bag over his shoulder, stumbling backward a brief second as the weight pulled against him. Dasher picked up his shotgun and exited the vault, eyeing the manager as he passed. The man lay in the same position as when he'd entered, not daring to move even in the slightest.

"Freeze!" An officer yelled while aiming his gun at Dasher's chest.

Dasher dropped his shotgun and fell to his knees, keeping his hands high above his head so as not to get shot. The bank was full of cops, fourteen by his count, unless there were more outside or hiding. The one nearest him took hold of his wrists and pulled his hands behind his back, slapping on a pair of cuffs. The tightness of the cuffs made him feel claustrophobic, bringing an uncomfortable dampness to his flesh and it became hard to breathe. As if he had to search for each breath and then pull it from wet sand. The officer behind him pressed hard on his back and forced him to lie on the floor, ripping his black ski cap from off his head to expose his face. The bank's floor was freezing against his cheek, giving off a pungent smell of cleaning fluid, maybe some kind of polish.

"Looks like you chose the wrong friends, amigo," the officer whispered into his ear, his breath reeking of pickles.

Dasher looked up, moving his vision between the legs of numerous officers until he caught view of the street. Their getaway car was gone and so was his crew. They'd taken off like panicked cowards and left him holding the bag, literally. Dasher felt like crying, pressing his face back to the floor as he knew he was beaten. The previous sensation of entitlement and prosperity was now overshadowed by a redwood of remorse and terror. He of all people should have known that there is no loyalty amongst thieves. And no matter how grand and glorious his dreams may be, he was in the end, nothing more than a common thief.

10

Two days in solitary was hard enough, but knowing there were twelve more days made him ill. Travis moved into a sitting position and rested against the wall. After a few hours of sitting in pure darkness you began to wonder if your eyes were open or closed. Either way there wasn't a difference. Two weeks for a brief brawl may seem extreme to many, especially when compared to the penal systems back on Earth where prisoners were allowed to tear off limbs before intervention, but this was off-world. There were two forms of punishment for a direct violation of the rules. The first was a two to three week run in solitary. The second, for either being a repeat offender or by breaking the core rules such as rape and murder, was death. Not a simple injection like back home. Here they tossed you into the airlock and opened the outer door. Such a painful death they'd only had to administer once. A miner he'd never met before, some hothead little shit from New Jersey, got into an argument with a smaller man over something stupid. To end the argument, the moron had taken a food tray and slammed it into the other man's face, sending bone fragments into his brain and killing him instantly. He swore up and down it had been an accident, and it probably was, but in an environment as dangerous as this they couldn't afford any further incidents.

Travis subconsciously brought a hand to his neck as he remembered the look on the man's face as they had opened the door. It took one minute for the man's lungs to explode, but it had felt like an hour to Travis. Andrews had insisted that every man watch the punishment, to see how serious they took such matters. Travis wondered about Andrews' real intent. Maybe a display of power over men more than twice his size, to make him feared amongst the workers. Travis didn't really care what his motives were as long as he didn't pull any further demonstrations. Travis shook the image from his mind, not wanting to re-play the grotesque footage like a horror flick. There had to be a better memory to maul over, something when times had been slightly brighter than they were now.

Travis closed his eyes and leaned his head back, running through his life with Annie, the earlier memories, finding one that made him smile. Seeing her with long hair trailing out behind her as the wind ran through it, catching the sun every so often turning it golden. She'd been four months pregnant with their first child, Ethan. At least that would have been his name if he hadn't been stillborn, but that was months away. This memory, with Travis driving the white convertible they'd rented and Annie with her round stomach in the passenger seat, was a good one. Something that even at this moment made him laugh out loud.

They'd been in their early twenties and were only married a few months. The original plan had been to marry in August, but the discovery of Ethan had moved the date up to April. Annie had been quite upset when she thought the wedding dress, the perfect wedding dress, wasn't going to fit. But everything had worked out for the best. It was a beautiful day in April and they were on holiday, driving down the Virginia coast with their futures bright ahead of them.

"Honey?" Annie placed a hand to her mouth, looking shocked.

"What is it?"

"Pull over!"

Travis pulled onto the gravel shoulder and ran around the front of the car, opening the door for his wife. She took hold of his hand and scurried into the nearby brush, bending over the wildflowers to vomit. Travis thought absently that if they weren't covered in puke, he would have loved to pick them for her. Too late for that now, but it still brought a cute idea to mind. He hurried over to his wife and knelt down behind her, rubbing her back in slow, circular motions.

"Oh that pizza kills," Annie moaned as she took a seat in a patch of grass.

"Sure it wasn't the whole bag of sunflower seeds? Or the popcorn…"

Annie pinched his stomach playfully. "When you have cravings then you can talk."

Travis delicately maneuvered his hand through the damp wildflowers, hovering over them like a fickle bumblebee in search of that perfect flower. He found a dry one and plucked it, putting it behind her ear with a smile.

"There, now you look fantastic." Travis held out his hands and connected his thumb and index fingers, looking through the square at his wife. "Aw, picture perfect. But I must say, next time you want some flowers you can simply point to them."

"Maybe, but pregnant women mark things, like ravenous beasts!" Annie extended her arms while shaking her hands. "Now help me up, my butt's asleep."

Travis took hold of his wife's hands and stood, pulling her to her feet. She dusted off her pants and was a bit caught off guard as he leaned in for a kiss. They held each other for a moment, locked in a long kiss with the sun shining down on them. Standing on the side of the road, their clothes lightly coated with dust and pollen, vomit on Annie's shoes. This was a perfect moment. He'd give anything for another vomit tasting kiss.

Now Travis sat in a dark cell millions of miles from that road, from his Annie. He gave into the darkness slumbering within his heart and let the tears roll down his face. No shame is showing weakness when you're locked inside a black room, cut off from everyone like a carrier of some deadly virus. He let himself go limp and slid down the wall, lying on his side with an absent sigh. Travis wondered if he was approaching day three and felt heartache as a horrible thought seeped into his mind. What if this was still day one? No way of knowing for sure. Not till they open that door to tell him he's no longer in time out. He'd been given four meals, so that had to be two breakfasts and two dinners.

"Please be the second day," Travis spoke, taking comfort in the sound of his own voice. Something other than just the dark silence, confirming that yes, he was still there.

11

"What did he just say?" Andrews asked, leaning back in his office chair while aiming a dart.

"I don't know. Couldn't catch it," Alvin lied. Alvin didn't want to pass along the sad words Travis had muttered in despair. There was no enjoyment watching a proud man weeping on the floor of a dark cell, not for Alvin anyway.

"Problem is they treat this place like a fucking health spa." Bowers took a seat on the table beside Alvin, leaning in to see Travis on the monitor. "Especially those military fucks."

"Home office has no clue how dangerous it really is out here." Andrews threw the dart and smiled with satisfaction as it hit the picture of Jesus square in the nose. "This place is hell."

"Yeah, no shit," Bowers laughed, cutting it off quickly as the expression on his superiors face showed annoyance.

"They give these men psychological evaluations every month. They can play pool and drink their little frozen drinks. Classical music on the overheads and pictures on the walls to remind us of summer days and springtime picnics. But it's all a crock of shit." Andrews stood from his chair and walked over to the dartboard, pulling the five darts delicately from the picture so as not to tear it. "All it takes is for one miner to go ape shit crazy. Just one." Andrews held out his finger, waving it between them. "One son of a bitch goes insane up here and we're all fucked. Mark my words gentlemen. We are all that stands between civilized conduct and complete anarchy." Andrews took a seat, aiming his first dart.

"I think it's more stable than that, sir." Alvin turned from the monitor, crossing his arms about his chest.

"These men outnumber us thirty to one." Andrews threw the dart, hitting Jesus in the wrist. "That'll keep him on the cross!" Andrews let out a chuckle.

"I'm not worried. These men are here to work, plain and simple."

"It's a prison...plain and simple. Call it an "Off-world facility" or fucking Disneyland. A prison is a prison. Only we're in general population with these common thugs."

"These men aren't inmates," Alvin snapped.

"Are you deliberately trying to chap my ass today?" Andrews lowered the second dart and gave Alvin his full attention. "Three hundred of these bastards are here from the company to work, I'll give you that. But what about your little buddy there and his men? These men are trained soldiers sent here on some deal with the company. They're trained to kill. One of them decides to take us out and we're all screwed."

"There's no point, sir," Alvin explained. "There's nothing to take over. Nowhere for them to go."

Andrews threw his second dart and stood from the chair, standing beside Alvin to look down at the green video footage of Travis in his cell.

"You go ahead and trust them if you wish. But if it were up to me I'd have every man and woman on this red rock locked up for all hours of the day. Let out in a ten unit rotating squad for work detail, keeping them in the minority while we keep them in line." Andrews' eyes went glossy. "Watch them closely boys. Men can be like dogs if put in the right situation. Obedient, loyal. But when the chips are down and they feel threatened, you bet your balls they'll turn on you. That's why the company has issued such strict punishments. To keep these rabid beasts at bay.

It's our jobs to let them know that there is a presence here to watch over them, to judge them." Andrews tapped his chest. "Out here, we're God."

"You bet your ass we are," Bowers smiled, ear to ear with a dopey expression.

"Yes, sir." Alvin spoke the words but didn't agree. Andrews could carry on for hours with his little God trips and sense of superiority, but Alvin knew a good person when he saw one. Travis and his men were not cold-blooded killers. They were just in the wrong place at the wrong time and are now forced to suffer the consequences.

"Give him another week in there to think things over." Andrews tapped the screen with a cruel smile. "That should make him think twice."

"Yes, sir." Alvin watched Andrews as he took a seat, tossing his darts at the picture of Jesus on the cross as if to show them that God didn't exist out here. Andrews disagreed, strongly even, but he wasn't about to open his mouth.

"Break their spirits." Andrews aimed his fourth dart. "Before they revolt and break our faces."

12

Annie sat up and pressed a startled hand to her chest, breathing hard. Her flesh damp from a warm sweat. Annie recognized her room through the darkness and settled a bit. It had been just another nightmare. She exhaled with annoyance and fell back onto the wet sheets. The moist fabric felt uncomfortable against the bare skin of her arms and neck, sticking like well-cooked spaghetti to a kitchen wall. Annie closed her eyes and took some controlling breaths. In and out, slowing the rate her chest rose.

Annie opened her heavy eyelids and looked to the clock mounted across the room—four fifteen in the morning. She shook her head with agitation and closed her eyes, trying desperately to fall back into the black abyss of sleep, but she couldn't. There was no going back once she'd hit the three-hour mark. So once again, as was her morning routine since Travis had departed, she sat up and swung her legs over the side of the bed. Exhaustion weighed heavy on her, dangling from her eyes and muscles like mountaineers desperately clinging for life. Not even after her fourth cup of coffee would she be able to shake them. Annie stood and shuffled toward the bathroom, stepping over piles of laundry she'd been meaning to get to, stacks of photo albums she'd put on her list to finish. Nothing seemed to get done anymore. Erica from next door often told her not to let the small things bother her. That little messes and junk filled drawers can be a good thing, creating little projects for her here and there to take her mind off things. Annie would have agreed if her house fluxed in between clean and dirty, but lately it had been a stalemate.

Annie let out a yelp as she stepped on the hairspray cap. She kicked the lid away and entered the bathroom, turning on the shower. Annie stayed for a moment, leaning into the shower to let the warming water drop to her hand. The warmth was such a comfort from the cold morning air. When so much of her life had gone cold, she learned to enjoy the few warm moments. That first moment when she would step outside and the sun's rays rolled across her face, or the smell of the brewing coffee. Simple pleasures were hers. No court could take those away. Annie shook the daydreams from her head and closed the shower curtain, cursing softly at the damp carpet. Now she'd have to clean that before it began to mold. One more project added onto Annie's distraction list. Not really wanting to, Annie undressed and faced the mirror, standing naked with a slight slouch. Tilting her head from side to side offered no comfort.

"You look like shit." Annie frowned at the words she spoke, hating the tone. It was the voice of a beaten woman, not of the strong woman Travis had married.

Annie ran a hand down her smooth stomach, sucked in and held a breath as she turned to the side. There was a good three-pound weight gain since her last mirror assessment two weeks ago. Not a huge weight gain to most fat Americans, but Annie was a petite woman that showed every pound. A heavy sigh escaped her lips. This is what depression does. Whether she wanted to believe it or not, the signs had become quite clear. Gained weight, messy house, her usually high-maintained wardrobe replaced with the comfy robe and worn slippers; all pointed to depression. It took her from the high peak of happy normality and pushed her down, causing the tumble. And like a snowball, she had picked up weight, dark thoughts and clutter while racing uncontrollably, faster and faster. She knew that if she hit the bottom, it'd be too late.

Erica from next door likes to pep it up by saying her house kept her busy, but she was on the same mountain, falling just as fast if not faster from the weight of her denial. She and Erica were both military wives, only Erica's husband had been killed in action two years ago. The thought sparked a deep sadness. Thinking of Travis six feet beneath the ground. Annie shook the negativity from her mind and stepped into the shower.

Twenty minutes later Annie had exited the shower, dressed in her comfy sweatshirt and black pajama bottoms and went downstairs to start the daily routine. She went into the kitchen and flipped on the small television, fumbling with panicked fingers to lower the volume as it burst into life. Her immediate reaction was to look up the stairs with her ear cocked toward Logie's room, waiting for the inevitable thump as he hopped out of bed. There was no thump, just the sound of her breath and the morning anchorman on the channel five news. Annie opened the fridge and got the coffee beans, the expensive coffee beans. Probably the only luxury she afforded herself, but well worth the little extra. If it kept her going, how could she deny it? Annie ground the beans and allowed the television a slightly louder voice, turning the volume from level fourteen to a whopping eighteen.

"Very compelling." Gregory Cunningham gave the camera his award-winning stare, shuffling papers as he prepared to move forward. Eyes sparkling as if they were filled with glitter. "Here are some clips from the last political rally in Washington D.C. with the third party candidate Manuel Marques of the Green Nation Alliance. Who as of this moment is the frontrunner in the polls."

The image switched to a very handsome man, his face honest and caring. He wore a black suite with a green tie. "This country can no longer afford to pretend that our planet is not in need of assistance. Assistance from every man, woman and child. Earth doesn't care if you're black or white, rich or poor. This planet provides for us simply because that's what it's here to do. Mother us. Shelter us. Keep us breathing with the air given to us from its trees. But things have changed." Manuel hit his hand on the podium, adding passion to his words. "Our latest environmental tests confirm that our ozone layer is all but gone, depleted by decades of harmful chemicals and pollutants. Our oceans have high levels of acidity never before seen in our lifetimes, making it toxic to the poor creatures that have no other home. The very soil we stand on is quaking beneath our feet from the mounds of trash and chemicals we bury every day." Manuel took a brief pause, closing his eyes to let the emotion simmer within him. "A time for change is coming. A change that every American, no matter their lot in life, has the ability to get behind. We are a nation of thinkers and dreamers and it is time to become united, to put an end to the pollution today, so that our children will have a brighter future." Manuel's closing statement was barely audible over the explosion of applause.

Gregory Cunningham came back on the screen, his head slightly tilted to say, "yes, I understand and agree." "We move to our top story. Massive earthquakes devastate Vienna and Hong Kong. Vienna experienced an eight point seven yesterday afternoon while three hours later Hong Kong was hit by an eight point four. Seismologists are baffled and offer no immediate explanation as no active faults run beneath either city. We're going live to our European correspondent, Simon Chester, who is standing in the devastating aftermath of Vienna."

"Yes, thank you Gregory." Simon wore a thick coat and squinted against the heavy rain. "I'm standing in the heart of Vienna, across the street from the remains of the Vienna Opera House. Much of this ancient city is now shattered and broken in the wake of such an awful act of nature."

The image changed to an overhead shot from a helicopter, giving the home audience the overall destruction of the once great city. Annie was taken aback by the damage. To see such a beautiful city known for music and romance reduced to rubble made her teary-eyed. The image changed to the classic news, jumbled footage of men and women running from a collapsing structure, people on the ground as they sheltered an injury. No one did human misery better than the news. But then the scene changed, showing something quite different, a four-mile crack in the earth on the outskirts of the city. The camera zoomed in on the opening and the screen went black, nothing visible within the long trench.

"A similar trench has formed two miles outside Hong Kong," Simon said loudly, trying to be heard over a screaming woman in the background.

There was a loud thump above her, the unmistakable sound of little feet as they ran to the bathroom. Annie looked at the clock and couldn't believe two hours had passed since her rude awakening. Logie would want his morning regiment of syrup with a hint of pancake. Annie grabbed the pancake mix from the pantry and began stirring, smiling at the typical morning sounds as Logan came down the stairs. Yawning, his hair sticking up in the most random way.

"Making pancakes," Annie announced, speaking over her shoulder with a smile.

"Can I have a piece of cake?" Logan smiled, rubbing his fingers together greedily.

"Not for breakfast, pook." Annie couldn't keep the smile from her lips.

Logan gave her the usual dish of sass, looking down to the white tiles with a hangdog expression. "Cake!" Logan stomped.

"Why don't you go in the other room and play with your toys?"

"Fine," Logan moaned, suffering defeat as he turned away and headed off into the living room.

Annie set about making the pancakes, stirring the batter as she listened to her son playing on the floor behind her. Logan's imagination was something she bragged about to Erica. Her son could come up with the most elaborate scenarios for his little toys, soldiers fighting on distant planets. Annie listened intently to the words her son spoke as he took on each individual character, one of them always being his father. It was such a relief to hear Logan always placing daddy as the heroin rather than the monster society saw him as. The last thing in the world she would ever want was for her son to believe the things those snooty bitches at his preschool said while pointing at them from across the lot. It was common knowledge why he was up there, but as always the truth had been widely edited and reworded before going to the papers. Travis needed them to believe in him, to love him.

"You need to come drink your milk." Annie flipped the banana filled pancakes on a plate and carried it to the table. "Come on, we can't be late this morning. Or did you forget that Buckaroo Bill is coming to your class today?" Annie's eyes widened with childlike excitement to get her son into the spirit.

"He's bringing a ton of ponies with him." Logan took a seat, eagerly digging into his pancakes. "He has like two ponies." Logan took a bite, smiling while bouncing his head from side to side. "And I get to ride them!"

Annie smiled, her depression temporarily overshadowed with the love of her child. Seeing his excitement over such a small thing reminded her of exactly why she needed to stay strong. Logan was her medication and she needed him every day.

13

The darkness began to play with his mind. Shadows moving within the dark, looking like people passing by when he knew no one was there. Travis supposed their station's psychologist would say his mind was trying to cope with the isolation, something that sounded smart and involved several long words. Travis rolled onto his back and looked up, assuming there was an up. Fifteen days had passed. He'd counted the number of times they brought him food, once in the morning and then again at night, thirty meals total. Travis has spilt his food numerous times, reaching out without sight, knocking over the glass of water with misguided fingers. He'd finished his breakfast about an hour ago, his clothes caked with fallen food and his fingers sticky.

The door to his cell opened, pushing back the dark interior with the blinding halogens from the hall. Travis rolled onto his side and shielded his vision, instantly harboring a massive headache.

"We need you to drive a loader."

Travis recognized Alvin's voice. "Would you ask such a task of a blind man?" Travis smiled, not yet daring to turn toward the light. Black, silver and white swirls filled his vision, dancing about each other like fish in a bowl that's far too small.

"Well if it were up to Andrews I wouldn't be asking you at all. But I pointed out that you hold a class four rating on operating the loader. Therefore you don't have a choice." Alvin couldn't keep the pleasantness from his voice, but it was short lived. Seeing Travis on the floor like some kind of POW brought a sick taste to his stomach.

Travis rolled onto his back, letting his arms fall limply to the side. He let out a grunt as he moved into a seated position, his eyes still tightly shut. Slowly, like a sensitive skinned man easing into a hot tub, he opened them. The white blur took shape, focusing in on the man waiting patiently in the hallway. The expression on Alvin's face was one of compassion.

"Do I look that bad?" Travis joked, holding out his hands to Alvin.

"Not your best, that's for damn sure." Alvin stepped into the small cell and took his hands, pulling until Travis stood. He kept a tight grip on his arms as it looked like his legs may buckle, but they held.

"Pins and needles." Travis pounded a fist into his thigh, wincing from the sleeping numbness as it faded. "You'd think your legs would have the decency of staying awake with the rest of your body. But no, they have to be all special." Travis released Alvin's hands to grip the wall. He looked up into the corner of the cell and saw the small camera. He didn't want Alvin's generosity and good spirits to drive a wedge between him and the other guards, thus removing the only kind man in authority from their presence. "Thank you."

"Sorry about this," Alvin frowned, shaking his head at the sight or Travis' pain. "Afraid we don't really have a choice when it comes to severity."

"Yeah. I heard you get your balls cut off if you miss the toilet." Travis pushed off the wall, feeling confident in his stance.

Travis stepped out into the hall, taking a moment to enjoy the recycled air, that familiar stale aroma drifting up his nostrils. The hall light filled the cell and showed the messes made from inmates past. Blood and feces stained the four walls. Filthy words written in uneven sizes and spacing from blind authors. Travis shook his head at the smeared food he'd left behind, embarrassed by the many puddles of urine at the base of the toilet, but it was clear by the stained floor that he hadn't been the first messy inmate.

The cells for solitary confinement were synonymous with the name, located at the farthest corner of the facility, opposite of the living quarters. The basic idea was to keep it as quiet and dark as possible. As if they didn't already feel completely alone and isolated being trapped in a massive structure on a distant planet. Travis walked slightly ahead of Alvin, providing the cameras all throughout the facility the impression that he was being transferred rather than accompanied.

"They don't have audio do they?" Travis motioned to a camera as they passed beneath it.

"No, these ones don't. Only the solitary cells, living quarters and public rooms." Alvin let out a small laugh. "Not that any of us actually watch them that closely."

"What about Christina's living quarters? Who's watching that footage?"

"Not us," Alvin answered quickly, wanting to smooth over any possible discomfort. "It was decided by home office that Christina's video feed should only be accessible by Dr. Hoffman for psychological evaluation."

"That sounds decent enough," Travis stated, knowing it was better than having that creep Andrews drooling over her as she slept. Christina, just like the rest of his unit, was there solely because of the deal he'd made. So therefore it was his duty to make sure all of them were taken care of and protected. That included Sean Jefferies. Hence the reason he could not bring himself to turn him in for a get out of jail free card. "What about Sean?"

"Sean…" Alvin shook his head. "That little pisser is one angry bastard."

"Yeah, I'm well aware."

"He was released three days ago."

"Before me?" Travis was caught off guard, wondering if maybe he'd heard him wrong.

"Afraid so. Andrews thinks you're very dangerous." Alvin gave him a wink.

They stopped before the elevator doors at the end of the hall. Alvin swiped his security badge and entered the four-digit code, the last four of his social security number. He'd been told not to pick such an obvious code, but he felt his credit score would be secure enough out here on the red rock.

"Who designed the landing platform?" Travis asked as they stepped into the elevator.

"Someone that never had to visit," Alvin said with a hint of envy.

The elevator only went up and down between two floors, taking them from the main level of the facility to the only sublevel that led to the landing platform. The elevator doors opened and they stepped out into a small room called the "staging room." The wall ahead of them was floor to ceiling glass, very thick. Beyond the glass wall was an enormous hangar measuring the length of two football fields. Sealed off from the atmosphere of Mars by two of the largest steel doors Travis had ever seen. The kind of doors you might expect to see in some kind of fantasy movie where a large monster is released upon the village below. A red light began pulsing through the hangar's interior, accompanied by an ear piercing alarm.

"Couldn't they have gone that extra step and made this room soundproof?" Travis clasped his hands to his ears.

"That would have made too much sense," Alvin yelled, covering his own ears. "Besides, what if one of our many blind miners were to wander down here and couldn't see the light?" Alvin didn't know if Travis heard him or not over the excruciating and annoyingly repetitious siren, but he laughed anyway.

The large doors slowly slid along the wall, exposing the darkness of the canyon. The opposite wall could faintly be seen if you were close enough to the large doors to squint. A metallic bang ripped through the cavernous interior of the hangar as the doors stopped. A moment passed and the bottom of the ship came into view, bobbing up and down like a tree branch in a storm. Then the entire vessel became visible, cautiously maneuvered through the opening that was slightly larger. Travis couldn't see the faces of the men in the control room located directly above them, all of them looking down from a similar room made of glass, their faces assumedly tense and sweaty as they auto-piloted the heavy beast in safely. Any damage to the outer hull could cause damage beyond their abilities to fix and might prevent take off. Or worse, cause the contents inside to shift and possibly break, things they needed here and now on the facility and it would take far too long to wait for a new shipment. The ground trembled as the large ship set down, the vibration tingling the bottoms of their feet.

"We have touchdown," Alvin announced with relief.

The large metal doors of the hangar slid shut, rumbling closed like a hungry giant's stomach. The doors connected and hissed with a rush of air. The red light and the siren shut down.

"Room has been sealed." Alvin opened the door to their left and entered the hangar, approaching the loaders set up against the wall. "You're up cowboy."

There were five loaders standing stiff and alert like five robotic soldiers. They were of equal size and shape, all of them eight feet tall with the ability to lift two tons; each with a thick reinforced steel outer frame controlled by a single operator, securely fastened inside the machines center.

"I would think you'd know how to operate one of these bad boys." Travis stepped onto the steel arm of the loader and pulled himself into the seat located dead center of the machine. He strapped himself in with the thick harness and powered it up. "One of these babies could do some damage." Travis raised his arm, thus lifting the mechanical arm of the loader to mimic his movement, and waved to Andrews in the control room.

"He could shut you down with the kill switch, you know that right?" Alvin smiled, not wanting to look up at Andrews but dying to see the annoyance across his face. "Or if he really wanted to, he could open the outer door and have us sucked out into the canyon. So long Charlie!" Alvin's good humor faltered as the thought struck up some bad visuals.

"What egghead decided to put the hangar in the side of the canyon wall and not on the surface? You know, let the ship come straight down and then lower it in or something."

"Not that I can speak for all eggheads, but I think it was decided that with all the sandstorms it would be safer to drop the ship into the canyon to cut down on the wind resistance. To avoid crashes or having the ship topple over."

"You really think a gust of wind could knock

this puppy over? That's like a mosquito ramming a brontosaurus." Travis pressed his thumb to the ignition, pausing a brief moment for his thumbprint to be accepted by the loader's control consul. The loader hummed loudly, stepping forward in synch with Travis' feet. Travis looked down to Alvin as he walked beside him, feeling like a parent walking his toddler to school due to the difference in size. Travis stopped as two security personnel operating loaders entered the ship, exiting a moment later with crates secured between their loader's hands.

Travis left Alvin behind and stepped up the long ramp to the ship's upper cargo hold. This was the smallest of the two, still able hold over three hundred crates of supplies and atmospheric equipment. Many times he'd wondered why they would pack the ship to the gills and make one long trip rather than waste the fuel. Morgan had stated that it was most likely a security measure. Six months worth of supplies meant that if a group of miners went insane they couldn't hold up for three years and completely destroy the place. If everything is reported as ship shape then they get the next six months worth. Checks and balances set up by home office. Travis figured that was as good of an explanation as any.

Very cautiously, Travis reached out with his giant arms and gently gripped the first crates by the sides with the rubber fingertips. The crate lifted into the air as if it were made of feathers. With his first load secured between his powerful grip, Travis stomped down the ramp and set the crate on the transport shuttle. It looked like a golf cart pulling a flat wagon, but it got the job done.

14

Ronald and Lori Anderson had been planning this fabulous family vacation since their first child had been born. Ben was now six years old and his little brother Jonas was three. Their friends thought it would be a waste of time taking a small child like Jonas to Disneyland. "He won't remember a thing," Jillian had told Lori. But then again, everything Jillian told Lori was in the negative. Jillian had been their neighbor for eight years, introducing herself the minute they exited the moving van, telling them all the downfalls of living in Cleveland. Lori took it with a grain of salt, just glad to have someone to talk to. She'd left her friends and family behind in New York for this big opportunity of Ron's. Pack it up and move it out. One minute they had their shit together, the next they were packing up their cozy apartment on the East side, the one her best friend Veronica had described as a "cottage on the thirtieth floor," then they're driving halfway across the country because Ron got offered a director position in a billing office. So she'd said yes, leaving her close and comfortable life behind to meet Jillian and the rest of the old shills on their block. The first few years were impossible, mixed with depressing loneliness and intense fighting. They were on the verge of a divorce when she'd been blessed with Ben. Life, for a while, had been wonderful.

Lori spent the next few years living for her son, filling her long and lonely days at the park or at the mall. Ron was working fifty to sixty hour weeks and they never saw each other. Lori began to sink back into a deep depression. Her thirty-three year old body moving from perky to soft, wrinkles caused by stress began to form around her mouth and eyes. Then came the announcement of a second child. Lori would admit this to no one, not even herself, but Jonas wasn't wanted. She knew it would only prolong the inevitable split between her and Ron. But when she'd seen his sweet face for the first time her troubles were once again put on hold. Her depression stuffed in the diaper bag until she could find a moment to herself to revisit it.

Now they had finally pulled together as the family they'd always pretended to be and drove across the country to California. The children had been excited the entire trip, despite the long hours they'd been cooped up in the backseat. They had their portable video players and their communication units, holographic game consul and 3D-Wand to keep them busy. Lori and Ron mostly sat in silence, asking each other every so often if they needed to pull over and switch seats. This wasn't the trip for confrontation or yelling, not when they were stuck together for days with the children sitting behind them. So they drove on in silence and played nice; both of them letting out a long sigh of relief when they'd reached the park.

That had been five days ago and it had been a wonderful time. Lori now sat in the passenger seat with the window down, taking a long sniff of the California air. The smell of the coast made her happy. They had departed Disneyland to spend three days at the ocean. The kids had never seen a real ocean before. Not one with tide pools and warm sand. But surprisingly their trip, weather wise at least, has slightly soured on their third day. Dark clouds had rolled in and turned from a sad grey to pure black. They'd remained above them, like a black cloth thrown over a bird's cage. Thankfully no rain—until this moment.

"Figures," Lori sighed, sticking her hand out the window to catch the big drops.

"The beach will still be beautiful," Ron said with

a little more pep to his step than normal. He knew his usual comments would only take away from their family fun, so he pushed himself. This trip was not about him. "I bet they'll have tons of starfish in the tide pools." Ron looked up into the rearview, smiling at two boys that were not paying attention. Ron turned back to the road, forcing a smile.

They sat in silence as they drove through the Laguna Beach Canyon, looking up at the rich houses sprinkled along the hillside.

"Do you know how many of those fall from mudslides?" Lori stated, nodding as if they'd all answered in unison.

"Or to fire." Ron looked back to the rearview. "Every year there are fires in this canyon."

"Why don't they just move?" Ben asked, never taking his attention away from his 3D-Wand. He was currently playing against his friend Simon. Holding a flute-like instrument in his hands while two holographic figures fought each other in mid air.

"I guess it's worth the risk to live in such a sought after place."

"Pretty stupid," Ben said absently, trying to set up a punch-kick combination.

Ron didn't approve of the word stupid, but he nodded in agreement. He himself didn't feel too sorry for the people that always settled down in the most dangerous places. Lessons to be learned from those that perished so long ago in the city of Pompeii. Still, they sure had some lovely homes.

Ron exited the canyon and took them along the beach, parking in a lot a few blocks from the ocean. He figured it was worth the walk if it saved them money. The entire walk from the car to the beach Ron had expected several digs from Lori about how cheap he was, but she'd kept quiet. Maybe this trip was what they needed. Like a refresher course on why they'd gotten married in the first place.

"What's going on, dad?" Ben asked, standing on his tiptoes at the crosswalk to try and see over the large group of onlookers standing shoulder to shoulder on the sidewalk, looking motionless toward the ocean.

Ron just shook his head. He took hold of Jonas' hand and hurried across the street, pulling them through the crowd. Ron's face took on the same stunned expression of the other onlookers as he stepped onto the sand, looking out at an endless stretch of damp earth. He'd forgotten about the rain as he stood there.

"Where's the ocean?" Jonas asked with his voice small.

"I don't know." Ron shook his head.

Police sirens were closing the distance, some units

driving down the sand. Lifeguards were standing all over the beach, looking down at thousands of dead fish and other marine life as they flopped helplessly on the shore.

"Look daddy!" Jonas pointed off to their left. "It's a whale."

Ron saw the great beast in the distance, laying there in pain.

"What is this? Pollution or the moon?" Lori placed a hand to her mouth.

"God only knows."

15

Wilbur Peters was completely clueless when the phone rang, waking him from one of the most erotic dreams his boring mind could conjure at the most critical moment. His dick may have retired but his mind still plugged away. Some creation of multiple research assistances and a few celebrities, mixed here and there with some pop singers and a tennis player, then he had her. The most beautiful woman. More importantly than anything else, she wanted him. How did he know? Because it was his creation. The dream had started out like most of his life, behind the desk in his office. But in she walked, wearing black slacks and a tight white dress shirt. As soon as she'd started to unbutton the God Damn phone rang, ripping the woman from his mind and scaring the hell out of him.

"Who is it Wilbur?" His wife of thirty years moaned, falling back asleep instantly.

"Hello?" Wilbur was startled, seeing by the alarm clock that it was just after three in the morning.

"Dr. Peters?"

"Yes, who's this?"

"You are to go downstairs and get in the car." The man on the other end of the phone was direct.

"What car?" Wilbur jumped at the knock on the front door. "Who is this?" His tone moved from shaky to angry.

"What's going on?" Elvira rolled onto her side to face him, her eyes widening.

Wilbur held up a hand to shush her. "Why is someone at the door? Where am I going?"

"Presidential order 2138, sir." With that given, the man hung up.

"What's wrong?" Elvira was getting terrified, fearing someone close to them had died.

"I have to leave," Wilbur spoke slowly, going over the orders in his mind.

"Leave? Now?" Elvira sat up, gripping his forearm tightly until she got some answers. "Are you having an affair?"

"Don't be a moron. You know I've got E.D." Wilbur tapped his crotch with agitation. "It's classified."

That was all he had to say. Years of being gone for long hours, sometimes days at a time, had trained her for these moments. But he'd been retired for ten years. She couldn't fathom what could be so damn important to wake up a seventy year old geologist and ask him to rush out the door.

Wilbur rolled out of bed, pressing a hand to the small of his back as he stepped into his slippers. The floor was so very cold at these early morning hours. He looked to Elvira and shook his head, letting her know this was not his idea. There was another series of knocks at the door, loud and urgent. Wilbur cursed under his breath as he shuffled into the walk-in closet and stood before his limited wardrobe, all hung up and organized by what matched what. As brilliant as he was, he could not grasp the concept of style. Elvira had taken it upon herself to organize his closet and spare him the embarrassment of his own design. Fine by him. One less thing for this old man to worry about. Should he go with the "business briefing" look or the "field researcher?" Since they'd bothered him so late in the morning he decided to be casual, grabbing the "field researcher" ensemble of jeans and a grey sweatshirt.

Wilbur blew his wife a kiss and told her not to worry. Probably just some concerns over the seven point three Utah was hit with yesterday. Living just outside Las Vegas, they'd felt a tiny bit of the rumble themselves. He gripped the handrail tightly as he made his slow decent down the stairs. The knocking was getting rather annoying.

"Yes?" Wilbur said with annoyance as he opened the door.

"Dr. Peters, if you could please come with us."

Wilbur nodded, grabbing a trench coat off the rack as it had started pouring. He locked the door behind him, moving slowly behind the young man with the impatient knock. He held the back door to the black Lincoln town car open for Wilbur, shutting it with a single hard push that shook the car. Wilbur didn't much care for this young man, watching him run around the back of the car to hop in. His hair was slicked back without a single misplaced hair, his black suit free of lint. Worst of all were the dark sunglasses. Presence was once thing, but who the hell needed dark sunglasses before the sun came up? Wilbur just shook his head with disapproval, buckling himself in as the boy took off.

"Where exactly are we going?"

"Our destination is just outside Provo, Utah."

"So it is about that earthquake."

"I'm not at liberty to discuss anything further than the location, sir," the young man snapped, sounding well rehearsed.

Wilburn spent the next several hours with his forehead pressed to the cold glass, looking out at the city as it gave way to nothingness. Just long stretches of desert. He felt the desert was a beautiful place, geographic features that had been shaped and twisted over time, dunes moving with the wind. The early morning sun had been incapable of penetrating the dark cloud coverage. It loomed above them and made the asphalt look so deathly black, as if it'd just been laid. Water came down in buckets, pounding on the car like a million little fingers. Wilbur yawned, shaking his head. Three in the morning was far too early for him to get out of bed and get moving. He closed his eyes and fell asleep, letting time and the road pass by without paying them attention. The sound of the rain soothed his agitated mind. So many drops falling from the sky to create a beautiful melody, lulling him to sleep. He fell hard, slipping down into the depths of his subconscious. Just as he had when he was a young boy, always out like a light on long road trips. Some things never changed.

"Sir?"

"What!?" Wilbur nearly fell from his seat. When he saw the driver looking back from the front seat he calmed himself, pressing a hand to his heart. "Don't startle an old man. Don't you know better?"

"We're here, sir."

Wilbur looked out the window, squinting to see through the dark. He saw some white tents fluttering madly in a strong breeze, maybe forty yards away. There were bright lights stretching off into the distance for as far as the eye could see just beyond the tents. The military presence was thick. Hummers and jeeps parked in packs. Soldiers dressed in ponchos stood stiff and alert before the tents, many others set up more tents or hurried to cover equipment as a tarp gave way. It was hard to make out any specific details under the cover of night. "It took you all day to get to Provo?"

"It's only eleven thirty, sir. That's AM." The driver motioned with his head toward Wilbur's window. "They're waiting for you in that first tent."

Wilbur furrowed his bushy brows and opened the door, his clothes soaked almost instantly. He cursed loudly over the rain as he hurried as fast as he could across the muddy terrain. More than once he'd had to slow himself in fear of slipping. Whatever this was, he wouldn't be much help to them laid up with a broken hip.

"Thank you so much for coming." Dr. Andrea Saccucci held out her hands to welcome him.

"It's been such a long time." Wilbur took hold of her hands and gave them a good squeeze. "But I must say this is not my idea of the perfect location for a reunion."

"I feel this is the perfect location," Dr. Katrina

Ludwig said with a single nod. "We must go where the work is."

"Is there work to be had?" Wilbur raised an eyebrow.

Andrea and Katrina shot each other a glance as they pulled open the flaps that led from the first tent into a much longer tent. In the tent's center was a long table lined with monitors and core samples, chunks of rocks with detailed labels taped to the many containers. Wilbur stepped forward and eyed the monitors, not really sure what he was looking at. Just a long black void it seemed.

"You're looking at the five mile crack running through the earth, located just a few feet outside this tent." Andrea crossed her arms about her chest, enjoying the bewildered look across her mentor's face.

"Are you suggesting this formed from the earthquake yesterday?"

"There's no question about it," Katrina added, pointing at the first monitor. "This crack is an exact duplicate to the ones in Hong Kong, Vienna, Galveston…the list goes on and on." Katrina tapped the screen. "This is more than just a mere crack in the Earth's crust. We're here to see if there's been any change to the earth's core or mantle. A continental shift unseen by this planet since the supercontinent of Pangaea."

"That's not possible," Wilbur muttered, but the look in her eyes told him this was a possibility.

"I hope you're right. Because if this is a continental shift..." Katrina took a deep breath, not wanting to focus on the negative. She was by nature a negative person, but only because she always knew how to combat it with a workable solution. But if the plates of the Earth were shifting as they did so long ago, no amount of positive spin would save them. "NASA is monitoring all solar output and the gravitational pull from the moon, but so far there's nothing unusual. There are over forty-three such cracks across the globe, including several being monitored beneath the ocean."

"Which ocean?"

"All of them," Andrea added with a sense of severity. She shook her head under the weight of it all. "That's not even the most baffling part."

"Something's worse?" Wilbur found it hard to believe.

"Something's burning down there." Katrina nodded, letting the information sink in to the old man's mind.

"My dear, you of all people should know that there is always something burning beneath the Earth's surface."

"No, we mean something other than magma is

giving off black smoke. Large amounts of CO_2 are being released into the atmosphere. That's why it's so dark."

"What the hell could be doing this?" Wilbur turned from the monitors and opened the tent's flap, looking out into the blackness. Through the rain he could briefly make out the shape of the crack.

"We don't know, but the President is asking for an answer. That's why you've been called out of retirement. We need the best minds, so dust yours off and let's get started." Andrea elbowed Dr. Peters with a warm smile. She admired this man since her early days in the field, following his lead as he'd shown her the ropes. "Let's put our game faces on."

16

Annie couldn't take her eyes off the television. The footage was just that shocking. There were moments in history when people just had to bear witness. The moon landing in '69, the Berlin Wall coming down in '89, and the first woman on Mars in '18. Now, on this historic and tragic day of May 4th, 2038, Annie watched a large crack in the Earth running through the heart of Paris. The camera kept going back to the Eiffel Tower, now slanted but at least still standing. Five miles worth of city pulled into the depths of the Earth. The president of France was about to release a statement, but Annie didn't care to hear it. She knew he would add nothing of importance. Just a bunch of fancy words and no explanation. What he was really doing was trying to curb the minds of the people from panic to understanding. False understanding, but better than chaos and mayhem as the people run through the streets in fear.

"This is the end," an old woman muttered, rocking back and forth.

Annie pretended not to hear her. The last thing she needed was some lengthy doomsday speech in the middle of this electronics store. She'd only gone in for a pack of solar snaps for a remote control car she'd bought Logie after she'd dropped him off for preschool, but the crowd swarming around the televisions had pulled her in. Now, twenty-seven minutes later, Annie set the solar snaps down and hurried out to her car. She saw the line and had debated over the lengthiness of getting through. If she didn't leave now she'd be late getting Logan and she hated having to wait outside with those bitchy moms.

The radio was the same on every channel, talking about the crack in Vienna, then the most recent one in Paris. Annie turned the dial to her favorite classic rock station, only the stupid DJ was talking about a new crack discovered in Chili. There were cracks in almost every country. Annie turned off the radio when the idiot on the classical station posed the question if these "cracks" should be called something else, like a "trench." It was all such pointless dribble and Annie hated speculation. No one was in possession of the facts. If they had them they certainly weren't going to share it with the general public. So it would be up to the media to fill everyone in on what they thought might be happening. Just a long game to see who can create the most plausible explanation. Crack or abyss? Who the hell gave a shit! A hole in the ground was a hole in the ground, no matter how they tried to spice it up with their own perspectives. Tragedy to humanity was about one thing: how can we put our own spin on the same info to get the most attention. Annie was already on ends with all forms of media. They'd painted her husband and his unit as monsters. As if they'd intentionally intended to kill civilians.

She pushed it from her mind. Why dwell on something that you couldn't change? Only it followed her everywhere she went. The gossip circles of the stay at home moms had a wider range than an atomic bomb. Spreading faster than herpes at a summer camp. She pulled up to Immanuel Lutheran's Preschool and found a spot right up front. It was a bit startling to see she'd made it with seven minutes to spare. She must have put the late foot down and gone a bit too fast. Lucky she didn't get pulled over. Last thing she needed was to get pulled over right in front of her son's school.

The moms were out in full force. They stood before the front doors with their carefully planned outfits and their high-maintenance hair. Salon ready at home. Annie didn't dare budge from her car, not since she'd had the "incident" three months back with that bitch. Her son was some snooty little cuss too. She'd been waiting outside like the rest of the pack when she'd overheard her husband's name. She turned and inquired to the reference. The skanky ho delivered a snooty remark about how they let just anyone into this school, especially the son of some murdering savage. Annie smiled, gave a polite nod and rushed her. Stopping with her arm in mid air just to scare her, but the clumsy moron stumbled over the small fence around the flowerbed and fell. The only injury came from embarrassment and anger over dirtying her new white capris. She'd raised a stink to the school and tried to seek legal action, but the truth of the matter was that Annie had never touched her. But to avoid any further unpleasantness, especially in front of her son, Annie stayed in the car. She saw her standing there with one of the other moms, Brenda. Annie gave an exaggerated smile and blew her a kiss. Brenda sneered and turned to her cronies. It had not been her intention to cause any issues, but she'd crossed the line. Much can slide by. But if you utter a bad word about her husband or son, well…you'd better be ready to rumble.

The doors opened and out came the children. They held hand painted art projects and newsletters to give their parents. All of them so happy and joyous. Logan was no exception, running toward the car with a wide grin. She held out her finger and Logan stopped, taking a second to look both ways before crossing the church parking lot to the car.

"How was school?" Annie turned and leaned over the seat, fastening his seatbelt through the car seat.

"Not bad." Logan gave her a big lower lip, lowering his face to hide his sadness.

"What's wrong?" Annie reached back and placed a comforting hand to his cheek.

"Isaac tore my art project!" Logan crossed his arms about his chest, moving with great drama.

Annie knew she should be supportive of her son and comfort him, but she laughed. It hurt his feeling to see her laugh or smile when he shared his feelings, but sometimes she couldn't help it. It was like a hiccup. An automatic response when she thought something was extraordinarily adorable, or even if it was extremely depressing.

"Don't laugh at me!" Logan snapped, lowering his head even more.

"I'm sorry." Annie controlled her facial expression, reminding herself to be stern and serious. "Sorry, I was just thinking of something funny I saw on the way to pick you up." She looked into the rearview and saw he wasn't buying it.

Annie backed out of the space and began driving. As soon as she pulled out into the road, a big fat raindrop hit her windshield. Then it hit all at once, hammering down like a tropical storm. It was becoming hard to see, even with the windshield wipers moving to full capacity. So very odd they were having so much rain. It had been pouring for almost two days straight. Picking Logan up had pretty much been the only break, so she was thankful for that. Very surprising to see so much water accumulating on the road. She looked to a hill on their left and saw it cascading down like a water park. Annie looked up and saw her son looking through his backpack in the rearview, his previous anger toward Isaac put aside.

"You want some ice cre –"

The wheel spun beneath her hands and the car lost control, spinning in complete circles to the right. Both of them screamed in shock and terror as Annie pulled desperately at the wheel. They drove over the shoulder and into a ditch, the driver side colliding with a cement barrier. Annie tried to open her door, pushing frantically without a budge. Her mind so overcome with panic she couldn't figure out why the door wouldn't open. Logan's tears were thick with terror. Annie's own mind struggled to comprehend what had happened. The heavy rain continued to pound down on them without mercy or concern, rolling down the windows until there was no visibility. Their flustered breathing had fogged up the windows. With the door sealed shut her mind began to race, feeling trapped. It was as if the water itself had wrapped itself about their car like a serpent and pulled them into the embankment.

"It's okay." Annie's voice gave little comfort, as it was thick with uncertainty.

She unbuckled her seatbelt and crawled over the front seat, kissing her son's cheeks as she ran her fingers through his hair, checking for any cracks or dents. Nothing but a frightened child. His eyes red and swollen as he hitched in shallow breaths. It pained her to see her son so afraid. Annie could see people running toward them from the highway, peeking in through the glass to assess the situation.

"Everyone okay?" an older gentleman asked, his face pressed to the window.

"We're fine," Annie yelled over the rain and her son's harsh tears. "It's okay. Everything's fine. I promise."

17

This just outright blew chunks. No positive spins or flowery way to look at it. Dasher had once again been screwed over and left to rot, story of his life. And bad luck just seemed to be out to get him. Now he was really screwed, locked in the Massachusetts Correctional Institution in Norfolk, awaiting trial for his failure to rob a bank. He must have looked like such an incompetent fool, running out of the vault with all that money, standing before over a dozen officers without a chance in the world. He'd read somewhere that Malcolm X had done a stretch in this very prison.

Dasher walked over to the small window and peeked out, watching the heavy rain run down the thick glass. A thin trail of black smoke rose in the distance, barely visible through the storm. Something about the thin stream of black smoke didn't sit right. Dasher was terrible when it came to geography, but he knew what he could see. It looked as if it was smack dab in the center of Norfolk. At least it looked like a small fire, but everything looked small from his little window.

"This is such shit!"

Dasher let out a sigh of annoyance as he turned from the window, taking a seat on his bunk while his cellmate paced before the bars looking like the most pathetic lion you'd ever seen. Miles Kraft was in for a battery charge against his girlfriend. As hard as it was to believe such a thin piece of shit could have gotten violent, apparently he'd really worked her over. "Beat the whore for giving some dude the eye," he'd told Dasher. Said he'd hit her with a belt 'til she fell limp and cowered like a dog.

"Women are like dogs," Miles had said, leaning against the bars four hours ago. "They need to be trained or they'll piss all over you." He absently tapped at his penis, getting off slightly at the display of dominance. "Beat them hard."

He'd been calmer then, waking from a deep sleep and a heavy bout of snoring, looking at Dasher like he hadn't seen him the other day. Now he'd gone hog wild, slapping at the bars while grunting. A deep noise within his throat that made him sound like a primate.

"Let me out of this fucking cage!"

Dasher just laced his hands behind his head and watched the show. Apparently Miles had completely forgotten he had a cellmate. Miles just ranted and raved, displaying the widest range of nervous ticks Dasher had ever seen. He shook his hands repeatedly, scratched under his eyes, and then his chin, hopped up and down, shook his head from side to side, grunted like a savage. Finally, Dasher's all time favorite, he put his hand down his pants and played with himself. On one joyous occasion he'd actually let his pants drop to his ankles as he went to town. Dasher had done his best not to bust out in mocking laughter. He figured it wouldn't keep their tight living arrangement nice and pleasant if he lay there, pointing and laughing at his little manhood. So Dasher had bit his lip and thanked God when a passing guard told him to pull them up or lose it.

"She's lying!" Miles pressed his face to the bars, working his lips between them to maximize volume. "She told me she liked it rough." Miles closed his eyes and hopped up and down, looking like a man waiting in line to pee. "A man is allowed to be a man." Miles shifted gears, moving from the innocent man being set up to the guilty party with his rights being abused. "Ricky Ricardo used to slap that Lucy bitch around!"

Dasher shook his head. Watching Miles was fun

and all, but even crazy got old after a while and he was tired. He didn't sleep well on these hard bunks. Concrete and a thin misshapen thing they called a mattress just didn't cut it for restful sleep. It was hard enough to be locked up in a small room with a total nut, but did they have to take his restful sleep away as well? Maybe he'd wronged Karma in another life? Odd how bad things seemed to happen to certain people all the time, as if some kind of allergy. But there was much about life that baffled him. It had nothing to do with his lack of education either, just observations on how the world seemed to operate. Like beanpole Miles for instance. How a scrawny waste of flesh like him could even get a girlfriend, let alone one he could torment and abuse, was well beyond him. Dasher racked his brain to see how any woman would find the man attractive. In the end he supposed some people were so desperate not to be alone they'd settle for anyone, or anything in this man's case.

Dasher was one to talk of course. He himself had been incredibly lonely at times, often wishing he had cash for the women he sometimes passed on the street. An hour of pretend love was better than no love at all. But there had been moments in his life, long ago and now faded and cracked like an ancient photograph stored in a damp box, back when things had actually been rather pleasant. Lately he'd been so busy trying to survive that all his daily worries were piled on top of the few good memories he had, losing them in the shuffle. Dasher closed his eyes and remembered something worth digging out. A time when he'd been as happy as a boy in his situation could be.

Dasher had been seven years old when he'd met Paul Zuluaga, one of his mother's frequent visitors. Unlike most of the gentleman callers his mother received day in and day out, Paul was a writer. At least that's what he said he wanted to be. Most of the men that visited his mother came for drugs, shot up, snorted or ingested their treat, then asked Dasher for some sexual release. He'd been held down dozens of times, once while his mother sat across from them on the couch with a doped out grin, but they'd never managed to get into his pants. He'd been quick and always managed to slip out of their shaky grips. But Paul was a calm soul. He had heard of his mother's house through a mutual strung out acquaintance, so he'd come by one night looking to score some blow. Two weeks passed and Dasher saw him again, sitting on the floor with his head back, eyes closed with a slight twitch. The next morning, Dasher had gone out into the living room to see if there was any food in the cupboards, usually he came up dry. Today there was half a box of soda crackers. Dasher couldn't believe his eyes. He took the box and tucked it under his shirt, tiptoeing out of the kitchen to go back to his room.

"What do you have there?" Paul asked, sitting up from the couch.

Dashers first instinct was to bolt, take his food and hide in his room like a rat dodging a hungry cat. But there was something different here. Paul sat on the couch and looked like a poor guy out on his luck. Dasher pulled the box from his shirt and took it over to Paul, stepping over a passed out woman on the floor. Her skirt was pulled up, exposing her bare ass for the world to see.

"Got a name kid?" Paul asked, patting the cushion beside him.

"Harold," Dasher said softly, not wanting to wake his mom in the next room.

"I'm Paul." Paul shoved two crackers in his mouth, closing his eyes as he savored the only food he'd had in a day. "Thank you for this. Really."

Dasher just nodded, not really sure what to say or how to act. He still wasn't entirely certain this man wasn't going to grab him. His heart was fluttering like a butterfly, keeping him in a readied state in case he needed to move. But despite the fear and uncertainty of this man's intentions, Dasher had done as he'd instructed. Because in an environment such as his home, he'd become submissive. Bowing down and accepting all behavior because that's all he knew. Every bit of kindness offered to him came with a price, some kind of request or forceful advance. So yes, he'd agreed to sit beside this man, but he knew the game. Fewer beatings if he went along with half of their request. When he'd been six, a man had told him to rub his feet like a good little bastard, and when he'd refused, the man threw an empty beer bottle. Striking Dasher above the right eyebrow and knocking him out. Now he lowered his head and obeyed, but there was something in this man's face. A look that told Dasher he too had been put down and forced to live a life he didn't want. Paul's eyes were heavy with exhaustion.

"Do you live here?" Paul motioned about the stained couch and drug addicts passed out on the floor, looking like the world's skuzziest sleepover.

"With my mom." Dasher looked down to his lap, feeling small, as if he wasn't supposed to admit that.

"Hey look, I'm sorry for this." Paul subconsciously sniffed, rubbing his nose to hide his embarrassment. "I feel like an asshole, passing out on your couch and all." Paul leaned his head to the left to catch a glimpse of the boy's face. "Do you want to watch some TV or something?"

Dasher shook his head. "The TV doesn't work."

Paul nodded, feeling guilty for having this addiction before a child. "Can you read?"

"A little bit."

"Well, I have a library card." Paul pulled out his wallet and displayed the card proudly, happy to feel somewhat normal. "How about a short walk to get some fresh air." Paul looked past Dasher to his unconscious mom in the other room. "Unless you think your mom would mind."

"No, she won't be up for hours." Dasher looked up and smiled. A genuine smile too, something he hadn't done in quite some time.

So he and Paul had taken a nice walk in the morning and read some books in the library. Paul showed him the young adult section where some of his favorite books from childhood were. Dasher could barely read the books Paul handed him, but it didn't matter. The books themselves were like tangible acts of kindness, physical proof that a boy like him could hold something nice and normal between his grubby fingertips. He'd been so happy in this moment, stemming from a single act of pity from a man that felt guilty for his own pathetic life, seeing it reflected to him in this young boy's eyes. Dasher had seen Paul a few more times, but then he'd disappeared. Like so many of the people that frequented their house, he just moved on. That one act meant more to him than all the miserable years before and after put together. Thinking about it now, laying on a hard prison cell bed with his cellmate grumbling over his situation, Dasher couldn't help but feel depressed. That was the best he could do? One stupid act of kindness from some strung out fuck that was probably dead by his own vices?

"I'll teach you!" Miles grunted.

Dasher opened his eyes and looked toward the bars, but Miles had moved into the far corner of the cell, standing with his back to him. Mile's posture told him exactly what he was about to do. Hands pulled in toward his crotch, his shoulders bent forward with his head touching the wall.

"What the fuck do you think you're doing?" Dasher barked, shaking his head.

"Ha!" Miles bounced on the balls of his feet.

"Don't you even think about it." Dasher sprang from his bed, crossing the room in a single motion.

Dasher grabbed Miles by the back of his pants and pulled him away from the wall, angry by the puddle on the floor. He pushed Miles into the bars with a heavy thud.

"Help! Rape!" Miles screamed like a woman, his voice cracking.

Dasher brought a hard blow into the man's right

kidney, silencing the screams as if hitting the off button. Miles coughed harshly as he fell onto his back, crying and thrashing. Unable to tolerate his cellmate's behavior another minute, Dasher dropped to his knees and punched the scrawny freak hard across the face. Miles let out a single moan before passing out. With a grimace, Dasher gripped the waistband of his pants and pulled them up, covering his limp penis.

"Did you hit that fool?" The man in the next cell called out.

"Yes." Dashed stood, wiping his hands on his legs.

"Thank you!" The man said with a laugh.

The good humor was infection, spreading to the corners of Dasher's mouth. He looked down at Miles Kraft and wished the man's girlfriend could have been present for this. Lord knows she must have wanted to smack his annoying ass for years, or however long they'd been together. How any woman could put up with such a tool was nothing short of amazing.

"That's what you get," Dasher told Miles, nodding as if he'd ended a lesson and dismissed the class.

Now their cell had taken on the unmistakable musk of urine. Not that it smelled like a flower shop before, but it least it had been less pungent. Dasher laughed with the formation of a plan, feeling giddy like a child at a sleepover about to play their first prank. He knelt down and grabbed Mile's by the wrist, careful not to touch his hands while remembering one of his nervous ticks. Dasher dragged him along the floor and dropped him to rest over the puddle of urine.

"Next time use a toilet," Dasher laughed, turning his back on the sad excuse of a man.

Dasher approached the window, wondering how long the rain could keep falling. For days it had been nothing but continual rain, pounding down without mercy. He didn't need to squint this time to see the thin line of smoke in the distance. Definitely from a fire, looking as black as it did. Even with all this rain the world could still burn.

18

Travis loaded the last crate onto the transporter. It had taken four hours to load the entire shipment of four hundred and eighty one crates between him and the two security officers. With a very steady hand, Travis maneuvered the robotic exoskeleton onto the transporter, lifting one heavy foot onto the center, holding a moment to make sure he was balanced, then stepping up. The giant arms and shoulders slouched with a mechanical whine as he powered down the systems, looking as if he'd depressed the machine with a bout of verbal abuse. Travis unbuckled the harness and slipped to his feet, landing with a heavy thud. Both legs are tingling and sore, half asleep from four hours of being stationary. The back of his uniform was soaked with sweat, sticking to his skin and starting to itch. What he wouldn't give to be back on Earth and have Annie wash this bastard with some fabric softener.

"You guys really need to train some more people on these bitches." Travis took a seat on the transporter.

"Then what would we need you for?" Alvin asked.

"This place would be pure hell without me here and you know it."

"It must be so nice to live in a world of pure delusion." Alvin got behind the wheel of the cart and powered up the fuel cells.

Alvin put the small lever into drive and turned the long transporter in a giant circle, leading them out through a long hallway that led to the main train station. This hallway was built for this purpose in mind, creating the shortest route between the supply ship and the train to disperse supplies. Travis slouched down until his head rested on the cool metal of the transporter, looking up at the lights overhead as they passed by. This wasn't so bad. Compared to solitary this was paradise. A part of him was feeling guilty. Here he was lying back on a transporter while his entire unit dwelled beneath the surface with heavy equipment and stale air fogging up their facemasks. Every second of comfort made him feel guilty for the choices he'd made. Luckily, only Sean felt the way he did. When he'd presented the decision to his unit it had been met with open mouths and shock. There was anger, fear, excitement. But those feelings all washed away with acceptance. Only Sean stewed on raw hatred, boiling over like a stew left on the stove with the heat turned up.

"First floor, ladies apparel." Alvin announced over his shoulder as he slowed the transporter, waiting with the engine idling as the heavy security door slid into the wall.

Alvin drove the whisper quiet transporter up a slight incline and turned toward the train's platform. He exited the transporter and handed transit papers with invoices to the train operator.

"Taking supplies to Facility Three, the scientific sector," Alvin stated.

The operator took the papers and looked them over thoroughly, looking up for a brief second to give Travis the once over. Travis shot him a friendly wave. The operator signed the transit papers and handed them back to Alvin.

"Bringing the train into the station, stand clear of the tracks." The operator spoke in a flat tone.

"I don't think this is what he wanted to do with his life." Travis hooked a thumb over his shoulder to the operator.

Alvin held a finger to his lips and turned his eyes to the left, motioning toward Andrews standing stiff and alert against the wall. Alvin looked to Andrews and nodded, but received no response. Only the usual heated stare. Travis kept his eyes low as the train approached, knowing that Andrews was not the kind of man to toy with. He'd been the sole reason his stay in solitary had been extended and he did not want to go back. But why the animosity? He'd never said two words to the man, nor had he been the direct cause of any trouble. Yet there was such anger toward him. Toward all those stationed there. Best not to pour gasoline on a dangerous situation. Travis looked out of the corner of his eye as Alvin drove the transporter carefully into the back of the train. Travis hopped off once inside and stood behind the long cart, waving his hands for Alvin to secure it into position. The thick wheels rolled into the four grooves and metal clamps locked the transporter into place.

"Train leaving main station. Take your seats and secure your helmets." The operator's voice filled the train through the overhead speakers.

Travis grabbed a helmet out from a compartment in the back, turning it slowly until he felt the rush of air. The back compartment had eight suits and helmets to match, but usually no more than four people went out on the train at one time. He took a second helmet and handed it to Alvin. They both made their way through the four cars and took a seat in the front where the windows were the biggest. The train began to move, entered the dark waiting tunnel for the airlock doors to close, then the slight incline and a bright light. It was like a rebirth, springing from the darkness toward the light at the end of the tunnel. Emerging into a new world.

"Sorry for the silent treatment." Alvin looked out the window at the red soil and distant mountains. "Andrews is just being a real asshole lately."

"Lately? I had just assumed he was born that way."

"I wouldn't be at all surprised."

"Don't sweat it. Technically it's your job to keep us quiet and in line."

"It's not my job." Alvin shook his head, turning in his seat to face Travis. "I'm not here to be some prick ass prison guard."

"Why are you here?"

Alvin held out his hands, motioning to the world about them. "Look at this, Travis. We're on Mars. Travelling along the surface of a distant planet, working toward making a breathable atmosphere." Alvin had a distance in his eyes. "How could I pass up the opportunity to be a part of something so important in the survival of our species?" Alvin brought himself back to the present and looked to Travis. "To make a new home for children such as Logan."

"Well I must say you've put a much better spin on our situation. I always focused on the negative. Like I couldn't bring myself to really look further than the punishment to see the grand scope of things."

"Don't feel too bad about it. Most people can't see but two inches before their own noses," Alvin smiled. "Take our mutual friend Andrews and his tight bunch of security numbskulls."

"You're one of those numbskulls too you know," Travis interrupted.

"Don't go lumping me in with those assholes or you'll find yourself floating home." Alvin gave a serious nod, enjoying the conversation. It had been a few weeks since his last chat with Travis and he'd wanted to catch up, but Andrews had strict regulations on fraternization with the workers. He felt that close relationships or good terms could lead to an unsafe feeling of comfort, one that could be exploited. "Anyway, back to Captain Asshole. Now there's one pessimistic son of a bitch." Alvin shook his head. "He's under the impression that he's the last thing standing between colonization and mutiny."

"I think Andrews is long overdue for a psych evaluation."

"He has them as often as you or I do, so I guess he's not that psychotic…or he's very smart."

"The insane usually are." It was disturbing to think their safety and overall existence on the facility might rest in the hands of an unstable man. Especially when that man already didn't care much for him. "At least we're in this together."

"Until the transport ship heads back at least." Alvin looked to his lap and nodded. "Yep, I'm being transferred out."

"Your request?"

"It could be worded like that." Alvin looked up with anger in his eyes. "Andrews has encouraged me to return to the home office. His formal report states that I am acting in an unprofessional manner and am thus creating a dangerous work environment. The home office has too much invested to take a single cautious step, so it's just easier to ship me out and replace me with a mindless thug," Alvin sighed.

"Is there any way you can fight this?"

"Andrews has gone to HR dozens of times with reports of improper conduct, little violations here and there. By themselves they're nothing more than a slap on the wrist, but he's created a very impressive paper trail. The man's methodical."

"Sorry."

"Hey, don't think it's a total bad thing. I get to go home to warm showers, pizza, green trees…"

"Fast food, television, hotdogs and baseball." Travis closed his eyes, sharing a laugh. "Seriously though, this bites the big nasty. It's going to be pure hell once you're gone. At least you bring a voice of reason into the security office. Without you, he's probably going to work us day and night."

"That can't happen." Alvin shook his head. "Home office monitors the psych evaluations and the HR reports very closely. They'll know if there's a change in the worker's moral. Besides, they always have your special reports to fall back on."

Travis fell silent, feeling as if he'd been caught stealing or lying. "You know about that?"

"I do. I read it while going through your file."

"Oh great. Wait till Andrews finds out about this." Travis knew this meant trouble. No telling what he might do if discovered one of his grunts was an informant. It went against every fiber of his being to be a little snitch in the first place, but it did provide all those that lived there a little security. "He'll have me killed."

"Don't worry about it," Alvin smiled. "I've re-moved the mention of it within the overview. Plus we don't have access to your psych sessions. Others might, but he doesn't."

"How did you know about that?"

"I snuck a peek through the files during my last session. Dr. Hoffman had to leave the session to an-swer an important call from off-world. Sorry, I was just curious."

"I still think —" Travis was cut off by the train's overhead speaker.

"Shutting down transportation. Debris covering track twenty-three meters ahead. Please be patient as sweepers are dispatched."

"What the hell?" Travis asked as the train gave a final lurch, jarring enough to pull them from their seats. Travis took hold of the metal handrail and steadied himself. "Please tell me we haven't broken down out here? I don't think we can call for a tow."

"This is actually quite common." Alvin gripped the handrail and lifted himself up, peaking out the front window as the trains grill pulled apart. "Watch this."

A miniature train car came out from within the train and sailed ahead down the track, moving with purpose. It looked to Travis like something he might buy his son to drive around in. It came to an abrupt stop and sat motionless for a full minute.

"Deploying sweeping units," the automated voice informed them.

The small train rose up in the front as a high-powered air blower lowered itself to the track, looking like a mechanical elephant. It slowly crept forward, blowing high-powered air at the large mound of dirt that had accumulated over the track.

"Every so often the dust storms leave a generous helping of dirt and rocks on the tracks." Alvin point-ed out the window. "The train could probably just plow through, but if it happened to go off track… well, would you really want to be the one out here when that happened?"

"Yeah, it's a long walk back," Travis agreed.

"Track has been cleared of all debris." The train stated a moment later.

They watched the small train lower as the air blower pulled back inside, and then it zoomed toward the train, disappearing within. The grill lowered and closed with a loud clank of metal.

"Resuming transport. Please be seated," the train warned a second before it took off down the track.

Travis and Alvin both fell into their seats, looking at each other with the same expression of surprise. Travis yawned, shaking his head to push out the exhaustion.

"You won't hurt my feelings if you want to get in a good nap." Alvin looked up at the small visual display showing their location on the track. "You have about four hours 'til we get there."

"I'm just afraid you'll try and have your way with me or something."

"Oh please. You're not my type."

Travis let out a single laugh as he leaned his head against the wall. He felt like a goldfish inside an empty fishbowl with his head bobbing about inside the helmet. He could take it off and be fine, but there was always that fear in the back of his mind, a sudden break in the glass or a tear in the hull. He'd spent too many hours watching the briefing videos to take a chance on that. All that footage of "what would happen." So Travis put aside the pain in his neck and closed his eyes, pulling his focus off the pain in the small of his back or the dry taste in his mouth left from the recycled air. Exhaustion took hold and pulled hard. He let go and fell into a well-deserved sleep.

19

Travis had been in a small cell, the lights on but it felt so very dark. There was a cot, but he didn't want comfort. He didn't deserve it. Five people, six if he counted himself, had their lives taken and thrown in a blender because of his foolish leadership. Travis sat curled in the corner of his cell, pressing his forehead to his knees. Thinking about how he'd let them down was all he could do to keep the tears back.

It had been two weeks now. Two weeks since they'd been ordered to go in hot. Travis and his unit were the best of the best, stealth and highly trained in black ops. This had been a standard mission. They were ordered to fly low, infiltrate a mercenary camp and leave no survivors. More importantly, leave no evidence of who had done the deed. But that was their specialty. So they had flown in below radar, Sean Jeffries behind the stick. The orders had been confirmed and they touched down outside the village.

They moved through the jungle like panthers. No one knew what hit them as they went in hot, taking the small grass huts one at a time without prejudice. But then Travis had entered a hut full of cowering children, their hands about their head. This wasn't right. Travis had ordered his troops out into the center of the village and called for a ceasefire. They surveyed the villagers and saw no militant rebels, no mercenaries or drug runners. Just women and children cowering before them.

Travis looked up from his spot on the floor as the door to his cell was opened.

"Good afternoon, Daniels." General George Campbell entered, closing the door behind him.

Travis stood, saluting the general.

"At ease son. No need for formalities." The General grabbed the only chair from its spot by the door and took a seat, letting out a sigh as he settled. "This is one messy fuck storm we have here."

"We followed orders, sir," Travis said firmly from his seat on the floor.

"I know. You did what any good soldier would have done. But our special ops never look good in black and white. That photo of you and your troops, standing in the village with their guns aimed on civilians –"

"That photo was taken out of context. I had

already issued a ceasefire."

"Well this picture screams a thousand words and ceasefire ain't part of it." The General showed genuine compassion. "The United States issued no such order to invade and will therefore not stand behind you. You and your unit will be held accountable for militant acts and possibly treason. It's a PR campaign to try and salvage bad press."

"Sir, permission to speak freely." Travis was choked with anger.

"Permission granted."

"This is complete bullshit, sir. We were given orders to go in there and clear the village and that's what we were doing. If anything, we should be seen as merciful for calling off the mission and issuing a ceasefire against those friendlies." Travis took a deep breath. It still seemed so impossible.

"That's the whole problem son, you were 'seen.' Don't matter if it was an accident or bad information. Right now the President of this here country has to defend your actions to prevent any future retaliation. If you boys had gone in there like smoke and burned the place to the ground it wouldn't have mattered one bit, just another jungle battlefield or country in unrest. Now you've gone and made yourselves the poster child for this incident. America is to blame." The General shook his head. "I'm sorry as hell, son. You're one of the best I've ever had under my command."

"What's to be our sentence?" Travis shook with the possibilities. He was trying hard to prepare himself with the death sentence he knew was coming. The mention of treason made his heart ache. Nothing could be further from the truth. He'd given his life to his country.

"That's actually why I'm here." The general had an odd look about his face, like a grandfather about to offer his grandson a family secret. "There might be something I can do to help you and your unit escape a more than certain death sentence."

"Yes, sir?"

"TransWorld Incorporated has just started staffing their off-world facility. Mining and colonization preparation. They hold some very expensive contract with our government for supplies and funds. As it stands, they need qualified personnel that will be able to adapt and function under extreme environment conditions and isolation. Given your expert training and your current situation, I've secured you and your unit a seat on the next transporter."

"You're talking about the Mars project?"

"Better than death son. Besides, this institution represents a sizable investment to the United States government. I set assurances to the right people that your presence there might help to keep the miners and other staff in line. You're a natural leader, Daniels. More importantly, we feel it might be prudent to have one of our own keeping tabs on the situation. You will send direct reports to me and me alone."

"I'm not a snitch, sir."

"It's not a matter of ratting out the prison druggie, son. You'd be doing every man up there, including your unit, a great service. A checks and balance system against those in charge and the men in the mines." The general placed a hand on Travis' shoulder. "You could help keep those men safe. And this offer has a shelf life of about ten seconds."

"I'm making this decision for me and my entire unit?" The weight of such a choice gripped his throat, restricting the airways. So much depended on the next few words he chose to utter. Not just for him, but for the lives of those he swore to protect. He'd already done a piss poor job as it was.

"Yes. This is a onetime offer for you son."

"What choice do I have?"

20

"Wake up sunshine." Alvin tapped Travis in the side with is elbow.

Travis opened his eyes and felt disoriented, unable to make out anything but a dark room and his heavy breathing. The train was stopped, sitting in the dark tunnel before the airlock. Travis felt moisture on his checks and face, sighing as drool lined the inside of his helmet.

"You must have been having a rough dream."

"Just a very bad memory."

"Sounded like it." Alvin offered a compassionate ear but withdrew, sensing this was as much detail as Travis was going to give.

The airlock door opened and the train pulled into the station, passing beneath the powerful air blowers to rid the train of any lingering Martian soil or possible contaminant. Dust could cause some very serious problems in these facilities if it got into the air vents or someone's lungs. Not to mention severe radiation carried in the soil. At no more than two miles an hour the train pulled up to the station, stopping with a single hard lurch.

"Welcome to Facility Three." Dr. Zatzkin held out his hands with a very gracious smile. "Please excuse any enthusiasm on my part. But it's been far too long since we've had visitors here in the scientific sector."

"Nice to see you again, Doctor." Alvin handed the doctor the invoices.

"Oh this is going to be a joyous day," the doctor smiled. "We've been hoping to get some new equipment for our soil samples and most importantly are the CO_2 filters. We would hate to die of carbon monoxide poisoning."

"That would be a bitch," Travis added, always feeling foolish and slightly stupid in the doctor's presence.

"Yes it certainly would, Mr. Daniels."

"Alvin, Adams is on the comms for you," the train operator said from behind his podium.

"Okay. Excuse me, doctor."

Travis removed his helmet and set it beneath his arm, feeling like a space invader to planet boring. He waited patiently while Dr. Zatzkin read through the papers and Alvin spoke to Adams at the main facility. Moments of levity always bothered Travis. Standing there with nothing to do or say, wishing he could shrink away or turn invisible. Not that he minded a good conversation with the doctor. He did get a bit technical at times, but he never spoke down to him or treated him as an inferior. The doctor just loved his work and he loved to talk. But now no one was talking and that left Travis alone in the center of the room like a sore thumb. If his outer uniform had pockets he would have gladly shoved his hands into them. Instead he pretended to read the warning sign behind the operator's station. The sign told anyone bored enough to read it that it was unsafe to stand behind the yellow line when a train was entering the station.

"Well Doc, looks like you're stuck with us," Alvin announced as he walked over. "A heavy storm has just kicked up a mile or so north of the facility and it is therefore too dangerous to make the trip back. Travis and I have been granted approval for an overnight stay." Alvin didn't seem all that upset about the news. In fact, a grin peeked its head, twitching at the corner of his lip.

"Well how wonderful." Dr. Zatzkin stuffed the papers beneath his arm and clapped his hands together. "Looks like we'll be having a little slumber party."

"Well I should probably suit up and move those crates before we break out the pillow fights and the marshmallows," Travis said with good humor.

21

Dr. Gordon Dennis was sick to his stomach. He sat in the passenger seat of the small helicopter, gripping the seat until his fingers turned white. A bucket was on the floor for easy access, held in place with shaking feet as the copter darted and dropped from the heavy chop. The pilot was holding the stick in a death grip, doing all he could to keep them steady as they pushed through the thick cloud coverage. The windshield was coated in rain, as if he'd taken them through a carwash. Gordon felt the tuna salad he'd had last night start to work its way through his stomach and into his throat. The urge to vomit again was too overpowering, bringing him forward while he hurried to raise the bucket. He vomited for the third time since their three-hour helicopter journey. The liquefied foods had now given way to the dreaded dry heaves, ripping pain through his abdomen with every uncontrollable lurch.

"I'm so sorry for this." Gordon set the bucket between his feet and wiped his mouth with the back of his arm.

"It's nothing I haven't seen before," the pilot yelled over the storm. "Usually it's nowhere near this bad."

"Oh great." Gordon tightened his grip on the seat, fearing that at any moment a mountain or a plane would appear in the dense cloud coverage and end their journey real quick. A foolish thought of course. Even through his panicked mind he knew they flew mostly on instrumentation and knew exactly what was out there, whether they could see it or not. "Oh God!" Gordon's entire body clenched in fear as they hit an air pocket and plummeted, the pilot quickly adjusting altitude.

"Where did you come from?" the pilot asked.

"I flew in from Boston to San Diego. Then to Honolulu and now I'm bobbing about the sky with you."

"Long journey. But I wouldn't worry; we're only a few minutes away."

Those had been the best words he'd heard in the past fifteen hours. It had been almost an entire day since he'd gotten the call from Kenneth Bongard, his longtime colleague and friend. Kenneth was aboard the USS Bridgewater as a representative of the

National Oceanic and Atmospheric Administration, or NOAA to keep it simple. Gordon had just sat down to a game of chess with his seven-year-old son. He'd only taught Jackson how to play the game a few weeks ago and already he was challenging his father. Gordon had just set the board up after breakfast in the entertainment room when the phone rang. Kenneth had told him that President Noll himself had issued an executive order to have the top minds in all fields dispatched to different locations around the globe. What choice does one have when told the president is asking you to move? Without any real idea on where he was going, Gordon had packed a light duffle bag and went outside to meet his escorts. Fourteen hours and fifteen dreadful minutes later brought him to where he was now, hanging on for dear life in the heart of a storm.

"USS Bridgewater dead ahead. ETA ten minutes," the pilot said.

The helicopter dropped below the clouds and drifted down toward the faint outline of a vessel. The ship was a navy issued science vessel. The rain pounded on them and made visibility impossible. Gordon hoped they were able to touch down smoothly so they wouldn't have to ditch in the ocean. Frightful images of a burning crash plague his mind, over and over again in a dozen different ways. He gulped and pressed the back of his head to the padding of the seat, bracing himself as best he could. The small grey blur now a long grey blur and closing in fast.

"Have you made landings in weather like this before?" Gordon's voice shook and vibrated.

"Many times. Just hang on and we'll be there in three minutes."

The words did offer some comfort, but they were blown away by the next harsh gust of wind, shaking them like a rattle.

"We have you on approach and you are cleared for landing," the radio buzzed, the man's voice cracking with heavy static.

The next two minutes were perhaps the scariest moments of Gordon's life. The copter came in low, hovering above the square platform located at the front of the vessel with the standard 'H' set dead center, as if too many other flying vehicles were just aching for a parking spot. Even in this moment of sheer terror, Gordon managed a nervous smile, thinking how hilarious it would be to look down and see a handicapped space. The good humor died as the copter dropped rapidly then steadied. Dropped and steadied, a vicious cycle that seemed to last forever. Finally, perhaps the greatest sound he'd ever heard, the metal skids pressed against the platform and the shaking ceased. Gordon let out a sigh and closed his eyes, thankful to be alive. He jumped as the door was pulled open.

"Dr. Dennis?" A man yelled over the pounding rain, shielding his eyes with his hand.

"Yes." Gordon hopped out of the copter, falling to his knees as his legs had fallen asleep. He grumbled to himself and felt foolish, taking hold of the man's hand as he helped him up. Nothing like trying to look professional while taking a nosedive in the rain.

"Your team is assembled in the mess hall. Follow me." The young man had to cup both hands over his mouth to be heard, the hood of his thin windbreaker whipping about his face.

Gordon followed him over the slippery deck, running hunched over as if it did any good. Thirty seconds in this weather and you might as well be holding a bar of soap. Gordon entered the ship and pulled off his coat, peeling it like the skin of an orange. He tossed it to the ground without a second thought, his mind too distracted and rattled with lingering nausea from the journey. This was still all so new to him. He'd been called out on some government exercises before, simulations and "what if" contingency plans. But this was no exercise. Every face he passed in the narrow halls of the ship wore the same expression: fear.

"It is so very nice to see you again, Dr. Dennis," Kenneth smiled, extending his hand. He looked strung out and exhausted, his breath reeking of black coffee.

"Nice to see you." Gordon took a seat across from Kenneth, watching with interest as the room was cleared and the doors were sealed. "You're not going to kill me are you?" Gordon said nervously.

"It's not me you have to worry about." Kenneth shook his head, not wanting to verbalize what he'd been dreading for the past two days. "The temperature of the world's oceans has risen by seventeen degrees, even in the depths. The Oceanic Climate Center in Florida has registered this change through their series of buoys in the Atlantic and the Pacific." Kenneth swallowed, flattening his shaky tone with a mental block, not wanting to tear up before a respected colleague. "This thick cloud coverage and heavy rain is a direct result of the ocean's rising temperatures and it's only going to get worse."

"My God almighty!" Gordon placed a hand to his mouth. "How could this happen? Some kind of solar flare?"

"We thought so at first, but then we discovered these." Kenneth slid a stack of pictures across the table.

Gordon thumbed through them one by one,

giving them all a thorough once over. He tapped the last photo and struggled to formulate the question. His usual quick responses and sometimes snooty intelligence was lost in a haze of uncertainty and disbelief. "These sonar images…they're all from one single abyss?"

"No. Twenty-seven identical openings in the ocean's floor have been discovered over the past few days. The President has every available ship with sonar capability actively pinging the ocean floor." Kenneth shook his head. "Poor whales are probably dead from all this sonar activity."

"Poor whales?" Gordon shook his head. "Here we are faced with the worst global catastrophe in human history and you're worried about the whales?"

"Doesn't matter anyway. If our sonar's don't harm them the rising temperatures will. Beaches across the globe are lined with dead critters. And if this evaporation isn't controlled soon we'll likely lose sight of the sun in a matter of days. Only a matter of time until all the countries of the world are plunged into darkness…or drown from flooding and continuous rainfall."

"What's happening in those trenches?" Gordon picked up the last photo and held it close.

"It's as if the planet's core is exposed and the water turns to steam as it fills in the trench. But we don't believe that's the case. An opening running that deep in the Earth…twenty-seven such openings would rip our planet into multiple chunks. The rotation of the Earth's core would have ceased or cooled, but all internal functions are unchanged. This is something different." Kenneth tapped the photo. "We are working on a plan, but it's laughable at best."

"What could possibly save us?" Gordon's voice shook with despair. The treacherous helicopter ride long forgotten in the wake of this new nightmare.

"President Noll's top scientific adviser has postulated that a series of underwater charges set along the abyss may cause a cave in that might inadvertently seal whatever is venting this heat."

"A five mile opening that runs miles into the crust, if not further, and the best plan we have is to try and stuff it full of some rocks?" Gordon leaned back and ran a hand through his damp hair. "Is there no other alternative?"

"That's why you've been plucked from your comfy slumber. The President is searching for any and all alternatives in case the primary plan doesn't work." Kenneth's eyes spoke volumes. He offered a stare that said he too believed the explosives would fail. "I'm hoping that with your expertise on the ocean's floor and trenches you might come up with something."

Gordon set the photo down and leaned forward, interlacing his fingers. "I'm not a religious man, but I'd have to say that this one is in God's hands. But as I'm a scientist and I don't have God's number, I'll see what I can do."

22

Compared to his small cell in the main facility, the room they'd provided Travis with was a suite. It actually had a mattress and box spring, the kind you might find in a two star hotel. The sheets were made of cotton and had recently been washed. They gave off a scent that reminded him of lemons and spring. An odd combination for sure, but it brought a pleasant sensation. He had to laugh at himself, remembering all those lame ass commercials where the wife pulls the laundry out and loses herself in the amazing fragrance. Travis closed his eyes and laid back with his hands behind his head, feeling comfort for the first time in a very long time. There was no rush. No feeling that at any moment the lights might flash on and off and he'd be called into action to fix a broken oxygen valve or assist in septic repairs. He was going to close his eyes and savor the lack of activity and the absence of urgency. But the little nap on the train over had sabotaged his sleeping pattern. Travis opened his eyes and stared up at the ceiling, moving over the uneven surfaces and counting the cracks in place of sheep. After a few minutes he'd given into his restlessness, deciding to go out into the small kitchen and help himself to whatever scientists considered a late night treat.

Travis was pleased to see that these rooms had the ability to be opened by the occupant, unlike the cells in the main facility. More trust amongst the educated he guessed. He peeked out into the hallway and saw no one, just a windowless stretch of hall. He shut the door gently and walked lightly toward the kitchen. Unsure why, but he felt like a child sneaking downstairs to sneak a piece of cake. Only instead of a time out, up here you received death. He shook the thought, remembering where he was. These men were not here to torment. They were here to further their research and turn Mars into Earth's little sister. Blue and breathable if possible. Travis didn't even try to understand the process. How they planned to take a red, dead planet and turn it into "Earth 2" was so far beyond him it was ridiculous. Right now he thought it suited him more to figure out where the kitchen was. Travis stood for a brief moment, looking down the hall to his left and then to his right. Both were identical. He shrugged his shoulder and turned to the left. Then he lifted back his head and put his nose up into the air, smelling the unmistakable sent of freshly baked bread.

"No way!" Travis smiled, turning the corner to see Dr. Zatzkin holding a fresh loaf of bread. "How'd you get the bread machine?"

"I brought it with me," he smiled, setting it down on the table closest to the only window in the kitchen. "Come, have some. It's best when it's hot and fresh."

"Do you have any butter?" Travis hoped, taking a seat. Saliva was already beginning to build in the corners of his mouth.

"Now that we are out of."

The doctor pulled the bread apart with his hands, wincing as the steam scorched his fingertips. He handed half the loaf to Travis who took it without hesitation. Dr. Zatzkin held up his piece of bread and tapped it to Travis' half in a toast of toast.

"I've read your file," Dr. Zatzkin said over a bite of bread.

Travis was a bit taken back. "How?"

"Dr. Hoffman and I use the same software. His reports to the home office are completely visible… if one knows how to look." Dr. Zatzkin wiped some crumbs from his mouth and then shook them from his white shirt. "I'm sorry for your imprisonment."

"It's not a prison sentence. It's a 'voluntary service

to our country,'" Travis mocked the words from his training.

"A prison is a prison no matter what you call it," the doctor said. "But that doesn't mean you're a condemned man. If either one of us were to walk outside we'd suffer the same agonizing death. So I hope you don't feel you're in this alone."

"You can go home on rotation."

"That's true, but that will never happen." The doctor was pleased by Travis' questioning expression. "I've spent my entire life fantasizing about this planet. Imagining myself as an astronaut in an exotic colony, fighting Martians and saving Earth. The dreams of a young boy have changed significantly, but I never lost sight of my goal. And here I am, over fifty-seven million miles from the small town I grew up in."

Travis couldn't keep the joy from his face, spreading over him like the warmth of the sun. The doctor wore such genuine pleasure. It was touching to see someone have so much passion and pride.

"You're a part of this too, howbeit so small is irrelevant."

"I know, my unit and I have discussed it many times. But it's still just a manual labor camp. Only here we get to wear funky outfits and annoying helmets. I do think it's amazing that in a few years this planet may be the next home to the human race."

"Yeah…" the doctor sighed, stuffing a big chunk of bread into his mouth with a deflated expression.

"What is it?"

The doctor finished the bread and wiped his mouth, holding out a finger as he took a sip of water. "As a scientist, I have every intension on creating a livable environment. But that doesn't mean I want to subject this planet to humanity."

"Earth is dying –"

"Yes! Exactly right. And do you know why the planet is being choked to death from all the air pollution and the lack of resources? Humanity! The most lethal virus unleashed upon the universe. Worse than a brush fire."

"That's a little backwards don't you think? I mean, you are human after all and you're up here."

"Yes, I am human. I too am part of this ever-spreading disease. But unlike most of the people on our dying home world, I'm not contagious. Meaning I won't infect this virgin planet with crumpled up fast food wrappers and plastic bottles."

Travis was very surprised by the shift in the doctor's demeanor, a complete one hundred and eighty degree turn from his normal peppy attitude. When someone was passionate about something they took on added strength to their character and felt justified.

"This world has gotten by just fine without the

addition of a shopping mall or a super highway. No traffic jams to destroy the fresh atmosphere I'm helping to create. No light pollution blocking the trillions of stars we enjoy every night. To subject this planet to such harsh atrocities makes my stomach turn. Yet, by following through with my work I'm doing just that. I'm building the foundations for which humanity will strike its claim." The doctor looked distant as his eyes grew heavy. "Ultimately, I would be the one responsible for the rape of this planet."

"You're pretty hard on yourself."

"Should I go easy? Doesn't the responsibility fall on those responsible."

"It's your job."

"We both know that sometimes doing our job can be worse than simply walking away." Dr. Zatzkin looked to Travis for a moment and felt bad for what he'd said. "I'm sorry if I've offended you. It's just not often that I have someone to actually rant and rave too."

"No harm done. I'll take a heated conversation over my small cell any day."

Dr. Zatzkin nodded, turning his attention to the window and then up at the stars. He was silent for a long while, looking them over as if hypnotized by their twinkling brilliance. He'd spent most of his life laying on his back looking up at the stars. Almost every clear night God had granted him as a child, he'd climb out his window and lay on the roof of the barn. There wasn't too much else to look at in Deerfield, Kansas. But he'd grown up as everyone eventually did, went to MIT and graduated summa cum laude in three years. But as he looked up at the sky in whatever big city he happened to be passing through, his beloved stars had been hidden through a yellow haze. The human race had taken his night sky.

"Do we deserve another chance?"

"What do you mean?"

"Should we offer this planet up as a fresh beginning, knowing full well that over time it will suffer the same fate as Earth? Or should we pay for the damage we've done?" The doctor looked to Travis with a cold heart. It seemed so oddly out of character. "Does humanity deserve to die?"

"I've already faced a death sentence once and I didn't much care for it. But I would like to think that I'm looking at the world through wider eyes." Travis nodded, sympathizing with the doctor but unable to take such a grim stance. "I feel that a person is capable of change, if faced with the right persuasion."

"I couldn't see anything more persuasive than the loss of one's planet." Dr. Zatzkin frowned, his morose falling into the shadows of his normal good nature.

"I have to think there's hope. For my son's sake."

"That is probably the best reason I've heard for being out here yet." The doctor held up his glass of water. "For the children of Earth!" He laughed, feeling the dark cloud over his thoughts lift and dissipate.

"I'll drink to that."

23

Omar's fear of flying had him paralyzed. He gripped the armrests without mercy, clenching his teeth until he could barely breathe. Most of the time he could distract himself with a crossword puzzle or a holographic putting game off his wrist communicator, but not when the plane was bouncing around like it was. He turned his eyes toward his wife and couldn't understand how she could be so damn calm. It angered him to see her reading a magazine while he held on for dear life. What made her so fucking special? He wanted to grab her by the shoulder and give a hard shake, scream at her for messing with him. For making him feel so inferior.

"Do you want something to drink?" His wife had to lean in for this, not wanting to embarrass him to the old woman sitting in the aisle seat.

"No."

"Are you sure? They have those tiny –"

"I don't need a stupid little bottle of booze," Omar snapped.

Kim just tilted her head and went back to her magazine, hating her husband when he was like this. Unfortunately for her he was like this more and more often. It wasn't just when he was scared. Omar was actually worse when he became frustrated, exploding over the simplest of things. Only two weeks ago he'd been unable to open a jar of pickles and so rather than taking a moment to loosen the lid with some warm water or tapping it on the counter, he decided the only rational thing to do would be to throw it into the kitchen sink. It had opened the jar all right, but no one wants a pickle from the sink. But she was learning to live with it. She'd taken her wedding vows two years ago and she'd said yes. Things might have been different if they'd included the phrase: For better or worse, or if thy husband becomes an asshole that smashes things. But even then she would have said yes. Forty percent of the time he was annoying or rude, but the sixty percent when he was sweet overshadowed it all.

"Why did we have to take this fucking trip!" Omar snarled, clenching his eyes shut.

"You're the one that wanted to go to Nassau, remember?"

Omar just shook his head slowly, looking like an

angry child sulking after a punishment. He let out a high-pitched gasp as the plain dropped. The pit of his stomach rose into his chest. Kim grabbed the armrest herself, moving on reflex from such a drop. Flying never bothered her. She knew the pilot had no intention to die and the statistics were great. Planes practically flew themselves. But she'd never seen such bad weather. She looked out the window and saw nothing but black storm clouds and water as it rolled over the thick plastic of the window. A shadow washed over the plane, blocking the light for a brief moment.

"What the hell was that?" Kim pressed her cheek to the glass and looked up, hoping they hadn't crossed into another plane's flight pattern due to the storm.

"What? What is it!?" Omar leaned over her, bobbing his head up and down like a hungry bird. "Is there something wrong with the plane?"

"No. I just thought I saw –"

The plane dropped as something hit them from above. Everyone in coach, afraid of flying or not, covered their heads and screamed. Kim peeked out from beneath her arm at the roof above the aisle. Her heart raced as it began to cave in, crumpling like a tin can. The plane lost cabin pressure as the center was slashed open. Three seven-inch talons wiggled back and forth to free themselves of the plane's roof.

They pulled out only to be jammed through the plane's right side, piercing three passengers in the window seats of rows 15F, 16F and 17F. The claws were pulled free of the plane and the impaled passengers lulled forward, twitching from the strong toxins coursing through their systems.

"Please God!" Omar screamed.

The plane was spinning out of control. Kim and Omar held each other in fear of being sucked through the tears in the roof. Then the roof was pulled open like a box top. Kim felt a hard jerk as Omar was pulled from her tight grip. When she opened her eyes she saw the seat beside her was empty, her arms warm with her husband's blood. Unable to stop herself, she looked up. An open beak was the last thing she would ever see.

24

"How'd you sleep?" Alvin asked from his seat on the train.

"Probably the best night's sleep I've had in a year."

Travis had meant it. After his late night snack with Dr. Zatzkin he'd gone back to his room and fell instantly to sleep. He'd slept deeply and had a pleasant dream of his wife. Not the usual nightmares or dark nothingness. Travis looked up as the train passed through the airlock of the main facility, the air blowing away the comfort from last night and reminding him of the harsh reality of his sentence. Travis and Alvin were both very surprised to see Andrews and three other security personnel waiting at the train station.

"A welcoming committee, for me?" Travis said with a serious face.

"Report to Mr. Chen and get back to work immediately." Andrews said to Travis while looking at Alvin.

"Yes, sir." Travis knew he meant business. He gave a single nod and hurried on his way.

"Is something wrong?" Alvin felt a bit intimidated by the look in Andrews' eyes, as if he were heated and full of rage.

"I have called an emergency security meeting. Now that you're back we may proceed."

Andrews turned without another word and headed out of the station, followed closely by Gomez and Rodriguez, two very annoying brownnosers. Alvin unscrewed his helmet and took a deep breath, allowing the facility's air to fill his lungs. He set off in a jog and slowed to a fast walk after he caught up. He thought it best to keep a distance of a few feet. Andrews led them into the security conference room and shut the door, locking it behind them.

"Everyone take a seat." Andrews walked to the front of the small room and waited till the last man took his seat. "At O'nine hundred hours Earth time we received a secured message from home office. It has been stated that all rotations have been temporarily cancelled and the supply ship is to remain in the hangar. They have deemed air travel unsafe due to unexplained atmospheric conditions." Andrews took note of their stunned faces and felt assured they were paying attention. "Home office has instructed us to issue a yellow alert. Allowing only small groups of workers out in rotating increments. Until such time as home office deems necessary. Questions?"

"You mean we can't go home as promised?" Gomez asked.

"I think you're missing the grand picture here. If the supply ship is unable to take off then that means not only are you stuck here with the rest of us but it means that, for the time being, there are no more supplies coming."

"This is just temporary...right?"

"I know what you all know. So I suggest we take this seriously and start tomorrow's shift on yellow alert. We'll break up the work schedules into units and rotate them as instructed. Any questions?"

The room was silent. No one really knew what to ask. Andrews had been given a simple message and he'd relayed it. Anything beyond that was a mystery. Alvin sighed softly, not wanting the other men to pick up on his agitation. The last thing he wanted was to be stuck under Andrews' thumb for God knows how long. In all honesty, Alvin had begun to look forward to heading home. Looks like that was going to be placed on hold.

"I will keep the communications link open between us and the home office and I will continually check for any updates. When I know something...you will know." Andrews leaned against the table nearest him, folding his arms about his chest. "Tomorrow things are going to be very different around here. Expect hostile behavior from the men and don't be surprised if we see some resistance. But we will follow home office's orders to the letter and we will do our jobs well. Now let's get to it."

The men stood and shuffled out, talking amongst themselves or running over the meeting in their minds.

"Alvin, if you would remain?"

Alvin let out a grunt of annoyance, but had the good sense to keep it within his mind. He managed a polite smile and took a seat, hating how it put him at a lower level than Andrews. Letting him look down on him like a principle at a delinquent student.

"I have some concerns," Andrews started, looking up to the ceiling as if trying to word this delicately. "I happen to know that you and some of the men have a relationship. I have no real issue with you playing nice as long as you remember where your loyalties lie. I'm worried that these new orders are going to put a division between us and the men, thus creating conflict. Are you going to have any problem keeping these men in line?" Andrews tilted his head slightly and gave him the eye.

"Not at all, sir. I know what I'm here to do."

"Excellent." Andrews scratched the back of his

neck, looking uncomfortable. "Look, I don't know how to put this delicately. But if you and any of the men are engaged in any sort of homosexual behavior –"

"What the fuck are you talking about?" Alvin snapped, shaking his head from complete surprise.

"Mind your tongue."

"I'm sorry, but that is completely unnecessary."

"Maybe to you, but to me it's extremely important. We're in a very fragile environment here and I need to know where everyone stands. So if you can tell me that you're with us one hundred percent, then we can end this conversation and whistle a happy tune like it never happened."

"No, sir, nothing like that at all." Alvin didn't want to dignify such idiocy with a response, but it was better to just end the conversation and walk away angry.

"Excellent. I'm very glad we had this conversation." Andrews was happy, knowing full well he'd embarrassed him. "You may go back to your duties."

"Thank you, sir." Alvin hurried out of the room, not wanting to be anywhere near that prick.

Andrews stayed put, watching Alvin's back as he hurried out into the hall. Stupid ass running away from him like a little girl. He hoped they fixed whatever little issues they were having back home, because he couldn't stand this crap much longer, not when they'd promised him men who would follow his orders. They needed to keep this place cold and efficient. No room for feelings and that sissy shit. Friendship was for elementary school students, not for miners abandoned millions of miles from home. He knew Alvin wasn't, but it gave him great pleasure to piss off that hippie homo. Andrews wished he could just banish the bastard and anyone else that might give them trouble. May they all be on their best behavior and fear him until this thing is over. Because for the time being they were on their own. And out here, he was God.

25

Travis was set back into the daily grind, riding the elevator with his helmet securely fastened. Normally the sudden drop of the elevator, accompanied by the unpleasant rise in his stomach, would bother him. Not today. His mind was racked with guilt over what Alvin was probably going through. Alvin was the only ally they had on this red rock. Losing him meant there was no buffer between the minors and the security personnel. Not that Travis was all that afraid of Andrews and his goons. In a straight up fight they wouldn't stand a chance. But much as it was with the food service industry, don't fuck with the people that handle your food. The security officers, although mentally lacking and not combat trained, had access to every aspect of their lives; the food they ate, the quarters they slept in, and maybe even the air they breathed—if they had the access. Travis wasn't entirely sure on that one, but he certainly didn't want to find out the hard way. Protection aside, he was going to miss Alvin. He'd come to be a pleasant face in an otherwise drab place. Someone you could talk to about sports, new and hilarious trends in fashion. But mostly they talked about family.

Travis gripped the handrail as the elevator came to an abrupt stop, gravity tugging at his knees. Travis straightened as the doors opened, greeted with that always pleasant gush of air.

"You're late, Daniels," Mr. Chen grumbled, marking something down on a clipboard. Not that he could read his own writing when wearing his gloves.

"Unavoidable. I was ordered to transport supplies to the third facility. You can talk to Andrews if you need a note from mommy."

"Get your gear and get moving smart ass. Tunnel seven." Mr. Chen shook his head and went back to the clipboard.

Travis craned his neck as he walked by, struggling to contain his laughter. The cold and often grumpy Mr. Chen was drawing a torso with massive breast, the nipples overly large and comical. Travis couldn't hold back any longer. He let out a few short bursts of laughter. You just had to. Especially in such a depressing environment, otherwise you might go mad. But whether or not Mr. Chen agreed was a different story, so luckily he hadn't seen him sneak a peek at his artwork. Travis opened the equipment locker and took out his laser drill, wondering who had gotten the pleasure of operating the giant hand. Most likely Christina since she had the most training and probably the steadiest hands. As long as it wasn't him, he hated the thing. Travis set his drill into the small cart and fastened the safety harness. The cart took off like a bat out of hell, zooming down the dark tunnels carved from the Martian soil. Travis wished he could feel the rush of the wind against his face instead of against the glass of his helmet. Sadness washed over him as he realized he might never again feel a breeze across his skin.

"Do you even work here anymore?" TJ asked as the cart pull up along the track.

"Do you?" Travis unlocked his drill and pulled it from the cart. A moment later it was called back to the elevator.

"You know this place would be pure hell if you didn't have my perfectly timed humor."

"Wow, TJ. Is that what you're calling it these days?" Christina laughed at her own insult, glad to be ragging on someone. These men were her family. No one knew her the way they did, watching out for her wellbeing like a bunch of big brothers. Playing around, dissing each other with colorful slang and dirty jokes made them feel normal again. Just another day at the office. "What was the outer facility like?"

"Like the Ritz Carlton compared to this shithole." Travis thought back to his late night chat with Dr. Zatzkin and wished he could visit with him more often. "They had tea and warm, fresh baked bread."

"Oh hell no." Jerome shook his head. "Please tell me you did not sit over there and enjoy some fresh baked, steaming, straight from the oven bread!"

"No, I didn't." Travis paused. "It was fresh baked, steaming, straight from the bread maker!" Travis laughed as he powered up his drill. He held the drill firmly and turned toward the designated wall, firing the short laser beam into the thick iron. It chipped away slowly and fell to the ground in heavy chunks.

Christina wore a large glove over her right hand and with every movement, a large robotic hand that was connected to the mining cart would operate to her movements. The hand reached down and gripped the metal ore, lifted it and dumped it into the cart with a clanking thud.

"Keep your eye on the hand, Christina. Jones from tunnel three said some of them have been shorting out," Morgan warned, always the den mother.

"Yes, daddy."

The four men went about their work and kept the conversation minimal. Jerome and TJ were working side by side, chipping away the same wall while cracking jokes about who could land the biggest chunk of ore. Morgan stood to Travis' right while Christina stood behind them all, picking up the rocks they dropped like a mother cleaning up after her kids. Christina reached out to grab a fallen piece of iron when her arm spasmed, twitching beneath the glove. Reacting to the subtle movements, the metal hand lashed out, running along the wall and then finally crashing through the nearest strut.

"Everyone move!" Morgan screamed, dropping his drill as the ceiling above them began to crumble and fall.

Morgan dove into Christina as the shaft began to cave in, large rocks dropping all around them. The shaft filled with dust, making it impossible for them to do anything other than curl up against the wall and hope for the best. The rocks fell for only a few seconds, but time was impossible to tell without sight. It had gone completely black with the overhead lights now smashed and buried.

"Everyone sound off!" Travis yelled.

"I'm okay." TJ lowered his hands from about his faceplate, unable to see a thing.

"I'm kicking." Jerome said with a deep breath.

"Morgan? Christina?" Travis was growing nervous. "Answer me."

"Mr. Chen." Morgan was yelling into the built-in communicator on the back of his right wrist. "We've had a cave in on the seventh track and need emergency extraction. We have a medical emergency."

"Understood. Cart's on its way and the medical staff has been alerted," Mr. Chen said evenly, his normally calm voice now slightly elevated.

"Stay with me, Christina." Morgan panicked, holding his hands to the crack in her faceplate, careful not to apply too much pressure or he could cause more damage.

Travis fumbled about the top of his helmet and flipped on the small light, seeing nothing but floating dust. He waved his hands frantically before his face, seeing the vague shapes of one person on the ground with someone sitting over them. Travis approached and clearly made out Morgan's terrified face as he looked down at Christina's body, twitching beneath his hands. There was a thin crack in her face plate and she was breathing irregularly, her eyes rolling back in her head.

"Morgan. Your arm." Travis dropped to his knees, gripping the tear in Morgan's suit. "You're going to depressurize."

"Oh God, that hurts." Morgan closed his eyes and ground his teeth, the pain in his arm was tremendous. "My arm is broken."

"Hold it together." Travis turned, never so thankful to hear the grinding wheels of the cart as it approached. "Help me."

The four men took hold of Christina and lifted her into the cart, securing the harness about her chest. They all piled in and held onto whatever they could as the cart was called back to the elevator. They must have looked so funny as the cart pulled in, all huddled together like a bunch of teenagers riding in a convertible. Mr. Chen was at the elevator, the doors open and waiting.

"The med staff is topside." Mr. Chen hurried over. "We need to get her into the elevator now, before the Martian soil contaminates her lungs."

"No shit, bub." Jerome was angry. This bastard didn't care about Christina, only that it looked bad to have a casualty during his shift. "But we're all going too."

"Think of this as a sick day," Morgan said as they stepped into the elevator, all of them holding up Christina. Morgan's arm hurt something fierce, but he still held onto her left leg. Morgan looked Mr. Chen in the eyes as the elevator doors slid shut, giving him a look that told him to try and stop them.

For once the elevator couldn't have been slower, or at least it felt that way to Travis. None of them had anything to say. They looked down at Christina and prayed for the best. Her eyes remained closed, but she was not peaceful. She bucked and thrashed beneath their grip. Her skin color had gone from her usual olive tone to a pale grey. The elevator came to the standard jerky halt and the doors opened. Travis was a bit surprised to see the medical staff, comprised entirely of the facilities only doctor, waiting for them with a gurney. Not like he had anything else to do other than wait around for "the call."

"Get her on the gurney and remove her helmet," Dr. D'Ambrosio told them.

The men lay her flat as Jerome unscrewed her helmet, tossing it aside. They rushed Christina down the hall toward the infirmary, all of them glancing down occasionally to see if her condition had improved, but there was no change. She drew in short, raspy breaths.

"Hold up." Security officer Gomez stood outside the infirmary, holding up his hands to slow them down.

"Move out of the way," Dr. D'Ambrosio ordered.

"Move in doc, but the rest of you hold fast." Security officer Rodriguez stepped into view from an adjacent hallway. "You too Morgan. Have that arm checked out, but the rest of you stay where you are."

"I'll keep an eye on her. Don't worry." Morgan gave them a nod and entered the infirmary, holding his arm and wincing from the pain. He hadn't noticed at the time since he'd been so concerned with Christina's welfare, but he was feeling a shortness of breath, dizziness, nauseous and an uncomfortable pressure in his throat and chest.

Travis watched two members of his unit disappear behind the doors of the infirmary, sealed off from them and out of his control. This had been from no action of his, but he felt responsible as he always did. Like a father, he wanted to look after them, take care of them and make sure they didn't suffer.

"What's this all about? Why are you keeping us out?" TJ was agitated, looking past Gomez to the small window in the infirmary door, catching a glimpse of Morgan as he sat on a gurney.

"You are all to report back to your cells until further notice."

"What are you talking about?" Jerome was getting pissed. This was not the day to mess with him.

"This facility is on lockdown until further notice," Gomez said coldly, repeating the order like a good little robot. "Please return to your cells and you'll receive further instructions."

"Have we done something wrong? Travis asked.

"Please return to your quarters immediately," Rodriguez repeated Gomez's statement, using a firmer tone. The two security officers stood their ground between them and their wounded friends beyond the door. "Move it back, now."

Travis nodded, turning to Jerome and TJ, placing a hand to their chests to restrain them. They both had a hot temper and didn't respond well to false authority. Travis pushed them back into the hallway, leaving some space between them and the security personnel. The last thing they needed was a clash of words that led to a brawl, which would inadvertently lead to someone's death.

"We're leaving," Travis spoke to his men, keeping his tone level. "Let's go. There's nothing we can do here now." Travis pushed Jerome and TJ away from the infirmary, giving the security officers an obedient nod, telling them that they were going to be good.

Travis peeked over Gomez's shoulder and made eye contact with Morgan. As if sensing the tension from out in the hall, Morgan simply nodded, telling Travis to go and be safe. He waved a hand and lay down.

26

It had been three days of solid work, staring into a microscope over samples. Dr. Peters was far too old to go so long on such little sleep. Worse than exhaustion was the strong headache behind his eyes, repeatedly pinching like being stabbed with the blade of a knife. Poor Silvia was going out of her mind, cursing the government for being so damn foolish. She laid the usual guilt trip on him, telling him how empty their bed was and how she couldn't sleep without him there. He'd called her a few hours ago, eager for the break. They'd spoken for a good forty minutes, but he couldn't let her nag on. Time was growing short. The mysterious canyon was not letting up in its spewing of moisture and smoke. The rivers in the surrounding areas had all flooded and washed out the valley to the south. Thousands of homes now underwater, millions across the globe. The government could issue flood warnings and set up emergency relief stations, but it wasn't going to help. Nor was this cover-up going to last. After two weeks of continual rainfall, people might begin to wonder if something more was afoot. If the rain didn't spark the world's interest than the lack of the sun surely would.

"Do you need me for anything?" Katrina asked, standing from her cot with a deep yawn. She set down her journal and stood beside Wilbur, looking down at the samples they collected from deep within the canyon's walls. "Anything at all?"

"Nothing. Not a goddamn thing. And what's worse is that I have no idea what the hell we're looking for."

"All we can do is hope for the best."

"Hope for the best?" Wilbur laughed, but there was no humor there. He turned from his microscope and went to the flaps of the tent, pointing out into the pounding rain. "The general public may not understand what a long rainstorm and some cloud coverage can do, but I do know."

"All we can do –"

Katrina was cut off by a high-pitched scream.

"What the hell was that?" Katrina ran to the tent flaps and pulled them back, sticking her head into the rain to try and see anything through the darkness. "Hello?" Katrina yelled.

"What is it?"

"Where are the soldiers that were stationed out there?" Katrina stepped back inside, her hair soaked.

Wilbur grabbed the radio and checked the channel. "Hello this is Dr. Peters." Wilbur waited a moment for someone to respond, receiving only static. "This is Dr. Peters, does anyone copy?"

"Where are they, Wilbur?" Katrina was nervous.

A woman was screaming close by. Her voice so full of fright it made them both break out in goose bumps. Before either of them could ask the same question, Andrea fell into the tent, her face and clothes soaked in blood.

"Oh my God!" Wilbur dropped to his knees and took hold of her hand, falling backward as she scrambled along the floor, flailing her arms madly. Her eyes were wide in terror and she seemed to be lost in thought, looking past them as if someone was there. Wilbur placed a hand to her cheek and felt his heart ache at how bad she was trembling. "Where are you hurt?"

"This is not her blood," Katrina said, wiping the blood from her cheeks.

"What happened? Some kind of accident with the crane?" Wilbur felt ill with the site of her.

"It came for him." Andrea shook, the words muffled by her chattering teeth.

"What did? What are you trying to say my dear?" Wilbur wiped the hair from her eyes.

"She's scared shitless." Katrina couldn't take her eyes off her colleague's face. She'd worked beside her for so many years and always saw her as someone who had her shit together. A strong, vibrant woman. Now she looked like something from a horror film wiggling about on the floor like a fish out of water. "Where are the soldiers?"

"All gone." Andrea began to sob. "They came up from the trench and took them."

Wilbur wanted to consul her, tell her everything was alright, but then came an unearthly howl. It made the hairs on the back of his neck stand up, the first thing to go erect on his body in some time. His hands had begun to tremble as he heard the harsh and unmistakable sounds of something breathing. Whatever had done this to his dear Andrea was now close enough to be heard over the rain.

"Get on the radio and get some help down here," Wilbur whispered.

Katrina went to her bag beneath the cot, riffling through the crap she'd collected over the years and didn't need, aggravated she hadn't listened to her girlfriend and gotten rid of it. Finally, feeling like she was never going to find it, her fingers gripped her identification card.

"Call Dr. Morrow," Katrina spoke to the card, waiting anxiously as a holographic head of Dr. Morrow rotated slowly above the card's center, still no answer.

"What are you doing?"

"Calling for help."

"Who the hell is Dr. Morrow?" Wilbur whispered, his heart beating in his throat.

"He's the head of this whole shindig. He'll be the one to call in the troops from the right people. Otherwise who the fuck do I call? I don't know the main line to the army."

"Hello?" Dr. Morrow's voice drifted up from her card.

"Oh thank the Lord. We're in big trouble here."

"What is it? What's wrong?"

"Quiet!" Wilbur shushed, holding a finger to his lips.

Katrina followed his wide-eyed stair to the tent and froze, seeing the shadowed form of something large and oddly shaped being cast on the fabric. It stood over seven feet tall and walked hunched over with terrible posture. Its breathing was harsh and wet. Katrina began to shiver as the beast stopped and lifted its head, sniffing the air. It turned toward the tent and snarled, letting out a clicking from its throat.

"Please tell me you carry a gun?" Wilbur asked Katrina.

"Pepper spray," Katrina offered, knowing it was useless.

"It's going to eat us!" Andrea moaned, rolling onto her side, not wanting to look at the silhouette.

Wilbur wanted to offer her some words of comfort, but there were none. Wilbur looked from Andrea to the tent as he heard the fabric tearing. The beast ran its claws down the side of the tent, its long fingers showing. Its hand was like nothing they'd ever seen. Three-inch nails, four knuckles and only three fat reptilian fingers. The creature cut the fabric clear down to the ground. It reached in with its other hand and pulled it apart.

27

Gretchen Laboo thought she looked damn good in her new running shorts. Showed off her ass something fierce. Four months ago and she would have never worn anything so revealing, but she'd been working hard. Not a diet, because those things never worked. She'd be ten weeks into one and then eat a candy bar, something with chocolate for sure, and then it was over. There was no going back once she hit that first mistake. Those days were all over since her discovery of the channel four infomercials at three in the morning. A jittery old woman that looked incredible despite her age. Gretchen had watched with much interest, learning the secrets of juicing everything while eating many little snacks a day instead of three large meals. It worked because it wasn't a diet but a way of life. And she needed a change of life big time. No longer would she spend another New Year's Eve alone or another birthday come and gone without a special someone to take her to dinner. A change of lifestyle brought a change of clothes. A sexy new change in style brought her the attention of Randall Holiday, the coworker she'd had her eyes on for the past three years.

Here he came, walking toward her in his tight shorts and tank top with a large umbrella held over his head sporting their company's logo on the top. Lately their law firm had been giving them the cheapest gifts. He smiled and waved as he saw her, making Gretchen's heart flutter. This was the man of her dreams. Three years of being the chubby friend, the funny girl that everyone loved to have around but didn't want, was now about to change. She used to get all giggly when he'd sit next to her at one of their company's monthly potlucks, but he was here on his own time.

"I was hoping you weren't going to cancel on me due to the rain," Randall said.

"Oh please. If I canceled because of the rain I'd never be able to exercise."

"Well let's get a move on." Randall looked up to the clouds. "What the hell is up with this weather anyway?"

"God has a lot of tears," Gretchen laughed, her voice uneven from the jogging.

Gretchen leapt over a deep puddle and slipped,

giggling like a schoolgirl as Randall took hold of her arm to steady her balance. She picked up her pace and stayed close to him, using his umbrella as the perfect excuse for their proximity. His cologne smelt so wonderful. Strong and masculine, but not over-bearing. It may have been pouring like a son of a bitch, but in her lovesick mind, Gretchen saw them running down a flower-lined path with the sun shining. That was until she slipped and fell, skinning her knee on the pavement.

"Are you okay?" Randall took a knee, puddle be damned. He took hold of her hand and helped her up again. "Maybe we should go in and have some coffee or something. I think it's too wet out here."

Gretchen looked about Central Park and took notice for perhaps the first time. Her mind had been so distracted with sexual fantasies of her and Randall in the back row of a movie theater that she hadn't seen the extent of the rainfall. Deep puddles stood on the borderline of being called ponds. The few people running through the park were actually heading to someplace else, rushing by with an umbrella or brief-cases held overhead. As if a small square held over their body was going to do them any good across a massive park like this. She laughed at how old-fash-ioned they looked, but the laughter faded as a thought occurred to her. She hadn't seen a day without rain in quite some time. How long had it been? Three days of continuous rainfall? Maybe four? All her exercising had been done in the living room with her shades drawn and the music blasting, so other than her hour long commute to work she hadn't been too concerned with the bad weather.

"Did you feel that?" Randall skidded to a stop, smacking Gretchen in the forehead with a point from his umbrella. He held still a moment, holding out his hands as if for balance.

Gretchen held her breath, wondering what he was talking about. "I don't –" Gretchen stopped as the ground beneath them shook. Just a slight rumble. As if a large truck were driving through the center of the park. "Maybe it's an underground pipe rupture or something?"

"Well whatever it is, I don't want to be here when it breaks through."

As if challenging Randall's request, the ground beneath then let out a large ripple. Earth was moving like a wave across central park. Both Randall and Gretchen had been knocked onto their asses. The cement path beneath them cracked and crumbled, rising and falling. As if the earth's crust was a sheet stretched over a waterbed and children were jumping on it. Trees began to bend and sway, their branches whipping back and forth. Gretchen hitched in a breath as a homeless man running for cover was decapitated by the violently flailing branch of a nearby tree. Her stunned wonder might have lasted longer if not for the tree nearest them snapping in half and crashing down a few feet from where they stood.

"We have to get out of here," Randall yelled, jumping to his feet while reaching for Gretchen's hand. He pulled her to her feet and took off running.

Their casual jog turned into an Olympic event. Instead of jumping hurdles, they hopped from one flat spot to the next to avoid the cracks forming beneath them. Gretchen looked behind her and screamed, her mind unable to process the sheer reality of it. The ground was collapsing in on itself, following them and gaining speed. Gretchen ran full out, moving until her thighs burned and her stomach began to cramp. In the back of her mind, buried beneath so much confusion and fear, she found a peculiar thought. She wondered if this was maybe some kind of practical joke. A modern version of War of the Worlds? The homeless man had been some kind of mechanical stunt; his head made of paper mache and his blood nothing but corn syrup. They'd look so foolish in the interviews afterward, telling everyone at home how they thought it was so real and they would never go to the park again. Offer the good folks in the studio audience a wink. But that thought was squashed by an avalanche of the here and now. No little prank or mental creation could be this real. The ground was bubbling up beneath their feet. She couldn't overpower the urge to look back at the traveling crack. It didn't make sense. All the energy in her legs gave out, fading to fumes. All that hard work, changing her lifestyle and finally wearing something that is supposed to show off her new and improved body, and now there was this big fucking crack!

"You can't stop now!" Randall took hold of her hand and pulled her along.

Their footing became lost as the ground beneath them opened like a savage mouth and swallowed them whole. All they could do was grab onto each other as they fell into the darkness. Had this not been her final few seconds in this world, Gretchen would have been so very pleased to be in Randall's arms.

28

This was the most horrific thing Annie had ever witnessed. She herself had been to Central Park back in college. A few of her girlfriends had dragged her up there to meet some guys. It had been so beautiful and awe-inspiring. So odd to see something so lush and peaceful smack dab in such a busy city. Now this? Something you'd expect to see in some third world country recovering from the aftermath of an earthquake or a volcanic disaster. An aging celebrity walking the city streets to tell you how your change could save their lives. You weep and your heart truly aches, but then you remember your favorite show's on at eight. But New York didn't fall into that category. Those aging actors from those depressing commercials called the city their home. It was right out of a movie, completely unreal. But this was straight from the local news station.

"What you're seeing is the channel five news

helicopter flying over what used to be Central Park."
Alexander Gunn, channel five correspondent spoke
slowly, his voice breaking up from the bad connection. "There's no telling how deep the trench is or if
it will continue to spread through the city. As of right
now, we do not have an accurate report of casualties."

"This is unreal." Annie shook her head, speaking
to herself without hearing the words.

"We will now go live to President Noll's address."

The screen shifted from the white and panicked
face of the anchorman to the calm and political mug
of the president. He stood proud and confident in his
expensive black suit, his face stern. This was a well-
rehearsed look. Telling the American people to not
only believe his words, but to love them.

"My fellow Americans. As of eight o'clock this
morning, I have issued an order to have the FAA
halt all air travel until such atmospheric events can
be explained and resolved. The tragedy of Blue Skies
flight 213, Montana Airways flight 112 and Pacific
Sea flight 528 will not be repeated. In response to the
earthquakes that continue to rattle the United States
as well as the planet, I can only stress that we're doing
everything in our power to discover the root of this
global phenomenon." President Noll took a moment
to collect himself, looking very concerned. "Earlier
today, New York City, Detroit, New Orleans, and

Seattle were devastated by, what we have thus determined to be, a shift in the Earth's crust."

"Bullshit!" Annie turned off the wall screen and threw the remote, hitting the wall with a dull thud.

"That's a bad word," Logan informed her, signaling to the world that he'd awoken from his nap.

"You are correct and I apologize." Annie gave him a hug as he sat beside her on the couch. She jumped at the unmistakable pop of gunfire, faint but too damn close for her comfort.

"What was that?" Logan could sense his mother's tension. His little heart raced at the sight of her discomfort.

"Probably just a firework, pook –" Annie nearly fell off the couch as someone knocked on the door, hard and with urgency. Annie took a long and slow breath, pressing her hand to her chest as if to pin her heart in place. "Who is it?" Annie gripped the small bulk of metal from the lockbox and stashed it in her pocket; the PM40 Travis had gotten her when she was doing some night classes so many years ago. It held five bullets in the clip and did the job, but it still looked so pitiful in the palm of her hand. "Who is it?" Annie asked a few feet from the door.

"It's Erica." Her voice was trembling.

Annie hurried to the door and undid the locks, pulling it open to a woman in fear. Erica and her seven-year-old daughter, Abby, were standing on the porch. Annie barely had time to step aside as they rushed in and slammed the door shut behind them.

"What is it?" Annie grabbed Erica by the shoulders, pulling her from the door. Erica's flesh had gone cold and clammy. "Abby dear, please sit next to Logie on the couch. Your mommy and I are just going to the other room here."

"I want her in my sight!" Erica nearly shouted. Her head twitched back and forth as if she were possessed.

"Okay, that's fine. Let's just stand in the kitchen so she can see you and you can see her. But let's please remain calm for their sake." Annie leaned in close and said this last bit for only Erica to hear. Without waiting for an answer she put an arm about Erica's shoulders and pulled her into the kitchen.

"Is your front door wood or steel?" Erica looked back over her shoulder, not wanting to lose sight of Abby.

"It's wood." Annie looked to Erica with a furrowed brow. "Kept you out didn't it?" She always thought humor was a great way to ease someone's tension and fear. But it didn't work in this case. Erica remained on edge, overly anxious. "What is going on?"

"Someone broke into our house." Erica could

barely finish the last word. Her lips trembled so bad they'd gone numb. All strength had run out of her and she collapsed to the floor, sliding down to rest against the center island. Such a proud woman, she was now shaking and fragile.

"Calm down. It's okay now." Annie peeked over to the children and saw they were watching television. Poor Abby looked as if she were in shock. Her face void of expression. Annie got onto her knees and took hold of Erica's hands, rubbing them compassionately to get some warmth back into her flesh. "Just tell me exactly what happened."

Erica took a deep breath, held it five seconds and released with a loud sigh. "Abby and I were up in her room, going through some of her old clothes to donate them. I heard glass breaking from the living room. So I went into my closet and got the gun." Erica took a moment to collect herself. "I crept downstairs and saw the man's shadow. Before I could even think of what to do, he turned and bolted toward me. I...I shot him in the throat." Erica's eyes went glossy. She looked passed Annie and no longer saw the kitchen. "He fell to the ground and lay there gasping, clawing at the air. Then he just looked at me." Erica hitched in a breath and looked to Annie, grabbing her by the shoulders. "He looked into my eyes as he died."

"Did you call the police?"

"There was no one there." Erica knew she had to explain. "I called, but the number was busy."

"That's bullshit. They're the police for Christ sake." Annie was angry. She hopped to her feet and grabbed the phone off the counter, quickly dialing the easiest number anyone could know. Her face changed, angry scowl stretching into wide-eyed confusion. "There's only an automated voice." Annie hung up the phone.

"All circuits are busy. Please remain on the line or try your call at a later time," Erica mocked, shaking her head from side to side as she cried. "Who do you call when you can't call the police?"

"Are you sure the man's dead?"

Erica nodded. The lifeless look in his eyes as he lay there, staring up at her, would never leave her mind. She'd gone to the gun range with her husband dozens of times, but they didn't supply you with living targets. This had been her only kill.

"Okay, well there's no rush for medical aid then, so let's slow things down and collect our heads." Annie rubbed her chin to try and kindle some thoughts. "First, you and Abby need some towels and dry clothes. We can throw your sweater and pants in the dryer. Second, I want you both to stay here with me until we can get someone on the phone. Unless you have somewhere else you want to be? Your sister's?"

"My car's having work done. Timing belt is being replaced."

"Mine is still out from the accident." Annie shivered as she thought back to hydroplaning off the road. "So I guess the best thing for us to do is to just sit tight and wait."

The lights flickered, fading in and out until they died to darkness.

"Calm down!" Annie yelled, wanting her voice to carry over the children's nervous cries and Erica's rapid breathing.

"Oh my God! He's coming to get us." Erica was on the verge of hyperventilating.

Annie called out with her hands held up above her head, speaking in her best mommy voice. "Everyone, calm down. It's only the power knocked out from the storm. That's all it is." Annie was firm, whispering down to Erica, "calm down and keep it together for Abby's sake."

Annie moved slowly, walking with her arms outreached before her. She ran her fingers along the kitchen counter, knocking over the dirty glass left out with a sigh of annoyance. The cold brass handle of the junk draw was such a relief. Now she wished she'd actually followed through with one of her numerous to do lists. In this case, the drawer was overflowing with crap; coupons, empty sandwich bag cartons, plastic straws and a large amount of unknown miscellaneous. The small lighter felt so good in her hand. The little thing she knew to be there but thought she'd never find. Annie lit the candles she kept along the counter, carrying a raspberry one into the living room. The children flocked to the flames light like moths, making darn sure to stay within the small circle of light.

"Where's your gun?" Annie knelt beside Erica, handing her a small candle.

"I think I dropped it on the floor by the stairs." Erica shook her head. "I don't really know for sure."

Annie nodded, not wanting to do what she knew had to be done. "I need you to sit on the couch with the kids and watch the door."

"Where are you going?" Erica raised her voice.

"To get that gun. We might need it and I only have six more bullets upstairs." Annie tapped the lump in her pocket as if Erica knew what was tucked away. "Plus Abby is going to need some clothes and something to play with. To keep her mind preoccupied. Now, do you need anything from your house?"

"Please don't leave us." Erica sounded like a frightened child.

"I have to. But is there anything else?"

Erica shook her head. Annie reached out and helped Erica to her feet. She handed her a dishtowel and told her to wipe her eyes before leading her back to the couch, nestling between the two children. Annie got on her knees and took hold of Logan and Abby's hands. They felt so small and warm, making her smile.

"I have to run next door for just a moment, so please just stay right here. The power is out and I don't want anyone wandering around. You might get lost or eaten by the laundry monster." Annie tickled their stomach as she laughed. The children both giggled and squirmed beneath her attacking fingers, lightening the atmosphere considerably.

"What if I have to go potty?" Logan asked.

"Just hold it 'til I come back. Deal?" Annie held out her hand, winking at her son as he shook it. "Don't open this door unless you hear me say this exactly: It's Annie from this house. Got it?"

Erica nodded slowly, taking slower breaths as she felt calmer. Annie was happy to see the mood shift from frantic panic to a scared house. No different than if they'd just watched a horror movie. Annie crept to the door and unlocked the deadbolt, but she kept the chain latched. She peeked out into the darkness and squinted through the rain to the house across the street. No power on the whole block. Once she'd confirmed it hadn't been just her house, she unlatched the door and shut it behind her. The locks clanked and turned the instant the door was shut.

Annie just nodded.

The story Erica had told her was now starting to sink in, hitting home more and more with each shaky step. The rain was coming down so fast there didn't seem to be a break in between drops. Like walking under a waterfall. She was soaked through before she even reached the sidewalk. But it didn't bother her. Barely even registered through the unbelievable tale her neighbor had delivered. One of the reasons she'd purchased this home was because of the low crime rate; basic breaking and entering, some domestic stuff, but never anything as odd as what Erica had told her. Had she suffered some kind of lonely woman snap? Was her son now in the hands of someone completely unstable? Well she hadn't made up the part about calling 9-1-1. Something bigger than a nut job breaking into her home was going on here.

"You moron!" Annie called herself, agitated she hadn't brought a flashlight.

Thankful she hadn't been a complete idiot; she pulled the lighter from her pocket and produced a flame. She cupped her face to the glass window beside the door and peeked in to Erica's front room, vaguely making out the shape of the man lying before the stairs. Annie stepped back onto the porch and tried the knob, turning easily beneath her grip. The ever spreading pool of blood circling the man's head was confirmation enough this prick was dead. No need to bend down and place her hand to that creep's wrist or neck. Oddly enough, he didn't look like the type to break into someone's home. He was clean-shaven, wore designer jeans and new white sneakers. His wedding ring had evenly spaced diamonds around the entire band. He smelled of expensive cologne and had a nice watch. Annie searched the man and the surrounding areas for a weapon, spying Erica's guns. But that was it. This man had broken into her house unarmed and dressed in normal street clothes, nothing worn about his face to try and hide his identity. It wasn't sitting right with her. It looked as if he might have been running from something or needed something. Maybe asking for help?

Annie picked up the discarded weapon and tucked it into her pocket. She stepped over the man and hurried up the stairs. First place she went was the top of the closet, searching for the lockbox. But it wasn't there. Annie turned and stepped into the room, looking in the dim glow of the lighter's flame. There was something out of place on the bed, a dark lump in the blackness. Annie saw the box sitting wide open with the spare bullets inside. Erica had been so frazzled and rushed she hadn't thought to put it back, let alone pick up the gun she'd left laying beside the dead man in her home. The normal Erica would have never been so careless. Not with Abby. The only thing she had left in this world, the living part of her husband that could go on. Annie pulled both handguns from her pockets and set them inside the box with the additional ammo, tucking the box under her arm. She went to the closet and filled a laundry basket with some clothes, tucking the box in the center to keep it hidden from the kids. She went to Abby's room and looked for anything that might be precious to her. A few stuffed animals from the bed, a wooden puzzle and some toys. Whatever clothes she could pull from the dresser.

Annie felt like a penguin, waddling from side to side across the lawn with the basket full of this and that held out before her. Annie had set four towels across the top, hoping to keep the clothes dry. But the rain was relentless. It was so dark from such thick cloud coverage. Annie had to think hard whether it was day or night. Since their car had skidded off the side of the road they'd spent the last few days hunkered down inside. After the first day of cartoons and frozen pizza, time just seemed to mush together.

Annie set the basket down on the porch and knocked three times. "It's Annie from this house." Annie said extra loud, not wanting to be left outside longer than she had too. Her shoes had been soaked through and the squishing water between her toes was not pleasant.

"Thank God." Erica threw open the door and gave Annie a tight hug. "Was he still there?" Erica locked the door behind her, checking the chain and deadbolt twice before facing Annie.

"Yes, he's dead," Annie whispered, looking back over her shoulder to the kids on the couch, raising her eyes to Erica and hoping she'd catch the hint. "Did he say anything to you?"

"Was he still alive?"

"No, no. I mean when he had entered the house."

Erica shook her head, but there was doubt in her eyes.

Annie didn't feel there was any real point to bringing it up. What had been done could not be taken back and she needed Erica to remain calm. Annie carried the laundry basket into the kitchen and dug through the layers of clothes. She pulled out the box and set it on the counter next to her own lockbox, tapping it so Erica would know where to find it. Then she debated if maybe they should be hidden. But how would she have acted if some random guy shattered a window and came inside. Knowing full well she was Logan's only line of protection, Annie left the boxes on the counter. She knew that if the roles had been reversed, she too would have pulled the trigger. No one fucks with her child. A smile pulled at the corner of her lips, but she kept it hidden. The thought of her walking the streets with a shotgun just looked too out of place. She picked up the phone and pressed redial, shaking her head to Erica.

"How about some camping stories?" Annie howled like a wolf as she took her seat on the couch, setting three boxes of cookies between them. "I hope you don't mind staying the night for a little slumber party." Annie spoke to Abby, hoping to push away the vacant stare, "your mommy and I just feel it's safer to stick together."

"Okay," Abby spoke without emotion, like a robot.

Annie and Erica shared a glance, hoping this was all going to be over by morning. They'll be able to call the police and let them take care of the man that had broken into Erica's house. Just a simple case of self-defense. She hoped everything would be back to a state of normality, but she couldn't dismiss the distant sound of gunfire.

29

This was the moment of truth. Three days of no sleep, sitting over a stack of paperwork with cup after cup of coffee. Gordon Dennis was about to set their only hope on a plan that he himself didn't think was worth the shot. But there literally was nothing better. After reviewing a mountain of data, he'd come to no other conclusions. Now all he could do was pray.

"They're starting," Kenneth said from the doorway.

"Let the games begin," Gordon said sarcastically, setting the pen down as he stood.

Gordon closed the folder over the four pages he'd just written. After realizing there was little help he could offer, he'd decided to put his affairs in order. Gordon had taken some paper and written a long letter to his ex-wife and two children, telling them everything he'd always wanted to tell them but couldn't. It had always been so hard for him to express his feelings. So much easier to face a blank piece of paper than the face of a loved one. Hopefully the world wouldn't end before he could mail it. He felt like the world's biggest pussy and worst father. Too late to make amends now. Typical though, having his whole life to be the man he always should have been only to realize it when there was probably no time left.

Gordon followed Kenneth through the thin hallways, turning sideways from time to time to pass by a cluster of naval officers or other researchers. Everyone on board, whether they had a doctorate in oceanography and marine biology or simply the cook, all of them had an ocean of doom in their eyes. Gordon kept his head low as they pushed their way toward the bridge. He didn't want to look them in the eyes. It had been his brilliant mind the President himself had called upon to come up with a solution, so the fault must lie with him. He had looked over the data and felt baffled. No explanations, nothing he'd ever seen before. Earth had thrown him for a loop many times in the past, but never has it pulled the rug out from under him.

"Blue Boy's 1, 2, 3 and 4 have successfully reached the ocean floor. You can watch them on the monitors," Captain Keeble said as the two doctors entered the bridge. "The thermite charges are being secured along the trench wall at a quarter mile interval, as specified by your calculations doctor Dennis."

"I'm not a demolitions expert. But with the density of the canyon's walls and the blast radius, it should be sufficient to cause a uniformed cave-in. But this is all just speculation."

"You have made a continual note of that, doctor," Captain Keeble snapped, agitated by his lack of confidence.

Gordon felt the tension and let it go. What good was it going to do them all now? Besides, he knew the captain's agitation was not solely directed at him. He followed the captain's gaze out to the rough sea, almost entirely blocked from view by the heavy rainfall and dark cloud coverage. Gordon looked down at the four remote camera links to the Blue Boys. Four remote piloted submarines with strong arms and advanced robotics specifically designed for deep-sea submersion, they could work in atmospheres no human could enter, without exploding from the immense pressure at least. The operators here in the bridge were doing a fantastic job of securing and then arming the thermite charges. It might actually work! This stupid ass plan that seemed so military, "let's just blow the fucker up," might actually work.

"What the hell?" The operator to Blue Boy 3

took off his display helmet. "I've lost all remote capabilities."

"Bring it back online, pronto!" Captain Keeble hurried over to the operator, leaning over his shoulder to review the linking computer. "Remote arms or not, where the hell is the video feed?"

"All communication between our systems and this unit have been severed."

"These subs don't just power down and go to sleep."

"The only explanation is if the onboard circuits have been removed or destroyed." The operator set his helmet on the consul and turned in his chair. "Since no one could have removed it, the remote link must have been destroyed."

"Johnson!" Captain Keeble made a tight fist, channeling his rage. "Can you confirm early detonation from any of the thermite charges?"

"No charges have been detonated sir."

"This isn't possible," the captain said softly.

"Captain, Blue Boy 2 is down." The operator took off her helmet. "Lost all feeds."

"We just lost Blue Boy 1," the operator said with a heavy sigh. "I can't explain what I saw…" The young woman shook her head, closing her eyes as she examined the final moments of footage before it went blank.

"Run back the footage." The captain ran over to the operator and stood behind her, leaning in so close they may as well have been dancing.

The footage rewound quickly, passing by so fast in a jumble of dark footage. She pressed play and they watched the strong arms securing a charge to the wall, nothing they hadn't seen before. In a flash, something shot out of the darkness and slammed into the lens, ending the transmission.

"Play back the last four seconds of footage and go frame by frame."

The operator did as instructed, moving the images of the ocean floor and the strong arms over the thermite charge to one after the other. All of them looking similar. Then a blur of motion.

"Stop! Enhance that!" the captain shouted, standing erect and pointing down at the monitor while shaking his index finger. "Now what the hell is that? Gordon, get over here and tell me what this is."

Gordon ran to the monitor, bumping into the captain but he didn't take notice. On the monitor was the blurry image of a hand.

"Well?"

"I can't say for sure, but it looks reptilian. Like a three-fingered hand." Gordon tapped the screen. "Looks like a really big hand, resembling a talon with those long claws." He shook his head, unable to come to terms with such a bizarre occurrence. "This has to be an error. Some kind of signal interference."

"Captain? We have some very unusual sonar activity."

"What is it?" Captain Keeble was feeling ill. He was a confident, strong man that demanded a certain presence. Now he couldn't keep the cold sweat from his brow.

"Something's coming up, something very large."

Before the captain could question, the ship was struck from beneath, knocking the vessel onto the port side. The captain was hurled through the window and disappeared into the sea with a handful of his crew off the bridge, all of them screaming. Gordon fell against the wall, shattering three of his ribs. Water began filling the bridge, shorting out equipment. A red warning light went off, screaming out to them in an automatic siren that there was something terribly wrong. As if being knocked on its side wasn't indication enough.

"Kenneth," Gordon spoke in a soft whisper. It hurt just to talk, but he had to. Kenneth lay only a few feet away, pinned against the sonar equipment. "Kenneth?"

Gordon leaned to his left, struggling against the pressure gravity was inflicting. He'd never felt so much pain as he did in his chest, sharp and agonizing.

Kenneth lay motionless. Gordon gripped the wall as the ship shifted and groaned, the ear-piercing shriek of the steel hull being torn. A hand rose from the water, bigger than any creature he'd ever seen. It could have rivaled the fossil record. It was different than the hand they'd seen on the sub's video footage. It's gigantic hand looked reptilian as well, dark green and covered with thick scales. The hand had five curled fingers; the nails pushed their way through the fingertips like that of a tiger. It slapped down on the bridge, pulling all that remained into the cold, dark waters.

30

"Careless pricks," Andrews sighed, looking down at security feed from the camera placed outside the infirmary.

Andrews was finding less tolerance toward Daniels and his military brats each day. This was his baby, his special project, and he didn't want these Special Forces fucks in here to mess it up. They needed skilled miners, men trained for the job. People that wanted to be here to make the difference, not those forced into labor like a chain gang. They'd gone and caused a cave in which would set them back. Now was not the time for any inconvenience. They were on their own for God knows how long. It might take every ounce of ore and oxygen to keep them alive until they could send out the supply ship and then wait another year to get a fresh batch. Six months there, six months back. It was becoming quite clear that there would be some rough times ahead. Life for all of them might have improved greatly if those idiots had been killed in the cave in. More rations to go around, less people using oxygen. Maybe except for the woman. She wasn't as bad as the rest of those morons.

Andrews pressed a button on the monitor and switched angles, moving from the camera in the hallway to the one in the infirmary. Morgan was lying beside Christina, sheltering his arm with his eyes closed. Andrews leaned in close as the doctor worked quickly to pull off her suit. Christina lay motionless with an oxygen mask secured to her mouth and nose. She flopped about as the doctor jiggled her suit over her legs. Andrews felt aroused, watching her chest bounce.

"What a dumbass," Gomez laughed as he entered the room, shaking his head.

Andrews quickly changed the footage, turning in his chair to hide his erection.

"Any updates?" Rodriguez took a seat at the monitors across the room, scrolling through the bulletins and latest transmissions. "How can there be nothing here? Not even that stupid newsletter we always get."

"Switch to channel three and move up the board." Andrews swiveled in his chair to face them, his penis back to its usual state of agitated slumber. "Check for any transmissions." Andrews looked lost, staring off into the wall. "Look for anything at all."

"What's happening here, sir?" Gomez could read Andrews expression.

"We've been cut off. Severed like a wounded limb."

"They wouldn't leave us out here. These facilities are far too valuable." Rodriguez shook his head, thinking it had to be some kind of training exercise. To see how they'd function if left alone to fend for themselves.

Andrews turned back in his chair, ignoring their worried faces. He had to keep things running smoothly. If he didn't, all hell would break out and the miners would turn against them. If they hadn't already? Perhaps having a trained leader like Travis Daniels around was too dangerous. Nothing he could do about it…for now anyway. There were more important things at hand. Now that they had all their pigs locked in the stalls, the next order of business was to find out what the hell this was all about. They'd never been without a continual link to the home world's main station. Policies and procedures coming through daily, requests and status checks on the facilities, but there had been nothing. The link had been severed on their end. He thought a different approach might be worth a shot. Andrews scanned the airwaves to hopefully pick up any transmissions from earth, television or radio, but there was nothing.

"We have some magic happening here," Gomez yelled back over his shoulder. "It's a secure channel to the Alliance Space Station."

Andrews stood from his chair and motioned for Gomez to move. He took a seat and fine-tuned the connection, turning a blur of static and colors to a close-up of a man's face.

"This is Yuri Kopylov, Russian cosmonaut aboard the Alliance Space Station, do you copy."

"We read you. This is Andrews, head of security at the Martian Facility. What is your current status?"

"That is very funny," Yuri said without a trace of humor.

"Excuse me?"

"Are you making a joke, Mr. Andrews?"

"No, not at all. We need to know why we've lost contact with Earth."

"Well that would make two of us." Yuri looked behind him, down a dark corridor, but shook his head. "My crewmates have been reacting badly to the situation. The news is less than encouraging."

"What news? We haven't been able to see any transmissions."

Yuri didn't want to say it. He looked behind him again, looking nervous. "Not sure you want to know what's happening down there."

"Please, what's going on?"

"Not that we have been fully informed ourselves, only bits and pieces from some random news stations. But it appears that the Earth has been suffering massive quakes. One such quake tore a hole in the ground and swallowed up the White House just an hour ago. Your President is not said to have survived. I am sorry."

"That wouldn't explain the loss of communication." Andrew thought for a moment, wondering how something like that could have happened. Personally, he didn't give a rat's ass about President Noll. He thought the man to be nothing short of a colossal moron. He couldn't imagine the state of panic the United States must be in right now after losing such a monument. He himself remembers the first time he saw the White House as a boy. It had been such a sight to see.

"You have received no formal communications from TransWorld?" Yuri was a bit surprised.

"We did receive one message a few hours back. It was very general." Andrews thought hard on the wording. "Home office instructed us to move into a lockdown and to keep the supply ship docked. Something about 'atmospheric conditions' being too severe to pilot the ship back."

"Atmospheric conditions huh?" Yuri smiled,

shaking his head from side to side. "Is that what they told you?"

"What is it?"

"I am going to patch through a direct feed from our outer camera. You tell me what you think of this 'atmospheric condition.'" Yuri hit a series of buttons and the screen went black for just a moment.

"Oh my dear Jesus." Andrews was shocked to say the least. "What is happening over there?"

Gomez and Rodriguez huddled up behind him, leaning in over his shoulders to look down on the screen. The continual footage looked the same no matter what region it was focusing on. The once beautiful sphere of blue and brown magnificence was now a black swirling ball of storms. There was no sign of landmarks, no absence of cloud coverage. The lightning strikes lit up the darkness repeatedly, over and over again. None of them had ever heard of a planetary storm.

"How long has this been going on?" Andrews was shocked, his mind racing. He didn't know what to think. They may have well been looking at an alien world.

"A few days, but this is the first time we've been unable to see a break in the clouds."

"This is more than just a storm," Andrews said softly, fearing the worst.

"I think we should keep this channel open at all times. As we have lost all communications with NASA, we need to stay connected."

"I agree." Andrews rubbed a hand over his face. "Please, let me know if you hear anything."

"Yes, of course." Yuri looked sad. "I wish we weren't so far apart. I'm starting to feel very isolated here."

"What's the station's compliment?"

"Twenty-two, but they're all being very quiet. Suffering from shock."

Andrews nodded. He himself was having trouble believing the footage.

"Andrews. I'll be in touch very soon."

Andrews nodded, turning from the monitor to face his men. All three of them shared a stunned expression. They were truly on their own now, cut off from Earth. Now they needed to survive. At all costs, Andrews was going to do everything in his power to keep them alive until this nasty business was resolved. If it ever could be.

"We need to round up the rats," Andrews smiled.

31

Morgan had been out of the game for far too long. He'd gone soft. Not something you thought about, it just happened. Ten years ago he could have taken a bullet to the arm without a flinch, able to channel his pain into focused anger. Now he lay on a gurney with a broken arm, sheltering the wound like a five year old with a bad boo-boo. The only thing to alleviate the terrible throbbing was the unconscious face of his sweet Christina. Since she'd first entered their unit, he'd come to look upon her as his daughter. Her innocent face anything but. Never had he been so impressed with a woman then he was with her. She'd saved his ass on more than one occasion, ending an intense session of hand to hand combat with a flirty wink or a hilarious joke. Now she lay motionless. So unlike her to be so still, looking weak and frail.

"Is she alright?" Sean asked from the doorway.

"No change," Morgan answered, rolling onto his side with the good arm. "The doctor said she'll pull through, but there might be some permanent damage to her lungs."

"What kind of damage?" Sean's eyes were heavy with concern.

"I don't know." Morgan smiled, sensing the love radiating off him. "Why don't you come in and sit a spell. I know we could both use the company."

Sean entered the room, pulling up a chair beside Christina. He'd lowered his hard exterior in the wake of the news, fearing the absolute worse. He took hold of her hand, upset by how cold her flesh felt to his fingertips. It felt so good to be close to her again, despite the circumstances. Holding her hand reconfirmed why he went on living. She was his only lifeline in this shithole. To lose her would be unimaginable. It would be all he'd need to go into his cell and slit his wrists. There would be nothing left for him, not in this existence. Hell was no concern in the afterlife. Not when every moment of his natural life was spent there. Looking at her day after day from across the cafeteria, wanting to cross the room and take hold of her hands. He loved her. With every ounce of his soul. But he couldn't bring himself to enter back into their circle, to be with Daniels. Not after the deal he'd made that had sent them to this red prison. Daniels deal had been an admission of guilt when there was none. Sean refused to be called a murderer when they all knew it to be a lie.

"You're going over it in your mind." Morgan turned his head to get a better glimpse of Sean's face. "Being with her reminds you of what happened."

"I don't need to be reminded of what I can't forget...or forgive." Sean spoke softly.

"Seems like there's not much you can do about that now." Morgan winced from the pain in his arm as he struggled into a sitting position, rolling his legs over the side of the gurney. "What Daniels did was for the best of us all."

"Don't hand me that shit again," Sean yelled, his rage boiling over. "I like you Morgan, just as I like every other member in our unit. But I will not sit here and go over the same bullshit in hopes of trying to move on. Move on with what? Anyone and everyone that's ever known me now thinks I'm a brutal murderer. Worse, we weren't even given the chance to defend ourselves. He didn't even try."

"Open your eyes. We weren't going to get a chance to stand trial. They wanted to keep this quiet. Daniels was offered the choice to plead guilty and get a one-way ticket to space, or deny everything and have us all executed. He did it to save your life."

"What are you talking about?"

"They offered him a deal. Come to Mars and report from the inside and watch the miners, or have all of us be put to death." Morgan nodded, smiling at Sean. "Yes, that's right. If he hadn't done it, you and Christina would be dead." Morgan lay back down, letting out a groan of discomfort. "We'd all be six feet under."

"Six feet under? Like my father?" Sean stood from his chair. "Travis' little deal made us look guilty to the eyes of this country, including my father. He became so disgusted with what he'd heard... You see, they'd published those photos, put them all over the BBC. Night after night, watching our faces standing in the middle of that village like a bunch of blood-thirsty monsters, until he could finally take it no longer. He dressed himself in his dress uniform, went into my old bedroom and took a seat on the bed." Sean wiped a fresh tear from his eye. "He put a bullet through his brain. But the last thing going through his mind, other than that bullet, was how ashamed he was of his son."

"That was not Travis' doing." Morgan looked Sean directly in the eyes. "That was all the work of those fucking tabloids. Blowing the truth completely out of proportion to make Americans look like total bastards. Poor people like your father are always caught in the middle, but do they care? Not as long as they can sell their papers."

"It's not something I can just get over." Sean turned to Christina and looked down at her peaceful face, so thankful to see her chest rise and fall. "I want to, so very badly I do." Sean shook his head. "I just can't do it."

"Well its well within your power to do so." Morgan rolled onto his side. "I'm going to try and get some rest, so feel free to visit with Christina. It won't bother me." Morgan pressed down on the pain medicine release valve. "Especially when these drugs kick in." Morgan closed his eyes and let the medicine slip into his system. Warm and soothing, masking the pain in his arm.

Sean looked back to Morgan and nodded, knowing deep down inside he had been right about a great many things. There had never been a greater time in his life then his years with the unit, part of the team. They'd watched each other's backs and shared their lives, becoming a family. But Travis hadn't taken the place of his real father. No one ever could and now he was gone, dead because of what he'd allowed to happen. Sean felt the pain swell in his throat like an apple he'd swallowed, uncomfortable and thick. It was best to push it aside and focus on the only good thing he had left. He took his seat and ran a hand through Christina's hair, brushing it away from her eyes. He had no medical training whatsoever, so there was no indication as to how serious her condition was. Sean knew they were never to remove their helmets subside. Training had burned it into their brains. Now he knew it wasn't just paranoia. His sweet Christina was suffering from Martian soil inhalation, all those chemicals and ground ore absorbing into her lung tissue.

"I'm not sure if you can hear me, but I want you to know that I'm right here." Sean looked back to Morgan, keeping his voice low. But Morgan was on his back with his eyes closed, his mouth slightly open. "I want to say how sorry I am for not being there for you. Like today." Sean felt himself tearing up. Her face so calm, too calm. There was no response to his voice. "Can you hear me?"

Christina lay there without response, her chest rising and falling in a slow rhythm. Sean pulled his chair closer to the gurney, bringing his lips a few inches from her ear so his words would remain private. He was not the kind of man to let emotion flow easily; a remnant from his father's training on how to be a good little soldier. But this was love and therefore took precedence over all else.

"I remember the first time I saw you." Sean smiled, thinking back to what a prick he'd been. "I insulted you right off the bat. Told you there was no way a scrawny bitch could keep up in a unit like this. Then you twisted my arm behind my back and forced me to the ground." Sean laughed softly, remembering how embarrassed he'd been. Talking trash only to be beaten down by the woman. "I think I fell in love with you that very instant."

The lights dimmed, replaced with a red flashing alarm.

"Attention, all personnel are to report to their private living quarters immediately. Cease what you are doing and report to your living space. This facility is in a level five lockdown until further notice."

Sean recognized the voice as Andrews, the tone cold and full of urgency.

"What's this all about?" Morgan opened his eyes and lifted his head, swaying from side to side as he fought the medication.

"I don't know, but I don't like the sound of a level five lockdown, whatever that means." Sean turned his attention back to Christina, the red lights bathing her pale skin. "I guess I have to cut our visit short. I'm sorry." Sean touched her cheek, wanting so badly to stay, to be by her side, but the red siren above told him it was not to be.

32

Thursday night, date night. Pretty much the only night Russell and Veronica set aside to spend one night doing nothing else but spend time together. Russell would put down his holoscope and Veronica would stay off her wrist communicator, if only for a few hours. Other than this one night a week, most people in their building would have thought they didn't exist. Both worked from home, had two of the three bedrooms in their condo converted into offices and stayed inside almost all the time. Dinners consisted of who delivered. Date night was their only exception to the norm, a reminder that they were in fact a couple. Children would have reminded them daily, but neither one thought that was going to happen. Since day one, Russell and Veronica had agreed that bringing a child into this world was a cruel joke.

"Did you hear someone screaming a few seconds

ago?" Veronica yelled from the bathroom, curling her hair.

"Huh?" Russell had barely heard her. He stood before the bedroom mirror working on his tie.

"Nothing." Veronica shook her head, turning off her curling iron with a dissatisfied sigh.

Veronica was never the type of girl that liked to dress up and "make pretty," a term her mother used to toss about almost daily and it made her sick. She was more of a T-shirt and jeans kind of girl. To be more to the point, she was a straight up slob. Had always been one too. As a little girl she'd pull out all her drawers and toss the clothes on the floor. Russell understood this because he was a slob as well. Both their offices were monuments of clutter. Textbooks piled on the desk as well as the floor. Old newspapers and magazines lay in mounds, none of them newer than four years ago. They both strongly felt that the media was comprised of morons breastfed by Satan himself. But that's what made them a workable pair. They were both disgusting and they accepted that. It wasn't so much love. More that Veronica knew everything about Russell that bothered her and it wasn't enough to make her leave. Vice versa no doubt, but they'd never talk about it. Not something they would bring up, especially on date night. Even the heavy rain outside wasn't going to stop them tonight. It may have been the perfect excuse to keep them in for the last few days, but even she needed to stretch her legs.

"Okay, let's cut a rug." Russell stood by the door, blue jeans and a tweed jacket over a black T-shirt. His version of dressing up.

"The day you go on the dance floor is the day the world ends." Veronica gave a sour smirk as she passed, grabbing her coat from the rack beside the door. "There it is again." Veronica stepped into the hall, tilting her head up to the ceiling.

"What are you talking about?" Russell asked while locking the door.

"Did you hear that? It sounded like screaming and gunshots."

"Come on," Russell laughed, linking his arm around her while pulling her toward the elevator. "We live on the tenth floor for crying out loud. Even if someone was out there screaming their head off, you'd never hear it from up here." Russell pressed the button for the elevator. "You're probably just overly stressed because that dick of an agent is pressing you for an ending."

"Well the novel should have one, don't you think," Veronica snapped, stepping into the elevator with her head down. Russell had been right of course. She'd been so stressed out over the last chapter that she hadn't gotten a good night's sleep in three days. Veronica would sit on her computer and play around, go shopping when she should have been typing. Distractions kept her from the frightening truth, those horrible two words that stalk writers like a plague: writer's block.

"Are you okay?" Russell was concerned, reading her expression of doubt and dismay.

"Fine," Veronica lied.

It was a shitty start to a wonderful night out and Veronica felt bad about it. Most of her life was either spent feeling guilty or pissed off, the latter always ending up with a guilty feeling. But that's what had always made her such a great writer. Her anger toward the world and her mounds of guilt led to honest, truthful writing. Emotional people could relate and wanted to buy. But there was nothing spewing from her these past few days but doubt. She looked up and watched the number descend with them, from seven to six and so on.

"Do you smell that?" Russell sniffed the air with his extremely large nose, looking like a bloodhound on the trail of some fugitive. "Smells like smoke."

"Maybe you had a thought and the sticks are burning." Veronica's laugh quickly died off as the smoke filled her nose as well. "What's going on?"

The elevator moved from the second to the first

floor, the doors parting to pure chaos that neither of them would have ever expected to see in their lobby. A car had driven through the main entrance and sat a few feet from the elevator door, completely engulfed in flame. This was not something they ever expected to see in their lifetime, let alone in Wisconsin.

"Shut the doors!" Veronica reached passed him and stretched for the button.

"Are you mad?" Russell gripped her arms, digging his thumbs deep into the flesh. "We have to get out of here before the whole building goes up."

Russell released Veronica's arms and hurried out into the lobby, running with his arm before his face to shield the heat. The car was upside down, the tires still spinning. Russell got as close as he could and knelt down, pulling away from the intense heat to try and get a glimpse inside. The charred remains of the driver lay curled in the fetal position on the roof, looking well beyond any possible hope of rescue. Russell pushed away from the burning wreckage and looked for a fire extinguisher, spying one lying on the ground with some foam on the nozzle. He went to touch it, wondering why someone had started to put out the blaze and simply took off, but a nearby shriek altered his focus. Someone was standing on the sidewalk, staring directly at him. He couldn't make out any features through the smoke but he could feel the weight of eyes on him. The person sprinted forward, moving with unnatural speed and agility, and then it bent down to run on all fours.

"What the fuck?!" Russell screamed as the creature leapt through the hole in the front entrance.

It looked like a human dinosaur, elongated and reptilian, yet humanoid. Russell watched it fly through the air, up and over the car with a trajectory directly for his face. Feeling as if he were moving beneath water, Russell grabbed hold of the fire extinguisher. He fell onto his back and compressed the black plunger. White foam sprayed into the beast's face, blurring its vision while causing it to miss Russell by mere inches. Veronica shrieked and dove out of the way as the creature slid along the lobby, slamming into the elevator wall.

"Close it!" Russell screamed, tilting his head to look back at her, the world upside down by his vision on the floor.

Veronica scurried to her feet and reached inside the elevator, cringing in terror from the creature on its back, kicking and slapping the air blindly. Her finger pressed a floor at random and she withdrew her arm as the doors closed, making that brutal bastard some other tenant's problem now. Veronica looked to Russell and broke out in tears, her body shivering. There was no comprehension for what she'd just dealt with. The uncomfortable warmth from her proximity to the car brought her back to reality.

"We need to get going." Russell moved into a sitting position, freezing as he heard another shriek in the distance. "Like right now!"

Veronica stood and took hold of Russell's hand, pulling him to his feet as they maneuvered over the broken glass and chunks of wall scattered down the cement steps. They both stood for a moment, looking out on the city they'd called home for the past six years and wondered how this could have happened. While they'd been locked away in their penthouse condo like a couple of hermit crabs, something had sent this city into a panicked frenzy. The downtown district was one large fire, all the buildings burning like giant candles. People were running through the streets with their arms either carrying whatever belongings they could grab or held high above their heads as they fled. Veronica and Russell ran across the street into the community park, ducking behind a playhouse to gather their thoughts. Both of them oblivious to the heavy rainfall.

"What is happening?" Veronica tried to control her breathing. Short, quick breaths were all she could manage.

"Did you see that mutant freak?" Russell closed his eyes tight, forcing out the smoke and soot. It stung something fierce. "I've never seen anything like that before. Must be something from the government."

"Look!" Veronica pointed back to their building.

They sat in stunned silence as their building, their home, caught fire. Even with all the rain, the fire continued to spread. It was horrifying to watch, but it held their attention. People's screaming voices rang out through the night. Helpless and fearful. Veronica took her husband's hand and watched as people flung themselves from their windows. This had been partly their fault and they both knew it. Russell could have taken the fire extinguisher and gone to work, spraying that damned car till he had done all he could. But they'd both fled into the night like a pair of thief's. Now they were going to sit in the cold, damp grass and watch these people plummet to their deaths. Veronica was so thankful for the bushes and shrubs at the park's edge that kept their impact from her vision. The wet thud made her shiver. The noise of their bodies colliding with the sidewalk would haunt her till the end of time.

"God forgive us." Veronica whispered.

"Amen." Russell finally turned away. "There's nothing more we can do for those people." Russell stuck with his best quality, the ability to find excuses. "We didn't crash that fucking car into our building. Plus we weren't the first ones to work that fire extinguisher. Why hadn't they gone for help?"

As if to answer his question, a creature shrieked from only a few yards behind them. Russell took hold of Veronica's hand and stood hunched over, looking over the roof of the little wooden playhouse. He saw the creature standing in the park, looking from side to side. It lifted its head into the night air and sniffed like a dog. It was far too close for their comfort, no more than thirty feet away. The rising flames from their building cast some light into the park, illuminating the features of this bizarre beast. It was dark green with small black dots, long, muscular legs. It looked like a giant frog to Russell. Its thick chest pushed out, rising and falling quickly as it continually sniffed the air. The face was nothing short of grotesque. The head was shaped like a wolf's, elongated around the mouth like a snout, but there appeared to be no lips. A permanent snarl came from its protruding teeth, uneven and black. The eyes were the most disturbing part, neon green. Glowing in the dark as if radioactive, which had been Russell's first initial thought as to their origin. The beast cocked its head and let out a shriek that eerily sounded like an infant's cry. It took off toward the buffet of falling victims across the street.

"That was a different one. How could there be more than one of those things?" Veronica was slipping into shock, her eyes going distant.

Russell ignored her. He couldn't take his eyes off the way it moved, how it started out in a standing position and then fell forward into an all out beast-like sprint. It must have stood over eight feet tall to be so comparable to the trees around it. Russell's thought process was broken as something growled out of the darkness.

"Come on, we have to move." Russell pulled Veronica by the arm, but she didn't follow. "Wake up damn it!" Russell slapped her face back into consciousness.

"Ouch." Veronica grabbed her cheek, looking him in the eyes and asked him how dare he hit her without so much as a word.

"Please, we have to go."

Veronica followed her husband closely as they ran across the park, unsure of where they could possibly go. Most of the buildings around the park were now ablaze as their condo fire met up with the burning blaze from downtown. Across the park was a corner drugstore with the lights still on. They picked up the pace and ran harder than they ever had in their lives. Their lungs burning. Russell was the first to reach the store, tugging on the door to no avail.

"Please. Someone let us in!" Russell screamed, pounding on the reinforced glass like a savage. "Someone help us."

An older man wearing a red apron with the drug-store's logo set in the center stood from behind the counter and hurried to the door. He knelt down and turned the small latch, barely able to move out of the way as the couple bolted inside. The store's clerk quickly locked the door.

"What is happening out there?" Veronica cried, burying her face in her husband's chest. "What is happening!?"

"We don't know." The clerk stood, gripping a near-by display of energy bars for balance. "That fella back there was the first to come in here over an hour ago. Said they took his wife right away." The old shopkeep-er limped back behind the counter and took a sip from his flask. "I didn't see them 'til a few minutes ago run-ning past while dragging some poor woman behind it, like she was a sack of garbage on its way out to the curb. Oh, the site of her mangled face…" He looked down to the counter and began to weep.

"Does anyone know what those things are?" Russell asked, looking over the shelves of overly priced items to the scattered people. "What are they?"

"No!" Veronica screamed, backing away from the front door.

Russell turned and saw the beast they'd heard snarling in the park staring at them from across the street. It walked across the pavement slowly, snarling to show its impressive fangs. This creature was different than the one from the lobby. As it stood beneath the streetlamp, it became apparent this creature was not some random mutation. This was a hunter. It stalked them with those same green eyes its larger brother had, glowing in the dark like the stars Russell used to put in his room as a kid. Beneath the lamppost it looked as if someone had skinned a lion, only this time the lion had something to say about it.

"This is something different," a man said from the back of the store, his voice a rollercoaster of terror.

"No shit, Sherlock!" Russell shouted, backing away from the door. "We've got the tall daddies and their dogs."

"These doors are shatterproof, right?" Veronica needed to know that there was more between them and this approaching monster than just a thin pane of glass.

"It's bulletproof too," the shopkeeper said with a sigh of relief.

The beast obviously hadn't heard the old man's confidence in the strength of the glass. It sprinted the remaining distance and leapt forth, smashing through the glass without effort. It cornered them, blocking their only way out. With a deep growl emitting from its thick throat, the dark beast moved in.

33

Two days spent cooped up in her house with nothing but the continuous drop of the rain. Thudding on the wood shingles without pause. Annie sat at the window by the front door as Erica put the two kids to bed. They'd decided to take shifts, knowing someone should always keep watch while the children were safely tucked away up stairs. So Annie sat watching the water rise. It had gone from a minor annoyance to a massive catastrophe. Soon they wouldn't be safe in their own home. The water level had now spilled over the curbs, creating a river down the street. Two days spent in the dark. No power since Erica and Abby had showed up. More frightening than that was there was no news. Not even on the radio or the digital broadcaster. Nothing but static on every channel. Rain could be to blame for knocking a tree into a power line or some flooding, but not from stopping broadcasters from delivering the news. Whatever was happening out there was happening everywhere.

More gunfire. Much closer this time, making her jump with every pop. Crazies always scattered once the power went out, operating under the cover of darkness as if they were shadows. Annie absently ran a finger over the gun in her hand, soothing herself with its presence. It wasn't much, but a bullet was a bullet. Erica's gun had sure proven that point on the poor bastard lying on her floor. Maybe he'd deserved it, maybe not. Bullets don't slow down to reason. They just do their job without thought.

"They're finally asleep," Erica said with exhaustion. She grabbed a chair from the kitchen and joined Annie by the window. "Anything interesting come sailing by?"

"No, nothing but the rain." Annie didn't want to say what she was about to say, but they needed a plan. "If the rain doesn't let up soon, we're going to have to leave."

"Go where?"

"I don't know. Maybe there's an emergency shelter set up at the high school or the fire station on River Road. On second thought, River Road doesn't sound like our best bet."

"Anything on the radio?" Erica was hopeful.

"No, not a goddamn thing."

"That isn't possible."

Annie agreed, but what good was it going to do them. They needed a plan. Aside from the rising water they'd run out of basic supplies. It was hard enough to get Logan to fall asleep, but doing so without his nightly apple juice/water was an impossibility. There wasn't a whole lot she could make them for dinner without the power being on and the items in the fridge and freezer were starting to turn south. They needed to go somewhere with a working generator and some food, some place situated on higher ground.

They both looked out the window as something screamed nearby. It was like nothing they'd ever heard before, ear piercing and beastlike.

"What the hell was that?" Erica stood from the chair and pressed her cheek to the window, cupping her eyes to see through the rain. There was nothing out there but the raging river that had once been the street.

Erica hurried into the kitchen and unlocked the box on the counter, filling the gun with the few rounds she had. She hurried back to the window and swayed, anxiety taking a hold on her.

"What the hell could make a noise like that?"

"It could have been anything." Annie wasn't convinced. It had definitely been some kind of beast, but nothing they should be able to find around here. "Maybe something's broken loose from the Woodhaven Zoo; it's only fifteen miles up the road."

"It didn't sound like a bear to me?" Erica fell back on her paranoia, one of her most annoying traits. Every cough and rash became a life-threatening flu or outbreak. "Something unnatural is happening here."

"This rainfall is unnatural." Annie looked up into the black clouds. "I'm waiting for God to give us building instructions so we can board the ark."

They both shared an uncomfortable laugh, the sound so full of despair and phoniness. But the laughter quickly faded as the same shriek sounded much closer. Then something stepped into view, walking down the middle of the road without any hesitation to being knee deep in rushing water. It stopped in mid stride, lifted its head into the rain and began sniffing. It stood perfectly still for a moment, hidden in the darkness of night and blurred by the rain, but they didn't need a clear shot to know it was not human. No person could stand so tall with their chest jutting out so far. The beast turned and sprinted toward the house across the street, jumping in through the window. A split second later they heard gunfire and a woman screaming, then silence.

"What the hell is happening here?" Erica was

shivering, the gun darting back and forth in her grip until she finally dropped it.

"Shush." Annie held her finger to her lips and pointed. "It's coming back out."

The creature stepped out of the window and onto the grass. It reached back into the house and gripped something, pulling it up and over and finally dragging it behind. Annie didn't want to be seen, but she couldn't help but dart her head from side to side, agitated the power was out.

"It's got old lady Watkins and her husband!" Erica shouted, instantly covering her mouth.

Annie looked up at her with cruel intentions, telling her in a single glare that if she put her son at risk again she'd toss her noisy ass out into the rain. Erica nodded, removing her hand slowly while taking a deep calming breath. They both looked back in time to see the creatures stepping out of view across the street, pulling the old woman and her husband along like a meat wagon on a string. Annie noticed that it had hold of their faces, dragging them along by their jaws. She couldn't tell from this distance if they were alive or dead, but she hoped for their sake they'd passed on.

"It went into their home and just took them?" Erica took a seat. "What was that thing? It certainly wasn't from the zoo."

"Keep your voice down!" Annie warned.

A woman was screaming, sounding close. Her voice silenced with another shriek and then nothing. There was no telling how many of those things were out there, taking full advantage of the rain and darkness. Maybe these creatures and the rainfall were linked. Stood to reason since both were completely out of the norm. Annie put her thoughts aside as another beast, if not the same one, began down the street without any fear of being seen. It sniffed the air, searching for its next meal. Only this time, it turned its head and spotted them.

"Oh shit!" Erica couldn't breathe. She fell to the floor and tried to pick up the gun, but her fingers had gone numb, losing all eye hand coordination as if the gun were nothing more than a hologram. Finally, she was able to grip the handle.

The creature raised its head and let out a deep snarl, sounding wet and full of rage. It lowered its head and made eye contact with Annie, its green eyes glowing. She couldn't tell for sure, but she could sense it was smiling at her. She didn't see any lips, just sharp teeth, but she swore it was smiling. It leapt forward and closed half the distance, breaking out in a full out sprint. Erica and Annie opened fire. Annie hit the beast three times in the chest and twice in the forehead, whereas Erica struck the creature three times in the chest and missed until her clip was empty. The creature slipped over its own feet and slid along the grass, colliding with the wall beneath the window.

"Fucking thing took all our bullets to bring it down!"

They both jumped as it stood and punched through the glass, grabbing Erica by the collar of her sweater. It pulled with unnatural strength, ripping the sweater off her back. Erica fell onto the chair, shattering it beneath her. She scrambled to get away as the beast jumped through the window and reached for her. Annie grabbed the metal lamp off the table and yanked the cord from the wall, slamming it down on its face. The creature lashed out and slapped her hard, knocking her over the couch and onto the coffee table. Erica, sensing a momentary lack in its concentration, took one of the wooden legs from the chair and stabbed upward. The beast recoiled with a deafening roar, gripping the protruding wood with both its hands.

"Here!" Erica tossed Annie a chair leg as she took one herself, plunging it right beside the first one.

Annie let out a savage roar of her own as she jammed the jagged piece of wood directly into its throat. She held it for a moment, turning it clockwise to inflict the most damage. She pulled the chair leg back out and prepared for another jab, but the creature fell to its knees, moaning for a brief moment before collapsing on its side, letting out its last breath. Black liquid seeped from its wounds, looking like oil.

"Broke into the wrong fucking house bitch!" Annie yelled, kicking her foot across its face. "Stupid –" Annie's celebration was short lived as she looked up to the window and saw two more of them standing in the road, both of them staring at her. "Run!"

Erica stood, slipping in the creatures blood as they both ran for the stairs. They could hear the creatures snarling on approach, moving so damn fast. As they reached the top of the stairs they heard a thunderous crash. Both demons had jumped through the wall with ease, sliding into the living room after stepping in their fallen comrades' blood.

"What's going on, mom?" Abby sat on the top bunk of Logan's bunk bed.

"What is that?" Logan was standing before the bed, tears running down his face.

"Come here!" Erica held out her hands to Abby and caught her as she jumped down, setting her down and shooing her away from the window. "Both of you, by the closet. Hurry!" Erica ordered.

Annie and Erica got on either side of the bunk bed, both of them tilting it toward the bedroom door until it fell to the ground with a mighty crash.

"My bed!" Logan covered his face and cried harder.

They pushed the top bunk into the door and then pushed the dresser on top of it. They pushed Logan's thick art desk between the bottom of the bunk and the back wall, leaving no wiggle room for the door.

"Now we're trapped up here," Erica moaned.

Annie ignored her and ran to the window, dropping to her knees. She pulled the metal grating off the floor and pushed out the screen on the window. She took the rolled up ladder and tossed it out the window, letting it unravel on its way down. Annie could hear the creatures kicking open her bedroom door and it made her so angry. Those twisted monsters messing up her personal belongings. They had no right to be in her home.

"Get on my back and hold on very tight. Don't let go," she told Logan, leaning forward so he could climb on. She locked his hands beneath her chin and stepped over the ledge. The ladder was already slippery underfoot from the heavy rain, but she managed to get a good grip.

Annie was barely down three rungs before Erica kicked her leg over and stepped onto the ladder. They moved quickly, increasing their decent as they heard the creatures tearing through the upstairs. Annie knew that makeshift barricade they constructed wouldn't take them but a moment to smash through. She just hoped it bought them enough time to reach the ground and run out of sight. Annie looked beneath her feet and saw there were only a few rungs left, but she heard the door splintering up above. She let go and landed hard, forcing herself to fall forward so as not to crush her son. Annie stood and stretched her ankle as Erica hopped off the ladder.

"We need to find a place to hide." Annie left Logan on her back, gripping his small hands about her neck. She was afraid the surprisingly strong current of the water would carry him off. Plus after seeing that creature up close, she didn't want to let her child out of her sight for even a second.

34

Dasher deserved better treatment than this. To be locked away in a cell with a moron that had wept in his bed for two days was just cruel and unusual punishment. At least the scrawny bastard was now silent, lying on the top bunk fast asleep. This had been his first peaceful moment since they'd locked him up. Well, as peaceful as it could get in a prison. The inmates were all at their bars, yelling out into the hall that they were starving. He too was hearing his stomach growl. They hadn't had anything to eat since yesterday morning, but it had been a very odd day. They'd been pulled from their cells and marched down into the cafeteria as always, loading up their tray with brown this and grey that. Dasher sat next to a super fat white supremacist, but he didn't bother him. He'd eaten in silence, watching the prisoners and guards. Their behavior caught his attention. Instead of standing over them on the second level, staring down with their usual smug authority, they stood next to each other, talking furiously with their hands. Something big was going on, you could tell in their demeanor. Then their conversation ended with a nod of confrontation. But that's when it got rather strange. The guards kept their eyes low, looking at the windows when they should have been looking at them. He hadn't thought too much about it at the time. They were sent back to their cells, locked in and left there. No sign of a guard since yesterday.

Dasher turned toward the window, rubbing his stomach as he went. He was starting to get sick from a lack of food. Dasher had to stand on his tiptoes to get a good view of the world beyond, but it wasn't something he had wanted to see. The rain was still coming down, harder than before it seemed. If that was even possible. He'd been in a week's worth of rain before, but never when it hadn't let up. The grassy valley between the prison and the woods looked like a lake. What was more disturbing was the shape of Norfolk just beyond the trees. The fire had consumed the city, spreading to every building despite the rainfall. Now the forest was ablaze. Dasher was thankful for the new lake between them and the spreading inferno, but he couldn't help wonder why this was being allowed. Where were the firemen? Dasher didn't give a rat's ass for cops, he'd known too many crooked ones from his days on the street, but you had to respect firemen. They did nothing but put their ass on the line to save yours. But where were they now?

Something caught Dasher's attention, running from the woods in the distance. It ran on all fours like a dog, bolting like lightening through the newly formed lake, heading directly toward the prison. Then three more came running out from the woods, splashing through the water without pause. Their speed made it impossible to see what they were; too large to be dogs. Dasher thought maybe the fires had sent some bears running for some new digs, but he'd never seen a bear haul ass like that. If he'd been allowed more than one call he'd go out and call National Geographic. Dasher turned away from the window, his mood now as cloudy and dark as the weather outside. He stood by the bunk and looked at the back of his cellmate's head, his hair looking so filthy and unkempt. Dasher ducked down and lay on his bunk. He couldn't keep the depression from a few days back out of his mind. It's true; he'd been offered a phone call. But when he'd picked up the phone he realized there was no one to call. No friends that could come visit him. No family that would even give a damn.

Dasher looked on the brighter side, thinking about all those poor saps that lived within Norfolk. He could see them staring at their homes of twenty years, or their apartments, watching them go up in flame without anything they could do. They'd lose their decorative bath soaps and photo albums, expensive art, extra bed linen and all the other crap they'd managed to accumulate and stuff into a drawer. One thing about living on the street that he could pass along to all humanity was the ability to make do with the little bit he had. But it was sad to think of the all the children that would probably be homeless before the end of the day. That was something he didn't wish on them. The fire sparked a new thought. He nodded as the idea planted an image within his mind. He could see all the guards outside the prison, spraying the rooftops with firehouses as an extra precaution. But deep down he knew that wasn't the case. The rain had been soaking the entire building for days. Wherever they had decided to run off to, they'd better come back soon because his stomach was giving quite the lecture. It wasn't like he could find something to eat in the kitchen. He couldn't even open the door. Dasher thought of resorting to cannibalism and couldn't help but laugh, letting a single "ha" burst through his tight lips. The last thing he wanted to do was wake up his annoying cellmate, but sometimes you needed a good laugh. There couldn't be but a few bites of meat on his scrawny ass anyway. Not to mention he was sure it'd be stringy and tough.

Something dropped onto the back of his hand. At first he didn't see anything but a dark mole, but when he turned his hand to the side the mole had moved. On closer inspection the mole wasn't a mole at all, it was a bead of blood. Then another had dropped, spilling on the floor. Followed by a thin stream that began to pool. Dasher swung his legs over the side of the bed and leaned far to his right to avoid the blood. He stepped on the bottom bunk and pulled himself up, looking down at the pale flesh of his cellmate's face. There was a large chunk missing from his right wrist. The blood had been soaking into the mattress for some time and was now starting to seep out from beneath.

Dasher hopped off the bunk and gripped the bars, pressing his mouth between them. "Hey! We have a dead man in here!" Dasher yelled.

The hallway was deserted. Dasher pressed his cheek to the cold steel and looked as far down as he could, seeing arms protruding from the other cells but no one in the hallway. No one. Something was definitely wrong here. Dasher had never heard of guards just up and walking out. Even if it were some sissy strike or something, someone would be in to look after them. They couldn't just leave them here to rot. Dasher stepped away from the bars as a beastly growl echoed through the hallway. It was like nothing he'd ever heard before, definitely not human. Curiosity got the best of him, bringing him back to the bars for a peek at what could possibly make such a growl. Maybe one of those bears he'd seen earlier had wandered into the cellblock.

"Any of you boys see what the hell that was?" Dasher yelled to no one in particular.

"Sounds like a fucking lion," the man in the next cell said, his voice shaken.

They all fell silent as they heard a shriek from just outside the cell door, loud and painful. Dasher stepped away from the bars and covered his ears, winching from such a high frequency. He jumped from a metal crash, a cacophony of twisted bars. Dasher ran to the bars and looked down the hallway, seeing the back of something very tall and green as it entered the first cell.

"Help me!" A man screamed, shrill and full of terror.

His words were cut off with a heavy thud, followed instantly by another shriek. Dasher lowered his hands in shock as the creature emerged from the cell, snarling at him with sharp fangs. It turned toward the hole it had made and walked out, pulling the unconscious body of the prisoner behind it.

"Oh sweet Jesus." The man in the next cell began to cry. "What the hell is that?"

"It pulled the cell door off," Dasher spoke to himself, trying to comprehend the strength it would take to do that. "Ripped it right the fuck off, like a damn screen door."

Three more creatures entered through the hole in the wall, darting their heads about like birds. They leapt onto the bars of the next cell and tore it open, pulling the bars free from the wall. Again Dasher was subjected to the horrific screams of a man in torment. He could hear the wet tearing of flesh as one of them bit into the prisoner's abdomen, sampling some white meat before pulling him out by his ankle. Dasher backed himself into a corner, his head turning from side to side in disbelief. This was some new form of torture approved by the senate. A new "scared straight" program or something. But the creature's shriek in the next cell expelled that theory. Dasher looked up to the body of his cellmate and wondered if he had known this was coming.

Dasher broke his paralysis as the creature's elongated shadow spilled across the hallway before the bars of his cell. He leapt forward, grabbed the thin mattress from his bunk and pulled it back with him into the corner. He shivered beneath it like a child hiding under the covers from the boogeyman. Dasher held his breath, clamping his top and bottom teeth together with mental superglue. It was impossible not to cringe as the door to his cell was pulled free. The loud clanking of metal as it was discarded in the hall. The thud of approaching footsteps made him shiver. Its breathing was harsh, sounding labored and wet. A slight gurgling expelled from within its throat. Against his better judgment, he lowered the corner of the mattress. The beast gripped the bottom bunk and paused, sniffing the air. It stepped into Dashers bunk and leaned over his dead cellmate. It pressed its snout to his back and took long, savory sniffs.

This was it, his one and only chance. Dasher laid the mattress on its side and hurried toward the opening. He didn't bother looking back. What good could it have done him? He slid in the hall, slipping in a prisoner's blood and other mysterious fluids. Dasher fell hard on his butt and collided with the wall. He quickly gained his footing and ran through the hole in the wall. There was no sign of the other creatures, just the smears of blood on the floor, leading him through the prison like a painted line. There was another hole on his left that led outside into the rain. Despite the immediate terror, Dasher couldn't keep himself from pausing ever so briefly to lift his face into the downpour. It awakened his senses, washing off the dirt and grime and maybe even his guilt. He felt reborn, stepping into a world that had changed and might make a place for him. Some higher purpose. The moment was broken as he heard a roar from behind. Dasher dove behind some shrubs, splashing down into a six-inch puddle of water. He pressed his face into the icy water and lay still, holding his breath as the creature emerged with his dead cellmate's foot in its grip. It stood in the opening they'd made, lifting its snout into the air for a good sniff. Dasher kept perfectly still, barely making out the creatures form over the water and through the shrubs. This tense moment seemed to last forever, lying there in a cold puddle as some kind of beast stood just a few feet away, smelling his scent. Dasher pleaded with whatever God there might be to just let it pass on by. The random deity must have heard his pleas because the beast gave out a final snort before running off toward the woods.

Dasher rolled onto his back and let out a long breath, not caring that he lay submerged in a muddy puddle. The sensation was invigorating, tingling his flesh. It took a distant roar to bring his mind back to the present, shedding away some of the lingering shock of seeing the beast. Never had he imagined such a creature, something so strong and evil. It had pulled the door to his cell free and clear as if ripping off a band-aid. Why they had come into the prison in the first place, whatever they were, was still a mystery. Easy prey he guessed. Grown men standing behind easy to remove bars, like a living buffet.

Dasher fell forward onto his hands and knees and began to crawl, keeping low besides the building. He was so thankful for the heavy rainfall and the dark, heavy clouds above working together to conceal his progress. Dasher lifted up onto his feet, breaking out into an all out sprint. He felt like Jesus, running on water at times.

"Make for the trees. Make for the trees," Dasher repeated as he ran up a slight slope, remembering the forest across the meadow and the burning city beyond it. "Oh shit!" Dasher slid to a stop, losing his footing on the wet grass to go tumbling forward onto his face.

Dasher had remembered the valley had now become a lake, separating him from the coverage of the woods. He looked back over his shoulder as a creature stepped out of the prison. A prisoner slung over its shoulder like a sack of dirty clothes while it pulled two lifeless bodies behind it. Dasher crawled into the lake, shivering from the icy water. He dug his fingers into the muddy bank and inched himself along, allowing his body to float just beneath the surface. He felt like a child playing some kind of submarine game in the tub, only instead of a loving parent taking notice it was a tall reptilian creature. Dasher pulled himself along, his mouth beneath the cold water with only the top of his head visible. His plan was to pull himself along, moving stealthy like a floating leaf atop the surface, hopefully going unnoticed until he reached the woods. But it was slow goings, looking like a floating sloth, pulling himself along for what felt like an eternity. The shrieks of those creatures made him jump repeatedly. They sounded a bit too close for comfort.

Dasher pressed his fingers deep into the loose earth and held his breath, pulling himself beneath the icy water while holding perfectly still. He'd heard something splashing in the water just behind him. His body trembled uncontrollably, waiting there without any visual confirmation of what might be closing the distance. The splashing grew louder until a three-toed reptilian foot passed by his face, walking by without taking notice. It dragged behind it the shredded remains of a prisoner, one Dasher hadn't seen before. The man's head was being pulled along the lakebed; his eyes open. Dasher looked him directly in the eyes as he passed, staring into his glossy, dead eyes. It took every ounce of his being not to lift up his head from the water and run, to free himself of such horror. The water turned a dim pink as the man's head passed by; blood trailing from countless gashes and tears throughout his body. Dasher let out a mental sigh of relief as the beast disappeared from view.

Dasher lifted his head above the water and coughed; an explosion of stale water erupted from his mouth. He bit his lip and looked about the water, thankful to see the creature entering the woods without hesitation. Dasher couldn't take the pressure. He stood and bolted toward the nearest batch of trees, his feet splashing through the water. He felt incredibly exposed; the only thing moving in a vast valley now covered with water, moving dinner to any creature that might happen to take notice. Thankfully nothing saw him rise up from the water and make a mad dash through the open air, his prison-issued outfit clinging to his skin. The air chilled him to the bone, numbing the flesh. His thighs chaffed from the wet fabric and the friction of his full out sprint. He made it into the trees and kept going, unable to stop his legs from pumping. Fear had taken a tight grip over his motor functions, moving him through the dense forest and uneven ground. Heavy rain and low branches made it hard to tell where he was going. For all he knew he might burst out of the trees and splash back into the same water with a view of the prison. His foot snagged a root, tripping him hard. Dasher fell flat on his face and slid along the damp leaves as if he were in a water park. The long slide through the woods came to an abrupt stop as his right shoulder collided with the base of a tree.

"Son of a bitch!" Dasher rolled onto his back and held his shoulder, clenching his teeth together while shivering.

Dasher tried to sit up but the pain consumed him, swirling about his mind like a dust storm. He fell back into the damp earth and began to cry. Tears ran freely like the rain dripping down through the trees coverage above. An emotional release he couldn't contain. For five minutes he lay in the rain, crying like an infant and unable to stop. Too much had happened. Horrors he had never expected to witness. Dasher wiped his eyes and laughed, thinking it was such a waste to dry his eyes while lying in the rain. The will to sit up had left him. He wanted to just lie there, fall asleep in the woods and wake up to a normal world. A creature shrieked its inhuman cry, tearing through the trees.

"God protect me," Dasher spoke to the dark sky, squinting his eyes against the rain.

Dasher rolled onto his good shoulder, pushing himself up into a sitting position. He hadn't realized how tired he was, how drained the last hour had left him. Being in the presence of such atrocities milked his mind like an utter. The sound of grunting brought him back to reality, getting him to his feet. Both legs were sore from his sprint from the prison, burning like acid. But he kept going, pushing himself harder and faster, occupying his mind with hopes of a better tomorrow. Maybe he'd stumble out of the woods to find a military outpost ready to take out the creatures in an orgy of firepower and explosives. It was surprising even to him that the first thing he'd want to see after breaking free of prison would be the authorities. But at least prison guards fed you and didn't eat you.

But there were no authorities. Nothing beyond the trees but a slight slope and a black highway littered with wrecked vehicles. The muddy slope slipped out beneath his feet and carried him down with it, rolling head over feet with the mud, screaming out in pain from the collision of his bruised shoulder and the ground and finally rolling onto his back and sliding down to the highway's shoulder. Dasher rolled onto his feet and crawled up the muddy embankment to the dark highway. The road was thick with cars. He walked from car to car, looking through the windows to the empty drivers seats. Almost every vehicle was smashed or burning, charred remains of twisted metal crumpled with the car in front of it. Dasher came to a Porsche and shook his head, always wanting one but now that he was able to take it, the damn thing had two flat tires and the windshield was smashed. Besides, the keys were gone.

"Where the hell is everyone?" Dasher asked himself, climbing up onto the roof of the Porsche to get a better view of the highway. "Hello!?" Dasher cupped his hands to increase volume, but no one answered back.

He hopped off the hood and stood for a moment, placing a hand over his eyes to block the rain at least for a little while. He turned in a complete circle, but there was nothing, nowhere to go and no help. Dasher walked between the cars, hoping to find one that wasn't damaged too badly or wedged in so tightly he could take it. Finally, lying on its side with a key still in the ignition, a Harley-Davidson motorcycle sat unharmed. Dasher smiled for perhaps the first time in weeks, bending down to grip the handle bars and lift the bike onto its wheels. It's been so long since he'd last ridden a motorcycle and he'd forgotten how damn heavy they were. With his shoulder still burning from the bruised flesh, he flung his leg over the bike and took a seat, bouncing a bit from the shocks. He turned the key and let out a laugh of pure delight as something was finally going his way. The comforting vibration of the bike beneath his legs felt fantastic. Something tangible and real. Something normal in a day that had been anything but. With an exhale, Dasher revved the engine and took off, driving slowly down the shoulder. He had to maneuver through debris, luggage and car parts littering the shoulder and road like confetti. Mixed with the heavy rain, it made it impossible to travel faster than five miles an hour. Fear kept a continual presence within Dasher's mind, tapping on his head like an aggressive salesman wanting to come in. More than anything he wanted to gun it, leaving the prison far behind. He was a fugitive after all. Hopefully they'd understand why he'd been forced to run through the woods like a frightened little bunny, going easy on him if he were to be recaptured. But then again, going by the looks of things, they had bigger problems.

35

Annie was running short of ideas and time was short. The night air was cold and her son was shivering, hungry and tired. They had run as far as they could, knocking on every door they'd passed without an answer. Either no one wanted to help them or there was no one left. Half the doors they knocked on were left ajar, blood on the porch. One such door had a human hand left on the doormat, just lying there like a newspaper. Annie had been thankful the kids hadn't seen it. They were already rattled enough. Logan had been crying ever since they'd climbed down the ladder while poor Abby was all but catatonic. Erica held her daughter tightly to her chest, covering her head with her own coat while enduring the heavy rain. Erica's flesh had gone numb minutes after they'd left the house, but it didn't register. Nothing did past the concern for her child's wellbeing.

"We have to get out of here," Erica shouted over the rain.

"Where?" Annie turned from the last house on the block, agitated no one had answered her pleas for help. "Where the hell is everyone?"

"The kids need to get out of the rain!"

"You think I don't know that?" Annie calmed her temper, not wanting to yell at Erica in front of the children, especially when they needed to stay calm, at least for their sake. "There's that grocery store just up the road."

"Anything. We just need to go." Erica was on the verge of hysterics.

Annie nodded, sensing the vulnerability coming off her friend in waves. She needed her calm and cool if they were going to stay safe. Annie jumped and grabbed hold of her son as gunshots rang out, close by from the sound. The shots were followed by a shriek and then a woman screaming. More gunshots came from the other direction. It seemed this chaos was everywhere. Annie felt panicked, unable to think. She looked down into the face of her son and felt apologetic, as if this was in some way her fault.

"We need to go." Erica tugged at Annie's arm.

Annie nodded, taking hold of her son's hand. They walked down the sidewalk and headed across the street, passing more dark houses and open doors.

The world had gone dark in what seemed like a matter of hours. The houses sat without lights, streetlamps dormant. Whether or not the blackout had been caused by these creatures was irrelevant, but God help them if they were clever enough to knock out the lights. Annie didn't want to think about it. All she needed to focus on was the safety of her son and nothing more. Getting Logan out of the rain and into a safe location was the only thing that mattered, the only objective and concern. The notion to sneak inside someone's home was all but too inviting, but there could be anything lurking inside. With the power out, there was just too many dark corners to hide in. Annie figured the grocery store was their best bet. It had food, clothing and medical supplies. Plus there was nothing else closer and they were out of options. Annie tapped the gun in her pocket just to confirm she had something on her side, some form of protection out here in the dark. Screaming for help sure wasn't going to do anything.

They had made it to the corner without incident, looking across the street with a heavy heart at the burning remains of the Good Earth Grocery Store. The flames lit up the darkness, flickering shadows across the street and warming them despite the freezing rain.

"Get down," Annie whispered harshly, pulling

hard on Erica's arm.

They dropped to the pavement and pulled themselves beneath a pickup truck. They had to squeeze together to keep hidden beneath the truck, laying over their children to shield them as best they could. Annie tucked her arm beneath Logan's cheek, keeping his face out of the three-inch deep water. She held her finger to her lips to shush them, motioning with her head toward the street. Erica peered out beneath the truck and saw four creatures walking down the center of the road. They walked on their hands and feet, hunched over like dogs. They stopped and sniffed the air, lifting up to stand on their hind feet. Their naked forms showed no sign of gender. Annie had seen enough horror movies in her younger years to know these weren't your average hillbilly murderers or toxic mutation. These were something different, some kind of creatures from within the earth or demons straight from hell. The one standing out front, the leader of this little pack, let out a series of grunts and snarls. The three behind broke off and ran into the night, heading down more suburban streets to treat themselves to some more human snacks. Annie kept her eyes glued to the one that remained, standing in the middle of the road while sniffing the air. In a flash it leapt forward and ran across the street on all fours, heading for the pickup truck.

A car turned the corner and peeled out, hydroplaning from the water on the roadway. The creature turned as the car plowed into it, rolling end over end to crash into the grocery store. Annie shielded Logan's head as the car exploded, sending wooden boards from the store out into the air, falling all around them and onto the truck. Logan and Abby screamed beneath their mothers, crying out in fear as the flaming wreckage slammed against the truck, falling into the cab until the truck itself had caught fire.

"We have to move." Annie could smell the burning upholstery from the seats above her, knowing full well it was only a matter of time until the flames reached the gas tank.

Annie slid out from beneath the truck first, crouching low and making sure the coast was clear before taking hold of Logan's hand. Most of the wooden boards scattered about the street had been extinguished by the rain and deep water over the road. Annie lifted Logan up into her arms, turning in a slow circle to try and weigh their options. Her heart rate quickened as two creatures emerged from the shadows, walking slowly toward them with their heads slightly cocked. They sniffed the air with savage hunger, smelling their flesh.

"Get up. We have to run!" Annie screamed, unsure where the hell they could go.

"Hurry!"

Annie turned toward the voice, spying the darting light of a flashlight from the hardware store on the corner of the next block. She took hold of Erica's hand and pulled her through the water, yanking her out from beneath the truck. The creatures shrieked in unison as they ran forth, sprinting after them and quickly closing the distance. Annie pulled her gun and fired behind her, unable to aim while running as fast as she could. Logan felt heavy in her arms, but he was not going to slow her down. Quite the opposite really. His weight added purpose and urgency, a reminder why she needed to make haste. Her love for her son made her legs pump that much harder, splashing through the water on the road without slowing.

"Drop. Get down!"

Annie and Erica fell to their knees and ducked, cradling their children's heads as the men standing outside the hardware store opened fire. The barrage of bullets flew overhead by inches, hitting the beasts head on as they charged. Annie turned and watched in a panic as they drew near, coming forth despite the automatic weapons slamming round after round into their bodies and heads. Still they kept coming. Annie gripped her son tightly, knowing it was all she could do. As their distance closed in to only a few feet, the creatures fell forward, sliding along the water to come to rest four feet from Annie. She looked down at the creatures as they took their last breaths. Their glowing eyes dimmed and faded as they died.

"Hurry. You have to get inside before more of them come," a man yelled from the doorway, holding a shotgun. "Please!" He held out his hand to them.

Annie took one final look at the dead beasts, their bodies so different than anything she had ever seen. Their teeth protruded through the skin above its mouth, no real lip to speak of. They were sharp and uneven, black guns with bits of flesh and cloth stuck between them. These were hunters plain and simple. Annie was thankful to turn away, taking hold of the man's hand at the entrance of the hardware store.

"There's plenty of food and water inside." Skip Bateman shook Annie's hand. "Name's Skip and this is my store. You're welcome here." He was sincere, happy to spare the two children any more horror. Skip was a single man, but he loved children. Always had.

"Thank you so much." Annie was truly grateful, knowing full well they had no other options.

"Thank you for your kindness." Erica was close to tears.

The four of them stepped out of the rain and into the warm glow of candles set throughout the store. It was so comforting to be around people again, a small sense of normality.

"You'll find some water bottles over by the register there." Skip shut and locked the front door, lowering the security gate made of chain link. "Feel free and help yourself." Skip pulled on the gate and confirmed its security. He took a deep breath and set down the shotgun. With a slight smile of humility, he picked up the shotgun and set it behind the counter. "I'm not accustomed to having little children around."

"I understand." Annie set Logan on the ground and took a deep breath of her own, settling her heart for the first time in many hours. "Have you heard any news about what is happening here?"

"Nothing." Skip bent down and opened a cooler beside the counter, getting himself a cold bottle of water. The arthritis in his hands made it hard to twist the cap. "The last thing we heard on the radio was from some station in Washington D.C.. They said these creatures are running through every major city. Coming out of those goddamn cracks in the ground. Pardon my French."

"What are they?" Erica pleaded, needing to have some kind of answers. Her mind begged for clarity or it threatened to shut down.

"No one has said for sure." Skip shrugged. "Demons, underground monsters. I haven't a clue."

"Shut up! All of you," Sam Mitchell shushed,

waving his hands about. "Put out those fucking candles or they'll come back." He ran to the window and peeked out, darting his head frantically to see every angle.

"Calm down." Annie held out her hands. She instantly disliked this man, sensing panic, fear, and stupidity.

"Don't shush me bitch. We risked our safety to save you and your brat."

"Zip it." Skip held up a finger in warning. "I will have none of that in my store."

Sam bounced a bit in his stance, angry and wanting to lash out at them but remembering his place. He was grateful to Skip for opening his doors to him, allowing him to hide from those beasts after they'd destroyed his Mercedes. Damn thing had just come back from the detailers. Polished and pretty, then those fucking demons. So very typical. Sam turned from Skip and looked Annie dead in the eyes, giving her a hard stair. But Annie returned his glare, burning holes through him with her eyes, delivering a promise that if he ever called her son a brat again she'd rip him apart. Seeing that she meant it, Sam gave a final huff and walked off, disappearing down the aisle marked "plumbing."

"Please don't take offense," Skip apologized. "Some people were just born that way."

"What's his name?" Eleanor Schultz asked as she knelt before Logan, cupping his chin with her elderly fingers.

"I'm Logan."

"Oh what a big boy you are. My name is Eleanor and it's a pleasure to meet you." Eleanor shook his cold hand, happy to be changing the mood from anger to pleasant. "We have several tents and sleeping bags set up in the back of the store." Eleanor gripped the counter so she could stand, her knees cracking. "Pleasure to make your acquaintance."

"I'm Annie and this is my son Logan. This is Erica and her daughter Abby."

"You're all welcome here. Some people tend to forget that manners are what separate us from those creatures outside." Eleanor hooked a thumb toward the plumbing aisle.

"Thank you both for your kindness. I think we'll take you up on your offer for a place to crash. We're all so tired."

"Your little ones need a good rest. And you will all be safe here."

"That's right," Skip added, confident in his store as he had been since its opening twelve years ago. "We have a rotating shift for watching the front entrance here. Plenty of weapons and the weak spots have already been boarded up." Skip sighed, looking

KEVIN J. HOWARD

back over his shoulder to the boarded windows. He'd
seen one of those things flip a car onto its side without effort. Would some boards of wood hastily nailed
to the walls do anything than offer them a little piece
of mind?

"Oh thank God." Erica ran a hand through
Abby's hair. "We're both so tired."

Annie and Erica took some waters and cold
sandwiches from the cooler before walking through
the aisles to the back of the store. The further they
got from the front entrance the darker it became, the
candles' light barely touching the tents set up in the
back of the store. Annie stopped and knelt down,
lifting Logan up into her arms. An arm's length was
too far a distance to have her son, not after their mad
sprint through the rain. It had become far too dark in
here, passing through the center of the aisles where
the candlelight didn't reach them. In a brief moment
of panic, Annie gripped her son a little too tightly to
her chest.

"Mommy!" Logan squirmed beneath her arms.

"Sorry baby." Annie loosened her grip.

They came to the end of the aisle and stood a
moment, looking left to right at all the tents and
sleeping bags, huddles of families squatting on the
floor with their heads down. It looked like an intern-
ment camp. Damp cheeks everywhere, heavy silence

broken with occasional sobbing. A three-year-old girl was curled up on a sleeping bag to their left, rocking slightly as she held herself tight. Her mother sat beside her with a hand running through her hair, but her attention was on the distant windows. She too thought the boards were too flimsy. But there were no other options. Her handgun was out of bullets and the creature she'd put six bullets in was still out there, limping along.

Annie led her ragtag group of four cautiously over the occupied sleeping bags. She released a breath of relief as they came to a three-person tent that was currently unoccupied. No sleeping bags set up, but that didn't matter. Right now she could collapse on a mound of broken glass and sleep long and deep. As long as they were indoors next to people she'd be fine.

"Do you trust these people?" Erica set Abby on the ground.

"I don't think we really have a choice." Annie got down on one knee and cupped her hand beneath Abby's chin. "Are you okay, sweetie?" Annie frowned as there was no response. "It's okay, dear. Why don't you go on in the tent and rest up."

"God, I hope she's going to be okay," Erica told Annie as she watched her daughter step into the tent, moving without a word. She leaned inside and kissed her daughter on the cheek, rubbing her back gently.

Not since she was a little girl had she been so cuddly and needy at bedtime. "Sweet dreams princess."

Erica pulled back as Logan crawled his way into the tent, pressing his back to Abby and falling asleep as soon as his little head hit the pillow. Both mothers leaned into the tent to watch their children sleeping. Their faces pale and exhausted, but peaceful. Annie wanted to cuddle into the small available space within the tent to hold him, cradle him to her bosom as tightly as she could, but for now he needed the sleep. Poor dear had had the worst night of his life. One no child should ever have to endure. She motioned with her head for Erica to follow her out of the tent.

Annie took a walk down an aisle to their left, passing hammers, nails, screwdrivers, and other miscellaneous tools. She reached the end of the aisle and turned down the next one, seeing lounge chairs and patio furniture. She grabbed two of the folded chairs off their hooks on the wall and hurried back to Erica, not wanting to leave her alone too long. Annie had seen the look in her eyes. So very close to snapping, losing her sanity in the blink of an eye if allowed the time to process what had happened to them.

"This is exactly what we needed." Erica smiled as she took the chair, unfolding it with a sigh of contentment. "I thought I'd never get to sit down."

"We're going to have to find some dry clothes for

the kids soon. Can't have them lying there all night in their soaked clothes. Might get sick."

"Yeah, sure," Erica nodded, her eyes wide and glossy. "I agree."

"Erica?" Annie placed a hand to her knee.

Erica broke down before she could turn to Annie, releasing a long hard cry she'd held on to for far too long. The weight of this evening had been too much to bear, pressing down on her as if carrying an obese man on her shoulders. Erica pressed her hands to her face and leaned to the side, resting her head on Annie's shoulder. Annie had set an arm around her, but she couldn't play the comforter. She too was exhausted, taken back by such a horrific chain of events. Tears rolled from her eyes in a steady stream, dripping off her chin to settle into the hair of her neighbor. In one night she'd gone from homeowner to refugee. In a span of hours, all that she'd worked so hard for, her house, Logan's safety and her own sense of what should be, now all tossed about like a mixed salad. Annie lowered her head to Erica's and closed her eyes, falling back into her exhaustion as if it were made of silk sheets.

36

Andrews hadn't brought much of an appetite with him. Too many hours spent watching news footage from around the world, each static report showing the same thing. Burning buildings despite the unrelenting rain, people screaming through the streets while unidentified creatures chased them. He had yet to see any footage of the creatures, nothing more than a tall brown streak as it ran past a camera. Andrews had had enough, at least for now. His eyes so dry they felt as if a hard blink might shatter them. So he'd left the comms room and taken a stroll down the hall toward the cafeteria. What an uncomfortable walk it had been. His every footfall echoed off the empty hall.

Andrews entered the cafeteria with his head down, blocking as much of the bright lights above as possible, his eyes red and irritated. At least the classical music had been turned off. He grabbed a

bowl off the counter and received a generous helping of mushy goop. Hard to have an appetite when
given something so visually unappetizing, but there
was a special treat today. The kitchen's maintenance
staff had discovered seven boxes of oatmeal cookies;
real, honest to God cookies that had been baked and
everything. Andrews placed the small cookie on a
napkin and set it beside his bowl, looking down on
it as if he'd never seen a cookie before. It looked so
small, centered in a square napkin no bigger than his
hand, yet this cookie meant so much to him. When
the world was tearing itself apart, leaving them isolated, he could still pick up this cookie and enjoy it,
close his eyes and take comfort in the pure ecstasy of
the small joys life could bring him. Just a little cookie.
A reminder of home, a flavor caressing his tongue
he'd thought he'd never again feel. Like discovering
a long lost lover. So much worth in such an everyday thing. He lifted the cookie, careful not to grip it
too hard or an oatmeal grain may flake off. His eyes
rolled back into his head like a shark as he bit down,
savoring every single bite as if this was the first dessert to have passed through his lips.

The moment was short lived, stomped flat by the
heavy work boots of a small group of ten miners as
they were led into the cafeteria. Andrews shoved the
last of the cookie into his mouth and swallowed it

quickly, not willing to give them the satisfaction of seeing him enjoy something. This was a very delicate environment, one that must be taken seriously and controlled by all means necessary. He himself must stay cold and vigilant, someone the men know not to mess with.

"I can't believe we have cookies." Edgar Reece set his tray down as he sat across from Andrews. "It's like fucking Christmas."

"Language," Andrews scolds, shaking his head. "Remember our place here. We lead through supreme example."

"Okay, sorry." Edgar lowered his head as he ate, taking on his submissive role as all the security officers did in Andrews presence. Something about him, an intensity in his eyes maybe, told them all that he was not the kind of man to have on your bad side. "Still, it's a nice treat."

Andrews didn't return his officer's attempt at small talk, just allowed him a brief nod of agreement. Edgar just ate, keeping his comments inside as he always did. He was so thirsty for good old-fashion conversation and all the other security officers were just as tight lipped as Andrews. Alvin was a decent fellow, but Edgar knew he was on the outs with Andrews and that's something he wanted to avoid at all costs, even if it was by association. So he would keep his loneliness to himself and remain a loyal terrier.

"I can't wait for this drill to be over." Edgar felt a natural smile bugging the muscles of his face to be allowed to surface, but he kept it down. "Must be a mighty powerful storm to delay transport of the supply ship and all."

"You think this is all over some storm? Are you serious?" Andrews bore into him with a scowl. "Open your eyes. This is far too serious to be affected by a little squall. Whatever is happening to Earth may be nothing less than catastrophic to put us on a work halt." Andrews leaned across the table, pointing his finger at Edgar. "We must keep the severity of this away from them!"

Edgar looked back over his shoulder, seeing the ten miners eating their food, normal men engaged in conversation, a laugh here and there. He had actually wanted to get up and join them, take comfort in their everyday conversations. But he turned around and faced Andrews.

"Look at this display," Andrews snarled, looking past Edgar to the table of miners as they ate. "They don't deserve such treatment." He knew Edgar wouldn't understand the complexities of his emotions, not with his limited range of intelligence. Another reason he wanted new security officers, men that heard orders and didn't know the meaning of a follow-up question. No room for second guesser's way out here. Andrews lost his appetite, pushing his tray across the table toward Edgar, his bowl half empty. "I have work to do." Andrews stood.

"Aren't you hungry, sir?" Edgar looked from the bowl to Andrews, filled with concern and hope. If he wasn't going to eat his rationed meal, you can bet Edgar would be there to pick up the slack.

Andrews didn't hear him. His eyes were locked on the long table of men. One of them, Jerome he thought, one of Daniels military brats, looked back over his shoulder and made brief eye contact. He watched him turn back to his friends and share a secret, leaning in to keep the conversation private. Then they shared a brief laugh. An actual laugh right before his eyes, most likely at his own expense. This was something he couldn't stomach, not at this moment with so many troubling thoughts.

"Is he still there?" Jerome asked, looking behind him to a blur of color, standing still and out of focus.

"Yeah and he looks pissed." TJ let out a single laugh, shaking his head. Leave it to Jerome to piss off the wrong people. "Wait, he's gone."

Jerome looked back over his shoulder and sighed. "I hate being stuck up here at the mercy of these guys."

"At least we're alive and safe from whatever this is all about," TJ spoke over a mouth full of food. He picked up his cookie with a childlike grin, holding it beneath his nose. "Just like momma used to make. Cold and stale." He smiled over the taste, enjoying it all the same. This was a real treat. A little taste of home.

"This shit is kind of scary." Jerome looked up at the lights. "Must be serious if we're running on auxiliary power. Otherwise why shut down the main breakers."

"Precaution maybe."

"Whatever." Jerome kept his voice low. "They don't know what the hell is going on and it's freaking them out. Just look at any of the security officer's faces. They're ready to crack."

"Andrews does look pretty unstable."

"Oh please, TJ. That asshole always looks that way. But most of his little bitches look crazy now too. Keeping us under lock and key, moving us around in groups. Day by day this is looking less like a mining facility and more like a prison. Only the warden is millions of miles away." Jerome shook his head, processing the possible scenarios of how this could play out. "I've never felt so far from home."

"I guess if worst came to worst they could always fire up the supply ship."

"Smooth thinking." Jerome smacked his head with a mocking smile. "Whose going to pilot the mammoth beast? You?"

"Sean could."

"Sean is a brilliant chopper pilot, but he's no astronaut."

"I bet he could fly just about anything."TJ thought back to one particular mission, watching Sean land the chopper in a safe zone barely large enough to allow the chopper entrance.

"Well let's just pray this is all some bullshit test from Earth. Checking the station's stability or whatever."

37

Andrews made tight fists, digging his well-groomed nails into the flesh of his palm, leaving half-moon shaped cuts. He took slow, steady breaths, calming his rapidly beating heart. He was having a panic attack. The hallway had become far too empty. Andrews looked left to right and then turned to look behind him; just a long, dark hallway from the cafeteria to his security command. The lights overhead were a dull reminder of how easily things could go from bad to worse. Even simple everyday things, such as light, became a precious resource. More valuable to him at this moment than a mountain of gold. What was wealth anyway when it came to survival? Money wouldn't help him in the darkness when the lights go out, and they eventually will. They could generate their own energy, but supplies where out. Machines break down and require new parts. If this communication blackout with Earth continued indefinitely, how long until the men turned on him, wanting more food or better conditions despite such limited resources? How long until the lights go out and he's left to scramble about in the dark with these men, these bastards?

Andrews pulled at the collar of his uniform, suddenly finding it very difficult to breathe. He turned toward the wall and pulled open a small metal box, entering a ten-digit code followed by a green button. The wall shook as the metal plating slowly rose up from the floor, revealing the red surface of the Martian planet and the blackness of space. Andrews pressed his hands and cheek to the cold, thick glass, tilting his head back to view the countless stars. So many of them. It was a rare occasion indeed to have the shielding lifted from the windows. Safety protocol recommended the shields be down to keep the facility and miners safe from sand storm debris or possible meteorites. This was the only portion of the facility that stuck up above the surface. Doing everything by the book, Andrews had insisted the shields be down at all times. But this was different. He needed to be shown that there was something beyond these grey hallways and dim lights. A world outside the window. One he could never walk on without the aid of an airtight suit, but there it was.

"Sir?" Alvin asked timidly, not entirely sure he

should be interrupting Andrews' little moment.

Andrews heard him, but didn't respond. Alvin was one of his men but he knew he wasn't with him. He could turn on him with the rest of the beasts. One minute a fellow officer, the next a snarling creature in the pit. No, he wasn't going to let this falsity into his midst. He was much smarter than that.

"Is everything okay?"

"Right as rain." Andrews lowered his head until his nose smashed against the glass. "Why do you ask?"

"Just checking in is all." Alvin took a subconscious step back, folding his hands behind his back in a nervous stance.

"I can't seem to see Earth." Andrews tapped the glass with his finger. "I know it's out there. Or at least I hope it still is. Somewhere out there in all that space…that blackness." Andrews turned his head to Alvin, his eyebrows furrowed. "Do you know where it is?"

"I think it's on the other side of the facility." Alvin hooked a thumb behind him, nervous by the distant look in Andrews' eyes.

"Why do you like them?"

"Who, sir?"

"The men here?"

Alvin shrugged. "I wouldn't say I like all of them.

Maybe a handful really. Why?"

Andrews shook his head, turning to look out the window. "I just find it's best not to get too attached to things, especially when they can turn on you like a rabid dog." Andrews nodded, a wide grin as dark thoughts came to him. "But then again. At least little pups can be put to sleep."

"Excuse me?" Alvin wasn't sure he'd really heard what he'd said, but he knew he had. He hadn't wanted to, but it was out there.

"Oh nothing." Andrews entered the same ten-digit code and lowered the shield. "Carry on and keep them in check while we're in alert."

"Will do," Alvin spoke up as Andrews walked off, lingering a moment in the hall as he watched him go. His stride unnaturally slow, just a bit off.

Andrews felt the weight of Alvin's eyes on his back but didn't dare turn around. He wouldn't give him the satisfaction of letting him know he'd gotten to him. Instead he slowed his pace, put a little hop into it. Maybe things weren't as black as the space all around them. He was safe from all this madness for the time being. Andrews turned the corner and entered the Comms room, thankful it was empty. He locked the door behind him and pulled up a chair. An instant feeling of comfort as Yuri's face came into view on the screen. But there was a sadness to it. Pale flesh hanging with exhaustion and stress. He had heavy bags under his eyes, as if his tears had painted his flesh a dark purple.

"What happened to you?" Andrews kept his attention glued to the dark bags beneath his comrade's eyes.

Yuri shook his head, closing his eyes with a deep breath. He looked up, locking eyes with Andrews for what felt like an eternity.

"Yuri?"

"I don't remember my homeland. Not from the images I've seen."

"What images?" Andrews leaned in close to the monitor, praying the link wouldn't be disrupted. "I haven't been able to receive any signals from Earth."

"I don't sleep anymore." Yuri closed his eyes and leaned back in his chair, running a hand through his damp hair. "I can still see the screaming faces of the women running through the streets before the beasts fell on them."

"What beasts?"

Yuri opened his eyes. "The dogs of hell."

"What are you talking about?"

"I've seen them, running through the streets on all fours." Yuri turned in his chair and pointed to a monitor behind him. "A television broadcast from Earth two days ago in Moscow. A woman holding a camera as she hid beneath a car. Watching, filming. All the people running past her, crying and screaming." Yuri lowered his head into his hands, crying softly. The blood on his cheek dampened, blending with the water to roll beneath the collar of his shirt. "Then she turned the camera to what they were running from. A beast made of twisted leather, dark green. Taller than a man and twice as thick. An abomination."

"This can't be."

"Oh, but it can. It is. I saw the creature lift a woman off the ground by gripping the top of her head, pulling it from her body like a grape off the vine." Yuri cleared his throat, taking a moment to collect himself. "The woman screamed and dropped the camera. End of footage. Since then I've seen nothing else."

"What is happening?" Andrews shook his head, running the Russian's story over and over again in his mind. He'd told him the whole story in English, but it still sounded so foreign to him. Something lost in translation.

"I do not know." Yuri closed his eyes and leaned back, moving his lips slowly as if singing a song, words spoken too softly for anyone else to hear. He sat there for a good three minutes, leaning forward with a solemn face. "We must consider ourselves the lucky ones. God's truly chosen people. The ones handpicked to survive."

"To survive…" Andrews thought the phrase over.

"Yes, to live. And we must be so very careful, especially you."

"Me?"

"Oh yes. In your position, so many men under your command, you must be careful."

"Careful of what?" Andrews shifted in his chair, an uneasy chill shooting through him.

"You think those creature spreading across Earth are monsters and demons, but they pale in comparison to the true darkness of man. The beast we all carry within. Lock enough of us up, say within a space station or an off-world facility, and you've got a real case of terror on your hands. A struggle for survival." Yuri leaned in close to the screen, his eyes filling the monitor. "Best to keep your men in line before they let fear get the best of them. Before they too become beasts. Otherwise, you too might find yourself running through the darkness with a monster on your heels."

Andrews nodded, turning from the monitor to the door, realizing how many of them were out there. Miners with physical conditions far beyond his own, making it far too easy to overpower him. Dogs. Beasts. Filthy parasites that could turn on him if things got worse. Yuri was right. The real danger wasn't a million or so miles off in space. It was here.

38

Morgan winced as he lifted himself up onto his side, watching another group of twelve or so miners shuffling past toward the cafeteria, their heads down. He wouldn't even call them miners anymore. The term doesn't apply when they're no longer mining. Watching them walk past, their expressions reflecting the exhaustion and concern they're trying so hard to conceal. No, not miners. They'd become prisoners. Their hands weren't bound, but they were prisoners all the same. The guards standing on both sides of the double line, two more guards in back. Zap sticks clutched tightly in their hands; long batons that gave off an electric jolt at the tip. Both the guards and the miners were nervous, causally looking up at the dim lighting, all of them wondering what was going on, and how much longer would they have to endure it. If tension were a female singer, the bitch would have been screaming.

Morgan dropped back to the bed and lay still as the guards peeked in. A quick glance as they passed. Morgan did his best comatose act, lying perfectly still with his eyes tightly shut until he felt their eyes pass over him. Morgan had become quite good at playing possum. Once, back when he'd been a younger man in the service years before he'd ever met Travis, he'd been caught behind enemy lines. He could hear the enemy rushing through the jungle, their voices yelling back and forth. Morgan's leg was torn and shattered, no way to run. He was bleeding badly. In less than a minute, he'd pulled himself beneath the bodies of fallen comrades and waited. His eyes closed, his cheek pressed to the damp earth. The blood of his friends dripped onto his face, rolling over his cheeks and into his eyes. He lay there for hours, holding his breath as they searched the wreckage and the nearby jungle. His eye burned from their blood, but he didn't dare move. Minutes turned to an hour, their voices long since gone, but he couldn't move an inch. He'd focused on his heartbeat and held it down, suppressed it almost to the point of stopping.

Morgan opened his eyes and was thankful to see the dim overhead lights of the med lab, and not the dead body of someone he called friend. Morgan turned his head and looked out to the hall, seeing nothing but a dark hallway.

"Christina?" Morgan whispered, looking from

the hall to the back of Christina's head.

When there was no response, Morgan lifted himself into a seated position, grunting a bit from the sharp pain in his shoulder. The flesh was black and blue but the wound was healing nicely. The broken bones in his shoulder were beginning to mend, but it still hurt like hell. But despite the intense pain, Morgan rolled his legs over the side of the bed. He sat a moment, catching his breath. Dozens of dangerous covert operations under his belt, and yet a simple move off a hospital bed had him winded. Age, it seemed, might have finally caught up with him. Still, Morgan pushed past the pain and stepped off the bed onto the floor, wincing from the freezing temperatures against the bare soles of his feet. This wasn't a caring hospital where they gave you grippy socks with a robe that exposed your ass. Here, you were lucky to get an aspirin. But they weren't up here to have creature comforts. They were here to look after each other. To keep the team alive, and that's what got Morgan moving across the freezing floor. Inching the distance of ten feet to the sleeping backside of a young woman he'd come to look upon like a daughter.

"Christina?" Morgan took a seat beside her bed, placing a hand to her shoulder. "Can you hear me, dear?"

"Morgan?" Christina rolled onto her back, her

eyes closed. She looked as if she wanted to cry.

"Yes." He smiled, taking hold of her hand. A gentle squeeze as the bones beneath the flesh felt brittle. "I've been here the entire time. Just waiting for you to wake up and smile."

Christina opened her eyes, smiling despite the fact she couldn't make out his face. Just a pink blur looking down on her with a familiar voice. Smiling hurt her face, something she never thought could be possible, but there it was. Still, it felt better to smile than to lay there in the dark, wondering if what she was seeing was real. Far too many times in the past few days she'd opened her eyes to a blurred reality, different men looking down on her. Their faces mixing together into one ambiguous form giving her injections, taking blood pressure, or maybe just checking in on her. Was this real now? Was Morgan looking down on her from above, or was this a familiar voice leading her into the great beyond?

"How are you feeling?"

"Pretty damn terrible." Christina's smile faded as pain rippled through her. "I've definitely had some better days."

"Haven't we all."

Christina gritted her teeth until the pain subsided, fading into the background but never fully disappearing. Only once in her life had she felt such an intense throbbing. Ten years ago when she'd shattered a molar during a mission while snacking on some almonds. She'd had to endure that agonizing pain while sneaking through dense jungles and staying silent. But that was her job, and she was good at what she did.

"My eyes must be in worst condition than I'd thought. I still can't see anything."

"It's not your eyes, dear." Morgan looked back over his shoulder, fearing the footsteps of an approaching guard. He hunkered down and waited for the footsteps to pass. "I guess there's no reason to look in here." Morgan felt comfortable enough to stand.

"Why are the lights off?" Christina tilted her head back and looked out to the hall, seeing the dim red lighting in place of the constant bright halogens they were accustomed to. "Where's the medical staff?" Christina rolled onto her side as she broke out in a coughing fit, her lungs burning.

"Here." Morgan turned and rushed to the sink, filling a glass of water and returning to Christina. He held the glass to her lips, gripping it with both hands to steady it. "Hold on, take it slow." Morgan tipped the glass to her lips and let the water roll into her mouth. "Breathe slow. Nice and slow." He let out a groan as pain erupted in his arm.

"Okay," Christina said in between breaths. She focused on her breathing and willed away the tightness in her throat. "My throat is so dry." Christina took a long sip.

"You know, for a while there, we thought you weren't going to make it."

"What did happen?"

"There was an accident." Morgan pulled away, running a hand through his hair. "The shaft caved in and you inhaled some Martian soil. Plus there was some slight decompression." Morgan's eyes filled with tears. "We almost lost you there, kid."

Morgan ducked down as footsteps drifted in from the hall. Christina rose up and looked over his shoulder as the guards led the miners back from the cafeteria to their rooms. To their locked cells. The guards walked with their heads down, looking tired and worn out. They all gave off a sense of dread.

"What the hell is going on here?"

"I don't know, but it looks bad." Morgan leaned in close, taking the empty cup from her hands. "It's been like this for a few days now, maybe a week. It's kind of hard to keep track of time from these beds."

"Has something happened?"

"I don't know. But whatever it is, it's serious." Morgan looked up at the dark lights. "If they're running on auxiliary power, there's more to this than a training exercise. Too much at stake to test the system for this long, not way out here."

Christina lowered her head back to the bed, overcome with dizziness. Her forehead broke out in a cool sweat.

"I just need some rest. I'm sorry." Christina closed her eyes and sighed. "I'm just so tired."

"It's okay. Just rest up." Morgan wiped the sweat from her forehead. "Nothing we can do about it now anyway."

Morgan sat with her a while, holding her hand. In a normal world, he would have gotten her some help, someone to check her temperature. A fucking doctor. But this wasn't a normal world and there didn't appear to be a doctor on call. Extremely odd for a medical facility. Morgan wondered when was the last time someone had been in to check on them. Were they stuck in there? Morgan stood and hurried back to his bed, lying down quickly as a single pair of footfalls headed toward them from the hall. Morgan lay on his right side, his good side, pretending to be asleep. He listened as the footfalls came to a halt inside the doorway. Morgan wanted to turn his head and look, to take a peek at the mystery man watching them from the doorway. Why weren't they bothering to check the vital signs of their two patients? The silence stretched out past the causal glance to an uncomfortable staring. But the tension eased as the footfalls began moving off toward the cafeteria.

39

Dr. Zatzkin tapped the bottom of the powdered coffee mate, shaking what little he could into his morning cup of coffee. This morning there was little more than a light dusting. He set the empty canister down on the table beside the pot with a huff, shaking his head. Had they been flung so far from Earth that they couldn't even get a semi-decent cup of coffee? Nothing but black coffee now? Had they fallen so far off the grid? Dr. Zatzkin cracked a smile, taking a seat at a small table against the window. His mental rant had come off quite dramatic, but a little entertainment would do this place some good. He was beginning to feel a little too isolated lately, running on auxiliary power as instructed by the main facility. Why they'd been forced down to dim lighting and rations had not been explained. No one ever seemed to fill them in on anything. Just because they were a long walk away didn't mean they weren't curious.

They were scientists for crying out loud. Who's more curious than them?

Feeling a bit uneasy, his stomach gurgling from indigestion and stress, he stood from the table and walked over to the orange juice dispenser. He took a plastic cup off the rack and held it beneath the nozzle, waiting patiently for a few drops followed by a hiss of air.

"Oh come on." Dr. Zatzkin tapped the juice release nozzle with his finger to no avail.

"Out of juice?" Dr. Keller shook his head as he entered the room, looking at the machine as if wishful thinking were a useful tool.

"We'll have to wait until the next rotation for juice now."

"That's very wishful thinking." Dr. Keller shook his head with a smirk.

"What is that supposed to mean?"

"The supply ship is still in the facility hangar awaiting clearance to depart."

He looked up from Dr. Keller's shaggy facial hair to the dim lighting. It occurred to him that they hadn't been issued their usual barrage of test schedules and performance reviews from the facility in Virginia. An odd thing really.

"Excuse me," Dr. Zatzkin said to Dr. Keller, speaking more to himself as he pushed passed the plump physicist on his way out of the cafeteria.

He turned down the hallway on his left and walked briskly, his white coat trailing out behind him like a cape. There were questions swarming about his mind, collecting like flies in the tangled webbing of his mind. Questions that were his job to have answers for as head of the research facility. Dr. Zatzkin briefly looked out the window to the red planet's surface; his mind occupied with concern. Usually he walked the structure with a calm, casual pace, taking in every landmark as he passed. Today it was a red blur on his way into the communications room.

"Morning Dr. Zatzkin."

"Good morning, Steven." Dr. Zatzkin gave the technician a brief smile. "Have we had any transmissions from Earth?" He crossed his hands behind his back.

"Nothing in the last thirty-six hours."

"I see." Dr. Zatzkin bounced on the balls of his feet, hoping to conceal his nervousness from this man. "Doesn't that seem a bit unusual to you?"

"No, not really." Steven placed a hand to his chin, rubbing out a thought. "I just figured it was part of their test. Like the lights."

"Will you do me a favor? Can you call them for me?"

"Sure. Just wait a few minutes for the satellite link

and the delay of the signal." Steven swiveled in his chair with purpose, turning dials and flipping switches, placing a thin receiver in his ear. He squinted his eyes and focused, holding up a finger as if queuing the other side. A few minutes passed and his finger slowly lowered, dropping limp to his side altogether. His focus replaced with puzzlement.

"What is it?"

"There's a good link, but no one is answering."

"What do you mean, no one is answering? This is a direct uplink to the main facility in Virginia. A direct call to TransWorld."

"I know, but no one's home."

A moment sat between them, heavy and uncomfortable. In their dumbfounded silence you could hear the many subtle noises of the structure. The air vents feeding through the filters, the coolant systems clicking on and recycling every thirty seconds, and the almost inaudible clicking of the sand being blown against the glass from the harsh winds outside.

"Okay, this is fine." Dr. Zatzkin nodded along with his rational thinking. "They're just testing our resilience in case we were ever cut off, that's all." Dr. Zatzkin looked passed the worried face of the technician to the instruments, their design and function so foreign to him. "Try this. Contact the space station to see if they have an active line of communication."

The technician was happy to oblige, turning in his chair to enter his commands into the system, clicking enter with a smile that immediately deflated as a small box popped up on the screen.

"It says that communication to the station has been blocked."

"Can't you run a bypass or something?"

"No, it's password protected."

"By who?"

The technician leaned forward as he searched through the system, leaning back with an answer. "Andrews."

The name ran a shiver down Dr. Zatzkin's spine. Thinking that their temporary isolation might not be a training exercise at all but something far more serious. What did Andrews know? More importantly, what did Andrews want to keep everyone from seeing?

"Do me a favor, keep a continual call in to TransWorld. Someone will get annoyed enough to pick up on their end."

"I'll stay on it."

Dr. Zatzkin nodded to the young man and left the room, walking the hall at a slow pace with his head down, mulling over the troubling thought that their fates may now be resting in the hands of a young technician. A man that looked as if most of his time was spent playing computer games or maybe playing with himself. What else did he have to do day in and day out in that tiny room? But regardless of how he spent his day, Dr. Zatzkin could only hope he gets a response from his pages.

40

So many gas tanks and not a single hose to siphon with; so goddamn typical. Dasher searched the next car, reaching in through the shattered driver's side window to pull the lock. He opened the door and put his knees on the seat as he rummaged through the messy interior. Clothes strewn about the floor, a crumpled map with a dirty footprint across the top. Fast food and candy wrappers, some drops of blood. Just as with the previous fifteen cars he'd searched, there was nothing of usefulness. At least the rain had stopped. First time in over two weeks, but the black clouds still stuck around, covering the world in twilight.

"Fuck!" Dasher pulled out of the car and slammed his fists down on the hood, cringing as the noise carried off into the distance.

He dropped to his knees and pressed his back to the door, holding his breath as a nearby roar drifted out of the trees. Sounding far too close for his comfort. He eased his hand toward the pavement, inching along with stealth, gripping the assault rifle he'd found a few miles back. Used to be, this kind of weapon required military service or some sort of mafia affiliation. Now they were just lying along the road, dropped by some soldier scared shitless at what had been coming down the road. Same with cash. He wished he'd put off his unsuccessful heist a few weeks. He only just passed a pile of hundreds at the base of a tree several miles back. He'd put his Harley on its kickstand and hurried down the shoulder of the road, standing above the money with a strong urge to bend down and stuff it into his pockets. But he laughed instead, uncontrollably until he cried. Seeing a few thousand dollars lying about the shoulder of a road was the perfect visual. Putting this whole shit storm into perspective. But a weapon was a different story. He'd already emptied the clip from the first handgun he'd found, unloading all twelve shells into the head of a charging beast, thankfully dropping it on the final bullet. Now he clutched the rifle, pressing it to his shoulder as a beast emerged from the opposite shoulder.

This one was different. Smaller than the other ones, like a hairless wolf. It walked on all fours, sniffing the air with an elongated snout filled with jagged fangs. Its eyes were a radiant green, larger than golf balls. So far, Dasher had seen the taller human-shaped bastards, the things flying high above, and now this sniveling dog-like monstrosity. Dasher rose up and watched it stock slowly along in the opposite direction, moving stealthily with its head lowered. It reminded him of a cat he used to watch outside his house, hunting birds and squirrels in the vacant lot. But this beast wasn't interested in sparrows or woodland creatures. Dasher followed its target, a woman far in the distance. As if sensing her stalker, she turned and saw the beast, charging in a sprint. Her awkward retreat was from something she carried, tightly clutched to her chest.

Dasher lifted up his weapon for a shot, but the beast was gone, springing with the speed of a cheetah. It cleared the hundred yards in seconds, tackling the woman while sliding its front claws down her back. Dasher panted as he ran, slamming into a nearby car to rest the rifle on the roof for aim. He pressed the trigger and let the bullets fly. A steady stream of automatic fire poured into the creatures back. Yet it still had strength enough to turn and charge him, the woman's clothes dangling from its teeth like designer floss. It moved forward a few feet before falling to the ground, its black tongue lulling out the side of its mouth. Dasher took another shot, hitting the dead creature square between its large eyes for good measure. He lowered his weapon and collapsed to the floor, taking long, slow breaths. Fear had a tight grip over his heart, squeezing as if trying to make some new form of juice. The pain subsided and he was able to regain his composure, rising to his feet. Dasher looked down at the dead creature. It had taken twelve bullets, direct hits into the beast's head and body, to bring it down. Dasher couldn't help but tremble before such a deadly foe, dead or not.

Dasher held his breath and listened, tilting his head slightly as something drifted toward him from down the road. Could it have been the woman? Surely not. Not when the thing had cut her deep enough to exposé her spinal cord. But there was something, like a cat meowing at the back porch. Hopefully his short burst of gunfire hadn't gotten the attention of another hunter, or something larger. Against his best judgment, Dasher tucked the stock of the weapon into his shoulder and crept down the road, hearing the soft sound rise in volume as he approached the woman. No doubt in his mind it was coming from her, despite the fact she wasn't moving. As he stood over her lifeless body, he could hear her crying softly.

Then he saw it. A little finger poking out from beneath her left breast.

"Oh my God." Dasher dropped to his knees and

gripped the woman's arm, rolling her onto her back.

An infant child lay in the road, covered in her mother's blood, screaming her head off. Dasher looked her up and down, running his eyes over her pink onesie; a cartoon rabbit set dead center in grey stitching.

"Oh shit" was all he could manage. "Um, shit!"

Dasher hopped to his feet and paced madly, looking rapidly from one shoulder of the road to the other, scanning the woods for anything that might be drawn in by such a racket.

"Shut up," Dasher said, running a hand though his sweaty hair. The baby hadn't listened. If anything, her crying only seemed to increase. "I said shut up!" Dasher's face grew red with rage, screaming down at the infant as if she could understand him. His facial muscles twitched and softened as he looked down to her. Both her arms rose up while she clutched empty air.

Dasher took a seat beside the baby, hesitantly placing a hand to her stomach. The fabric of her onesie was so soft, soothing to his fingertips. Briefly he felt like laughing, thinking this whole ordeal could end if everyone and everything could wear such comfortable fabric, putting aside all anger and rage for such warmth. But the humor was short lived as the little girl gripped his fingers, squeezing them. Dasher pulled his hand back, cringing as it brought out a high-pitched whine. Fearing another visit from those demon dogs, Dasher placed a hand beneath her back and lifted her into his arm. He set his rifle down and patted her stomach with his free hand, swaying from side to side while shushing her. A motion he'd seen women do throughout his life. One that was probably never used on him. To his recollection, he couldn't even remember being hugged by his mother.

Dasher spit on the infant's cheek, using his thumb to push some of her mother's blood off her face. Her skin was so soft. Untainted and hardened by society, everything he wasn't. A dark urge came over him, rising up from the depths of his mind like a storm. He looked to the child's mother and debated leaving her. Simply placing her back in the dead woman's arms while he used the noise of her screaming lungs to draw anything away from him as he continued his search for gas. His abandoned Harley lay on its side ten miles back, aching for him to return. He certainly couldn't ride it with this baby in his arms. Yes, leaving her was the right thing to do. The only real option. Moving quickly, he knelt down and set the baby between her dead mother's side and left arm. He grabbed his rifle and hurried down the road, moving faster as she began to cry again. Oddly, her crying seemed to grow louder the more distance he put between them, filling his mind until he could hear nothing else, not even the footfalls of his boots on the pavement.

"Shit!" Dasher screamed and turned around, staring at the small arms of the child as they flailed about in the distance.

He didn't want to leave the child there. It wasn't being done out of malice. It was survival, and during times like this you needed to look out for your own best interest. To stay alive at all costs, no matter what hard choices you had to make. And despite this harsh mental persuasion, Dasher found himself more than halfway back to where the baby lay crying, her voice like a siren blaring inside his mind.

"Big fucking softy." Dasher shook his head with annoyance as he knelt down and scooped the baby into his right arm. He searched the mother's sweater and pants pockets with his left. "Oh hell yes!" Dasher exclaimed with pure ecstasy, pulling out his salvation in a small plastic pacifier. "Thank God for small favors," Dasher said as he pushed the pacifier into her open mouth, so very glad to hear the subtle sucking over her shrill screaming.

Dasher slung the rifle over his shoulder and continued on down the road. He looked at the child and shook his head. She was covered in blood and dirt, her mother dead on the road behind them, and yet here she was falling asleep. All the nastiness of life overshadowed by the comfy texture of her plastic binky. At least for the time being.

"You might be better off back there kiddo." Dasher looked up, eyeing the long road ahead and nothing but abandoned vehicles that had either been set on fire or smashed beyond repair. "Just you and me…" Dasher looked her over and smiled. "I'll call you Siren." He nodded, thinking the name suited her.

She fell asleep in the comfort of his arms as he carried her down the road.

41

His living quarters were looking more like a prison cell every day. Travis sat on his uncomfortable cot with his knees pulled up to his chest, his arms wrapped about his legs. He's been this way for hours. At least it had felt like hours, maybe even days. Impossible to tell when there's no measure of time. No windows to watch the sun move across the sky and no clock on the wall. Nothing to occupy his mind but doubt and growing concern. Concern for the mental stability of their security personnel. Concern for the wellbeing of his unit. More than anything, concern for his two wounded soldiers still laid up in the infirmary. For as well as he knew anyway.

Travis looked up as his door opened. He sighed with relief, grateful to see Alvin's face, even if his expression was tired and worn.

"Your turn to get some grub."

"About time." Travis stepped onto the floor,

wincing from the cold. "I've gotten so hungry I've actually been looking forward to this slop." Travis smiled as he pulled on his socks and boots, but his smile was not returned. "Something you care to share?"

"Please." Alvin stepped out of the room and motioned for Travis to join him. "We need to keep moving."

Travis just nodded. He exited his cell and got behind five miners he didn't know; all of them stood with their heads hunched and their shoulders sunken. Travis' door shut and the march began. Slow, heavy steps down a long hallway toward the cafeteria. No one spoke. They all kept their eyes to the floor as they passed room after room. Men like them, locked up and waiting for their hour of freedom. Never had their distance from Earth felt so evident.

"Please have a seat at the first table after you've received your food," Alvin spoke loudly, his voice filling the large, empty room. "You have one hour."

Travis stood in line with the men, but his focus was on Alvin. He stood against the far wall, leaning against it with his arms folded about his chest, his eyes glossy. He was looking at them but he wasn't seeing them. The look of a man running off orders and a lack of sleep. Even from a distance of twenty or so feet, Travis could see the dark purple bags beneath his eyes. What did he know that they didn't?

Travis shrugged and moved with the men, grabbing his bowl of blended proteins, vitamins and slop. He sat at the far edge of the long table, not wanting to hear the soft conversations of the miners. Instead, he inched down the bench until his left buttock had to grip the edge or he might fall off.

"Why not join us?"

Alvin shook his head, clearing his thoughts and coming back to reality. It was apparent he didn't expect any trouble from this group of men. His posture showed no evidence of anticipation, no thoughts that at any moment he may need his catlike reflexes to swart a riot. Alvin looked as they did, shuffling about with no real reason as to why or what for.

"Al?"

"What?"

"Have a seat?"

Alvin gave a single shake, eyeing the exits to the room. He looked back to Travis and knew a simple head gesture wouldn't do. "I can't be seen fraternizing." Alvin whispered, speaking from the side of his mouth.

"Why not?"

"Because…" Alvin took a deep breath. He eyed the far door and took a seat, letting out a long sigh as he eased his hands on the table, settling in like an air mattress with a tear in it. "Andrews is calling all the shots here, and I'm already not one of his favorite little pups."

"Look, what the hell is happening here? Now we all know this isn't a drill. It's been seven days already."

"I don't know what this is." Alvin shot a glance back over his shoulder, double-checking he was the only security officer in the room. He turned back to the table and saw the five miners were staring at him, pleading for answers with their heavy eyes. "All I know is that there has been no communication with Earth for a week."

"What the fuck does that mean?" a miner asked, lowering his head as the others shushed him.

"I don't know. But the supply ship is still in the hangar." Alvin said this to Travis, not caring what the miners heard or followed. "Whatever this is, it's serious enough to cut us off."

"Kirsch?"

Alvin closed his eyes and took a deep breath, cringing a bit at the sound of Rodriguez's voice. He turned and looked over his shoulder, giving his fellow security officer a single wave. An awkward moment as he lingered, watching them from the doorway with his hands folded behind his back. Finally he returned the wave and left the room.

"Shit." Alvin turned back to Travis and pounded the table. "That's the last thing I need. Andrews' little lap dog running back to his master."

"Haven't you tried another satellite or alternate facilities? Maybe even the space station?"

"Andrews has an open line of communication with the space station –"

"But?"

"I don't know. He's just out of it."

"More than usual?" Travis wondered what could possibly be the norm for an asshole like Andrews.

"He's becoming isolated. Speaking in short, cryptic responses."

"All we can do is hope he keeps his shit together long enough for this all to blow over." Travis leaned back, sliding his mush across the table. His appetite smothered by the suffocating thoughts pressing down on him, thinking of a nut job like Andrews being their only voice to the outside world. Not even a report filed by Dr. Hoffman would do them any good, not now.

42

Was it blood? It looked red, but then again, it looked purple. Andrews wanted to ask, but he kept his mouth shut at the risk of insulting his only link to the outside world. Yuri, his only true friend. The one man that could possibly understand what he was going through. But that red scratch down his throat and those purple blotches weighed on his mind. Maybe some kind of food? Yuri had told him that the station had turned off its gravitational rotation to conserve fuel. It was very plausible to think some kind of liquid, shampoo or Jell-O, floated into his neck without him noticing. Could happen. Andrews rocked up and down in his office chair, his entire body nodding with his conclusion. He looked at the dim interior of the space station's communications center. A few blinking lights in the background, the same picture of someone's brother hung slightly crooked, the left corner just a tad higher than the right. A large, dopey smile on his face.

Yuri's face filled the screen as he took a seat. His expression was cold, exhausted. The look of man that's shed the last of his emotions.

"What's happened?" Andrews asked, his eyes pulling free of the Russian cosmonaut to look at the scratch on his neck. Maybe he scratched it on a piece of equipment while coming around the corner?

Yuri sat motionless for a while, looking down into his lap, his bottom lip trembling. He shook his head slowly as the tears began to fall. He lifted his face up into the camera and took a deep breath, trembling. "Have you ever held someone as they lay dying?"

Andrews leaned back, stunned by such a question. "No, not really. I mean… I've been next to people as they've died. I've even caused a few, but no. Never held them."

"You are lucky my friend." Yuri lowered his head. "I wish I could say the same. But our chief science officer, Patrick Lybecker, took his own life a few moments ago. You may know him. He was an American astronaut."

"No, I've never heard of him."

"Oh, well, doesn't really matter now. He's dead. Cut his throat with a jagged piece of mirror glass. I walked in as he dropped it to the floor. I caught him, in my arms, and held him there as he lay dying." Yuri lifted up his hands to the camera, maroon staining the normal tan skin. Both hands trembled. "I looked down into his eyes and watched his soul leave him. It's actually quite beautiful." Yuri gave a distant smile.

"Why did he do it?"

"The transmission we received. We caught a military transmission through a communications satellite." Yuri shook his head. "It hit too close to home for Patrick. A soldier's last report from a small town in Colorado."

"Can I see it?"

"Are you sure you want to?"

"Please, I have to."

Yuri hesitated for just a moment, running the footage in his mind and remembering his own initial reaction. But he'd been thankful for seeing. A morbid realization, but still, better to know the truth and come to terms with it than to hold onto false hope. He turned his back to the camera and entered some data into the computer, opening the correct files and finally patched the recorded feed into the communications link with the Mars facility. The camera went black, and for the briefest moment Andrews felt his heart pick up, fearing the connection between him and Yuri had been severed. Possibly for good. No one could simply repair the lines as if they were on Earth. No AT&T repair men circling the planet or making house calls. Andrews took a relaxing breath as the close-up of a young man's face filled the screen, an extreme close up of his right eye while he struggled with his units' communications satellite uplink.

"Please work," Private Luther Mihalyo of the 131st company said softly, nodding to himself as he saw the red light above the lens. "Okay, okay." Luther took a seat, resting his sweaty palms on his knees while looking directly into the camera. His eyes twitched. "My name is Luther Mihalyo and I'm in Boulder, Colorado. My entire unit is dead." Luther held his breath, holding back a fresh batch of tears. "Everyone in this city is dead. And those that weren't killed have been stuffed in cages, like fucking hamsters." The tears fell. "These massive things just came out of nowhere. Grabbing anyone and everyone, throwing them inside these cages. I can't —" Luther wiped his face and took a calming breath. "I don't even know why I'm recording this. Or who might ever watch it. I've heard nothing from the radios, no response from the surrounding units. Am I all alone?"

Luther fell from his chair, startled by a nearby shriek. His panicked foot lashed out and kicked over the camera, leaving the footage to be shot sideways with a view of the tent's flap. Andrews sat forward, watching in anticipation as the shrieking continued, outlasting the stamina of any human vocal cord.

Luther's boots stepped into view as he hurried toward the fluttering tent flaps. He pushed them open and exposed the world beyond. Andrews held a hand to his mouth, shocked by such a contrast to the world he remembered. Heavy rain fell from black clouds. The only light coming from large fires that burned the remains of Boulder. Luther aimed his machine gun out into the darkness, rotating slowly without a visual. A creature leapt from the darkness, pushing Luther back into the tent to land on the camera, severing the link.

Andrews had fallen from his chair, startled by the ferocity of the attack. The creature had been huge. At least twice the size of Luther. In the brief second of its attack, only its face and front claws were visible. An elongated snout with large fangs. Its face was completely hairless, and the reddish brown tint to its flesh looked as if the beast had been skinned alive.

"I wept when I saw it," Yuri said as he looked down to Andrews.

Andrews sat for a moment, the floor cold and uncomfortable through his thin work pants. He felt pinned down by the gravity of what has happened, or is still happening. With a shaking hand, he gripped the table and pulled himself up; thankful his weak knees hadn't buckled. He took a seat and looked at Yuri. He may as well have been looking into a mirror.

The face looking back at him was unshaven, exhausted, and a clinging shard of sanity in his eyes.

"What is that thing?"

"None of us have ever seen anything like it." Yuri leaned back in his chair, looking past the camera. "Are you a religious man?"

"No."

"Neither am I. Curse of the scientist, I suppose. But still, one looks at all this and wonders." Yuri gave a cryptic smile. "Maybe we were put here to survive this. To outlast the extinction of humanity."

Andrews had been concerned, hell, he'd been downright scared shitless with the sight of that footage, but never had the extinction of humanity entered his thoughts. The thought had been there, leaning against the back of his mind, but it hadn't hit home.

"Do you have women there?"

"Yes, only one."

Yuri nodded, leaning forward with a warm smile. "You are so very fortunate. I lost the last female of our crew six months ago. She went back to Earth on the last rotation. But you, you have the tools to sustain." Yuri shed a tear. "Keep her safe and you save us all. Keep her close. Because our salvation is now in your hands, my friend."

43

Annie lay on her side, propping her head up on her hand. She ran her fingers through Logan's hair as he slept, looking lovingly at his peaceful face, slightly envious of his ability to sleep soundly. But such is a mother's job, to shield her children from the terrors of this world. Even if that meant she slept very light, waking to every crack and pop from the fires outside. And there were so many of them now. In the six days they'd been within the hardware store, she'd see the distant red glow moving steadily closer. Apparently no one had informed the fire of the heavy rain, because it didn't seem to care. It moved toward them all the same. Forcing houses to collapse or wood to burst out into the street, startling her from sleep every few hours. If it wasn't the fires, it was the creatures. Their snarls or screeches tearing through the air. As always, each inhuman shrill was followed closely by someone screaming, their voice fading with

their life. Six days of constant hunting and screaming. Endless voices begging for help. With the power
out, fewer people came to the door. Smashing their
fists against the boarded up windows until they bled.
Annie had been on guard duty when a woman of perhaps twenty came running toward them. Annie had
watched her through a crack in the boards, hoping
she could make it. But out of the shadows came one
of the smaller ones, the "dogs" as they called them.
It hit her hard, sliding her along the pavement on
her back like a skateboard, coming to a stop a few
feet shy of the store. Annie pulled back, wanting to
help but not daring to give away their position. She'd
wanted to turn away, but the girl looked up. Their
eyes met. The creature sank its teeth into the back of
her neck and ended her life, yet her eyes still looked
to Annie. Her last hope on this world. Then she was
dragged back through the water filled street, pulled
into the shadows as they all were.

Annie pulled back her hand as Logan gave out
an annoyed snort, rolling onto his side to give her
his back. The "leave me alone" pose. Annie smiled
and respected his wishes, moving into a seated position. Her arm was falling asleep anyway. She stood
and stretched, lifting her arms far above her until
she heard that all too familiar snap. A smile surfaced.
Not long lived, but there. It had gotten to the point

where any remembrance of her old life or shed of comfort needed to be enjoyed. Especially since her new residence was the end of the gardening aisle. At least they weren't outside like so many people were. Drowning in some flash flood or being hunted by either the tall ones or the dogs.

Annie bent down and covered Logan up one last time. She knew full well he'd kick it off, but it's what mothers did. Satisfied he was covered for the next twenty minutes, Annie headed down the dark aisle. The soft flicker of light ahead made her smile. Arnold was on guard duty tonight, sitting before the front doors with his left scrawny leg crossed over his right. He wore tan slacks, black socks, and a red and blue striped knit sweater. A pipe clutched between his teeth as he read whatever novel he pulled from the shoulder bag he'd brought with them, his glasses pushed down the bridge of his nose so he could see. A small candle held close to the pages, barely giving off enough light to see the book, let alone read it.

"Ah, my dear Annie. Please, pull up a chair."

"I'm not disturbing you?" Annie asked as she took a seat beside him.

"Don't be silly. I'm aching for some human inter-action. These books are a fine way to pass the time, but boy do they leave me with such a headache. My eyes, you know."

"Mr. Lee, why read then if it hurts your eyes?"

"First, drop the Mr. right now. I think being huddled together like this allows for some informality. And second, I like reading. It comforts me when I'm nervous, calms me when I'm scared. More than anything, it reminds me of a time when we weren't hiding from the scary things of the night. I'm not just a man sitting before a boarded up door with a loaded rifle on the ground beside me. I'm simply a man reading by candle light."

"I like that."

Arnold nodded, putting his book in his lap. He tilted his head and read Annie's expression, seeing her concerned features as if the candle were a hundred watt bulb. He set a comforting hand on her knee and gave a good squeeze. Arnold wasn't concerned that she'd see this friendly squeeze as any sort of sexual advance. When you're sixty-eight, people tend to look at everything you do as either being cute or annoying, but never sexual.

"What's on your mind?"

"It's that obvious?"

"I'm sure if it weren't you'd be back there snuggling with your boy."

Annie looked to Arnold and thought of her father. How he used to lift her up and read to her when she couldn't sleep. "I'm just concerned for Logan.

And thinking about Travis."

"I'm sure he's thinking about you. Although, I wonder if they know anything about all this. It's not like they get the morning paper delivered."

"I hope they don't. Why fill him with worry when there's nothing he can do about it." Annie lowered her head, wishing more than anything that Travis was here.

A loud thump shook the building.

"What the hell was that?" Annie sprang to her feet and hurried to the door, ducking down to peek through a crack in between two boards.

"Something very large." Arnold gripped the wall for balance as the store rocked again.

Heavy footfalls slamming down on the pavement came closer. The ceiling tiles fell to the floor, startling the twenty people in the back of the store from their sleep. Annie looked back over her shoulder and heard their worried voices and a few panicked yelps. She hoped Logan had slept through the shaking, but she could hear him crying. Her guilt for not running back to console him was eased as she heard Erica soothing him. Annie turned back and peeked through the crack in the boards as a car came flipping down the street, moving like a matchbox car tossed by an angry child. Annie shook her head slowly in startled disbelief, watching the car slam through the front of a secondhand clothing store a few stores down. It occurred to her that whatever had thrown that car wouldn't have any difficulty pulling a few boards from the storefront, or ripping the metal security gate right off the front door. How safe were they against something like this?

"What the fuck is happening?" Sam ran down the aisle with a handgun aimed at the window.

"Lower that and shut the hell up!" Annie waved her hands as he ran toward her. "You'll give away our position."

"What is it?" Sam whispered, pressing his face to the window, darting his head about until he could get a view of the street.

Annie could hear the crowd growing behind them, speaking softly in anticipation. She wanted to turn and offer some words of encouragement but the continual shaking had peeked her interest. The very Earth seemed to shake, growing louder, growing closer. Annie pulled back as the largest foot she'd ever seen stepped into view. It made the animal planet's recreations of T-Rex look like a child's toy. The four massive toes sank into the pavement, splashing the standing water high into the air and hitting their window. Annie ducked down and looked up, never seeing more than the creature's leg. It took another step forward, a stride of twenty feet, maybe more.

Items behind her fell off the shelf as it passed. Behind it was a long and oddly formed tail, ending in three fingers. It flexed and crawled about the street, picking up debris floating by here and there, sizing them up before tossing them away. Everyone held their breath for the next few minutes as it lumbered by, stepping on and smashing a bank as it slowly made its way down another street.

"What in the name of Christ our lord was that?" Skip asked, clutching a hammer to his chest as if that would have done any good.

"How many different kinds of these things are there?" Annie whispered to Arnold.

"Three that I've seen so far. That thing, wow. What a behemoth."

"It's all over now," Sam yelled, pushing off the window with his head lowered. "If things like that are free to roam, then you know it's over."

"Keep your voice down," Annie hissed, motioning with her head toward Logan as he stood under Erica's left arm, Abby under the right.

"It's a bit too late for discretion, lady. That thing is just going to come back here." Sam waved his gun about as he spoke, sweating wildly as he grew red with anger and panic. He turned to the crowd, preaching his fear for supporters as they shook with terror. "Don't you all see? We're just waiting around for the inevitable slaughter."

"What do you suggest? We just unlock the doors and invite them in?" Arnold crossed his arms in agitation but spoke softly, calmly.

"We're safe for now and that's what matters," Skip smiled to the children. "Even the rain has finally stopped."

"Fuck the rain. Who cares about rain? I'm not worried the rain is going to break through that door and tear my guts out!"

Annie stepped forward and punched him in the stomach, knocking him backward into the register. Sam cradled his stomach as he collapsed to the floor, struggling to breathe. She stood over him and pressed her foot to his throat, stepping down just hard enough to pin him.

"Now you listen to me," Annie snarled, pointing down at him. "You keep your voice down and stay calm. The last thing we need in here is panic. Now if you want to go, I'm sure Skip would be more than happy to open that door and let you run off. But if you want to stay, you'd better remember your manners." Annie pressed her shoe down on his throat. "And if you cuss in front of these children again, I'll tear your guts out. Do we have an understanding?"

Sam did his best to nod, clawing madly at the foot on his throat. "Yes!" He croaked.

Annie gave a single nod and withdrew her foot, bending down quickly to snatch the revolver from his hand. "When you've demonstrated that you're a rational person, come see me and I'll give this back." Annie gave him a hard slap on the cheek before he could stand, turning her back to him since she no longer perceived him to be a threat. "Okay, listen up everyone. Please return to your sleeping bags and get some rest. Mr. Lee and I will stand guard. Please, go on and get some rest."

Annie stood for a moment, nodding to her fellow squatters and understanding their woe. She lowered her hands to her side as they began moving. She gave Logan a hard hug and a kiss on the check, patting his butt with a wink before Erica took him back to bed. Annie eyed Sam as he stood, shuffling off into the darkness of the store with his head lowered in defeat.

Annie didn't trust him. He had gone far beyond his level of mental control, broken his comfort zone. Men that paid for valet and first class plane tickets didn't transition well to sudden catastrophe. Their tailored suits torn and dirtied. Their stomachs growling while they flee their worldly possessions. No, Annie didn't trust a man that didn't know himself. It kept him capable of anything, especially as desperation gave way to fear. If she wasn't careful, he might turn on them.

"Let it go, dear." Arnold gave a tug at her elbow. "He's whimpering now, but I'm pretty sure you put him in his place."

Annie turned and let it go, taking a seat beside Arnold with a view of wooden boards. She crossed her left leg over her right and leaned back with a sigh. She wasn't even sure of the time. Night or day? The rain may have stopped outside but the black clouds stayed put.

"I think that might have been the biggest creature I've ever seen...or at least partially saw."

Annie nodded, still able to feel her feet lift off the floor the tiniest bit with every impact tremor.

"How can we possibly defend ourselves against something like that?"

"I don't know." Annie shook her head, wondering just how much damage their weapons could actually do against such a beast. "Let's just pray the military is getting the job done."

44

"Get that goddamn hatch sealed!" Lieutenant George Wagner looked up at Private Watts, shielding his eyes from the blue flame of his welding torch. "You six, take the left tunnel. The rest of you reload and do a shell count. We'll hold up here."

Wagner couldn't catch his breath. He'd been in constant motion for the better part of two days. He and his men had been holding steady in Time Square, firing like mad at anything that moved and wasn't human. Unfortunately, everything topside wasn't human. Those that hadn't ran or found a superb hiding spot were being dragged through the streets toward the crack in Central Park. Wagner had seen hundreds of people being hauled away, dragged behind the beasts while kicking and screaming. He'd put a bullet in those poor souls' heads. Every one. Better to spare them the tortures of whatever lay inside that crack. But now they had been forced down the hole, pushed

back through the streets of New York by a seem-
ingly endless advancement of those creatures. They
ran toward the unit at such speeds, unafraid of the
firepower they were setting down, charging soldiers
with machine guns and assault rifles. Hell, he saw
one of his men empty what had to have been thirty
shells into one of those human-sized fuckers. And
it still managed to sink its teeth into him. George
had hurried over and put a bullet square in the bitch's
head, finally killing it, but the damage had been done
to his man. They were killing machines, straight and
simple. When they'd been cornered, he ordered what
few men were left into the sewers.

"Trapped like fucking rats," George scolded himself, shaking his head.

"Manhole is sealed!" Watts yelled down, hopping
off the ladder to splash George with sewer water.
"Sorry, sir."

"Shitty smelling water is the least of my troubles,
son."

All the soldiers in the sewer, including George,
cringed as something slammed the pavement. The
concrete above them cracked. Another hard hit, this
time directly above them. The crack widened and
pieces of the road broke off, splashing all around
them.

"Everyone move! They're coming through,"

George yelled as he ran, his feet splashing through the ankle-deep sludge. Once a mixture of water and trash, the streets were now red from all the blood washing through them. Torn pieces of men and women's clothing floating about. A red strip of fabric from a woman's pajamas stuck to George's right leg. "Get down!" George cradled his head as the ceiling opened up. He fell face first into the muck, sliding along his stomach.

A leathery hand reached into the hole, one so big it touch all sides of the sewer. It wrapped its four fingers around three of his men, yanking them from the hole. George rolled onto his feet and went to charge, but the creatures cut him off. They jumped down into the sewer through the large opening and fell on his men, standing on them with their teeth tearing into their flesh as his men drowned. George raised his machine gun and opened fire, no need to aim as the tunnel had become wall to wall with them. He gave out a savage yell as he emptied the clip. George tossed down the weapon and pulled his service revolver. Dozens of them moved toward him with only twelve rounds in the clip.

"Fuck you!" George cocked the gun and pressed it to his forehead. "You're going to have to eat this meal cold," he screamed, pulling the trigger.

45

Had it been a week? Had she really been lying in bed for a week? Had to have been longer judging by the stubble on her legs and the dryness in her throat. If this was an infirmary, where was the medical staff? Why were there no fluids in her I.V.? Christina grunted as she rose up onto her elbows, her chest burning. Each breath brought with it a sharp agony to her sides. But she managed to hold herself up, long enough to turn her stiff neck for a view of the large, empty room. She fell back to the table with a heavy grunt, clinching her eyes tightly against the sheer pain erupting from her ribs and sternum. This was bad. Worse than anything she'd ever felt. Even more than when she'd been shot in the ass while fleeing a hot zone. The pain had been excruciating, but the humor lightened the wound. Her unit had a magic touch when it came to mocking physical pains. Emotional pains were not the same story. She could turn to anyone, even TJ with his smartass quips, and receive their open shoulder. She wasn't a crybaby by any measure. In fact, she'd never needed a shoulder to cry on. But she knew it was there.

Christina turned her head, wincing from the sore muscles in her neck. Someone was standing just beyond the overhead light's dim reach. The silhouette was standing with sunken shoulders, an apologetic stance.

"Who is it?" Christina could raise no more than a whisper, her voice raspy.

Sean stepped out of the shadows, a bowl in his hand. "I'm glad to see you're awake."

"I was afraid this was a dream," Christina smiled, looking over the familiar features of his face. "I was beginning to think I'd passed away or something. Where's Morgan?"

"They had him put back in his cell a few days ago." Sean took a small step forward.

"His cell?" Christina furrowed her brow, looking about the room to make sure she was in fact still on the facility. "What's happening here? Where is everyone?"

Sean pulled a chair over and took a seat, leaning in closer to her than he'd been in months. His important news was suddenly lost in the beautiful fragrance of her hair. It did in fact smell quite awful, more than a week without washing and the remnants of oil and sweat clinging to her scalp, but it was her smell. And to him, Christina was the personification of beauty.

"Sean?" Christina touched his hand, gripping his pinky with what little strength she could muster.

"I don't know, and what's worse is that no one will speak to us." Sean scooted the chair with the back of his legs and got on his knees, ducking down as far as he could to keep hidden from the hallway. "They've had us locked in our rooms for over a week now. They take us out only to eat, twice a day in small groups of ten. I'm on my dinner now. I don't have but a minute. Alvin was nice enough to let me slip out."

"Why aren't you eating then?" Christina asked, her dry lips cracking and splitting.

"I wanted to see you." Sean lifted the small bowl into view and set it on the bed beside her. "It's not a chocolate sundae, but it doesn't taste all that bad. I think it's some kind of liquid cake. Anyway, I thought you could use it more than I could."

Christina tensed as Sean dropped beneath the bed, leaving only the top of his head visible. She listened as the unmistakable thump of a security officer's boots went by in the hallway. There was a brief pause outside the door, just a quick check that their only patient was still in her bed before moving on.

"This place is going south." Sean lifted his head above the bed, resting his chin on the thin padding. "I have to get back before someone comes to check on us. I'd hate for Al to get busted on my account. Despite what the guys think, I'm not a total asshole."

"They don't think that." Christina felt like crying, measuring the sadness he carried with him was enough to break her heart. "I've never thought that."

Sean heard more footfalls from down the hall. He moved forward with a soft kiss, gently pressing his lips to hers so not to damage them. He pulled apart, standing for a brief moment with their eyes locked. He opened his mouth to say more, but the footsteps were coming closer. Sean took hold of her hand and gave her a brief squeeze before running back into the shadows.

Christina turned her head back to the ceiling and closed her eyes, exhausted by their brief encounter. She licked her lips, not caring that it hurt to do so. She wanted to taste him once more, to pull every last bead of saliva from his lips to carry with her. If this was the only way to keep them together, so be it. She loved the look they'd shared, feeling as if they weren't locked away on some foreign world but back home on a date. Something simple like being parked off the road at the end of a movie. But the movies weren't playing all that much these days, especially now that they were running off auxiliary power. She didn't need a technician to tell her all the lights weren't on. The lights didn't bother her as much as being locked away in solitary rooms, tucked away in their cells like prisoners. And who decided to make such a decision? Were they undergoing some form of shakedown from TransWorld? Didn't matter really. Whatever was happening would happen no matter what they decided to say. No one would listen to Form A-126 or whatever the hell she might be able to request from human resources. They were prisoners all the same. Only thing that changed from before her injury to now was that they'd finally begun to treat them as such.

"Shit!" Christina grunted as her elbow pushed out, knocking the bowl of what looked like dirty brown water onto the floor. "Oh God." Christina had lifted up and turned toward the bowl, falling back in a heap of pain. She gripped her chest and held her breath, willing the pain back into the darkness of her subconscious. The pain finally subsided, leaving her weak and drained, her eyes falling closed.

Time passed. How much she couldn't say, but it felt later. Christina felt pressure on her hand, a growing tightness around her wrist. She smiled, remembering Sean as he nervously stepped from the shadows with his little gift. Christina opened her eyes with the greatest of expectations, thinking that maybe he'd been given another opportunity to sneak away for another brief moment. But this wasn't Sean. It was Andrews looking down at her with a wide grin that didn't reach his eyes.

"What are you doing?" Christina pulled back from his touch, but he tightened his grip, wrapping his fingers over her wrist like a snake strangling its prey.

"Shush." Andrews leaned forward. "You need to rest. Conserve your strength."

Christina nodded, unsure what he expected from her. In her weakened state, she didn't have the energy to fend off any sort of attack should she provoke him. She managed a smile despite the dread growing in her heart. Fear rising like floodwaters from the pressure of his grip and the weight of his creepy smile. But what made the situation unbearable was the deadness in his eyes, like the look of a man with a terminal illness. He stood there, unflinching for more than ten minutes, staring down at her without a word. The pain in her wrist intensified as he gripped tighter and tighter, digging his nails into her skin.

"Ouch!" Christina wiggled from beneath his grip and pressed her bleeding wrist to her mouth, sucking the dripping blood. A visual queue to him if anything, but he never stopped grinning.

"You should go ahead and rest, Eve," Andrews nodded with his advice, stepping back from the table. His hands slowly falling to his side. "You're so very important to us now." Andrews closed his eyes. "So important to me."

Christina could only lie there, shivering from the most uncomfortable moment of her life. Never had she felt so vulnerable. Ten days ago she could have snapped this assholes neck with little effort, but her current state was what she had to work with and it wasn't much. Worse was that he knew it. A single tear rolled down her cheek as she prepared herself to be raped. But how could she? What could she tell herself to make it any better? There was no comfort to be had, only the growing dread rising from the pit of her stomach to seize her heart. What had started with a tender moment between her and Sean was now moving into the running for the worst day of her life. Christina tried to cross her legs, just one over the other, but they wouldn't move.

Andrews stood back, watching her squirm and struggle as he stared down at her. He stumbled over the bowl, grabbing the counter behind him so as not to slip in the watery cake. He stood and straightened, looking down at his feet and then off into the hall-way, as if he expected someone to be standing there. Then he turned and left, walking briskly out of the infirmary and out of sight. Christina listened to each heavy footfall until they were far enough away to be inaudible. Then came the flood. A heavy release of tears at the mental rape she'd just been put through. Although no physical penetration had taken place, he'd robbed her of comfort, put her through the possibility that at any moment he could take from her what wasn't his. Christina rolled her head to the side, tired of the dampness in her ears, but suddenly a ray of hope. A slight glimmer of light reflected off the shiny chrome of a scalpel lying forgotten on a small tray just a few feet to her left. Christina wiped her eyes, blocking the pain in her body with her mind shouting commands. *Move it you weak bitch!* Christina gripped the bed while reaching for the scalpel, swatting her hand through the empty air until she carelessly bumped the tray. The scalpel slid toward the edge and tottered, but it stayed. *Steady that hand soldier!* She reached out slowly, her hand shaking from the strain. Her fingers traced the cool metal and finally closed around it.

Christina pulled her arm back quickly, securing the scalpel beneath her leg before anyone else could come walking in. She lay still for a moment, shutting her eyes as she worked to slow her breathing. Her heart felt close to its highest setting, threatening to leap through her damaged chest and go running off down the hall. But a few minutes of slow breaths, calm thinking and overall focus over her body and its individual functions got things back in order. She opened her eyes and looked out into the hall, listening for that heavy footfall and thankful for the silence. With her eyes glued to the hall, she pulled the sharp blade from beneath her leg and tucked it between the thin mattress and the gurney. A weapon changed the score. Some careless medical staff member had left things in disarray and evened the playing field. Let Andrews try it now. Christina kept her eyes to the hall and her hand an inch from the bedside. Never again will he catch her so vulnerable. Never again.

46

Was this day seven already? Travis held out his hand and counted the fingers, only to pause, unsure what day it was. His internal clock had been thrown for a loop. No daylight from outside, no clocks to look up to, nothing but the dull light from his cell. He'd counted the small imperfections in the walls a dozen times, traced the crisscross pattern of the ceiling tiles over and over again. Anything to pass the time without falling back into memory. No sense being locked up and depressed.

Travis looked up as the door opened. Alvin stood there, his face tired and worn. This routine was beginning to wear on both sides and it showed.

"Dinner time, come and get it." Alvin managed a weak smile, but it quickly fell from his face.

Travis stood from his cot and joined the group of nine miners, all of them different each time. He wasn't sure who picked the eating rotations, but he hadn't seen a member of his unit since lockdown. He could only hope they were all okay.

"How's Christina doing?" Travis asked Alvin as he set his tray down on the table.

Alvin took a seat and leaned in close. "Last I heard she was doing fine."

"Last you heard?"

"Last night, Andrews gave orders for no one to enter the infirmary. He was dead serious about it." Alvin gave a nervous laugh. "He's become dead serious about everything. If he'll even talk to you that is."

"Shut your fucking mouth!"

Alvin and Travis looked up as two miners swept their trays onto the floor and began pushing each other.

"Break it up," Alvin yelled, hopping up from the bench with his electric prod in hand. "I said break it up!" Alvin stood between them and held them apart at arm's length, but the men were large and heated.

The only miner Travis recognized, he thought his name was something like Neil or Phil, pushed Alvin to the ground. Alvin fell hard, smacking his head onto the cold, hard tiles. Travis thought it was time to set aside his meek obedience and step in with his training before this got out of hand. But as he stood up to engage the two men, three security officers rushed into the room. Gomez, Rodriguez, and

Adams, all three of them had their lips permanently sewn to Andrews' ass. But Travis was actually happy to see them, at least until Gomez took things a bit too far.

Gomez hit the miner closest to him in the base of the neck, a hard hit with a shock from his electric prod. The miner yelped in pain and surprise, dropping to his knees. As quickly as it had started, the confrontation was over. But Gomez gripped the club and swung it hard into the back of his head, bringing the miner to the floor. Adams jammed his prod into the second man; the one Travis had fished for a name, and brought him to the floor as well. As if in unison, the two guards beat the miners, hands up and then back down. Over and over, hard blows to the head and face until the skin tore and swelled. The savagery wouldn't stop. Rodriguez stood with his back to the assault, standing between the officers and the stunned miners still hovering about the table. He patted the baton to his palm, egging them on if they were so foolish to come forward. Travis had to ignore every urge in his body to charge and stop the beating. Doing so would put his life, and yes, possibly even his entire unit's lives in jeopardy. Instead he dropped to one knee and took hold of Alvin's shoulder, nudging him until he opened his eyes.

"What the hell?" Alvin sat up with a hand to his

bruised head. He fought the urge to sit back down, feeling woozy and nauseous. "That's enough. I said that's enough!"

The two officers paused, their batons held up in a readied stance, blood rolling down the black metal to their tightened fists. Both shared the same expression of savage intent, their breathing hard and heated. But they lowered their arms and stood from the miners, standing informally like tuff schoolyard bullies unafraid of the approaching principle.

"Rodriguez, take the men back to their living quarters. You two have these men brought to the infirmary."

"Infirmary is off limits now. Andrews gave clear instructions," Adams said smugly.

"Not to the gravely wounded, asshole. Now move it!"

The men put up some resistance, finally dropping to their knees to grip the men by their wrists. They stood and pulled, dragging the miners along the cold floor. Travis took a look back over his shoulder as they were led out of the room. He didn't need the opinion of a doctor to know those men were both dead. Their noses had been smashed and shoved into their brains, along with their shattered skulls. It had been a savage beating, one he would never forget. Mostly, he'd remember standing there with his skilled hands by his side. What it all came down to is that those men were now dead because he'd chose to sit this one out. Travis lowered his head and headed back down the hall, wondering how much longer this was going to continue. How long until they were all lying on the floor with their heads caved in?

47

Alvin had been pumped since he'd left the cafeteria, fueled by rage. What he'd seen was not what they had signed on for and he wasn't going to stand for it. Alvin passed the infirmary and saw Christina laying there, her eyes closed. He wondered if maybe he should stop in for a brief look over. The pain in his head was excruciating, intensifying with every angry step toward the communications room. And then he wondered yet again where the doctor was. Hadn't seen the slightly competent Dr. D'Ambrosio in over five days. A bit odd he wouldn't be monitoring the only patient he'd had in months. But so many things had begun to go south lately.

Alvin blocked the pain in his head with the task at hand, putting his angry words into a well-organized presentation before Andrews could redirect. He stood before the communications room and froze, his speech slipping from his tongue to fall forgotten on the floor. There was just something off. Alvin cleared his mind of such pointless playground terror and knocked on the door, his body tense and ready for a confrontation. A moment passed and there was no answer. Alvin knocked again, three hard knocks, but still he received no response.

"Andrews?" Alvin pressed his thumb to the metal plate, a bit taken aback as the door opened to a dark room. "Hello?"

Andrews was sitting in a chair with his back to the door, his head slightly tilted. He gave no indication that he'd heard the door open or the knocks. No movement at all.

"Andrews?" Alvin's anger gave way to confusion, smothered by the growing fear that Andrews was dead.

Andrews pressed his big toe to the floor and swiveled around in the chair, lifting a hand to his face to shield the dim light from the hallway from his eyes. The darkness under his eyes and the stubble across his face said he'd been there for quite some time, sitting alone in the dark. He lowered his hand and looked at Alvin, taking a brief moment to take notice of who he was.

"Are you all right, sir?" Alvin spoke slowly.

"Right as rain," Andrews answered with a wide and creepy smile. "What is it?"

"We've had an infraction between two miners

and two security officers."

"What type of infraction?" Andrews looked annoyed, spinning slowly back and forth in his chair like a child that had better things to do.

"Well, basically, Gomez and Adams beat two miners to death." Alvin spit it out plain as day, hoping this type of news might spark a little human emotion, but Andrews only shook his head. "Sir, I said two miners were beaten to death."

"I'm not deaf." Andrews crossed his arms.

"I know, but steps need to be taken."

"Steps?"

"Incident reports need to be filled out and submitted to human resources. Gomez and Adams need to undergo a disciplinary review."

"Who should we send these incident reports to? The home planet that's no longer returning our calls?" Andrews gave a single laugh, shaking his head in annoyance. "There is no need to remove two of my best officers because some assholes were fighting. I suspect Gomez and Adams were well within their boundaries."

"Our job is to maintain production and safety."

"Don't you dare lecture me on the prime directive!" Andrews stood from his chair and stuck a finger in Alvin's face, pressing it to his chin. "I don't need instructions from a spineless little prick on how to make this place run smoothly. Without me, you'd all be dead in a week, torn apart by those savages."

"They're just men, sir." Alvin pulled back, holding onto the wild dog that had become his angry tongue. "Just men."

"They are so long as we keep them caged. But how long is that going to keep? The supply ship is still just sitting in the hangar, meaning nothing else is coming and nothing is going. Do you even understand the immense pressure of knowing that every scrap of food that we have at this moment is the most we're ever going to have? Do you?" Andrews looked past Alvin to the hallway. "All we can do is survive." Andrews took a seat and turned his back to Alvin, leaning forward to look at a consul that showed nothing but static. "As per the dead bodies, file whatever reports you feel necessary. Go ahead and fill them out, send them to HR, and clean up the mess." Andrews spoke without turning around.

Alvin just nodded, stepping out of the room and shutting the door. He stood for a moment, looking at the door and wishing he could lock it from the outside. It became clear that he was no longer a security officer. He too was under the control of Andrews, subject to whatever harsh rules or conditions he might inflict. Ultimately, he too was a prisoner. Only in this prison, it looked as if the murderers and crazies were in charge.

48

"What the fuck do you want?" Dasher asked Siren, bouncing her in his arm as he headed down Highway 90 out of Massachusetts. "I'd give you milk, but my tits aren't exactly lactating."

Siren didn't find the joke to be all that clever. She continued to cry, just as she'd been doing the last hour. And the three hours before that, and the entire day before that. Dasher did the little bounces, rocking her in his arms, but nothing worked. Last night he'd managed to secure them a luxurious room for the night in an abandoned motel. The motel had recently been burned nearly to the foundation, but two rooms near the back had suffered only minor damage. Still, black walls and the smell of burnt carpet was better than being cooped up in the backseat of some abandoned car. Siren had agreed upon the room as well. She'd stopped crying for a whole thirty minutes upon being set dead center on the bed. The comforter smelt of mildew and had stains from the water dripping through the holes in the ceiling, but it was still soft. Dasher had stood over her for a moment, afraid any movement might put her back into a crying fit. But the piss wouldn't hold off. Dasher hurried into the bathroom and threw open the lid, tilting back his head as he pissed into the bowl. He couldn't help but laugh. With the world turned to shit, would anyone really care if he just took a piss in the center of the room? What's the worst that would happen, they wouldn't give him back his deposit? Dashers brief humor was ripped away as he heard Siren screaming her head off.

"Oh come on!" Dasher yelled down at the crying infant on the floor. "Can't you stay put for two minutes?"

Dasher's first lesson in parenting: never take your eyes off the child.

Dasher had spent the remainder of the night on the floor with Siren in his arms, rocking her back and forth as he hummed a ballad from some long-haired rocker group from back in the day. She seemed to like the tune, because she fell asleep in his arms. He looked down to her closed eyes and smiled, not just because she'd finally shut up. There was something sweet about her. A peacefulness that calmed him.

The night passed too quickly for him. He woke

up to her screaming, flailing her arms about. He knew she needed something to eat, but he had nothing. Dasher searched the hotel and found a busted vending machine with a few candy bars and some chips. He crushed the chips in his hand and fed them to the baby, thankful it had been enough to soothe her, at least for the time being. Now they were miles past the motel and there was nothing on the highway but the occasional abandoned car.

"Wish me luck, little darling," Dasher said to his passenger as he got behind the wheel of a new Toyota truck. The key was dangling in the ignition like a cruel tease, ready to laugh at him when he turned the key and saw the gaslight instantly come on. For once, fortune was on his side. The engine rolled over and the truck hummed into life. "Thank the maker. Let's roll!"

Dasher put the truck in drive and pulled off the shoulder. Old habits made him look in the mirror before merging back with the highway, even though he hadn't seen another vehicle in days. He'd seen people, lots of them, but they were all trapped inside some gargantuan cage. They'd been dragged through an open field by the biggest creature he'd ever seen, deciding to take its massive lobster trap full of people for a walk. Dasher had wanted to help them, but there was nothing he could do. It had been one of

Siren's rare quiet times, and he'd been so thankful for it. That had been two days ago. With the black clouds holding steady overhead and the continual scene of abandoned cars left along the highway, the days were beginning to mesh together.

Siren began crying, lying on the seat beside him. He knew she wasn't supposed to be just lying there, but he didn't have a car seat. His stomach growled, rippling through him like thunder. Off the road about a hundred yards to his left, hidden within a thicket of trees, he saw a house. Unlike every other house along the road, this one didn't look torched. And if you weren't looking just right, it was easily missed. Dasher turned off the highway and made his own road, bouncing through tall grass until he drove up a slight shoulder and turned down a long, gravel drive-way. A cloud of dust had kicked up behind him. He looked in the rearview mirror and felt like an idiot, raising a massive red flag to any creature that may be passing by, but the damage had been done. He pulled the truck up to the front porch and let it idle for a moment. It was a nice Victorian home, painted white and well maintained. There was a porch swing and the front door hadn't been pulled from the hinges. That was always a good sign. Dasher turned off the engine and opened the door.

"Hello, is anyone home?" Dasher yelled up to the

front door. "Hello?"

He thought he saw the curtain pull back ever so slightly on the front window. Dasher stepped onto the porch and pressed his face to the window, cupping his hands about his eyes to block the light. At first there was nothing but darkness filtering through a dirty window, then something black blocked his view. Dasher pulled back and raised his hands, stepping back from the barrel of a shotgun that had been pressed to the glass.

"Okay, all friendly out here."

"Shut up!" A woman's voice.

Dasher squinted to see beyond the barrel to the person holding it, but the dried mud and collection of bird shit showed him nothing more than a vague shape.

"My baby and I need a place to sleep tonight." Dasher made sure to emphasize the baby.

There was a moment of hesitation. "I don't see a baby."

"If I step down from the porch, will you promise not to shoot me?" Dasher asked, slowly lowering his hands.

The barrel disappeared from the window. A moment later there was a rattle from behind the door, locks being turned, and a chain lock falling freely. The door opened a crack and the shotgun protruded a few inches, its twin barrel aimed at Dasher's chest. Dasher nodded and turned back toward the truck, opening the passenger's side door. He reached down and scooped his hands under Siren's back. She looked up at him with curiosity as he tucked her into his arm and shut the door with his foot.

"See, a baby girl." Dasher held Siren up with a smile.

He jumped as a shrill scream filled the air, followed closely by a massive roar. It made a lion sound like a pussycat. Dasher lowered Siren and looked to the door, his heart sinking as it closed. He turned to get back in the truck, startled as the door flew open. A young woman stepped onto the porch, her blonde hair blowing about her face as the wind kicked up.

"Come on, hurry." She waved her hand toward the house, keeping her eyes on the road. "More are coming."

Dasher smiled and hurried up the steps. "Thank you," he said as he passed.

She stayed on the porch a moment, eyeing the road and the disabled Mercedes on the shoulder. A second roar got her moving. She went inside and shut the door, locking the two chain locks and the dead bolt.

"Thanks again." Dasher was rocking Siren from side to side, thankful the excitement hadn't caused her to cry.

"Do I need to use this?" The girl gripped the barrel of the shotgun beside the door.

"No ma'am. I mean you no trouble."

She nodded, wiping her palms on her black sweater before extending it. "I'm Ann Marie."

"Harold, but everyone calls me Dasher."

"Why is that?"

"It's my last name."

Ann Marie nodded, the hint of a smile surfacing. She hunkered down and tilted her head to the side, instantly moving from hardcore survival nut to baby enthusiast. Her voice rose in pitch and her face became animated. Dasher smiled, unable to help himself. Siren let out a giggle, a sweet sound Dasher had never heard from her. She reached up with her little hand and touched Ann Marie's face.

"What's her name?"

"Siren."

"What?" Ann Marie looked back at him with her eyebrows raised. "What kind of name is that?"

"It just kind of happened."

"She's not yours, is she?" Ann Marie took hold of her little hands and massaged them, happy to be holding a little baby once again. "What happened?"

"Her mother was killed, so I took her."

Ann Marie straightened and released Siren's

hands. She looked Dasher in the eyes for a moment, nodding as if he'd told her something.

"I like you. I've decided that."

"Just now?"

Ann Marie nodded, moving past him into the kitchen.

"Do you have any food here?"

"Already on it. Have a seat and I'll get Siren some milk. I think I saw some formula in the pantry." Ann Marie disappeared in the kitchen.

Dasher took a seat on the couch, laying Siren across his chest to poke her belly in a playful manner. He was becoming a real softy, but who cared, he liked the little shit. She looked at him without judgment, something very few people in his life had ever done. She was tangible redemption, a second chance to do right by someone.

"This isn't your house, is it?" Dasher yelled toward the kitchen.

"No."

"What happened to the people here?" Dasher eyed the family photos on the wall beside the stairs.

"Why do you ask?"

Dasher squinted in the dim light, seeing the previous occupants were a much older couple, mid sixties by the photo. "Just trying to gain perspective."

"I have some milk here." Ann Marie entered the

room with a bottle. "Probably had grandchildren or something. Or maybe for feeding baby calves."

"They have cows?" Dasher took the bottle and positioned Siren in his arm, pressing the rubber nipple to her lips until she took it. "I didn't see a barn."

"I think it was washed out. The whole backyard is nothing more than a lake."

"So what's your story? I mean, how'd you end up here?"

"My brother and I were driving down the highway here, trying to get as far from the cities as possible. And we ran out of gas right there. That's our car."

"It's a nice car. Where's your brother now?"

Ann Marie took a seat beside him, poking Siren's little pink booties with a distant smile. Her shoulders became tense, rising up above her ears as the bad memories seemed to drown her. "We ran out of gas up there about three days ago. Greg and I saw the house, but one of those things was coming down the highway behind us. We ran for the house, but I didn't know..." Ann Marie closed her eyes and collected herself. "Greg turned back and headed further down the road, waving his arms for the creature to follow him. It did. Last thing I heard was him yelling out to me, telling me to find mom. Then nothing." Ann Marie whipped her eyes. "I went inside and hunkered down."

"I'm sorry." Dasher meant it.

"Me too." Ann Marie nodded, looking down into her lap as the guilt consumed her. "I should have gone back for him. I should have helped him."

She broke down, letting go of tears she'd been holding onto for three days, balling uncontrollably. Dasher raised his arm and wrapped it about her, pulling her in close to rest her head on his shoulders. Granted, they didn't know anything about each other beyond their first names, if they hadn't lied upon introduction, but even strangers can offer comfort. Another human to lean on when the world around them felt so alien. Siren didn't seem to mind. She sucked back the milk with her eyes shut, losing herself in its white goodness. Dasher just leaned his head back and closed his eyes. Overcome with the sudden urge to laugh. He felt like a father in some cheesy sitcom. Only this was real and completely unscripted. Still, the humor was there. Dasher suppressed the urge to laugh at himself, feeling it might set the wrong tone with Ann Marie, and he enjoyed her company. She was a rather pretty woman, maybe twenty-five. So he'd let her cry. Lord knows there was plenty to cry about these days.

49

"It's not a question of safety anymore. I think we need to seriously consider a scouting party." Annie had given the group her two cents, passing her ideas around the circle of adults, looking like an AA meeting. "We've been locked in here for eleven days now, and the fridge in the back is running on empty."

"There are only a handful of snacks left in the vending machines," Skip added, looking around the group for support.

"The rain has finally stopped and we haven't seen but two or three of those things outside. If we all create some cover, it might be very possible for a small group of individuals to sneak out and hunt for food and supplies."

"That's a great fucking idea, really top notch." Sam raised his voice, lowering it as the group shushed him. Sam looked back over his shoulder at the back of the store where the children were trying to sleep.

"So your best idea is to have us throw open the front door and open fire like wild cowboys."

"We'd only need to open fire to give cover to those that leave, in case something comes at them. So no, we're not going to have a hoedown and open fire at random." Annie hated this man. She kept her voice steady and her words slow, taking joy in making him look stupid.

"Regardless of how you do it, opening fire will do nothing more then tell them all where we are. They'll hear the noise and come running. Sure a few people might get away, but what good are supplies if we're all fucking dead!"

"I told you to keep your voice down, and watch that dirty mouth." Annie pointed at him from across the circle, her hand shaking in rage. The other twelve adults, excluding Sam due to his blinding ignorance, knew she meant business.

"I'm getting real tired of you telling us what to do, lady."

"I'm just telling us all what we need to hear. The facts are simple. We're low on food, our water supply is tainted due to the massive flooding, and the fires are growing closer. I know that staying put seems like the safest thing, but I'm telling you with all sincerity that it's not."

Annie felt horrible, laying out the difficult choices

before these good people like gruesome crime scene photos. She actually understood exactly what Sam was saying, even agreed with him, to a small extent. Her visual wasn't quite an old west celebration of gunfire and dancing, but there was a very large possibility it would draw the creatures in on them. But they were running low on options. People were getting restless, tired of being handed half a piece of bread and a bag of chips. The children were crying for more than cold oatmeal and candy bars, as shocking as that may seem. The floods had filled the water pipes with brown sludge, dirt, and God only knew what else.

"I guess it's time to decide who should go." Arnold leaned forward, rubbing his hands together, a nervous habit of his. "I'd like to volunteer myself. I know I'm slower than many of you, but I'm willing to put my name in there just the same."

"Let's not volunteer ourselves as if we're really going out there."

"If you don't like Mrs. Daniels plan, then how about coming up with one of your own." Skip sat up straight, pulling from his diaphragm to raise his voice up to what he would consider an angry tone. "All you do is point fault and gripe, and that gets us nowhere."

"Fine." Sam leaned back and crossed his arms. "If you don't want the sound voice of reason, then I'll just keep my mouth shut."

"Thank God!" Annie exclaimed.

"But you can bet your ass I'm not volunteering myself for your suicide run. I'd rather stay here where it's nice and safe."

As If cued by Sam's pigheaded opinion, the glass storefront shattered. The group of adults fell off their chairs in shock, scrambling to their feet as humanoid creatures leapt through the opening. Annie stood, hopping to her feet, ready to bolt toward Logan but kept in place by the collection of monsters. Four of them stood within the store, all of them eight to nine feet tall with similar, reptilian features. But it was their mannerisms that kept her lingering, at least for the briefest second. They turned toward each other, one grunting and clicking in his throat while the others nodded. So they weren't just savage beasts. Annie didn't stick around long enough to find out their likes and dislikes. She bolted toward the back of the store, running three times the speed of Mr. Arnold with his bad hip and twice the speed of Skip. Annie skidded to a stop and turned to help, but it was too late. One of the beasts had fallen on Skip, tackling him with a running start while sinking its teeth into the back of his neck. It lifted its head and looked to her, pulling veins and flesh from the back of Arnold's neck as they were lodged between its teeth.

"Annie!" Erica screamed.

Annie pulled free of the creature's cold glare and raced to the back of the room, dropped to her knees to skid into her son. She scooped him up and joined Erica as they ran for the storage room. She felt overwhelmed and dizzy from the screaming voices of men and women, gunfire ringing out throughout the store. Annie's ears began to ring, rising in volume until she couldn't hear anything but a high-pitched whine. Erica was covering her daughter's head and screaming something to Annie, but she couldn't hear it. Annie turned toward the backroom and stopped, her heart leaping into her throat. A creature emerged from the back aisle with someone's severed foot in its hand. Blood dripping from the shoe in a steady stream. It dropped the shoe and crouched, spreading its arms wide as it let out a massive roar. Even with her ears ringing she could hear the ferocity. Annie gripped her hip and panicked, suddenly aware she'd left Erica's handgun back inside her tent. Only ten feet behind her, but with this bastard on her heels it may as well be in Texas.

"Stay back." Annie stepped before them, her small group of dependents, and pushed them back.

If there was one thing she was good at, it was thinking on her feet. Annie inched toward the creature, aware of the fact that she was unarmed and the thing in front of her sported very large, sharp claws. It turned its head and eyed her, taking a step forward. Annie reached behind her to a gardening end cap, grabbing two troughs. With a flick of the wrist, she flung the gardening tools, catching the creature by surprise as they struck its torso and bounced off.

"Shit!" Annie screamed as she turned down the gardening aisle, the creature right on her heels.

She'd forgotten how thick these things' skin was, back from when she'd stabbed one in her own living room. Annie ran hard, knowing it was only a few seconds before she was within this thing's reach, but she'd thankfully chosen the right aisle. She gripped an axe off the rack and dropped to her knees, turning in mid slide while swinging with all her might into the creature's left knee. Thick skinned or not, the axe cut straight through the beast's leg. Annie hopped to her feet and swung the axe high overhead, bringing it down into the creature's back. She pressed down on its dark skin and pulled the axe free, slamming it back down twice more.

"Fucker!" Annie spat on the creature's back and turned toward the back of the store.

"Oh thank God." Erica placed a hand to her heart. She was sobbing heavily, both her and Abby.

Annie took hold of Logan's hand and pulled them toward the storage room, backing through the swinging door with her axe in a readied stance. The backroom was cold and dark, and there was a soft whimpering. Annie kicked the door open and let the light from the store seep in, casting a dim glow over a small child's face as she sat on the floor.

"Come with us." Annie tucked the axe beneath her arm and grabbed the little girl's hand, pulling her to her feet. "Where are your mommy and daddy?" Annie had seen the little girl in the store, but she'd been camping out at the opposite end.

The little girl pointed back into the store and Annie understood. She was now their responsibility. Erica took hold of the little girl's hand without being asked, knowing full well her role here was not as a protector but a tag-along. Annie let the axe drop from beneath her hand and gripped the wooden handle firmly. They had little time before the beasts behind them ran out of fresh meat and decided to explore. Annie ran to the far wall, searching for the release button for the corrugated delivery door. She found it, pressed it, and nothing happened.

"Goddamn power's out." Annie stomped her foot, feeling foolish for having glossed over such an obvious fact, but her mind was in panic mode. "Quick, help me get this up."

Annie took the axe and began slamming it into the padlock. Seven hard strikes and the lock snapped.

Her fingers stumbled over the lock, but she got it off. Erica joined her on the floor and they pushed up on the metal door, both of them grunting and straining. At first there was nothing but the sound of their own frustration. Then the door gave an inch, rising ever so slightly. They shoved their fingers beneath the opening out into the cool air and lifted upward. An inch turned into three, then five.

The building shook, followed by a deafening crash as the ceiling behind them caved in. Annie turned and dove toward the children, knocking all three onto their backs to shield them. Dirt and water fell down on them, but the roof above their heads stayed up. A monstrous roar rose above the scream-ing in the store.

"We have to move. Now!" Annie pushed off the ground and gripped the metal door, lifting with her legs until the five-inch opening became a two-foot gap. "That should be enough." Annie stepped back with a heavy breath, her arms and legs burning.

Erica lay flat on her back and rolled beneath the door, taking a moment to scout her surroundings before turning back and reaching for the first child. Annie let Heather, the recently appointed orphan of the store, go first. Selfishly in the back of her mind, she figured if anything should happen, better let it happen to anyone other than her or her son. Next came Abby, then Logan, and finally Annie. She felt so exposed, standing beside the building with nothing behind her but bricks and the open world around them. They needed to get moving, but this had been their first real glimpse of the outside world in days. The buildings that she herself had shopped in were crumbled and burnt, collapsed and running into the streets. The high water that had reached the storefront only a few days ago had receded, but there was still two feet on the roads.

"Look, across the lot." Erica pointed toward the back of Schuman's Clothes.

The black semi was only thirty feet away, but Annie had to squint to see it. She got the children running, lifting Logan up into her arms as it was difficult for his little legs to tread through the water. Heather was seven and moving along fine, same with Abby. All of them picking up the pace as the cries and screams from the store grew closer, and they felt more and more vulnerable the further they moved out into the open. Annie stepped up onto the metal step beside the driver's side door and said a little prayer, pulling on the door. She let out a laugh of joy as the door pulled open, yelping as the dead body of a heavyset man rolled out of the driver's seat. The children screamed as the fat trucker splashed into the water, soaking them all. Annie helped the children into the truck and climbed in, wincing from the dampness of the trucker's slowly drying blood on the seat. Annie had never seen a sight as beautiful as the golden glimmer of the keys as they dangled from the ignition. Now she could only hope her luck would hold out. They all held their breath, clenching tight as Annie turned the key.

"Thank God!" Annie turned to the children, shivering from the sensation. Just to have something working again, power where it should be, was enough to bring tears to her eyes.

Annie put the big truck in reverse, grimacing from the grinding of the gears as she struggled with the clutch. It took her a few noisy tries, but she finally got the semi backed up and turned toward the highway. Either from the noise of her inexperienced trucking or simply out of the victims, three creatures ripped the metal delivery gate clear off the wall and hopped out into the water.

"Hold on!" Annie pressed her foot down hard on the gas.

The creatures ran toward the truck with their claws reaching towards them, their teeth showing in anticipation. Annie gave a cruel snarl and gripped the wheel upon impact, yelling as the truck rolled over them. There was a shared cheer of celebration as they turned the corner of the store and headed down the road, but their good cheer was cut short. They looked up at the tallest creature they'd ever seen standing in the middle of the road, reaching into the open roof of the hardware store. It turned toward them, looking like a brontosaurus on two legs, with its hands full of people. These were the legs she'd seen pass the store a few nights back, like walking tree trunks. It opened its mouth and emitted a high pitch shriek. Then it raised its hands high above its head, people still squirming and struggling beneath its massive fingers, and lowered its fists down upon the truck.

"Oh shit." Annie muttered, pressing hard on the gas while turning the wheel toward the left sidewalk.

The beast's fists missed the truck by only a few feet, hitting the paved road with enough force to leave two massive craters. The shock from such a blow shook the truck and made it nearly impossible to steer. Annie lost control of the wheel and drove over the sidewalk and through the front of a pharmacy. Annie took hold of the wheel in a death grip, leaning back into the seat while yelling. Visibility had been taken down to zero as they drove straight down the middle of the store, knocking over the displays and shelving. Candy and medicine flew down on them, covering the windshield in a wide array of colors. The interior of the semi bounced and shook as they rammed through the store. Twelve seconds later they burst through the back wall, weightless for a second until they connected with the pavement. Had the semi been pulling a trailer, this would have surely tipped them. Annie steadied the wheel and turned them back toward the highway.

"Is everyone okay?" Annie gasped between breaths, her shoulder high beside her head.

She looked down at the side mirror, but it was gone. She rolled down the window and leaned out, looking back at the smoking remains of Richmond, VA. The giant beast had decided to let them go, turning its back to them as it reached into another building.

"What do we do now?" Erica asked, her words heavy with exhaustion. She reached behind her to take hold of Abby's hands, pulling her into her lap. She held her daughter tight, taking comfort in her presence.

Annie glanced briefly over to her neighbor and her daughter. The poor girl had become nearly a deaf mute since this whole thing had begun. Her normally cheerful smile was now hidden with dirt, and beneath that were trembling lips. She was thankful to have them. Even Heather. Annie looked up into the rearview at the young girl, feeling a deep since of whoa for the child. She was left alone. In just a few minutes she'd lost her parents and was on the run.

Annie couldn't imagine the sorrow, the overwhelming confusion.

"Everything is going to be all right now," Annie spoke into the mirror, hoping a few shallow words might offer the tiniest bit of comfort. But Heather just kept on crying. Her long blonde hair fell over her face, hiding her from the terrors of the real world. "I think I know where to go."

"Where?" Erica maneuvered Abby on her left leg, pressing her daughter's head to her shoulder where she was instantly asleep.

"Someplace with lots of weapons." Annie had to slow her speed, crawling along the highway to weave in and out of abandoned vehicles. Most of which she used the grill of the truck to nudge onto the shoulder, but she didn't want to risk damaging the engine. This was not the right time for them to suffer a breakdown. The solar cells had been depleted, but fortunately the truck had almost a full tank of diesel. "I know a place. Just a few hours from here where we're sure to be safe."

Erica took faith in her friend. She lowered her head back to the seat, pressed her cheek to her daughter's head, and joined her in sleep. Annie looked back into the rearview and saw Logan had also fallen asleep, laying back on the small mattress the trucker had stashed in the cab. Only Heather stayed awake.

She sat on the edge of the mattress, her knees pulled up to her chest, shivering. Poor child. Annie tilted her head as an odd thought surfaced, something so random and yet very obvious, slightly comforting and mortifying at the same time. Annie was a mother again. This was her new child. If not hers, Erica's. Annie had to suppress a laugh, knowing full well this was not the appropriate time to look at the lighter side. Still, she found it funny; looking back into the rearview at their newly adopted child, thankful this one came without the pains of childbirth.

Annie slowed the semi to four miles an hour, weaving between an overturned bus and the sad remains of a motorhome. It would be slow going, but at least the rain had stopped. She could be thankful for that.

50

D asher set Siren down gently between two couch
pillows. He stepped back, eyed the distance from
Siren to the hardwood floor, and added another pillow.
Trial and error from her little roll off a motel bed. He
told himself it was so she wouldn't wake up and scream
her head off again, but he knew that was a load of shit.
He liked the little bitch. Dasher smiled, folding his
arms. The "little lady." He was a father now, after all.

"I'm sorry," Ann Marie said from the doorway of
the kitchen.

"About what?"

"Crying all over you like a little girl, and then passing out." She rubbed her elbow, nervously moving her
hands about her arms. "I am thankful you're here."

"I am too." Dasher joined her in the kitchen, taking a seat at the table.

Ann Marie pulled some matches from the drawer and lit a candle. It flickered in the breeze, but the

flame held. She opened the fridge and stuck her hand inside, sighing only to shut the door.

"Generator's out." She took a seat. "Looks like we're back to the Stone Age."

"I'm just thankful to be off the road." Dasher's good humor faltered as the flame danced about. He leaned to his left and looked out the window. "Is this a good idea? The light?"

"You can't see the kitchen from the road. Should be fine."

Ann Marie looked over his shoulder to the living room. "You're very sweet to take her."

"Didn't really have a choice."

"Yes, you did."

Dasher was pleased to hear that he wasn't such a bastard after all. He set his hands on the table and nodded slightly, unsure what to say. Ann Marie was a very beautiful woman, wearing a soft cotton dress that showed off her form. A woman he would have never even been allowed to speak to in the old world, but times had changed. Ann Marie leaned across the table and kissed him, grabbing his face passionately, desperately. She pulled free and sat back, crossing her arms about her chest while turning her head in embarrassment.

"Sorry."

"No, it's perfectly alright." Dasher licked his lips, tasting the strawberry flavor of her lip balm. "In fact

I think that's one of the nicest things that has happened to me in years."

"Do you want to go down the hall?" Ann Marie bit her bottom lip, eager to have company in the only bedroom downstairs. She'd been alone for too long, scared and in need of someone, anyone, to press their security against her. Nothing against Dasher, she really did like him.

Dasher shook his head slowly with a soft whistle. "I take it back." He looked her in the eyes, seeing a slight retreat on her end as she feared some kind of denial. "That was the nicest thing."

Ann Marie stood from the table and took his hand. Dasher took one last peek at Siren as they passed her on their way to the bedroom. She was sleeping soundly with a thin blanket pulled up to her chin, her arms stretched out past her head. She looked so peaceful. Dasher turned his attention back to Ann Marie, pulling him along with an eagerness he'd never experienced. He had had his share of women, but it had never felt like any of them had actually wanted him. Maybe paying him back for some favor, asking him for a little drug money in exchange for some head, but never pulling him in like a wife on their anniversary after a romantic dinner. Only at the end of the world could a smalltime, luckless thug become a father and a husband.

51

It was truly dark now. It must have been noon, maybe two or three when they had left the hardware store. Annie had left her watch, as well as everything else they had, back in the tent. But Annie couldn't dwell on that now. She kept her focus on the road, her eyes squinting through the available light cast out from the semi's headlights. The fastest she'd gone in the past six hours had been a whopping seven miles an hour, but that had been short lived. She could see fires all along the horizon, cities burning turning industry to ash. Annie slowed the semi to a stop a mile shy of the turnoff. She rolled down the window and leaned out, squinting through the night to get a better glimpse of what ran across the road. Two deep gashes ran up the shoulder, across the road, and off into the distant field like two train tracks. But these were caused by something cutting into the earth. Or possibly by something dragged, but what could be so large? Annie rolled up the window and turned back to the road, gasping as one of the smaller creatures, the hairless dog type, leapt onto the hood of the semi. Annie put the large truck in reverse, knocking the dog from the hood. She put the semi in drive and let out a cruel chuckle as the semi gave a little bounce.

"What was that?" Erica spat, her voice groggy.

"Just a little speed bump."

"Where are we?" Erica lifted her cheek off Abby's head and looked out the window.

"Almost there."

Annie turned off the highway and headed up a winding road, pavement quickly giving way to mud. Thankfully this road was all but deserted. It was too narrow to work the semi through any sort of jam, but then again no one else really used this exit except TransWorld Inc. Annie knew they were trying to keep their location private, but with their money they could have sprung for a better road. At least they were making their way through the mud. Had she been driving her car, they would have gotten stuck the second the pavement ended. But they were moving along fine and the scenery was a pleasant change. Tall trees blocking the fires. It was as if they were going camping rather than seeking refuge, just a normal outing for her and her neighbor. Annie turned onto the facility's road, nearly missing the narrow turnoff in the dark. She drove slowly, leaning forward to see any sign of life up ahead. Even that asshole soldier that had pointed a machine gun at her son would do. But the large metal gate stood open; the metal twisted and warped.

"Are you sure this is a good idea?" Erica eyed the gate and the empty guard booth.

"This place has weapons here, trust me." Annie looked over briefly and gave Erica a smile, but there was doubt in her face. She couldn't take her eyes off the mangled gate. Something had either torn it open, or the soldiers had bust through.

Annie drove through the gate and down the road, pulling up in front of the building as she had a month ago. The front entrance was buried behind a foot of mud. Annie turned off the semi's engine and waited a moment, leaning over Erica to look in through the dark windows of the facility. There was a smear of blood on the wall beside the door, but no bodies. The silence was making her uncomfortable.

"Try the glove box. Maybe he had a gun."

Erica opened the glove box, pulling out several maps, a box of condoms, and some pills. No gun. Annie gave a huff and opened the door, easing her foot out slowly, hopping down into the mud. She pulled her foot free, thankful her shoe hadn't been pulled off by the suction. She crept around the front of the truck, shielding her eyes from the headlights while wishing she'd remembered to turn them off. No point being stealth if you're traveling in a spot light, unarmed to boot. But all that was about to change. Lying in the mud, discarded like a balled up fast food wrapper, was an assault rifle. Annie picked it up and ejected the clip, slapping it back in with a sigh of relief. Let those bastards come at her now. She enjoyed feeling the weight of the rifle in her hands and the pressure against her shoulder. Oh, it felt so damn comforting.

"Wake the kids, but stay put. I want to check this out first."

Erica nodded and rolled up the window, relieved she could do her part by staying put inside the locked truck. Annie could read this across her face and nodded, knowing it was best to keep her in charge of something easy and calm, like watching sleeping children. Annie gripped the rifle tightly with anticipation as she tiptoed toward the heavy glass doors. They opened easily. A bit alarming for what had once been a heavily secured building. She slipped in between the doors and stepped across the lobby, stepping over a pool of blood, looking black against the dark blue flooring. The glass sculpture of the hand holding the Earth had been shattered. She moved her eyes back and forth, walking past the conveyer belts and through the metal detector. Her heart raced as it beeped. Annie hurried through and turned in a slow circle, hoping she hadn't just rang the dinner bell for whatever might be lurking in the dark. A moment passed and nothing sprang forth to eat her. She knelt down behind the detector and flipped a black switch, shutting it down. At least the power was still on. Annie gave the dark hallway ahead of her a quick glance and then hurried out to the truck.

"Anyone in there?" Erica opened the door and stepped out, frowning as her foot sank into the mud.

"No one that I saw, but that doesn't mean they're not there. Still, we really don't have anywhere else to go." Annie thought back to the pool of blood just within the entrance as she hopped up into the truck, wondering if they should let the kids sleep while they search for something else. But where? "Come on little tiger, wake up."

"No mom." Logan swatted about his face, rolling onto his side to face away from his mother.

Annie dug her fingers beneath his arms to tickle his pits. The laughter that followed was such a refreshing treat, innocent and honest. She reached over the seat with both hands and took hold of her son, helping him up and over the seat. Heather and Abby opened their eyes and gave out simultaneous yawns. Annie reached out and brushed some hair from

Heather's face, offering her a warm, genuine smile.

"Are we home?" Logan asked, rubbing his eyes.

"No, we can't go home." It broke Annie's heart to say, especially when she knew he didn't understand. "We're just going to stay here for a little while. Like a campout." Annie ran a hand through his hair and set him outside, gently lowering him onto the mud. "Stay close to Erica."

"Can I stay with you?" Heather's voice was small.

"Of course you can, dear." Annie took hold of the young girl's hand as she climbed over the seat and hopped outside. "Abby, sweetheart?" Annie grabbed her hand, but the young girl was unresponsive, staring out into space. "Can you come with us please?"

Abby nodded without looking her in the eyes, moving up and over the seat, hopping out of the truck. She trudged through the mud to wait with her mother and the other children outside the main doors. Annie pulled the keys from the ignition and shoved them into her pocket before joining the others. She took point, leading them through the lobby with her rifle pointing the way. Past the small rooms where she had spoken with her husband to the end of the hall, on their left was a door marked Private. Annie shoed Erica and the children back as she tried the knob, turning it with ease. She kicked the door open and hurried inside, flipping the light switch on the inside wall. Overhead lights buzzed into life, revealing a row of six cubicles, three on either side, and beyond them was a single door.

"Follow me and stay close." Annie waited until she'd gotten a nod from all four of them.

Annie stepped past the cubicles slowly, ducking down to look beneath each desk. She didn't want any surprises. When she passed the last one, Annie took a deep breath and pushed open the back door. The room was dark. Annie stuck her hand into the darkness and felt along the inside wall, her fingers stumbling over the switch. As the room lit up, Annie turned to her son and smiled.

"Are you a hungry boy?"

"Yes!"

Annie threw open the door and stepped aside, motioning with her head for them to go on in. Erica lit up as she saw tables and chairs, vending machines, and even two fridges. It was like winning the kitchen you've always wanted on some game show. Erica approached the counter and pressed random buttons on the microwave, covering her mouth to stifle a cry. How such simple things could bring joy and comfort. A little reminder that pieces of your old life might still be out there, little conveniences after being without for far too long. Annie threw open the fridge and got down on her knees, thankful the power hadn't gone out. There was half a cheesecake on the bottom shelf, a quart of whole milk, takeout food in mysterious wrappers stuffed inside plastic bags. Sealed Tupperware on all three shelves. Truly a magnificent sight.

"I think this one might be teriyaki." Annie pulled open a Tupperware and set it on the table, letting them all get an eyeful. It wasn't teriyaki, but meatloaf mixed with mashed potatoes wasn't bad. Maybe two more days before the toss out date. "What do you say we heat this up?"

The children smacked the table and smiled, enjoying some home comforts. Even Abby was smiling, swaying side to side with an eerie grin, but smiling all the same. Annie turned to the microwave and opened the door, pausing as she thought she heard something.

"What is it?" Panic began filling her tone.

"Nothing, just a beeping sound. Can you hear it?" Annie cupped her ear and listened, hearing a repetitious beeping. Three defined beeps, a moment of silence, then three more. "Heat this up. I'll be right back."

"Be careful."

Annie nodded, giving Logan a kiss on the cheek before picking up the assault rifle. She kept her eyes warm and positive, yet the weapon raised some concerns for him. Annie opened the door and walked through the cubicles, following the beeping. It led her out into the hall, turning left through some double doors. She'd never been this far into the facility before, far beyond where the normal visitors were allowed to venture. She stopped and waited for the cycle to pick up, growing that much louder with each step. Finally she turned to a door on her left. The plaque across the door read: *Communication Uplink Center.* Annie tried the knob, but this one wouldn't turn. She took hold of her rifle and slammed the butt down hard on the knob. Three more hits and the wood cracked. The door swung inward.

52

Andrews didn't want to let his guard down, not for a second. Things were getting out of hand and the last thing he needed was for his own men to lose confidence in him. Dress sharp, look the part. Andrews gave himself a hard, focused look in the mirror. This was a confident man. A leader. He dipped a cloth into a glass of water and rubbed out a few stains on his uniform. The urge to take off his uniform and sit around in nothing but his underwear was hard to resist, but what message would that send? The prisoners would see that he's gotten soft. Next there would be a revolt, ending in his death and complete anarchy. He wouldn't let those savages win. Oh hell no, not on his watch. Because that's what they truly were. Prisoners. Savage monkey fuckers that would eat his heart if he let them.

"I am the Lord," Andrews muttered into the mirror, completely unaware he'd spoken a single word.

He set his cloth down and took a seat, spinning slowly in his chair. He hadn't left the communications room in two days and had no idea of the status of the facility. There were more important things to attend to. Andrews put his feet on the ground and leaned forward, running a loving hand over the monitor. Christina's face filled the screen, sleeping peacefully. She was his only real concern. She should be everyone's concern, if any- one was smart enough to realize the situation they were in. Since his last communication with Yuri, he'd turned his focus on her. His beautiful Eve. He'd have to rename her once this was all said and done.

The comms link blinked red, an incoming mes- sage. Andrews turned in his chair and eyed the blinking light, irritating him. He closed his eyes and slouched in the chair, ignoring the light. But there it was, over and over again. Beeping continuously. Didn't these assholes know he was busy?

"What?" Andrews hit the button, his tone irritated.

"Mr. Andrews?"

"Yes, now state your business."

"This is Dr. Zatzkin at the third facility."

"I know where you are!"

"I need Daniels and his men sent to me as soon as possible."

Andrews furrowed his brow, leaning toward the

speaker as he tried to comprehend the request. "Why specifically Daniels and his men?"

"For one thing, we have a ruptured coolant valve on the atmospheric processer relay system. I have a list here of all those trained on rewiring and patching such equipment, and Daniels and his men are all we have."

"Fine," Andrews snarled, biting his lip to keep back any unprofessional words. "But you can't have Christina; she's been injured."

"Understood. Please, send them immediately."

Andrews severed the link and slammed a fist down on the table. "Little prick!" He screamed, rocking back and forth, feeling violated. The science division was needed, whether he wanted them or not. In terms of survival, they provided the air they breathed and one day a workable atmosphere. Until that day came, he'd have to bend over and take it. But at least their request might play out to his advantage. Andrews leaned back with a dark smile, nodding along with the most ingenious plan his dark heart had ever concocted. On Earth they'd look at him as a monster, if anyone were left to do so, but here on Mars he'd be dubbed their savior. The one to pick his chosen few while casting the unnecessary out. Andrews leaned forward and pressed the overhead communications link.

"Kirsch, please report to the comms room immediately."

53

"You are a sight for sore eyes." Travis hopped off his cot with eager determination.

"I've missed you too." Alvin had meant to be funny, but there was no humor about him. "We need to get moving."

"What's happening?" Travis laced up his boots and joined Alvin in the hall.

"Like any of us peasants know," Jerome said with a smile, hugging Travis.

Travis laughed, moving from Jerome to TJ, then Morgan. He pulled free and hesitated, looking at Sean's back. He looked to the others and they raised their shoulders in unison.

"So what's going on here?" Morgan asked, wincing from the pain in his shoulder as he tried to keep up with Alvin.

"Dr. Zatzkin has requested all of you."

"Why?"

"Something about fixing a coolant valve." Alvin wasn't entirely sure he was saying it right.

"What the hell do we know about a coolant valve?" Jerome wasn't entirely sure what a coolant system even looked like.

"Nothing," Travis said, thinking why such a task would call for his entire unit. "I'm just glad to be out of that damn cell."

They kept silent as they walked through the cafeteria and through the door at the opposite side. Their heads dropped as they passed clusters of security officers, their arms folded about their chest and a scowl on their faces. They watched them pass with a smirk, as if they knew something they didn't. Travis never felt more like a prisoner than he did at this moment. Being locked in your cell was one thing; no one but your own mind to pass judgment. But passing these men, the tension coming off them in waves, sent a cold shiver down his spine. He didn't dare look them in the eyes, not after witnessing the brutal beating in the cafeteria.

In a short time they were all standing on the train's platform. Travis felt as if they were stuck somewhere after hours, no one out and about but security. The technician behind the podium didn't even pay them attention. Travis waited for the technician's automated tone to tell them to keep clear of the track, but the train pulled up before them without a single word of warning. Travis watched the man, unable to see his face as he read something across the top of the podium, some kind of book maybe. No need to worry about job security when they'd been cut off from Earth and there were no more rotations. Travis just kept his mouth buttoned tight and entered the train, keeping his eyes to the floor until the train began moving up the incline, emerging from the dark tunnel to the red surface of Mars.

"Okay, what the hell is happening here?" Travis broke the silence, feeling they were far enough from the watchful eyes of security personnel.

"I honestly don't know. Andrews doesn't tell us anything anymore. I never even see him."

"You must have heard something," Morgan asked.

Alvin leaned back, rubbing the tension from his neck. "Andrews barely spoke to me before all this shit went down. Now, he spends all day and night in that goddamn comms room, speaking with that fucking Russian, one of the astronauts in the space station."

"Surely they must have some clue as to what's going on. Some kind of communication with Earth." Morgan shook his head, trying to grasp the isolation as it seemed to wrap itself about him, smothering him. Information used to be as simple as picking up the telephone or buying the newspaper. But there were none of those things on Mars.

"Some of the other officers, those on Andrews' good side, have heard a little more. Like there's been no contact with TransWorld for over a week. No incoming messages. Nothing. I've been in the comms link only once in the past week, and there are no open links to the Earth facility. No incoming updates or duty rosters. No status requests or progress demands."

"I don't think they'd just toss us out like garbage." TJ lowered his head into his hands. "Why the hell is this happening?"

"I don't think they left us up here on purpose. You don't just abandon a multitrillion dollar facility." Travis looked out the window to the red surface, watching the soil lift off the ground in a swirl of wind. The dirt blew against the heavily shielded windows, something so similar to what might happen on a train trip through the Nevada dessert. Their worlds weren't so different.

"What's on your mind, Travis?"

Travis heard Morgan, but he ignored the question. The sad reality was that this was their home, whether they wanted to accept it or not. Being told they may leave when the atmospheric processors were fully active and automated was a joke. The planet was billions of years old as it was and there was no atmosphere. At the very least, working with the smartest minds and the best machines, they could hope to achieve this in a few hundred years. Travis kept in shape, but he wasn't going to be around for the breaking of a champagne bottle. Bottom line, what was happening on Earth really had no bearing on them.

"Travis?" Alvin cocked his head, reading the curious expression. "Are you okay?"

"As good as I can be," Travis said softly, turning back from his unit to the window. His previous joy of being freed from his small cell forgotten. A dark depression stretched out as far as the red landscape. Anger and sadness that whatever hell Earth was experiencing, was also affecting his family. And worse, he was helpless to protect them.

54

"No questions until I've finished this briefing. Understood?" Andrews waited until all his officers gave him a nod. He wouldn't utter another word unless he had their utmost attention. He took a seat on the desk at the front of the room, closing his eyes with a heavy sigh. This was important. He'd put on his best, cleanest uniform to keep the presentation professional. "I need each and every one of you to hear what I'm about to say. To take in the gravity of what we're up against."

The officers nodded, bracing themselves for the oncoming bad news. They all knew that Andrews was the only one that has had any communication outside the facility in days, and therefore his information was vital. Officer Rodriguez tightened his stomach muscles to keep his nervous stomach from grumbling. Last thing in the world he needed before hearing what could be life-changing news was a bout of the shits. Too bad you couldn't leave some things back on Earth, such as the runs.

"Earth is not going to come back on line."

"What's happened?" Gomez spat, looking down into his lap as he received a heavy scowl from Andrews.

"The planet has been overrun with some kind of creature. Its origin is unknown. Subterranean monstrosities, alien invaders, or possibly demons. Sounds like a goddamn joke, I know, but this is the truth of it."

Andrews gave his men a moment to digest the oddness of what he'd told them. To turn to the man beside them to softly mutter confusion and disbelief. They wore shrouds of shock and terror, tears welling up in their eyes.

"I've seen these creatures. It's disgusting, horrible footage. But I will gladly show anyone of you that may have doubts. It's that important that you believe me, because what lies ahead will take all of us." Andrews cleared his throat and stood from the desk. He wanted to stand before them as not just a man with a good idea, but as someone with a way out. He wasn't selling real estate, but providing salvation. "We have a chance to fix things before they have the opportunity to get out of hand. A real chance to save ourselves from a slow, agonizing demise."

"What are you talking about?" Edgar Reece asked

from the back of the room, his tone shaking from the previous news.

Andrews looked at his men, seven good men that had never let him down, men he had been pleased to work with and felt confident to carry out his orders.

"Our survival depends on our abilities to increase longevity." Andrews took a breath and folded his arms behind his back. "We need to dispose of the miners."

There was a moment of silence, hanging over them like a soundproof bubble. The men wanted to lean back and let out sighs of relief, laughing amongst each other at the odd joke their superior had played on them. Monsters destroying their home world, indeed! But there was no humor in Andrews' eyes. Just a solid glare, focused eyes weighing on them.

"You're not serious?" Gomez asked softly, hoping to be reamed for being so foolish.

"You must all come to terms with the fact that there is no help coming. The supply ship still sits in the hangar, collecting dust. We will no longer be receiving food rations, supplies; no rotations home. This is our new home. Like it or not, we're stuck here. But that's not what you should be upset about." Andrews waved his finger at them. "You have just over three hundred miners; rough, tough assholes locked up with only nine of us. Breathing our precious air. Eating our limited food and drinking your water. Three hundred men –" Andrews paced before them, nodding with the statement. "With them devouring our resources we'll be lucky to last a year. Without them, we may have a chance."

"Kill three hundred men?"

"How many men would be acceptable before you lay on the ground, grasping your throat for that last gasp of air? Ten? Twenty? Two hundred?" Andrews gripped Gomez by the shoulders and squeezed, frightening him. "How many men, Gomez? What is your life worth?"

"He's right!" Adams stood, turning toward the other officers. "We weren't put up here to police three hundred men."

"That's exactly what we were sent here to do." Oliver Hildebrandt folded his arms, shaking his head at such a savage notion. "We're here to keep the peace, plain and simple."

"What kind of peace will there be when three hundred men start to get hungry? Start running low on water?" Andrews forced Hildebrandt back into his seat with the weight of his glare. "These men are docile and tame for the moment, but how long can we keep them locked up? This is our only solution. Sacrifice some, for our survival." Andrews took a seat on the desk and let them murmur.

"They outnumber us thirty to one!" Adams shouted. "Who will they turn on first when they discover the truth?"

"We need to defend ourselves," Gomez spoke up.

Andrews let them rally, sitting there with his arms folded and a widening smile. They were beginning to turn, seeing things for how they really were. But four of his officers sat with their heads down. Three men wore heavy expressions of doubt and conflict.

"I need you with me on this. Hildebrandt? Jules? Stevenson? Are you not listening to what we're saying?"

"Killing three hundred men is not going to happen." Stevenson shook his head. A very large man, two hundred and fifty pounds of muscles. "This is not what I was hired on for, and I will have no part of it."

"I agree. I'm not an executioner." Max Jules was close to tears, disturbed by what he was forced to deal with. Never once in his forty-seven years did he feel as disgusted as he did right now, listening to men he'd once respected and called friends. "Where is your humanity?"

"Do you understand that we've been given a chance for salvation?"

"What's it worth? A few extra years until we all die? Alone and hell bound."

"You haven't seen the whole picture here, Max. We've been given a new home to start over, to cast off the shackles of the old way and live as free men."

"Ten men aren't a future."

"No, but we have Christina. A woman. Someone that can move us forward." Andrews rose from the desk and lifted his arms above him. "We will grow this society from Christina. She can be our Eve."

"You're insane." Jules stood from his seat and headed to the door. "And there is no way I will be a part of this lunacy. You can have my resignation or whatever, but I'm going back to my room."

"I hope you think this over." Andrews turned toward him as he left. He nodded to Stevenson and Hildebrandt as they joined Jules at the door. "Just make sure you make the right decision." Andrews gave them a cryptic smile, one that fell quickly as they left the room. He turned to the four officers that remained. "Now, we have some very difficult tasks ahead of us and we need to move quickly." Andrews folded his arms about his chest and gave a dark grin.

55

"Whose bright idea was it to make these stations so damn far apart?" TJ rubbed the back of his neck as the train eased into the station of the scientific facility. "These seats aren't exactly the most comfortable either."

"Bitch, bitch, bitch." Jerome smacked him on the shoulder.

Travis looked from the windows to Sean, catching him as he turned his head. Had he been looking at him? He certainly hadn't said a word to anyone the entire trip. Sean had just sat there, his cheek pressed to the glass with his mind elsewhere. Travis had seen something in their brief eye contact. Something, just possibly, other than hate.

The six men waited patiently as the train pulled up to the station, moving sluggishly until it finally came to a stop. They shielded their eyes from the blast of air as they exited the door, unscrewing their helmets and setting them on the ground. Travis was glad to see Dr. Zatzkin standing by the technician at the podium. He looked anxious, bouncing on his feet.

"I don't know what you're expecting from us, doctor, but we're not exactly coolant experts," Morgan said with a smile.

"Believe me, I'm very aware of that. As I've told Mr. Daniels before, I have access to your files. Now, if you all wouldn't mind waiting in the cafeteria. I need to show Mr. Daniels something."

"What is it?" Travis was curious, tilting his head with a furrowed brow as he studied the doctor's jittery movements. He looked like a child with a big secret, and he couldn't hold onto it a second longer.

"Please, it's easier if you just come with me."

Travis nodded, waving to his unit and Alvin as he and the good doctor hurried up a slight incline and down a long hallway. He hadn't a clue what could have rattled the nerves of such a calm, patient man like Dr. Zatzkin, but he trusted him. He and Alvin were the only two people on this red rock, aside from his unit of course, who he didn't suspect of secretly hating him. Even Dr. Hoffman with the well-decorated office had a sour expression from time to time. Travis just went with the flow, looking up from time to time as they'd pass a window, seeing the distant hills that rivaled the tallest peaks of Earth. The soil was hitting the outer shell rather hard, filling the hallway with the gentle clinking created upon impact. It was soothing, like listening to the steady fall of rain on any average day.

"Okay, here we are." Dr. Zatzkin held his finger above the doors keypad, looking past Travis to make sure they were alone. "No one else knows about this, save for me and the technician that received the response."

"What response?" Travis looked from the doctor's curious smile to the door. It was the communications uplink center. "What is it?"

"Best if you see for yourself." Dr. Zatzkin pressed the button and stood back as the door slid into the wall.

"Annie!" Travis rushed into the room, overcome with joy as he saw his wife's face filling the consol. "Oh my God, I've been so worried about you."

Dr. Zatzkin was grateful to see such a warm moment, enjoying the human element this facility had lacked for so long. He pressed the button beside the door and allowed Travis some privacy.

"I have missed you so much. Where's Logie?"

"He's here, with Erica."

"Why's Erica there? What's happening down there?"

Annie wiped her eyes as the tears flowed. "I don't

know, honey. There are these creatures everywhere. Some look like giant lizard people, dog shaped ones. And this one –" Annie covered her mouth to contain herself, shaking her head slowly from side to side. "Oh honey, this one thing was as large as a building."

"But you and Logan are all right?" Travis redirected, angry by his wife's distress. He should be there.

"Yes, we're fine now. I thought this facility should keep us safe."

"Are you safe?"

Annie shook her head. "I don't know what to think anymore. Everyone is gone. Those things tore through the streets and pulled people from their homes. Our neighbors…" Annie wiped her eyes, letting out a nervous laugh. "At least we won't have to make another house payment."

"What about the people at TransWorld? Isn't there anyone there?"

"No, it's deserted. Just like Roanoke. Everything is either deserted or burning."

"No one's left?" Travis looked up from the computer, lost in the gravity of what he'd just heard. "So we are all alone." Travis ran his hands through his hair, a nervous habit of his. "What the hell are these things? Aliens? Demons?"

"These mile long cracks started forming all over the world. Then smoke began filling the sky with ash and moisture. It's been raining for like two weeks solid, heavy rain and massive flooding, you should have seen our street." Annie gave another smile, short lived as she continued on with the bad news. "Then they started coming out of the cracks. Countless numbers, everywhere."

"I am so thankful you made it there. If I remember right, it's pretty secluded. And there should be weapons storage somewhere on the premises, perhaps the lower levels. It is a military owned facility."

"What should I do, Travis?" Annie thought of Logan as she'd driven down the highway, sleeping and vulnerable.

"Leave this comms link active and stay put. Gather as much food as you can."

"I wish you were here." Annie reached out and touched the screen.

"Me too."

"Liar," Annie smiled.

Travis tilted his head and looked past the computer, running his mind through a complicated plan, unraveling it.

"What are you thinking about?"

"Just stay close to the comms room. I'm going to have a little chat with the guys."

56

Christina was startled awake. She opened her eyes and struggled to sit up, but she couldn't. She could barely raise her head up enough to look down at her body. There were straps across her chest, abdomen and legs. She tried to untie them, but her wrists were secured to the gurney.

"Hello?" Christina thrashed beneath the restraints, struggling for even the tiniest movement. "Please, hello."

Panic began to grip her mind. She remembered back to the terror she'd felt when Andrews had stood over her, that look of want in his eyes. Had he come back to finish the job? Christina pressed her thighs together as tight as she could, thankful for the feel of fabric against her flesh. At least they hadn't stripped her naked, she could be thankful for that.

"Someone answer me." Christina could only raise her voice slightly above a whisper, and even that burned.

"Shush." A man spoke from behind her, out of view but nearby. "We wouldn't want you to hurt your lungs."

"What are you doing to me?" Christina lifted her chin as far as it could go, hoping to tilt her head back for a glimpse of the man behind her. It didn't sound like Andrews.

"Please don't talk to me." Adams moved into view, a syringe in his hand. "Shut up."

"What are you doing to me?"

"I said shut the fuck up!" Adams stuck the needle into her forearm and injected her with a clear liquid. "There, now I'm all done."

"Why are you –" Christina could feel a warm sensation in the back of her throat. The dim overhead lighting began to dance about the room. "Why to me?" She was feeling so tired. "Please…no."

She closed her eyes.

57

Hildebrandt had been scared. He hoped to God it hadn't shown in his expression, but it was there. The intensity in Andrews' eyes could have stopped his heart. Never had he seen a man standing so close to the edge of insanity. But that was the bare truth of it. The facility was now in the hands of a madman. And much like Hitler, Andrews was praying on the minds of the scared masses and had gathered a force. But Hildebrandt refused to succumb to his paranoid fantasies. Thank heavens for Jules and Stevenson. Being the only voice of opposition would have made him very disposable, but there was strength in numbers. It was funny really. He had never really liked Stevenson. Always thought of him as being kind of a smug jerk, like he was above them or something. Now he was thankful to have him.

There was a loud click in the ceiling, followed

immediately by the slowly dying fans of his air filtration system.

"Hey!" Hildebrandt hopped up from his cot and stood beneath the metal grate. He licked his fingers and held them beneath the vent, but there was nothing coming through. "What the hell."

"You had a choice." Andrews' voice came through the door. "Now you have to live with it. But don't worry, you won't have to harbor that regret for long."

"You son of a bitch." Hildebrandt ran to the door, slamming his fists against the thick metal. "You can't do this to me."

"Why not?" There was a humor to Andrews' tone, as if he were holding back a hearty laugh. "We've already done it to Jules and Stevenson."

Hildebrandt stepped away from the door, his arms falling limp to his sides. He dropped to the floor and looked up at the grate. This is how he dies? Trapped in his room like a rat in a cage. A tickle surfaced in the back of his throat, small at first, but steadily growing in intensity. Soon it became overwhelming. He meant to call out, scream something verbally damaging to Andrews and whoever else may be out there with him, but he couldn't speak. He collapsed to the ground, looking up at the vent as a thin trace of vapor drifted down. Bastards had cut off his oxygen and filtered through some kind of gas. Despite his best efforts to climb up on his cot and close the grates, he just couldn't summon the strength. He simply laid his head down on the cold floor and closed his eyes.

58

"All personnel are to assemble in the main hangar for a briefing of current events."

The miners listened to the automated message playing overhead, thankful to hear it. They filed out of their cells, clogging the thin hallways, and made their way toward the hangar.

"Everyone keep moving. Please stay in line and don't push." Gomez stood beside the hangar doors, motioning with his hands like an air traffic controller for the men to move on through. "Please move forward in an orderly fashion."

"I don't understand what could be so important that Andrews couldn't have told us over the comms link?" Dr. Hoffman asked as he approached the hangar. "Why the secrecy?"

"What I want to know is why he's receiving information before we are?" Dustin Gerke, human resources director and all around stuffy asshole, asked with agitation.

The small group of ten from the business facility approached the hangar with less than enthusiastic attitudes. They eyed Gomez up and down, wondering why a peasant such as he should hold information over them? He was just a hired hand. But they went through and joined the miners. Gomez gave a morbid smile, turning to face them as he pressed the button beside the door. Once the door had sealed shut, Gomez raced up the stairs beside him to the control room, his dark heart not wanting to miss the show.

"Are they all in?" Andrews asked, looking back over his shoulder as Gomez burst through the door, wheezing slightly from the sprint.

"Yes. Just had to wait for the second facility to arrive, but they're all in the hangar."

"Everyone except Daniels and his prick friends, but they'll be back soon enough," Andrews snarled, wishing they could have all been locked down there, taking care of this matter in one press of a button. But it might prove quite entertaining to dispose of them separately. He will certainly enjoy it; spend a bit more time on their deaths. There were no laws against cruel and unusual punishment out here.

"Is the ship sealed?"

"Yes. I checked it myself before programming the announcement." Rodriguez said proudly.

"Good. I'd hate for some of them to take refuge on board."

"So we're really going to do this?" Reece lowered his head, wishing he'd never spoken at all.

"Are you having second doubts, Reece?" Andrews turned to face him, folding his hands about his chest with a focused glare.

Reece shook his head, remembering the gurgle of Jules' throat as he'd died. He wasn't present for Stevenson and Hildebrandt, but he could imagine.

"Good boy." Andrews turned toward the large glass window that looked down on the hangar. "With a push of this button, I hereby cleanse this world of the remaining filth of Earth." Andrews held his palm above a large red button. "Salvation." He pressed his hand down upon the button.

Gomez, Rodriguez, Reece, and Adams rushed up to the large window, looking down upon the hangar as a panic broke out. The miners scrambled under the flashing yellow lights, stepping over one another as they rushed the doors, banging their fists upon the metal to no avail. Dr. Hoffman stood in the middle of the hangar, looking up at the glass window and to the security officers on the other side. He mouthed a plea, holding his hands together in the standard begging position, but there was no sympathy from Andrews.

"Airlock doors will open in ten seconds," the automated voice warned.

The miners were pounding on the walls, screaming to be set free. A group of men were climbing about the large supply ship, pulling on anything that may open and offer temporary security, but nothing gave way. The miners held onto whatever they could as the final seconds counted down to one. Dr. Hoffman stayed where he was, turning from the window to face the door head on.

"Ashes to ashes, and dust to dust," Andrews whispered, feeling a sense of peace as the large doors parted.

The sound of the miners' screams were drowned out with the suction from the Martian atmosphere. The majority of them were sucked out instantly, cast down into the darkness of the Valles Marineris canyon. Dr. Hoffman was yanked from the room, shooting through the doors as if a string had been tied to his waist. Andrews waved to the miners as they reached out to them, pleading for the door to be shut. Reece looked away, unable to process what he'd allowed to happen.

59

"Are you out of your fucking mind?"

"Sean, just hear me out. Please." Travis stood from his chair, holding his hands out to Sean as if he might take them. He waited patiently, pleading with absolute sincerity.

Sean stood for a moment, looking around the circle of chairs to find a reason to keep standing, someone to join in his opposition, but there was no one. The rest of his unit, including Alvin and Dr. Zatzkin, sat relaxed. All of them felt the same humorous shock to such a bizarre notion, yet they wanted to know more. Sean lowered back into his seat with a sigh.

"I know it sounds extremely crazy at first, but hear me out." Travis took his seat, resting his elbows on his knees to keep this conversation casual. "There is no one left within TransWorld, and so the conditions here are not ending anytime soon. We have to think long term survival here."

"I don't know chief." TJ lifted his head from his hands, shaking it slowly with a mind full of doubt. "Hijacking a massive ship and piloting it to Earth is fun and all, but what about those lizard things? At least we're safe from all that up here? Less they have a good travel agent."

"Aside from the whole demon army thing, no one here is qualified to fly that ship." Morgan hated to put down the hope of rescue, but he was a logical man, and as appetizing as this plan may be, there were many holes.

Travis turned his head to Sean. "In Sean's early career as a test pilot, he handled some of the biggest birds ever built. I know because I've read your file. AVN-332 and the Airship A14. Both have a similar configuration to the supply ship and both were capable of interplanetary travel. In fact, I believe you logged some space hours?"

"You're comparing apples to large ass spaceships." Sean let out a single laugh and leaned forward. "Look, those ships were behemoths, I'll give you that, but they were only half the size of the supply ship. And without the beacon from the home facility, I'll have to fly the entire way on manual."

"But you could do it." Travis was trying to drive home the point and spark some confidence.

"I suppose, but you're talking a long voyage."

"How long?" Jerome asked, his tone gaining excitement.

"If we burn primary engines and thrusters the entire way, you're talking maybe twenty-five, thirty days. But that's pushing the engines pretty hard. We could risk engine failure, possible fracture or even a meltdown. Not to mention that would eat through our fuel."

"But there's fuel at the main facility."

"Travis, this is just too risky." Morgan's expression sank, held down by his heavy heart. "I know you want to save your wife and son, but we'd be risking too much."

"Actually, I think we're better off trying for it," Dr. Zatzkin spoke up. "Look, I'm the last person here that wants to pilot an unsafe ship down to a world infested with building-size monsters, but Travis is right. We need to seek survivors and stock up on supplies. Now this facility is equipped with enough oxygen and food for about two years, but the oxygen filtration system will run out of filters in one year. Unless you want to die of CO_2 poising, I say we give Travis' plan further consideration."

"You only want to go for your wife and son." Sean was bitter, snarling. "Risk our lives to save your family."

"No." Travis quieted the room, holding out his hands. "You're right. I want to save my wife and child. And I need you to do it." Travis set his pride aside and crossed the room, dropping to his knees before Sean. "Please, I can't do this without you. I'm sorry for however I've wronged you, and you can hate me 'til the day I die, but please don't punish my wife and son for my mistakes." Travis was close to tears. He reached out to Sean and took hold of his hand. "Please, I'm begging you."

No one had ever seen this side of Travis. He was a tough man, someone who would opt for torture over the discomfort of his friends, but never had they seen him beg. This wasn't their tough lieutenant kneeling before them. This was the desperate act of a loving husband and father. Sean looked him dead in the eyes, pushing past the watering membranes and searching for a reason to hate this man. Just something to cling onto, to validate the way he's been feeling. But there was nothing there.

"Jesus." Sean withdrew his hand and crossed his arms around his chest. "Stand up you old fool. I'll do it. But this doesn't mean we're square. And I'm not doing this for you and your rug rat."

"Thank you." Travis wiped his eyes as he stood, giving Sean a long look of gratitude before returning to his seat.

"I'm not promising we'll be successful," Sean continued. "If we burn the engines full out, I can almost guarantee we'll run out of fuel before entering the Earth's atmosphere." Sean thought to himself for a second, rummaging through the possibilities. "I guess we could always dock with the Alliance space station to refuel. Of course I've never done that before, but why not. Let's add it to the long list of impossibilities. Hell, maybe I'll do it all blindfolded."

"I don't think that will be necessary." Morgan set aside his previous doubt to take in the growing consent of the group. "I'm all for bringing back civilians to the facility to spare them a life of darkness, but you're all forgetting one very large problem. Andrews isn't going to simply hand over the keys to the supply ship."

"No, but he won't have to. I can take them." Alvin felt it was the least he could do. "I know where the security card is for the docking bay ramps. I can steal the access cards, let you out of your cells, and we can go. It's not like he can come after us."

"What about Christina? She's still in the infirmary," Sean asked.

"She's stable enough to move. Last time I saw her she was able to sit up and talk." Morgan remembered their last little talk, wishing they'd been discharged at the same time.

"Okay then." Travis clapped his hands together.

"Still, I see some problems there."

"Come on, Morgan, grow a pair." TJ gave him a wink. "I say we get the funky hell off this red rock."

Travis moved from man to man, giving each one his undivided attention. "Morgan?"

Morgan gave him a thumbs up.

"Okay then, let's do it."

60

Annie had waited beside the open comms link, spinning slowly in the office chair for over an hour before her husband finally came back to her.

"Annie?"

Annie nearly fell from her seat, startled by the sound of his voice. She turned toward the screen and leaned in close, so thankful to see a warm smile. "What's happening?"

"Hold tight and save the champagne, we're coming to get you."

Annie's mouth dropped, pulled open by the severe shock. Had he been joking with her? "What are you talking about?"

"We're coming to get you. It's all worked out." Travis took a minute to set out the plan, not wanting to stumble over his words amidst his excitement. "We're going to take the supply ship and fly it down to the TransWorld facility. All you need to do is wait.

Simple as that."

"I doubt it's that simple. Especially since I'm sure they're not just letting you take their expensive ship for a joy ride. Are we talking a prison break?"

"No, not really. I've never heard of a prison break that involved the prisoner to break back in. But that's what we have in mind. Only it's going to take some time."

"How much time?"

Travis bit his lip, not wanting to tell her. She'd looked so hopeful. "Twenty-five, maybe thirty days."

"A month?" Annie's eyes went wide. "Wow, not really a trip to the corner store."

"I'm going to need you and Logan to stay hunkered down. Can you do it?"

Annie nodded, holding out her hands. "Do we really have anywhere else to go?"

"I love you so much."

"I love you too, honey." Annie kissed her hand and touched the screen. "I knew you'd be the one to save me."

"Just keep this link open and stay close."

"I promise."

"Okay, I have to go. See you soon." Travis was so overjoyed to hear those words coming from his mouth.

"Looking forward to it."

Annie watched him disappear from view, sitting there a moment longer as if he may have more to say, maybe to see if he'd been joking around or overshot their chances, but he was gone. Now all she could do was sit and wait, but for thirty days? Annie grabbed her assault rifle off the table and headed out of the office. She had to take a moment out in the hall to remember which way she'd come. Her sense of direction currently smothered with the information Travis had given her. But she quickly remembered. Annie hurried through the cubicles to the kitchen, thinking an hour had been long enough to keep Logan waiting. She tried the knob, but it was locked.

"Open up, it's me," Annie yelled through the door. "I have amazing news."

Erica opened the door, standing aside with a breath of relief. "You'd been gone so long I thought something had happened to you."

"Something did, but for the best." Annie sat at the closest table and waited till Erica and the three children took a seat. "How would you kids feel about going to Mars?"

"What are you talking about?" Erica was thinking this might be some kind of diversion tactic for the children.

"I just got through speaking with Travis, and he said to hold tight, because they're coming down to get us. In a big spaceship!" Annie turned to the children with an over-exaggerated show of joy. She reached out and tickled Logan and Heather, moving to Abby's stomach to let her join in the good times.

"Where's Mars?" Logan asked, looking down at his feet as if it might be one of his body parts.

"Mars is another planet, sweetie. Way out there in space. Do you remember the red one?"

Logan nodded, turning back toward a pile of plastic cups he'd been playing with, obviously unimpressed with the news. Abby and Heather turned to each other and began naming all the things they were looking forward to.

"How long 'til they get here?" Erica's smile stretched across her entire face.

"A month."

The smile across her face faltered, quivered a bit, and then fell to a frown. Erica took a seat and rested her head in her hands. "How do they expect us to survive here for a month?"

"It's our only plan. But at least we're safely indoors with weapons." Annie rubbed her neighbor's back, comforting her. "All we need to do is search this facility for food and stockpile it in here." Annie looked about the kitchen and its amenities, nodding with her plan. "I think we can easily last a month."

Erica looked up from her hands with a weak

smile, but at least it was there. Annie rubbed her back extra hard to change her mood from depression to good humor. But Annie wasn't as confident as she seemed. Behind her joyful smile was a growing storm of doubt and fear. Truth be told, she had no idea whether they were safe or not. A lot can happen in thirty days. And all she could was sit and wait.

61

Christina heard his voice long before she opened her eyes. That smug, darkness of Andrews' voice, only he wasn't speaking to her. Christina worked hard to force her eyelids open, thankful the overheads were on emergency power. After a few seconds of blurry vision, she saw Andrews speaking to three of his officers. She didn't know their names. Her first instinct was to scream out, ask them why she was still strapped to this damn gurney, but she pretended to be asleep so she could listen.

"Now that we've safely secured our Eve and the miners are all dead, we can tie up this last loose end."

"Dr. D'Ambrosio has taken his own life. Slit his wrists in his cell." Adams looked down to his feet.

"That's too bad."

"Also, Needleman has been killed."

"Who the hell is that?" Andrews drew a blank.

"The train technician. He's dead now sir," Adams

said with a satisfied nod.

"Excellent. Now we just wait to finish off Travis and his little military asses."

"How do you propose we kill them, sir?" Gomez asked timidly, knowing full well of their training.

"The comms room has a remote operating system for the train. It shows the train has left the station and is well on its way." Andrews rubbed his hands together in eager anticipation. "I think we should wait until the train hits the station, and then shoot them at close range with the repulse cannons. A shot set at full power should smoke their asses," Andrews laughed. "It's all so damn perfect."

"Why not just disconnect the train and let them starve?"

"Gomez, you moron. We can't risk anything happening to that train. Now get everyone into position. Except you Adams. I want you here, with her."

"Yes sir." Adams looked over to Christina, feeling a tingle in his groin. She wasn't his type, overly athletic with a bit less up top than he liked, but pussy was pussy. And there was definitely a shortage of that around.

"I said watch her, and that's it, understand?"

"Yes," Adams nodded, standing erect like a good boy.

Adams let his tension ease as Andrews stepped

out of view. He gave Christina a hard, long look before taking a seat. Why should the others get to have all the fun why he played babysitter? Adams looked up and eyed Christina's chest, watching it rise and fall. He felt heat radiating off his chest, rising up like floodwaters. The room became hot. He hoped she'd be a willing partner. Not all tooth and nails as he did his business. Maybe if they informed her that she was humanity's last hope she'd be more willing. Better to hear a moan or two rather than simply rape the bitch.

"Oh yes," Christina moaned, slowly twisting about on the gurney. "Feels so nice."

"Are you okay?" Adams stood and approached the gurney, keeping a foot between them. "Something wrong?"

Christina opened her eyes and followed his voice, smiling as she saw him. She licked her lips and moaned, closing her eyes. Her shoulders swayed from side to side, rhythmic movements like the swagger of a snake. Christina opened her eyes and let out a playful laugh.

"I don't know what you guys gave me, but it makes me feel so very naughty." Christina moaned, lifting her head back to play the part. "Oh I want a man." She looked to him. "Come closer, I want to touch you."

Adams stepped forward until his crotch was

against her hand. He lifted his head and closed his eyes as she rubbed the back of her hand against his pants. Adams lost himself in the most erotic moment of his pathetic life. An actual fantasy come true. A woman in bondage beckoning him near as she groped her captive; something he'd imagined many times while jacking off in the bathroom.

"Please, I need to feel you. Untie my hand." Christina looked up at him with a seductive moan. "Come on, how much trouble can I get into with one, little hand?"

"Oh shit." Adams looked toward the hallway and then down to Christina. "Fuck it. Let's find out."

Adams undid the strap on her right hand and let his hands hang loosely by his side, grinning down at her as she unzipped his pants. Adams lifted his head up to the ceiling and giggled, tingling all over as she reached into his pants, but then withdrew. There were a few seconds of silence.

"What the hell?"

Adam looked down as Christina jammed the scalpel into his abdomen. She pushed her hand up his body, running the scalpel up to his sternum. She released her hand and rolled over, untying the strap over her left hand, wincing against the aching in her chest. Once the strap over her wrist was clear, she moved onto her head. Adams stood frozen, his hands held over the scalpel that protruded from his body. He wanted to grab it, to scream for help, but he could only stand there. Shivering in stunned horror as the pain began to set in. It replaced all thoughts and emotions, consuming him until nothing else existed. Adams' eyes rolled back into his head as he collapsed to the floor, shivering briefly before laying still.

"Serves you right, asshole." Christina sat up and undid the straps over her legs and finally her ankles. "Next time try flowers and romance."

Christina swung her legs over the side of the gurney and hopped off, collapsing to the floor in a hard spill as her legs gave out. She rolled onto her back and coughed, crying from the impact of the floor and her chest. As the burning subsided, she placed a hand to the cold floor and moved to a seated position. She rubbed her legs, pushing the pins and needles from her limbs until she could move them. Rubbing, bending, and stretching them for over an hour. Sitting beside a dead body while she brought her legs back to life. Christina took a brief break, digging through Adams' pockets to remove his badge.

Finally, hoping to get a little more magic this time, she gripped the gurney and pulled, slowly moving into a standing position. She stayed put for a moment, holding her breath as she pushed off the gurney and headed for the wall, slamming into it and nearly losing her footing. She pressed her back to the wall and let out a quivering sigh, weeping gently from the pain in her chest. Cautiously, she stuck her head into the hall. If what they'd said about the miners was true, she'd be sure to have no problem moving down the hall without being seen. All the security personnel would be waiting in the station, waiting to murder her friends. Christina pressed her hand to the wall and hurried as fast as she could, her knees shaking. Her legs burned, shivering and threatened to give out. It was only a short distance down the hall, no more than twenty or so yards, but it felt like five miles. Her heart raced. At any moment someone could step out into the hall and catch her. How hard could it be to wrangle her up? Her top speed was no more than a mile an hour.

Christina paused, holding still as if that may somehow conceal her location. It was Andrews' voice and he was close, but no one came out. She increased her pace to a mile and a half, booking down the hall for someone in her condition. Each step brought a sharp pinch to her side. Every breath burned, as if it were filtered through sandpaper. But she finally reached the door. She pressed the keycard to the metal panel beside the door, relieved to hear the little click within the lock. She quickly stepped inside, jumping as the door shut behind her. Confident she'd remained unseen, she turned toward the machines and hovered a bit. Numerous computer monitors, flashing lights and dials. But she recognized the green digital map of the Martian surface and the dotted line representing the train's progress. The panel of switches to her left controlled the train's mechanics. The black button on her right was the communications link.

62

Alvin sat alone by the front of the train. He just wanted to clear his mind and prepare for the task at hand. It was all a bit too exciting to comprehend, sneaking around in the night like a bunch of thieves, taking the mammoth supply ship on a long trek to Earth. So many variables to consider, yet they'd made up their minds so damn fast. No one had thought to wonder what might happen upon their return. Andrews wasn't the type of man to let humility roll off him like a bit of rainwater. He may keep the hangar doors sealed and deny them reentry, thus killing them when their fuel runs out. As crazy as that sounds, Andrews may be that far gone. Or what if he caught them trying to run out? That would be a death sentence for sure. Alvin remembers the little demonstration they'd been forced to watch. How the miner's eyes had burst from his face, his veins exploding. Would a punishment for their crime call for something more painful? Maybe slowly opening the door up until their eyes explode, and then closing it—only to do it again? Alvin rubbed his throat, gulping uncomfortably at the thought of such a death. Especially since it was a very real possibility.

Alvin looked to his right, wondering if the men in the next compartment were considering the same thing. Maybe military men never considered the "what ifs," or maybe they just don't care. Either way, Alvin had the consequences tattooed on the front of his mind. It's all so comical, in a cosmic sort of way. He wasn't even supposed to be here. If this had happened six months down the road he would have been back on Earth, hiding out in a bomb shelter or something. Alvin laughed, thinking it funny that a bomb shelter might be a step up from this place.

"Hello? Can you guys hear me?"

Alvin jumped, startled by the female voice coming from the train's control panel. He hopped up from his seat and ran to the front, looking over the small board of switches and lights until he saw a blinking red one with the symbol of a microphone under it. He flipped it up.

"Hello? Yes, I hear you."

"Who is this?"

"Alvin Kirsch. Please identify."

"Alvin, it's Christina."

"Christina? What's going on?"

"Are the others with you?"

"Hold on."

Alvin ran from the control, bursting into the next compartment with a skid. Travis reached out to catch him before he tumbled forward.

"Christina...on the comms." Alvin pointed toward the front of the train.

"What?" Travis stood from his seat and headed down the train. "Christina?"

"Oh, Travis, thank God."

"What's going on?"

"Look, Andrews and his officers have killed everyone. All the miners. Now he and his men are waiting in the station to kill you."

Travis gripped the controls to steady himself, the words still rolling about his mind. It just didn't make sense. Anger began to build, growing hot like a fire in the pit of his stomach, fueled by each and every victim of Andrews' insanity. Men whose names he didn't know, but their faces were plain as day. He took each face and tossed them into the fire, building the flames until he felt ready to explode.

"Where are you?"

"I'm in the communications room."

"The system room, right?" Morgan asked, leaning over Travis' shoulder.

"Yeah, I suppose."

"You can operate this thing by remote then. Just stop the train and send us back to the scientific facility. Let him come to us."

"Won't do any good, Morgan. Andrews would be watching the map in the station and get suspicious. He'd just have his men kill Christina and then turn us right back around. No, that won't work. Besides, I want to face that prick."

"They have weapons," Christina said, remembering something Andrews had said through the fog of her awakening. "Something about repulse cannons, or non-lethal riot pistols. Besides, he doesn't want me dead. I'm to be their surrogate for the future. They want to rape me." Christina choked on the word. "Maybe you should just hide out in the scientific facility."

"No." Travis shook his head, running a thought through his mind, molding it. A sly smile spread across his face as the idea took shape. "Christina, you have access to all of the train's electrical systems?"

"Yeah, I think so."

"What do you have in mind?" Morgan folded his arms across his chest, recognizing the same crazy look on Travis' face from some of their most dangerous missions. The look that said "This is insane, but it might work."

"What do you say we go for a walk?"

63

The wrist straps crisscrossed about his arm, nearly cutting off Andrews' circulation. But the uncomfortable pressure building in his arm from the repulse cannons was nothing compared to the anxiousness. Andrews sat behind the technician's podium in the main station, staring up at the large digital map. He watched as the dot representing the train came closer and closer, putting more distance between Daniels' unit and the safety of the scientific facility. He suppressed the urge to laugh, loving the excitement and hating the anticipation. This was an ambush, just like all the great movies from his childhood; the bad guys coming toward them on the train while the good guys cut them down. Andrews and his posse of three: Rodriguez, Gomez, and Reece. Adams was there if they needed back up, but these military shits didn't stand a chance.

Andrews looked down at Needleman's body,

lying at his feet with an arm over his eyes. His throat had been cut, looking up at him like a second mouth. Blood looked darker in this room. Andrews shrugged, figuring it was just the dim lighting. He looked back up at the map, the green dot now flashing red.

"What the hell does that mean?" Andrews hopped off the stool and approached the screen, pointing up at the glaring red while demanding answers from his men.

"The train has stopped." Gomez scratched his head.

"Are they aware somehow?"

"No, sir." Reece had run back to the podium, putting up a readout of the trains systems on the screen beside the map. "The train's log shows it's deployed its sweeping units to clear debris off the track."

"Is this normal?"

"Actually it happens all the time. With all the dust storms, it's pretty common. Should only take a moment before it's back underway."

Andrews nodded, but he wasn't quite sure. He stood beneath the large screen, craning his head up to stare at the dot. The red light blinked back at him, as if Daniels himself were sitting on screen, waving with a smug look on his face. Five minutes had passed, stretching out as if made from industrial strength taffy, sticky and leaving a foul taste in his mouth. He tapped the repulse cannon against his leg, timing his impacts to coincide with the repetitious beeping. If those men had somehow discovered his plan, hoping to disable the train to avoid capture, then they didn't know a thing about him. He'd put on a space suit and walk out to that damn train before he let those assholes get the best of him. They were only a few miles from the station, and they certainly wouldn't expect an attack out on the surface. Andrews' impatience was overgrowing what was left of his judgment.

"There we go. See, only takes a moment." Reece pointed at the green dot, thankful things were literally back on track. Last thing he wanted to do was deliver bad news to an insane man. Not just insane, but armed.

Andrews watched the green dot drawing toward them, closing the distance. They'd be within the station in a matter of minutes. He couldn't contain the excitement. He bounced on his feet, his hands twitching. His dick began to tingle, pressing against the inside of his pants. Any other day he would have put some kind of unpleasant thought at the front of his mind, an erection blocker. But not today. This was his world now and he didn't have to hide anything from anyone. After all is said and done, he may just have to pay Christina a visit. Celebrating his new society with the first impregnation.

"They're going through the outer tunnel." Reece couldn't hide the nervousness from his voice. He didn't want to kill these men; God knew he didn't. But he was going to. Either them or him—that's how he saw it.

Andrews snarled with dark delight as the train rolled into the station. He kept his wrist behind his back, not wanting to spring the trap too soon. The train stopped, the doors parted and nothing happened. No one came out. Andrews leaned to the side to see into the next compartment, but that was also empty.

"What the hell?" Andrews shouted. "Reece, check the system for their personal locators."

Reece ran with purpose, shaking at Andrews' tone. He stood behind the podium, searching for all active personal locators within a hundred feet. He saw all of them standing in the station and all of Travis' unit within the train.

"Well, according to the computer, they're still inside the train." Reece took a step back, shaking under the heat of Andrews' glare.

"They're hiding in there, somewhere. All of you get your asses in there and tear that train apart!"

The three officers rushed into the train, moving to the front compartment and working their way toward the back. There was nowhere for anyone to hide.

The only place would be under the seats, but you'd be completely visible. Gomez nodded with his chin to the back of the train. They inched down the aisle way, holding their repulse cannons aimed toward a door at the very back, a door that was slightly ajar. Gomez stepped forward and threw open the door, revealing eight space suits with smashed helmets, the glass littered about their feet.

"Now," Travis shouted, hopping down from atop the train, the grey from his spacesuit nearly a perfect match for the train's metal exterior.

Travis' six travel companions hopped off the top of the train to stand beside Travis. The train's doors sealed shut, locking the three security officers inside. They ran to the door and began pounding on the windows. Rodriguez lifted his arm and aimed the repulse cannon at the thick glass, but the train began moving, catching them off guard and knocking them onto their asses. Andrews stood frozen in shock, watching his loyal soldiers being carted down the track and into the tunnel. Andrews turned and bolted, hearing their footsteps right behind his. He stepped out into the hall and slammed his wrist on the panel, sealing the door, locking it. He stood for a moment, looking through a small rectangular window at Travis.

"Open this door, Andrews," Travis ordered. "You

have nowhere else to go."

"Wrong. It's you that will have nowhere else to go," Andrews laughed, his eyes distant and watering with lunacy. "I know you're going for the supply ship. But it's too late for that. I'm going to blow it to hell." Andrews laughed, fogging up the glass with his breath. "Now we're all stuck here. Stuck in my world."

Andrews pressed his back to the door and cackled in hysterics, crying uncontrollably. Oddly, he'd never felt so happy in his entire life. But what would make him truly happy was sitting all alone in the hangar, and he wasn't about to let them have it.

64

Christina waited with her hand held over the button for the train's main doors, her nerves shot as she saw the train slowly pull into the station. She could see the men laying on the top of the train in their spacesuits, keeping still to stay out of view. So far they'd gone unnoticed. She held her breath as one of the guards searched the computer. Andrews yelled something, but the audio wasn't up. Christina turned up the volume and heard Andrews order his men on the train. This is exactly what they'd been depending on. Just as he'd planned it out, Travis fell from the train and gave the order. Christina slapped her hand down on the button, sealing the door and the officers inside. She may have hit the button a bit too hard, but her nerves were wound so tight. She turned a large dial on the control panel and set the train in motion, nodding with satisfaction as it rolled into the tunnel. The switch under her monitor allowed her to switch views. One flip of the switch took her to a camera mounted at the front of the train. A second switch, the one she'd been hoping for, took her to the train's interior.

"Come on!" Gomez shouted, pacing back and forth through the aisle.

Christina watched them panic, bouncing off the seats, tapping their legs nervously. Three minutes from the facility was far enough, especially without any suits onboard. Christina cut the power, watching with pleasure as the train slowed to a stop. She switched off the audio and sat back in the chair. All three of them ran to the camera, pleading soundlessly for someone to help them. No, she wasn't going to help them. These men who were more than willing to have her strapped to a table as their fuck doll got their justice. Now they knew what it feels like to be held against their will, completely helpless.

A quick movement caught her eye. She looked up at the monitor that showed the station's interior, startled to see Andrews standing on the other side of the door. They'd come too far to let such a monster run loose. Christina stood from the chair and stepped out into the hall, moving as fast as she could, gritting her teeth against the intense pain. She let out a moan, unable to keep such agony inside. Tears rolled freely, but it didn't stop her. She limped toward the junction where the hallway from the main station ran into the one that led to the comms room. Andrews' laughter charged down the hall, moving toward her under the heavy thud of his footsteps. He was running hard.

"You're all going to die!" Andrews laughed hysterically. "Oh yes, how smart you all are."

Christina measured his distance by the proximity of his rants. He was now only a few feet away, running hard on pure insanity and adrenaline, thus making him that much stronger and faster. But the same went for Christina. Her body trembled from exhaustion and fatigue, but her hatred for this man kept her upright. She took calming breaths, gaining speed as he drew near. His laughter chilled her spine. At exactly the right moment, moving as if they'd practiced the move together for hours, Christina stuck her arm out into the hallway. Andrews' throat connected with her arm, forcing his feet forward and up as his head slammed down on the cold floor.

Christina fell on her back from the force of impact, momentarily dazed as she struggled to get some air back into her lungs. She gasped, eagerly accepting the stale recycled air. Andrews moaned, lying on his back with his arms feebly flopping on the floor, his eyelids fluttering. Christina was thankful she'd been the first to get up. With her limited strength, he would have surely had the upper advantage. Christina rolled onto her stomach and took hold of Andrews' hair, making tight fists. Her hands turned red from the pressure. She let out a savage yell and slammed his head back down to the floor. Up and down. Smack. After the third hit, she rolled onto her back and began to cry, closing her eyes against the savagery. This wasn't her, beating an unconscious man's head to the ground, but things had changed.

"You fucking murderer!" Christina opened her eyes and pushed herself into a seated position. It took a minute to get her breathing under control, her lungs rattling. She looked down at his unconscious face, his lips moving. "Why?" Christina shook her head, knowing he couldn't answer her anyway, and if he could it wouldn't matter.

Christina grunted and cringed as she rose up on her knees, gripping the wall to steady herself as she stood. The hallway spun for a moment, simmering down to normal as the blood in her head settled. She kicked Andrews across the face before moving, not bothering to look back. He deserved to be beaten to death at least three hundred times, but it couldn't be done by her. Right now she needed to focus on her legs, getting them to work together and keep her up. Just thirty feet down the hallway, that's all, but her knees were beginning to buckle. Christina pressed her back to the wall and took a break, closing her eyes

as she slowed her breathing. The fall had been painful, bruising the skin between her shoulder blades
and now a raging headache. Christina looked down
the hallway, the door to the main station in sight.
She turned and slid toward the door, her shoulder
rubbing against the wall. This helped, keeping her on
her feet and heading forward.

"Hold on." Christina gave a wave through the
small window, pressing Adams badge to the plate be
side the door.

"Are you alright?" Travis asked as he stepped
into the hall, reaching out to catch her before she
collapsed.

"Fine, just very sore." Christina coughed, held her
breath a moment, and then nodded. "Andrews is back
there. He's unconscious."

"Damn! Even when you're sick, you're still kicking ass," Jerome laughed.

"Hey, men are easy, its cramps that scare me."
Christina grinned, probably the first genuine show
of affection she'd had in weeks.

"I need to get Andrews." Travis looked back over
his shoulder. "Sean, you want to take over here while
we get that son of a bitch?"

Sean was more than happy to step forward, ducking low to have Christina's arm slung over his shoulder.
He put his arm about her waist and supported her.

He looked up from her exhausted face to Travis, sharing a brief moment before he turned toward the hall. Travis gave him a grateful nod, looking from Sean to Christina before leaving. Sean watched him run off, wondering if he really could ever set aside the hate. Maybe this entire ordeal wasn't all Daniels' fault. One thing was clear; he and Christina were together again.

65

Andrews felt the discomfort in his pants long before the tightness of the ropes. An uncomfortable wetness in his crotch. He'd pissed himself. Andrews struggled to open his eyes, pushing with all his mental might to get them at half-mast. He saw the wide openness of the hangar. Nothing registered at first. Last thing he remembers was running down the hallway on his way to the ship. Had he already dismantled it? Andrews looked to his left and saw the giant steel bird sitting exactly as it had for the past few weeks. No signs of damage. So then what the hell was he doing just sitting there?

"What the hell?" Andrews mumbled, slurring his words as he tried to lift his arm and couldn't. "What the hell is going on?" Andrews opened his eyes all the way and examined his body. He was tied to a chair. "Who did this? Huh?" Andrews looked about, left to right, up and down.

"Homer Andrews, you have been convicted of over three hundred counts of murder." Travis' voice came out of the overheads.

"You military prick! Who do you think you are?" Andrews thrashed violently in his chair, falling to the side with a heavy thud, his cheek pinned to the cold floor. "I'm the head security officer of this facility, and it is my job to take any steps toward improving safety. I took the steps I felt necessary."

"Well then, due to your lack of good judgment, I sentence you to death."

"You have no authority," Andrews screamed, his voice filling the large hangar. "I'll get you for this. Mark my words, Daniels." Andrews looked up as the yellow lights began to flash. "I swear to God that I will kill you!"

Andrews' voice was drowned by the overhead siren, but Travis knew what he was saying. He didn't need to read his lips to know a good death threat, even from behind the thick glass of the hangar's control room. The yellow warning lights cast an eerie glow over them, bright flashes that hurt the eyes. Travis could feel the start of a headache, a slight pinch in the back of his eye, perhaps a slight twinge of guilt gnawing on his nerve endings. This man had killed over three hundred innocent men, yet Travis had trouble carrying out his sentence. He held his hand over the doors release button, wondering if they should lock him up or ask Dr. Hoffman to review him. Christina stepped forward and slapped the button with a satisfied grunt.

"You were taking far too long," she said, her eyes fixed on Andrews as the doors parted. "He doesn't deserve a second thought."

The doors opened and the powerful vacuum of space sucked him out, pulling Andrews and the chair from the floor. There was a moment of silence as they let Andrews' death sink in. They'd just killed the man who murdered over three hundred innocent lives, then waited to ambush them without any honor, eager to take care of the one last problem before starting his perfect world built off forcibly impregnating Christina. So yes, Andrews most definitely deserved to be sucked out into the canyon, to have his eyes explode from his head. He deserved much worse, but they were on a time crunch.

Travis pressed the button and sealed the room, waiting until the alarm ceased before turning from the window, not wanting to look down on the large empty hangar. He could picture the men he'd worked beside for the last year clawing at the door, stepping over each other like caged animals as the overhead lights went from yellow to red. A shiver went down his spine. He turned from such savage imagery and faced his unit. Seven little Indians left. Five highly trained military officers, one scientist, and the last of the Martian security force, stood together with the common goal to get them the hell off this red rock. To get them back home.

To Be Continued...

Also by *KEVIN J HOWARD*
FAITHFUL SHADOW

Kevin J. Howard's novel, Faithful Shadow, takes you beyond the splendor of nature to the terror that lies beneath, one that should have never been discovered.

Yellowstone is suffering from the largest forest fire in the park's history. Ranger JOE RAND, once passionate about nature and now drowning in alcohol after the recent death of his son, notices something is very wrong after a string of disappearances. When a fireman is found dead in the Old Faithful Inn after falling into a hole earlier that day, his body mauled and deprived of all its fluids, Joe knows he has no choice but to set down his flask and investigate. Joe and Lieutenant DALE CAFFEY of the Billings Fire Department go into the woods to search the hole the fireman had fallen into. They discover a series of tunnels lined with bones, the air thick with smoke. Joe and Dale conclude that the creature that had killed the fireman had left its subterranean dwelling to flee the overwhelming smoke from the fire above. The creature takes shelter inside the Inn, concealing itself within the darkened crevices, emerging only to feast on passersby. After staging an evacuation of the park, they lock themselves inside the Inn to hunt the creature. After just a short while it becomes frighteningly clear that, in fact, the creature is hunting them.

Learn more at: www.outskirtspress.com/faithfulshadow

Lightning Source UK Ltd.
Milton Keynes UK
UKOW031027060213